A PLUME BOOK

FORSAKING HOME

A. AMERICAN has been involved in prepping and survival communities since the early 1990s. An avid outdoorsman, he has spent considerable time learning edible and medicinal plants and their uses as well as primitive survival skills. He currently resides in South Carolina with his wife of more than twenty years and his three daughters. He is the author of *Going Home*, *Surviving Home*, and *Escaping Home*.

ALSO BY A. AMERICAN

Going Home
Surviving Home
Escaping Home

FORSAKING HOME

A Novel

Book 4 of the Survivalist Series

A. American

A PLUME BOOK

PLUME
Published by the Penguin Group
Penguin Group (USA) LLC
375 Hudson Street
New York, New York 10014

USA | Canada | UK | Ireland | Australia | New Zealand | India | South Africa | China
penguin.com
A Penguin Random House Company

First published by Plume, a member of Penguin Group (USA) LLC, 2014

CIP data is available.
ISBN 978-0-14-218130-0

Printed in the United States of America

Set in Bembo Std
Designed by Leonard Telesca

Here we are once again, for the fourth time now. I want to thank my family for their support through this process—it does take a lot of time. I also want to thank all of you who read the books for your support and encouragement. Additionally I want to take a moment for an unsung hero of all this, Kate Napolitano, my editor. Kate puts in a lot of hard work cleaning up the manuscripts and certainly deserves my thanks and yours! Thank you, Kate.

Lastly, a personal note. Godspeed, Robbie, we're still thinking of you.

FORSAKING HOME

Chapter 1

Immersed in total darkness, deprived of human contact, chained and afraid: this is how Jess, Mary, and Fred spent their days. Had it been a day, a week, or possibly worse yet, mere hours since they were they thrown into prison? Without being able to see the sun or even its reflection, time was a relative thing. Only the irregular checks the staff performed on them broke the monotonous routine.

Jess lay on the cold concrete floor, her hands clamped between her legs to try and keep them warm. The darkness was so complete that only by blinking her eyes could she even tell if they were open. Despite her current situation, she didn't regret the decision that landed her here. Given a chance she would do it all over again, without hesitation. The only thing that she felt bad about was that her friends were also detained. She now spent her time trying to think herself out of her predicament.

Mary was not faring nearly as well as Jess. She was, in a word, broken. Absent now were her cries and wails that had initially filled the halls. Her outbursts drew immediate reprisals from her jailers. Their methods of punishment ranged from hosing her down with cold water to what she was now suffering—having a rag stuffed into her mouth, held in place with duct tape. Her low, pitiful moans were nearly inaudible beyond the walls of her cell.

Fred, unlike her companions, was not idle. She had surveyed the entirety of her cell to the extent her chained hands would allow. Crawling on the floor, she ran her hand along the walls' edges, starting at the door and working her way around. She then used her body, keeping her head at the wall, to search the center of the room. The only thing she found in the room was a bucket, its purpose obvious. Once she completed the search of the floor she stood up and went around the walls. With her hands chained to her waist, Fred could only raise her hands chest-high. The walls were bare, she determined, the door the only feature she found.

The three were subject to random checks by the staff. Some encounters more abusive than others, depending on the guard. Of the methods used to punish them, the worst was the spotlight. At random, they would be ordered to stand and recite their names and ID numbers as a bright light was shined on their faces. The incredible intensity of light on their eyes after so many hours of complete darkness was painful. After these checks, white orbs were burned into their vision. Tears would run down their faces, their eyes watering uncontrollably.

Whenever a door would open, the women all experienced the same emotional response: panic. Despite their best efforts to remain calm, all three would feel the rise in their pulse and the quickening of their breathing whenever anyone entered the door. Without the use of sight, they could rely only on their hearing. They would listen to boots scuffing and crunching the sand on the concrete floor as their tormentors moved down the row of cells. Upon hearing the door open, they would get to their feet and prepare to deliver the information demanded. The faster they could recite their IDs, the quicker they would be left in darkness again. As bad as the blackness was, it was preferable to the torments they suffered in the light.

When they first entered the jail, they were dressed in jumpsuits. With the waist chain restraining their hands, they could not get out of them to relieve themselves. All three urinated on themselves, though each managed with great effort not to defecate. At some point—hours, days, they didn't know—their cell doors were opened one by one. They were ordered to kneel down, and their hands and feet were freed. Male officers then ordered them to strip, and they were each thrown a smock and a pair of pants. After this humiliation—the officers, of course, felt free to make comments about them as they undressed—they were again chained and left in their cells. This at least allowed them to relieve themselves. It was the only humane treatment they would receive.

They were each fed once a day via a bowl slid in through a smaller door near the floor, and with each meal, a sixteen-ounce water bottle was given to them. At the same time, their buckets would be exchanged for empty ones. No word was ever said to them, though Fred was beginning to think the person bringing their food and taking the buckets was a civilian worker. Those footsteps were not as loud as the ones from whoever shone the light in their faces. They sounded softer, more like sneakers. That, compounded by the fact that there was little chance the DHS goons would handle the buckets, made her confident in her opinion.

At this point in time, the three women had barely been able to communicate with each other. Fear of reprisal from their jailers kept them silent for the most part, though they did risk it on occasion. Usually after a meal was brought they would wait for a while, and then check on one another. Little was said other than *Are you guys okay?* Answered with hushed whispers of *Yes, you?* On this particular day, their routine was shaken up. From outside the jail, voices could be heard. This was certainly out of the norm. Fred and Jess both sat up, listening intently to the obvious struggle going on just outside the building. The door opened and the shouts of several voices poured in.

"Get his arm!"

"Hold him, hold him!"

"I'll kill you sons-a-bitches!"

From the sounds of the scuffle on the concrete, there was a hell of a fight taking place. Fred pressed her ear to the door, while Jess stood in the center of her cell, her eyes closed, listening intently.

"Dad! Dad!"

"Shane, where are you?"

"Shut up!" another voice shouted.

One of the men let out a guttural growl, the sounds of the scuffle growing nearer as bodies crashed into the walls and floor. A sickening slapping sound filled the building, followed immediately by a scream of pain. Fred cocked her head side to side. There was a pop and the unmistakable sound of a Taser.

"He broke my nose, you son of a bitch!" A voice shouted, "Move!"

The Taser was still clacking when dull thuds were added to the noise.

"Dad! Get off him, asshole! Get off him!"

The thuds stopped. "You want some? You bastard!" The shout was followed by a yelp, then more thuds and groans. "I'll teach you fuckers a lesson!" the man shouted. The sound of someone gagging now rose up, echoing off the walls.

"What are you gonna do now, huh?" The gagging continued.

"Get off him, Reese, he's had enough. Get off, you're gonna kill him."

"Good! They need to be killed!"

"Yeah, well, not yet." Fred could hear someone moving around, pacing. "Pour some water on him, wake him up."

Fred and Jess listened as the two men were dragged past their cells and dropped into their own. Both men were moaning and coughing. The doors were slammed shut and the officers, several of them from the sound of it, walked toward the door.

"I can't believe he broke my frickin' nose."

"I can't believe the old guy was able to knock you over and kick you like that. That's a tough ole bastard." The comment got a chuckle from the others.

"Yeah, lot of help you assholes were!"

"Whatever, you'll live. But you better hope that kid can talk when the interrogators show up," one of them said as the door slammed shut.

Silence closed in around them again. Fred listened intently for any sounds from the new additions to their personal hell. Jess was likewise listening. During the commotion, Mary had finally gotten the urge to fight again. It took a lot of effort, but she managed to pull the tape from her mouth and spit the rag out. Her mouth was dry as chalk and her throat hurt from the lack of moisture. She sat up against the wall and let out a sigh.

In the darkness, a voice croaked, "Dad? Dad, are you all right?" Shane coughed.

He was answered only by a grunt.

"Dad? Was that you? Are you here? I can't see shit, it's so damn dark."

With a heavy voice, full of pain, Calvin answered, "I'm here, son. Are you all right?" He let out a long slow breath, trying to ease the burning in his ribs.

Fred wanted to hear what they had to say, but at the same time, prisoners were not supposed to communicate. She was afraid of the consequences of this conversation.

"My throat hurts. One of those bastards choked me."

"I'm sorry, Shane. I think they broke my ribs," Calvin said as he tried in vain to find a position to relieve some of the pain in his side.

"Where are we?" Shane asked, as he fumbled with the cuffs on his wrist.

Calvin winced at the effort of moving. "I don't know. It's so dark, I can't see anything."

Jess moved to her door and put her mouth close to it. "Stop talking," she said in a loud whisper.

"Who's that? Where are you? Is there someone else in here?" Shane shouted.

"Stop yelling! They'll come back. Stop talking," Fred whispered urgently.

"Where are we? Who are you?" Shane asked as he stared into the blackness.

"You're in the detention center of the DHS camp."

Calvin raised his face. His eyes were closed tight as he resisted the waves of pain running through his side. "We're in the camp?"

"Yes, and if the guards catch you talking, they'll punish you. So be quiet," Fred said.

"Dad, you think we were set up by that old soldier?" Shane said, barely audible.

"I don't think so. I don't think they had anything to do with it. Remember Daniel talking about Morgan? He was with them when the guys from his group were killed by the helicopters, so he surely isn't part of the Feds."

When Jess heard Morgan's name, it was as if someone had thrown cold water on her. Her heart skipped a beat. It was too much of a coincidence. The old soldier had to be Sarge.

"Hey! You know Morgan Carter? And Sarge?" Jess asked in a voice louder than she intended.

There was a moment of silence, then a reply: "If you're talking about a crusty ole guy with a hundred 'n' first Airborne hat, then yes, we met with him today, him and Morgan Carter," Calvin replied.

As tears started to run down her face, Jess whispered, "That's them."

"You know them?" Calvin asked.

"Yes. Sarge and Morgan helped me get home right after the shit hit the fan. I haven't seen them in a long time, though." Jess thought for a moment then asked, "Why did you meet with him?"

"You guys need to quit talking before we get in trouble!" Mary called out in a hoarse voice.

Fred looked in the direction of her voice. "Mary, are you okay?"

Mary pressed herself into the corner of her cell. "Yes! Now shush!"

"How many of you are there?" Shane croaked.

"There's three of us. Is it just the two of you?" Fred asked.

"Yeah. Well, I think so, now. Dad, did you see Daniel?" Shane said.

"I saw him make it to the woods. Omar never got out of the truck. He's got to be dead," Calvin said.

"I think they all are," Shane replied solemnly, then added, "And so will we be, soon enough."

"What'd you guys do?" Jess asked.

Calvin slowly rocked his head back and forth on the wall, "Nothing, we'd just met with Morgan and the old man, Sarge. We pulled out onto the paved road and there they were, two DHS Hummers with machine guns. They just started shooting, no warning or anything."

"What about you guys? Why are you here?" Shane asked.

Jess couldn't reply. After a moment, Fred answered the question.

"We killed a guard, but he deserved it."

The answer caught Calvin off guard. A little smile curled his lips. "Good for you, girls, good for you."

Shane was trying to feel his way around the cell. "Do they ever turn on the lights?"

"No, the only light you'll see in here is from a damn spotlight they'll shine in your eyes," Jess said.

"Damn," Shane said, shaking his head, "how long have you been here?"

"We don't know, there's no way to tell time in here. The only way you can tell a difference between night and day is that it gets colder at night," Fred said.

"We're doomed," Shane said as he slid down the wall to the floor.

Chapter 2

I woke just as the sun was coming up. It was dark in the cabin, but with every passing minute, the light illuminated the room more. I decided to lie there for a bit: the sleeping bag was so warm that I didn't want to get out. I leaned against the wall and looked at the girls. They were mere lumps at the moment, but I knew who was what lump. I could see Mel's blonde hair sticking out of her bag, Little Bit rustling in hers. It was easy to tell the other two. Taylor always slept on her back, and there she was with arms sprawled and her mouth open. Lee Ann's bag was just a knot of nylon with her curled up inside. Outside, the river moved slowly by as birds and other creatures began their day. It was peaceful, and considering everything that was going on, I was happy.

That morning, Sarge and his guys would be leaving us. They were moving out to the National Guard camp to start preparing for their assault on the DHS camp. I wasn't going to be involved, and that was fine with me. I was growing weary of much of this new life, namely shooting and being shot at. For now, Jeff was going to stay, though, if I know that guy well enough, he'd soon want a piece of the action. Thad was still with us, of course, and I think he always will be. He's become part of our family. Danny and Bobbie have also become as close as family and I am so thankful for them. Having them with us adds something familiar, something from the Before that's constant and comforting.

Ready to start the day, I got up quietly and headed for the door. Slipping on my Crocs and coat, I slung the carbine over my head and stepped out. I could see Thad's big form sitting on the picnic table. Past him, fog drifted on the river. Hearing the door open, Thad looked over his shoulder, his smile glowing in the early morning light. I climbed up beside him on the table.

"How long you been out here?" I asked.

"I don't know. A while," he chuckled, "What does time matter anyways?"

Grinning, I nodded. "Guess you got a point there, buddy."

Thad was looking at the fog as it drifted on the water. "Smoke on the water."

"Yeah, looks like a river of smoke, huh?"

"That it does." He nodded. "So, the ole man and his crew are leaving today?"

"That's what he told me last night. I'm going to make a breakfast for everyone. The hens are starting to lay more with the weather warming. I figured we could send them off with full bellies."

"Sounds good to me. Want some help?"

"Sure. How 'bout you go see if the hens laid any overnight, and I'll bring the stove and stuff out here. There's even enough coffee for one, maybe two more pots."

Thad hopped off the table. "I'll do almost anything for a cup of coffee right now. Let's do it."

Thad took off for the coop and I went to the cabin for the stove. I set the stove up on the picnic table and opened the last two canned hams we had.

"Not bad, five more," Thad said, holding the watch cap open to show them.

"Nice, and there's another dozen in the little fridge. I'll run in and get them."

Thad had the stove lit by the time I got back, some of the rendered fat from the hog heating in the cast iron skillet. We cut the two hams up and put them in the pan, then started cracking eggs. Breakfast would be the eggs and ham scrambled together—a simple meal, but a good one. While the eggs cooked, I put on a pot of coffee. We sat in camp chairs while we tended breakfast. There wasn't any talk between us. We worked together in silence. The pan, popping and hissing, offered its own sound track to the morning.

"I'm gonna start a fire," I said, standing up. Thad nodded as I set about getting a fire going in the pit. It was roaring by the time Sarge and the guys headed our way.

"You guys hungry?" Thad called out as he stirred the eggs in the pan.

"Of course we are!" Ted said.

"Where's Jeff?" I hollered.

Mike shrugged, "Don't know, he wasn't in the cabin."

With the meal almost ready, I went back to the cabin and woke Mel up, grabbing a stack of coffee cups on my way out. Thad served everyone a plate while Sarge poured coffee. The guys all took a seat at the table and dug in.

"This is *good*," Mike said, holding up a forkful of ham.

"I hope so. It's the last of 'em," I said.

"We got more MREs down with them Guard boys. We'll get some to you guys," Sarge said.

"So, I know a little bit from Morgan, but I want to hear straight from the horse's mouth. What are you guys going to be doing with the Guard guys?" Thad asked.

"I reckon it's time to take the fight to them federal boys," Sarge said, taking a sip of coffee.

"Good luck. I hope you guys are careful," I said.

"We've got plenty of help now with the Guard behind us. We should be all right," Mike said.

"Yeah, but even with them, how do you plan to take it down? I remember reading somewhere that an assaulting force needs a five-to-one superiority to attack a fixed position," Thad said.

Sarge pulled the tattered hat off and rubbed the stubble on his head. "Well, we haven't completely figured that out yet. I've got an idea. We need to work on it still, but I can assure you one thing: there won't be any full-on frontal assault. We're not going to be rushing the wire like some damn war movie."

I spit into the fire, then looked at Sarge. "Why are you guys doing this? I mean, why stick your neck out? There's enough shit going on, why add even more risk?"

Sarge's head snapped up. "Why? What if it was you in there? What if your wife and kids were in there? Wouldn't you want the cavalry to come save your ass? How about because this is still a free country and the fucking government doesn't have the right to lock people up wholesale."

"I get that, but I mean why you guys? If the army wants to take over the camp, why don't they do it?"

Sarge dropped his head a little. "There's an old saying: all it takes for evil to succeed is for good men to do nothing." Sarge nodded at Mike and Ted. "Despite their appearance, these are good men."

I nodded. "I get it." Sarge smiled and looked into the fire.

"Whatever you guys do, be careful. Ain't no hospitals, you know," Thad said.

"Hey, Doc, them Guard boys got a medic down there?" I asked.

He shook his head. "No, but I wish they did. They just have some combat lifesavers."

I looked at Mike. "You guys better be *damn* careful, then."

"We will. I ain't looking to get killed yet," Sarge said.

Mel walked over to us, leaning in to give me a kiss. "Mornin', boys!" I handed her a cup of coffee. A few feet behind her, Bobbie and Danny were trudging over, both yawning.

"Sleeping in this morning?" Sarge asked with a grin.

"Sorry, my alarm didn't go off," Bobbie said as she sat down.

Sarge looked at his watch. "You're gonna be late for work!"

The joke got a chuckle out of a few of us.

"I wish I had to go to work. I'd happily mop floors and fold laundry today," Bobbie said.

Danny looked up. "Wonder what all those people you cleaned for are doing now."

"I doubt they're doing very well. They all had a lot of money and could have done a lot to prepare, but they lived for the day, not the next."

Thad fixed plates for the three of them and handed them out.

"You guys heading out today?" Danny asked.

"Yeah, we *do* have to go to work," Ted said with a grin.

Danny looked out at the river, chewing a mouthful. Looking back at Sarge, he said, "Be careful with my boat, old man."

Sarge looked over his shoulder at the Tracker. "I will, I'll get it back to you soon enough."

Danny nodded as he took a large forkful of eggs. "Good man."

"You guys taking any of the four-wheelers with you?" I asked.

"No, we'll be back at some point for my buggies, but you guys keep the four-wheelers," Sarge said.

"Cool, they'll be handy to have."

A sound in the woods off to our right got everyone's attention. I put my hand to my carbine, and Sarge stood up, craning his neck for a better view. After a tense few seconds, Jeff stepped out.

"That's a good way to get your ass ventilated," Sarge bellowed.

"Nah, you ain't gonna shoot anything you can't see," Jeff replied as he walked up to us.

Mike started to laugh. "Ever heard of recon by fire?"

Jeff cocked his head to the side. "Hmm, never thought of that." He plopped down on one of the benches. Craning his neck to get a look at the skillet, he asked, "What's for breakfast?"

"Sorry, man. We ate it all," Ted said as he stuffed the last bite from his plate in his mouth.

Jeff looked incredulous. "What?"

Thad took the heavy Dutch oven lid off the skillet. "Don't worry, I wouldn't let 'em do that to ya." He scooped out a plate for him and passed it over.

Jeff smiled as he picked up a fork. "Thanks, glad someone's looking out for me. Hey, Thad, any coffee in that pot?"

Thad poured a cup and handed it to him. "Anything else?" he asked with a smile.

"I'd like some pancakes." He held his hand six inches off the table. "A stack about that high."

Thad started to laugh. "You're shit outta luck with that."

"Actually . . . we can tomorrow," I said, which drew looks from nearly everyone at the table.

"You got pancake mix?" Jeff asked.

"Yeah, syrup too. You know what? We should make some tomorrow. The girls will love it."

"Of course you will, now that we're leaving," Doc said.

"I thought you guys would never leave," I replied with a smile.

"That's messed up! You've been holding out on us," Mike said with a smile.

I laughed at him. "I'm sure that Guard unit can whip up some hotcakes for you, big fella."

"Enough flirtin', you two! We got work to do," Sarge said, as he stood up.

"You guys need any help?" Danny asked.

"Nah, we got it. We'll check in with you before we head out," Ted said.

Sarge stopped by the pot and refilled his cup before heading to the cabin. The guys wandered off one by one as they finished their breakfast. Jeff, Thad, Danny, Bobbie, Mel, and I all stayed around the fire. Danny got up and kicked the ends of some logs into it until it was really roaring.

"What's the plan for today?" Jeff asked, holding a foot over the fire.

"I'm going to work on getting some firewood today. We need more," Thad said.

"I'll help. I could use a workout," Danny said, flexing. Bobbie rolled her eyes.

"We need *food*," Mel said. Bobbie nodded in agreement.

"I'll start looking around, see what I can come up with. In another couple of weeks it'll be easier to find food," I said.

"I'm worried about today," Mel said.

"Do we have anything left?"

"We still have some dehydrated and freeze-dried stuff like carrots, peppers, and onions, plus salt and some flour. There's nothing to really to make a meal out of except for rice and beans," Bobbie said.

"Rice an' beans, beans an' rice," Danny said in a singsong voice.

Mel looked over at me. "An' I'd appreciate it if we could limit your bean intake." This got Thad laughing.

I jerked my head back. "Me? You should hear your ass trumpeting when you're asleep."

Bobbie held a hand out in front of her. "TMI, TMI, let's just stop this before it goes any further."

I smiled. "You're just scared Danny's going to join in."

"Back to the topic at hand: we need food," Mel said.

"Like I said, I'll see what I can find," I said.

"Care if I come with you?" Jeff asked.

"Not at all. And hey, what were you doing out in the woods this morning? Becoming one with nature?" I said, shooting him a grin.

"Just out for a walk really, nothing special."

"See any deer or anything?" Thad asked.

"No, but lots of tracks. I did see an otter, though, down the river here," Jeff said, jutting a thumb over his shoulder.

"Oh, don't tell Little Bit," Mel said. "She'll try to take one home as a pet," she added with a laugh.

After a few minutes, Bobbie stood up, stretching. "I've got to try and wash some clothes today," she said.

"We're almost out of soap. That's going to be a problem soon," Mel said.

"We can make some," Thad said, getting Mel and Bobbie's attention.

"How?" they asked in unison.

"We got that fat from the pig and plenty of wood ash. It'll be easy. I know how to do it."

"How the hell do you know how to make soap? Were you in the Girl Scouts?" Jeff asked.

Thad laughed. "Naw, my grandmomma used to make it when I was little. Back then, I hated it. I wanted store-bought soap. But it always cleaned really good."

"Can we start it today? The more we can have, the better," Mel asked.

"Sure, let me get some wood up first and we'll start it up."

"I want to see this too," Danny said. "I've always read about it but never tried it."

"Well, today's your day," Thad said.

"What would we do without you, Thad?" Mel got up from her seat. "Well, I'm going to wake the girls up so they can eat before it's too cold."

The rest of us decided not to start the day's activities until Sarge and the guys left, choosing to hang around the fire pit chatting. A few minutes later, the girls came down and had their breakfast. It was a nice family meal. Little Bit climbed up into Danny's lap after she ate, still in her PJs. Her older sisters, being teenagers and therefore having a genetic aversion to waking early, sat by the fire, staring into the flames as the fog in their minds cleared. It wasn't too long after that Sarge and the guys drove their buggies up to the boat. We all walked down to the river as they were loading up.

"You gonna get all that in one trip?" Danny asked, looking at the huge pile of stuff in the beds of the two vehicles.

"Yeah, we'll make it fit. I don't want to have to come back," Sarge said.

We all pitched in, helping them load the boat. It was packed, but they did manage to fit everything in. Sarge stood back, looking at the overloaded boat. "We'll have to take it easy, but I think we'll make it."

"Yeah, you better go real slow. I don't want you guys to capsize before you even get your shot at the Feds," Danny said, shaking his head.

"Morg, can you move these buggies away from the river? We'll be back at some point to get them," Sarge asked.

"Sure thing."

"You still got the codebook I gave you when you left my place?" Sarge asked.

"I do, I think it's still in my pack. I never completely emptied it when I got home."

"Good. If you guys need anything, just give a shout."

"Same goes for you. We'll keep someone around them just in case you need to get in touch."

Sarge gazed out at the river. "It ain't the Suwannee, but it sure is pretty here."

I looked out. "Yeah, we've always liked it out here. It's peaceful."

"I could live here forever, I think," Sarge said with a snort.

We spent a few minutes shaking hands and saying goodbye to the guys. Sarge hugged Mel and Bobbie. He knelt down and looked at Little Bit. "You keep an eye on your daddy for me, okay?"

She smiled. "I will, Mr. Sarge! When will you be back?"

"We got some work to do, but don't you worry your pretty little head."

She smiled and hugged the old man. It caught him off guard at first, but then he wrapped his arms around her small shoulders. "I'll miss you," she said.

Sarge leaned back and ran his hand over her hair. "I'll miss you too."

He quickly stood up and got on the boat, and the rest followed. Little Bit gave each of the guys a hug as they got on the boat, telling them to be careful and to come back soon. It brought a smile to everyone's face, the innocence of a child not knowing the danger they were facing. Taylor and Lee Ann waved as the guys got on the boat, yelling good-byes. Taylor was fixated on Mike and flashed him a big smile. Mike winked at her. I saw it and narrowed my eyes at him. He saw me and put his hands up in mock surprise, and I shook my head, gesturing that I was watching him. Sarge started the boat and they were quickly out in the center of the river, barely moving faster than the current.

We all stood at the edge of the river and watched until they were out of sight.

"Well, they're gone," Jeff said.

Thad let out a huff. "For now." We all stood there quietly for another moment.

I couldn't help but think of what they were in for, remembering my last run-in with them over at Lake Kerr. Of course, these guys are the real deal—they do this for a living, after all. Maybe it was the image the DHS had built for itself, but there was a concerted effort to intimidate the American people. For the average person like myself, the thought of taking on an entire camp of DHS storm troopers was more than a little daunting.

The fact that Sarge and the guys didn't have a concrete plan was also a little worrisome. While I know they wouldn't take any chances, they certainly weren't afraid to hang their asses out to get the job done. This is what I was worried about. Despite my concerns, Sarge and his merry band of marauders were some sneaky, deadly bastards, and I was sure they would prevail.

"Come on, Thad. Let's get started on that firewood," Danny said, breaking the silence. Thad nodded at him and the two walked off.

I looked at Jeff. "You wanna go out and see what sort of grub we can scrounge up?"

"I'm game. Where do you want to go?"

"Let's take the kayaks. I want to look on the river. There's lots of stuff out there."

"Cool. You get the paddles and I'll put the boats in the water."

I nodded and walked toward the cabin with Mel to get the paddles.

"You think you can actually find some food out there?" she asked.

"Yeah. It may not be the greatest stuff, but it'll be edible."

She looked sideways at me. "I was hoping for more than *edible*."

I smiled at her. "I'll see what I can do. It's not like a grocery store, ya know."

She patted me on the ass and winked at me. "See what you can do."

"Well, since you put it that way . . ." I said with a laugh.

She handed me the paddles. "Now scoot!"

I walked back to the river's edge and laid a paddle in each boat. "You ready?" I asked Jeff.

He answered by quickly hopping into one of the boats and looking over his shoulder. "Push me out."

I shook my head. "Lazy prick," I said as I shoved the boat out into the current.

I got into my boat, laying my carbine alongside my right

leg, and pushed myself into the slow-moving river. Planting my paddle into the soft mud of the river bottom, I swiveled the boat to face upstream. The kayak I was using was an Old Town Predator, a sit-inside with a huge cockpit. One of the things I really like about it is that it's one of the few sit-ins you can actually stand up in, very handy for what we were about to be doing.

"Let's go upriver, there's a couple places up there that seemed like they could be good spots for some veggies."

Jeff was flailing the water with his paddle, cussing.

"You ever been in one of these before?" I asked with a smile, enjoying the spectacle before me.

"No, how'd you guess? And hey, I thought we were going to find some food."

"We are."

"You said veggies. That's what my food eats," Jeff said as he fought to keep the kayak upright.

"If you'll just relax, that boat will stay right side up. We can look for some game too, but plants are easier to get. They don't run and you don't have to shoot them."

"Easy for you to say. Lead on, O great one."

I instructed him on how to turn his boat and get it faced into the current. Once he was facing the right way, I gave him a quick lesson on how to maneuver and control the kayak. After a few failed attempts, we were on our way. It was nice on the water. Since it was still early, it was cool, and the fog was just starting to burn off. We paddled side by side for a while, my eyes scanning for a stand of arrowhead or wapato.

I eased over to the left side of the river, keeping my eyes on the water's edge. It didn't take long to find a stand of the arrow-shaped leaves. Now came the fun part.

"Over here," I said with a nod in the direction of the stand of plants.

I let my boat glide up to the plants, back-paddling to stop beside them.

"What're you doing that for?" Jeff asked as I shoved my paddle into the mud and started working it back and forth.

"We're getting wapato. Come over here and use your paddle like I'm doing."

"Wapato? What the hell is that?" Jeff asked.

"A lot like potatoes, you can boil and mash 'em or bake 'em. They're pretty good, they were a staple food of Native Americans all over the country. Typically it was the women that collected these, they would wade out into the water, use their feet to release the tubers, and collect them when they floated up."

"How do you know what they look like?"

I pulled a leaf off one of the plants. "See the shape of the leaf?"

"Yeah, it looks like an arrowhead."

"Exactly, it's the only thing in the river that looks like this. We want to get the tubers that are growing in the mud."

Jeff used his paddle like a pole, shoving it into the mud and pushing his way over to the stand of plants. He watched what I was doing for a moment, and then began digging into the mud. I was half waiting for him to turn the boat over. It wasn't long before he was stretched out with one side of the boat tipped almost in the water.

"Shit!" he shouted.

"Pull, dude, pull hard, or you're going swimming!" I said with a laugh.

He managed to get the boat under control and sat there shaking his head. "This is harder than it looks."

"Yes, it is, my friend. It's a little tricky."

Using my paddle, I swept some floating tubers toward my boat and picked them up. "This is what you're looking for. Let's see how many we can find."

Soon enough, tubers were floating all around us, ranging in size from the diameter of a dime to the size of a golf ball. We raked them toward the boats with the paddles and plucked them out of the water. It wasn't long before they were piling up in the boat.

Jeff was examining one of the golf ball–sized tubers. "Very cool," he said, and dropped it back into his boat. "Food you can just pick out of the river."

"They are as close to a direct replacement for store-bought spuds that you'll get. Let's see what else we can find."

I paddled slowly into the current, keeping my eyes on both sides of the river.

"How'd you learn all this?" Jeff asked.

"I studied it a lot. Me an' Little Bit would go out and see what we could find on the weekends. She had a lot of fun doing it, and it was a good excuse to get her out in the woods."

"But why? Have you ever used any of this before?"

"Food is freedom. Control the food, control the people. While a lot of people don't see it that way, if you think about our current situation, it really applies. How many people do you think have gone to the camps because they are hungry? Humans lived for tens of thousands of years before grocery stores, but take them out of the equation and folks panic."

"I see what you mean. Once the canned food or whatever was stored was gone, most people didn't know what to do. Hell, I didn't. If it wasn't for you guys I'd be fucked."

I laid my paddle across the cockpit and looked over at him. "But you're learning and not just sitting on your ass waiting for someone to come rescue you. That's precisely why I studied it. It offered a level of security for me and my family."

Jeff nodded. "I get it. All right, boss, what's next?"

We continued upstream, stopping once to pull a bunch of watercress. I explained to Jeff that it was a green that was similar to spinach. He shook his head. "This is so cool."

At a bend in the river, there was a large stand of cattail on the inside edge. We paddled over, pushing the boats up onto the bar created by the plants.

"You might want to take your boots off for this one."

Jeff looked at me like I was nuts. "You want to get in the water?"

I stuck my hand in the river and splashed him. "Yeah, you afraid? It ain't too cold."

"I'm not afraid, asshole. What do you want to do?"

"We're going to get some of the stalks, but mainly I'm after the roots."

Jeff took his boots off and began trying to extricate himself from the boat. It was like watching a turtle stuck on its back. I laughed at him for a minute then went over and helped pull him out.

"Thanks," he said begrudgingly. "Now what?" he asked, looking around at the water.

I grabbed a plant and cut it off about a foot above the water, then ran my hand underwater and grabbed the base and pulled. The plant came up, pulling other roots that were running away from the plant with it. I grabbed one of the pencil-thick roots and held it up. "We want these. See the little knots? That's the good part. Try and follow them out and pull them up. In another couple of weeks, there will be new shoots we can eat. They're really good."

We spent the better part of two hours pulling the rhizomes out of the mud. It was a messy job—the kayaks as well as our clothes were covered in mud by the time we finished. Thankfully the sun was warming up nicely. With the kayaks loaded, we headed back to the cabins. Going with the current made it a fairly quick trip, even with Jeff's occasional screwy paddling.

The girls were down at the river's edge as we came up. As the boat drifted to where they were standing, they looked at the tangled mass of roots and tubers and laughed.

"What is *that*?" Taylor asked, pointing to one of the tubers.

"It's going to be your dinner and part of your breakfast. You better get used to it," I answered.

Jeff whooped as he stepped out of his boat. "Oh man, I'm a mess!"

Little Bit pointed at him, giggling. "You're all muddy!"

"I'm the muck monster!" Jeff shouted as he started toward her with his arms out, walking like Frankenstein.

She squealed and took off running. I asked Taylor to go get the big washtub and bring it down. When she returned with it we loaded all the tubers, rhizomes, and finally the watercress into it and carried it up to the picnic table. Mel saw us walking up with it and met us.

She looked at the muddy mess in the tub and scrunched her nose. "What's all that?"

I held up a wapato tuber. "You remember eating wapatos a few summers ago? We were camping out at Lake Norris and dug some of these up and cooked them over the fire."

She nodded in recognition and pointed to the white mass of cattail roots. "That's right. What about that?"

"Cattail rhizomes. We're going to process them for starch."

"What are you going to do with it?"

"We'll use it in some pancakes tomorrow for breakfast. It'll make the mix we have go farther."

When the girls heard the word *pancakes*, they all got excited. "Really? Pancakes!" Lee Ann exclaimed. It was the first time I had seen her smile in weeks.

I looked at them and smiled. "With real syrup too." Taylor and Lee Ann high-fived.

I explained to Mel that the tubers would need to be peeled before cooking, and she immediately volunteered the older girls for that job. She said she'd take care of the watercress and that I needed to *deal with* the cattails, as she put it.

I took the tub with the tubers down to the river and washed them by shaking them in the water repeatedly. It was quite an effort to get most of the mud off, rubbing at them with my fingers and swishing them around in the water. Once they were as clean as they were going to get, I filled the tub with enough water to cover the rhizomes. I was wet and filthy by this point, and went back to the cabins to change. *It's a good thing Thad's gonna teach the girls how to make soap*, I thought, looking down at my muddy clothes.

When I came back out, relatively clean, Danny and Thad were sitting on the picnic table.

"You guys done getting the wood?" I asked.

Danny pointed to a massive woodpile over by the chicken coop. "That should take care of us for a few days."

"What'd you guys find?" Thad asked.

I pointed at the tubers that the girls were peeling. "We got some taters, some cattail roots, and some watercress greens."

Thad picked up one of the tubers. "What are these?"

I explained to him what they were and how we could use them. He and Danny both nodded their approval. I told them to come down to the river so I could show them the roots. On my way, I stopped by the woodpile and picked up a piece of oak about the diameter of my forearm.

Thad kicked the side of the tub of tubers. "What are you going to do with this stuff?"

"We're going to get the starch out," I said. Using the end of the wood, I started to pound the roots.

As I worked I explained to them the process: First, you pound the roots as thoroughly as possible, so the water turns cloudy white. Then, you remove as much of the fiber as possible and let the water settle. Once all the starch settles, you pour off most of the water and allow the rest of the water to evaporate. I told them that you could speed up the evaporation process by heating the tub, as long as you were careful not to scorch the starch.

"That's pretty neat," Thad said.

"We can use it to cut things like pancake mix. I'll make some tomorrow for breakfast."

"Oh, the girls are going to be so excited," Thad said.

"Screw that, *I'm* excited for pancakes. What else can we use this stuff for?" Danny asked.

"Anything you would use starch or flour for, like dusting fish for frying or thickening stews. The uses are really unlimited," I said.

After I pounded the roots out more thoroughly, the bottom of the tub had a soft layer of starch. Satisfied, I stood up and we started making our way back to the cabins. It was time for our soap-making lesson.

"I know you get lye from wood ash. What else do we need?" I asked.

Thad pulled a pillowcase from the table. "We need to fill this with ashes. And we'll need a few empty buckets."

We'd had a fire burning in the pit nearly nonstop since we moved into the cabins, so there was a lot of ash. When the pile of ash got too high we would dump it in a pile at the edge of the woods. We went to this pile with the pillow case and a shovel. Thad held the case open while I shoveled the ash into it.

Mel and Bobbie were at the table when we got back.

"You gonna show us how to make this soap?" Bobbie asked.

"Yes, ma'am," Thad said with a smile, "but it takes time. It isn't a fast process."

"What is, these days?" Mel joked, with a smile. "How long does it take?"

"The soap mix can be done in a day, but then you gotta pour it into a mold to set for at least another day. Then when you take it from the mold, it has to cure for a month."

Mel and Bobbie were both shocked. "What? A *month*?" Mel asked.

"Yeah, otherwise it'll burn your skin. It's got to cure. How much soap do we have left?"

"We still have some, but we'll probably be out of it in a few weeks," Bobbie said.

Thad smiled. "Then I guess we need to get this soap made."

Mel clapped her hands. "So! What do we do?"

Thad grabbed the large pot and nodded toward the river. "First, we need to get some water boiling." After filling it with water from the river, he set the pot on the fire. As we were waiting for it to boil, Jeff came back out in a fresh change of clothes.

"This the soap-making class?" he asked.

"This is it," Bobbie said.

"Do we get merit badges?" Jeff asked with a smile.

"No merit badges, but you will get to wash your laundry.

And from the looks of you and Morgan after your adventure today, your clothes need it," Mel said.

Soon enough, the water in the pot was boiling. Thad set the pillowcase of ash into one of the buckets, then asked Danny to pour the boiling water into it. Danny quickly dumped the steaming contents in as requested. Thad folded the edges of the sack over the rim of the bucket and looked up, "Go fill it again." Danny jogged down to the river and refilled the pot. When he returned Thad told him that pot needed to boil too.

While we waited for the water to boil, Thad explained the next step in the process.

"When that one boils, we'll pour it into one of those other buckets. Then the bag has to be dunked in and out of the water, like you're making tea."

We sat around talking while we waited. With so many eyes on it, the pot seemed to take forever to boil. Once it did Danny poured it into the sack as well. Thad grabbed the top of the sack and closed it up, then began dunking it up and down.

"Once this is done we need to boil everything down." Thad looked up at Mel and Bobbie. "Either of you have a big enameled pot?"

"I do, it's about the size of that one," Bobbie said, pointing to the pot used to boil water.

"That'll work."

"This is pretty cool, Thad. I always wanted to learn to do this. It was one of those things I always figured I'd get to." I looked over at him. "Just another example of putting things off till tomorrow. Sometimes tomorrow doesn't come."

"I know what you mean. I never thought of this as a skill I would someday rely on. It was just a way to keep something from the past alive, in a way."

I looked down into the slurry. "There's decades of skills lost that would make our lives easier. The rush to make life easier, more convenient, overshadowed those skills, and we're paying the price now."

Thad grunted. "Yeah, people made fun of folks who held on to the old ways, calling 'em hippies or whatever. I bet they are a lot more comfortable right now than most folks."

Thad poured the slurry into the pot Bobbie handed him. "We'll cook this down for a while." After scraping the bucket out with a stick, he set it on the fire.

"How long does it take?"

Thad looked up and smiled. "Till it's done."

Chapter 3

Ted guided the boat slowly down the river. Between the four of them and all the gear, the boat was almost overloaded.

Doc sat beside him with his feet stuck out on his pack. *Wish I had a flipping stick*, he thought. His thoughts drifted to a few months ago. Doc's tour was almost up before things went south, and he had decided it was time to get out. His parents were both gone now and he had no siblings. He had planned to fix up his parent's old place in Tennessee just as the shit hit the fan. To say he was bitter about the way things worked out would be an understatement.

Sarge sat in the front seat with his legs outstretched on the bow and the SAW lying across his lap. In the cool morning air, it was a peaceful ride down the river. *The calm before the storm*, Sarge thought.

The Guard camp was located on a sand plain six or seven feet above the river, spread out under the old live oaks and gum trees. On the previous visit, Doc had told Captain Sheffield that as nice as the area was, in the summer it would be crawling with ticks, and he was right.

The river became narrow and shallow, and soon, the landing ramp came into view. Captain Sheffield stood at the shoreline waiting for them. Lieutenant Livingston was sitting behind the wheel of a Hummer, and Ian, the adopted marine, was sitting in a second Hummer. Sarge stood as the bow of the boat hit the sand abruptly, launching him out.

Sarge landed on the sand, took one big step to slow his forward momentum, and stood up. "I meant to do that."

Sheffield shook his head. "It almost looked that way." He stuck his hand out, and Sarge took it with a grin on his face.

"Good to see you, Captain."

"Good to see you, First Sergeant."

Ted cut the engine and he and the guys started unloading their gear. Ian came down to help, and together, the four started carrying the gear up to the camp.

"Hey, Doc, I got a couple of guys I need you to check out when we get to camp," Livingston called out.

"Sure thing, what's the problem?"

"Some kind of stomach bug."

"Where are they staying?"

"We isolated them in a tent by themselves."

"Smart move. As soon as we get up there, I'll look at them."

With all the gear unloaded, Sarge got in the Hummer with Sheffield and Livingston while the guys rode with Ian.

"So what's the old man's plan?" Ian asked.

Mike laughed. "I don't think he has one."

"Let me guess: we'll make it up as we go along?"

Doc leaned forward to look at Ian. "And *how* long have you known Sarge?" All the guys started to laugh.

They drove through the camp, which was bustling with activity. People were visible everywhere. Tents were spread out under the old oaks along the river, civilian and military ones mingled in a loose organization. Numerous smoky fires burned throughout the camp. The smoke hung like clouds in the canopy of oak trees and Spanish moss.

They followed the brass in the lead Hummer up to the

command tent and parked out front. As soon as they got out, Doc asked to be taken to the quarantine tent. Ian pointed him to it, saying, "I ain't going in there."

Doc chuckled. "Pussy," he replied, pulling on a set of nitrile gloves.

Sarge, Sheffield, and Livingston went on the Command Post and sat down around a small table. Ted and Mike followed, taking a seat on a couple of crates.

"I'm all ears, First Sergeant," Sheffield said.

"We're going to need to work up a mission plan to try and take over the refugee camp located at the naval bombing range. Right now all I've got is the drawing you already saw. The brass says the camps aren't what they appear. Rumors of forced labor and relocations are coming out of several camps around the country. Worse yet are the rumors of executions."

Sheffield looked surprised. "Executions?"

"That's what we're hearing."

"We're going to need to do some recon on the camp. We need to get as much intel as possible," Livingston said.

"You said you have some equipment that will help with that?" Sheffield asked.

"I do, but before we commit to that, we need to send some guys out to find a place we can set it up. We aren't taking it in there blind," Sarge said.

"We can send in some scouts for a little sneak and peek," Livingston said.

Sarge nodded at him. "As we discussed earlier, send your marine and these two"—Sarge pointed to Mike and Ted—"and a couple of your best shooters. Five men should be enough."

Sheffield looked at Livingston, then back at Sarge. "How about four men and one woman?"

"I don't care if you send Sasquatch, as long as they know how to use a weapon and conduct themselves on a recon mission. Why, you got a gal you want to send out?"

"Yeah, Jamie. She's a spec four and the best shot in our unit. The guys hate it, but she's good. She's a big hunter, bow hunts every year," Livingston said.

Sarge turned to look at Mike and Ted. "You guys got any problem with a woman watching your six?"

Ted shook his head. Mike grinned. "Not me, I'm used to women looking at my ass."

"That's 'cause you're *all* ass, dipshit." Sarge looked back at Livingston. "Let's get 'em rounded up. We need to kick this off as soon as we can."

Ian stuck his head back in the tent. Livingston immediately told him to go find Jamie and the others he wanted on the mission. Ian nodded and waved for Ted and Mike to follow him.

•

Doc walked out of the tent and made his way to the CP. Sarge and the officers were standing out front. "Hey, Captain, who's responsible for hygiene around here?" Doc called out.

Sheffield looked at Livingston. "Sergeant Harmon was pressed into service for that duty."

"Where is he?"

Livingston stuck his head back in the tent and told a corporal there to go find him. "He'll be around shortly. What's up?"

"Those two have dysentery. I want to see the latrines and where you're getting water from, how it's treated and whatnot. Are the civilians running their side of camp any differently?"

"No, we all use the same SOP for camp hygiene."

"Hmph. Well, let's try and fix the issues. I'd prefer if you keep it to just two cases."

"I agree, we'll be swimming in a sea of shit if it spreads," Sheffield said. "What's the treatment for them?"

"They aren't in too bad a shape. They need plenty of clean water, and if you've got any Gatorade or anything similar, it would help."

"We have some of the powdered stuff," Livingston replied.

"That's good, we'll water it down. It will help them replace salts and whatnot."

"Doc, Mike, and Ted are going to go do a recon of the camp. I'd like you to stay behind and try and get this issue under control," Sarge said.

"No problem, Sarge," Doc replied.

A tired-looking black man in his late thirties walked up. "You need me, Lieutenant?"

"Harmon, Doc here said two of our people have dysentery. He wants to see the latrines and some other stuff. Show him whatever he asks to see."

"Not a problem. Glad to have someone around who knows what they're doing," Harmon replied. "Come on, Doc, I'll show you around."

Ian led the way through the camp, giving the guys the rundown on Jamie. "You guys will like her, she's funny as hell"—he waggled his eyebrows up and down—"and not bad on the eyes either. She's the best shot in the unit. She's also a really good tracker."

"Sounds like my kinda woman," Mike said with a grin.

Ian laughed. "She'll eat you for lunch, dude. Don't say I didn't warn you."

On the far eastern edge of the camp they came to a sandbagged bunker. Ian called out as they approached it, "Hey, Jamie, you in there?"

A petite brunette stepped out of the entrance. She looked dwarfed by all the body armor and the PASGT helmet on her head.

"Wha'daya want, Ian?"

"You've been volunteered for a mission. Come with us."

"Who are they?" she asked, jutting her chin in Mike and Ted's direction. Mike immediately noticed her brilliant green eyes.

"Your new best friends. Grab your stuff, come on."

She paused for a moment, not sure whether to believe Ian or not. He was notorious for playing jokes. Stepping back inside, she quickly reemerged with a pack slung over her shoulder. "Where are we going?"

"For a walk in the woods."

Mike stuck out his hand, which she shook. "I'm Mike, and this is Ted. We're going to go take a look at the FEMA camp at the old bombing range."

"Sounds like fun! Is it just us?"

"We need one more person. I was thinking of getting Perez," Ian replied.

Jamie nodded her head. "Grumpy ole fucker would probably like a trip out of here."

"Can you go find him and meet us at the CP?"

"Yeah, I'll round him up." She jogged off.

Ian, Ted, and Mike headed back to the CP. "Dude, she is hot as hell," Mike said.

Ian laughed. "Tell me about it. She's a tough chick too,

redneck as they come. Don't waste your time, though. Nobody has ever scored that one."

"Real nice, Ian. You just threw down the gauntlet. Now he *has* to try," Ted said, shaking his head.

"Challenge accepted!" Mike shouted from behind.

Ted shook his head, Ian laughed. "You better wear your Nomex underwear, brother, 'cause you're gonna go down in flames!"

Ted let out a loud laugh. "I can't wait to see this!"

Doc looked down at the small trench. "This is the latrine?" The visual was almost as bad as the smell wafting out of it.

"Yeah, I know it's crude, but it's the best we can do."

Doc looked at the slot trench, which was woefully unmaintained. It was obviously being used to urinate into as well.

"You know everyone is supposed to cover their waste when they use it, right?"

"Well, yeah, but some people don't."

"We gotta fix this."

"I'm all ears if you know a better way."

"Let's go talk to the lieutenant."

Harmon led the way back to the CP. Livingston looked up as they approached.

"Well, what's the diagnosis, Doc?" he asked.

"We need to do something soon. What you guys are doing to manage waste is not helping matters around here. It's probably why those two are sick."

Sheffield grunted. "Tell me about it, that damn latrine is nasty. I only use it when I absolutely have to. I'll take my chances and piss in the woods."

"That's another problem. You can't be doing that either.

You've got over a hundred people here. If everyone *pisses in the woods*, this place will be a cesspool." Doc paced back and forth. "We need to redo the latrine and make a urine pit where everyone goes." He looked at both officers. "Everyone."

Livingston and Sheffield both nodded, admitting their guilt in not following the standard procedures. "Just tell us what you need," Sheffield said.

"Hm. I need some empty drums, fifty-five-gallon ones, and some pipe too."

"We've got a few empties that used to have fuel in them. As for pipe . . ." Livingston trailed off, then looked at Harmon. "We got any pipe you know of?"

Harmon shook his head.

"We need some sort of aggregate too. I doubt there's any gravel lying around," Doc said, trying to think of an alternate.

"No, no gravel," Harmon replied.

Doc looked sideways at Livingston. "How about cans, like soda cans or food cans?"

Ian and the guys walked up.

"Need cans? We've got a stack of empty cans and aluminum trays from squad meals. Would that work?" Ian suggested.

"What the hell you going to do with that?" Sheffield asked Doc.

"Crush the cans, wad up the trays, and use them as filler for the piss pit. Harmon, you need to find a spot for the new latrine, get all the cans moved over there and have someone crush them all."

"Will do, we'll get started right now," Harmon said, nodding at the captain. Sheffield dismissed him.

Sarge stood off to the side during the conversation, as shit holes and piss pits didn't much interest him. Looking at Ian, he asked, "Where's this Amazon goddess hunter of yours?"

"She's on her way. She's rounding up the other guy we need."

Sarge looked at Ted. "What's your plan?"

"I figure we need to go out and poke around for a place to set up an observation point. We'll do that tonight and then keep an eye on them tomorrow. Maybe tomorrow night we'll move to the opposite side of the camp, see what we can make out."

"You going to take both buggies?"

"No, just the Hyena. Less tracks."

"Sounds good to me. Try and get a head count, equipment, whatever you can see."

"Will do. In that case, we need a ride down to the cabins to get the buggy," Mike said.

"I'll take you guys down in the boat. I need to get some stuff from Morgan," Doc volunteered.

"Works for me. Soon as your help gets here, you guys head out, and grab all the ammo and grub you want," Sarge said.

Jamie walked up with another uniformed man. He was probably close to fifty and had a haggard, hard look to him. Ian smiled at the two.

"Hey, Perez, you wanna go play hide-and-seek in the woods for a few days?" Ian asked.

Perez licked his lips and looked side to side. "Who's *it*?"

"They are. We don't want to be *it* in this game," Sarge said flatly.

"Damn, I hate the hiding part. I prefer to do the hunting."

"There'll be plenty of time for that," Sarge replied.

"You guys got all your shit?" Ian asked.

Perez held up a pack. "Everything I own."

Ian and Sarge looked at Jamie. She turned to the side slightly to show the pack on her back. "Oh, you know me, I got my makeup, some bras . . ."

A slight smile started to crack Sarge's face when Ian said, "Shit, Jamie, you wouldn't wear any makeup if you had it"—he paused and made a show of looking at her chest—"a bra, however—"

"Fuck you, Ian," she said, kicking sand into his face.

Sarge was smiling broadly now. "Oh, I like her, she'll fit right in with these misfits."

"They're your problem now," Livingston said with a smile.

Sarge looked at Doc. "Get 'em down the river, Doc."

After a quick check to make sure everyone had all the ammo and food they needed, the group climbed into a Hummer and they headed for the boat ramp. Doc took charge, navigating the aluminum boat upriver toward the cabins. Being on the water quieted the group. All conversation ceased as each person took in the view. The lilies swaying in the brown water, the old cypress trees, and the beards of Spanish moss hanging down in the current had a relaxing effect on everyone.

When they were almost to the cabins, Mike spun around in his chair. "When we get there, we should talk with Morgan. He knows the area and may be able to give us an idea of where to go to scope out the camps."

Ted had his feet up on the outboard. Without turning around, he replied, "Great minds, my friend. I was thinking the same thing."

Chapter 4

Tabor sat behind his desk, his usual post. He was camp administrator, and under the current circumstances, it was a job he was thankful to have. He was warm, dry, and well fed. He didn't have to deal with the scum running around, and he didn't have to grub around in the dirt to get his food.

"Hey, Ed!" he shouted at the open door.

Ed's head appeared in the open door. "Yeah, boss?"

"Go get Niigata up here. I want to talk to him."

"You going to give those new detainees to him?" Ed asked with a smile.

"Yeah, I talked to 'em, but they both gave me the same line. He'll get the truth out of 'em. No one is out *just riding around* these days."

Ed nodded. "Sure thing," he said, quickly disappearing.

A knock at the door diverted Tabor's attention from the stack of papers before him. Looking up, he saw Niigata and waved him in. "Have a seat."

Niigata came in and sat stiffly in the chair across from him. "What can I do for you?" he asked.

"I've got some people detained who I need you to question."

Expressionless Niigata nodded. "And what were they doing when you captured them?"

"Our security guys caught them driving on the road," Ed said from where he leaned against the door.

"I see. And this is a cause for concern?"

"They were armed, that's one issue, and they were driving a vehicle, which means they have fuel. They were out on the road using that precious fuel, so whatever they were up to must have been important to them, and that's what I want to know. I also want to know where they live. There may be a rogue element at play. We can't take any chances."

Niigata took in the information. "How exactly would you like me to accomplish your request?"

Tabor raised his eyebrows. "Do what you do. I just need to know that information."

"In that case, there are a number of methods I can implement. I'll begin with intimidation—"

Tabor started waving his hands in front of him. "No, no, no, I don't give a shit what you do, I just need answers to my questions. You figure out how to get them."

The faintest tension appeared in the corners of Niigata's mouth. "I understand. How many are there?"

Ed passed a form over Niigata's shoulder. "There's two, Calvin Long and his son Shane. You'll have to start with Shane. The boys got a little rough with Calvin. He's probably got some broken ribs."

Niigata reviewed the document, then looked up. "When would you like me to begin my interrogations?"

Tabor shrugged. "As soon as you can."

Niigata nodded and rose from his seat. "Is there any final disposition you would like for them?"

The question confused Tabor. "Huh?"

Finally Niigata smiled. "Do you want them to be alive when I am finished?"

Tabor sat there slack-jawed looking at the man before him. Ed answered his question. "It doesn't matter, so long as you are confident you've got the info we want"—Ed looked at Tabor—"right, boss?"

Tabor waved a dismissive hand at Niigata. "Yeah, sure. Now get to it."

Niigata bowed his head slightly. "Thank you, sir. I'll let you know the results." He turned and quickly left the office.

Ed came in and dropped into the chair. He looked back over his shoulder to ensure Niigata was gone. "That's one creepy bastard."

Tabor sat in his chair, leaning back with his hands behind his head. "Where'd they get that freak?"

"Remember Abu Ghraib?"

"Yeah."

"Well, he's the one you didn't hear about in the news. Rumor has it he extracted more info than anyone."

Tabor rocked in his chair. "Sick fuck looks like he likes it."

"Oh, he does. You should see him work, takes people apart like a mechanic would pull an alternator."

"Better him than me, I guess. I'm glad he's here."

"Me too. Now let's hope he gets the information we need."

The sound of the bar on the door sliding open echoed throughout the building. Jess was curled on the floor, trying to stay warm. Her eyes jerked open at the sound, but the darkness told her nothing of the visitor. Meanwhile, in her cell, Fred was sitting with her back against the wall and her hands resting on her knees. She turned her face toward the din. There was one other sound that instilled more fear in the girls than anything: the jingling keys. In their time spent in detention so far, one of the few pieces of information they could put together was that it was the cruelest guard who would signal his entry by jingling his keys as he walked down the row of cells. Jess inhaled sharply as the sound of keys became audible. The building was as quiet as a tomb, so any sound was magnified. The sharp clanging of the keys reverberated off the walls, accompanied by the sound of boots crunching sand on the cold concrete floor.

The jingling continued down the row, followed by the sound of metal on metal as a key slid into a lock. The door opened, the dry hinges grinding against one another. When the light hit his face, Calvin turned his head. It was an intensity he'd never felt before. With his hands cuffed to his waist, he couldn't raise them to cover his eyes.

Even though he couldn't see the men, Calvin heard them enter the cell. He tried to brace himself, but there was nothing he could do to prepare. He was grabbed by both arms and jerked to his feet. A painful moan escaped him as he was forced to stand. The fire tearing through his side caused his knees to buckle.

"Get on your feet, dammit!"

With as much effort as he could muster, Calvin moaned, "You fuckers broke my ribs. I can't."

With even more force the two men tried to pull him to his feet. The pain was so intense Calvin completely collapsed. He could feel his ribs popping.

"Son of a bitch, now what?"

"Get the doc over here to see if they really are broken," one of the men said.

The men stepped out and the door slammed shut. Calvin lay there trying to get his breath. He could only take small gasps of air. A full breath was a wish at this point.

"Dad! Dad, you all right?" Shane called out. He'd found his way to the door and had his face pushed into the edge.

The man that just left Calvin's cell stepped over and kicked the door. "Shut up!"

"Come in here and try that shit with me, asshole!" Shane shouted.

Silence answered him. Shane moved his face around the door, trying to determine if the man was still there. After a moment of silence, he was answered with a whisper, "Don't worry, boy, your time is coming."

Shane jerked his head from the door, surprised by the proximity of the voice. He recovered quickly and yelled out, "Big talk on the other side of that door! Open it up, cocksucker!"

Jess shook her head. *They have no idea what they're getting into,* she thought.

Soon, more voices came into the building. The door to Calvin's cell was opened once again, this time without the blinding light that had accompanied the earlier encounter. Before he could even react, a sack was pulled over his head. He could feel hands running over him and something being pushed down his shirt, then an incredible coldness on his chest.

A woman's voice told him to take a breath. He tried, but all he could muster was a gasp.

"Deeper."

Calvin shook his head and managed to say, "Can't."

A set of hands pressed on his side, causing him to wince and moan. After the brief examination, the people left, leaving the sack on his head and slamming the door.

Though muffled, Jess, Fred, and Shane could hear the guards and medics discuss Calvin's condition. "He's got at least two broken on one side and possibly some more fractures," one of them said.

"We're supposed to interrogate him today."

"You can try, but it'll probably kill him."

Another man spoke up. "Whatever, get the other one."

Hearing those words paralyzed Shane momentarily. His mind raced. *I'm not just going to sit here and wait for them to take me.* He felt around the door, trying to see if there was a handhold, but came up with nothing. He knew he couldn't run at them, but then he remembered an old football drill. He squatted down in front of the door, reaching out to make sure he was close, then took up the position of a lineman, his hands on the floor and his knees bent. With his feet shackled he had to keep them side by side, but he hoped he'd have enough leverage for what he planned.

As the key slid into the lock, he squeezed his eyes tight. The door started to swing open. Even with his eyes closed, the spotlight bore through his eyelids. Shane launched himself through the door. However, it was wider than he anticipated, causing the guard to be standing farther away. Shane's shoulder hit the man's knees. He managed to knock the man down, but he fell directly onto Shane's back, the spotlight crashing to the floor. The guard quickly recovered and drove an elbow into Shane's back again and again, taking all his breath away.

Shane lay on the cold concrete, trying to get air into his lungs.

"Thought you were smart, didn't ya, you little shit?"

A hood was quickly pulled over his head, and he was grabbed roughly by the arms.

"Get up, get on your damn feet!" one of the men shouted.

Shane was finally able to get a breath and managed to

stumble along. As a door was opened, the warmth of the sun washed over him. Even through the hood on his head, he could see the sunshine through the cloth. As he was pulled along he marveled at the feel of the sun on his body. For a moment he was elsewhere, but only for a moment.

Another door was opened and he was dragged inside another structure. The two men forced him into a chair, then spent several minutes undoing his restraints and securing them to the chair.

"He's all yours," one of the men said.

"Keep an eye on him. He thinks he's pretty smart," the other said. Shane's head snapped forward as one of them slapped him in the back of the neck.

Shaking off the insult, Shane rotated his head. The fabric of the hood was thick and he couldn't see anything, but turning his head allowed him to focus his hearing. His other senses were also more acute. The place had an antiseptic smell. It reminded him of the nurse's office from his elementary school.

The room was silent, but he knew someone was there. Shane wanted to say something, but he decided to wait for whoever was there to speak first. Instead, he focused on controlling his breathing and trying to relax. He was worried about his dad, and rage was building inside of him. They hadn't done anything to deserve this. Was it illegal to be driving down the road now? Even if it was, it certainly didn't justify all this. They hadn't bothered anyone. Some of their group members wanted to take the fight to the Feds, but Calvin had counseled against it. He assured them the fight would come to them, but that they shouldn't go looking for it. Unfortunately, when it did find them, they were caught completely by surprise.

After an uncomfortably long time, Shane jumped at what sounded like a chair scraping across the concrete floor. Footsteps followed and he listened as this person moved about the room. Despite his efforts to remain calm, his breathing began to increase, sucking the sack in with every inhalation. After a moment, the hood was snatched from his head. Shane closed his eyes against the light.

The man who pulled the hood from his head was balling it up, his back to Shane. As he tossed the hood onto a small table, he began to speak.

"Shane, my name is Raidon Niigata. You may refer to me as Niigata." He spun around and leaned back on the table, crossing his ankles.

Niigata smiled and began to speak again. "You and I are going to have a conversation. I will ask you some questions and you will answer them."

As he spoke, Shane was trying to remember what his voice reminded him of. Then it dawned on him: he sounded like Sulu from the original Star Trek series. This realization caused a small smile to creep across his face. Niigata noticed immediately and smiled back.

"Have I said something that amuses you?"

The smile disappeared immediately. "No, just an old memory is all."

"Ah, memories, yes, we all have them. Maybe we can talk about some of yours."

Shane didn't respond. He simply stared back.

A scowl wrinkled Niigata's face. "I hear your father is not well—pity. But that is what brought you and me together, isn't it?"

Shane shook his head. "*Not well?* That what you fuckers

call it when you beat a cuffed man? What happened to our rights?"

Niigata smiled again. "How quaint. I assume you are referring to your oft-misquoted *Constitutional rights.* I am certain you realize we are operating under a different set of rules at the moment."

Shane snorted. "Yeah, I've seen your rules in action."

"Then we can skip the pleasantries and move ahead," Niigata said, picking up an instrument from the table behind him.

Shane's pulse immediately jumped when he saw the scissors. As Niigata moved toward him, he struggled against the restraints, to no avail. Without saying a word, Niigata began to cut his shirt off, the blade of the instrument cold against Shane's skin. Niigata jerked the tatters of the shirt off him.

"What the hell are you doing?" Shane shouted.

As Niigata knelt down at his feet, he began to speak again. "Tell me, Shane, what do you know about interrogation?"

Shane watched in horror as Niigata began to cut up the left leg of his pants. Niigata paused and looked up expectantly.

"Uh, I uh, I know it's mainly psychological," Shane stammered as Niigata snipped through the waist of his jeans.

Very deliberately, Niigata moved to the right leg. "Very good. You are both right and wrong."

Trembling, Shane asked, "Why are you doing that? What the fuck?"

"We are establishing the basis of our relationship," Niigata said, as he stood he snatched the flayed jeans out from under Shane.

Shane let out an audible gasp, looking down at his exposed chest and legs. The room was cold and caused goose bumps to rise. He was thankful he still had his underwear on. In an effort to stop Niigata from going any further, he started to talk, fast.

"You haven't even asked me anything yet! Why are you doing this? You don't know I won't cooperate."

Niigata turned and laid the scissors on the table, much to Shane's obvious relief.

"Good point, but you can't fault me for thinking you would be resistant to answering my questions."

Calvin laid on the floor of his cell. He knew they had taken Shane away, but there wasn't anything he could do about it. He was in so much pain. His sides were on fire. With much effort he was able to get himself up into a sitting position. The effort required to do so was intense, and he sat panting against the wall. Once he caught his breath, he called out.

"Hello?" His voice was weak, and he wasn't sure anyone was even around to hear it. He called out again. "Is there anyone here?"

Fred and Jess both heard him and moved toward their doors. Fred answered him in a loud whisper, "Yes, we're still here."

Calvin looked around, unable to see anything in the blackness. "Where'd they take my son?"

"We don't know," Fred answered.

Jess sat at her door wringing her hands. Whatever was happening surely wasn't a good thing.

"Will they bring him back?" Calvin asked.

"I hope so," Jess whispered, to herself more than to Calvin.

Fred leaned against the door. "I'm sure they will," she said unconvincingly.

Calvin's chin dropped to his chest as tears started to roll down his cheeks. How could it be that one day ago, they were free, and now his son was going through God knows what?

Shane was tense, waiting for Niigata to start questioning him. But the man was in no hurry. He leaned against the table and stared Shane in the eye. After a moment, Shane noticed the small stand behind him. Turning, Niigata gripped the stand and pulled it around the table. The small stand was covered with a cloth. Niigata positioned it in front of Shane, pulling off the cloth to reveal an assortment of medical instruments and tools.

Shane stared at the implements lying before him. He started to feel light-headed and his ears began to ring. Niigata looked over the items on the tray, inspecting the occasional piece.

"It's time to begin, Shane." Niigata paused and looked at him. "How we proceed is entirely up to you at this point."

Shane's eyes moved back and forth from Niigata to the tray. His chest was heaving, as he was nearly hyperventilating.

"Let's start with the obvious: why was your group on Highway 40?"

Shane's mind was racing as fear crept in. "I didn't know driving down the road was illegal. You guys just started shooting. We didn't do anything wrong."

Niigata inspected the tray, then picked up another pair of scissors. Without looking up, he said, "You didn't answer my question." He looked at Shane. "I do not like to repeat myself, so please do not make me."

Shane licked his lips, looking at the instrument, but said nothing.

Niigata smiled and stepped toward him. "Remember how you said interrogation was *mostly* a mental exercise?" Niigata leaned over and swiftly cut the band from one side of Shane's underwear, causing him to jump.

"What the fuck, man?"

"You still haven't answered my question," Niigata said as he snipped the other side, leaving the front of Shane's drawers lying limp in his lap.

Shane was entirely off-balance now. His mind was running away, the fear of the unknown taking over.

"We were just out for a ride. We met some people and were headed home!" Shane shouted.

Niigata leaned back against the table and crossed his arms. "Very good. Who did you meet?"

"Uh, just some people. I didn't know them."

Niigata smiled again. "You have a pretty good poker face, Shane. It's a shame your eyes betray you."

"Huh?"

"You looked left, which tells me you made that up." Niigata stood up and turned to the tray. "It's not your fault: it's involuntary."

"No, no, it's the truth, I didn't know them." It was technically correct, but Shane didn't know how to convey that.

When Niigata turned to face Shane, he was pulling a pair of latex gloves on his hands. "Let's say that's true, you did not know them. Then your father, Calvin, he must know them?" He let the glove snap against his wrist.

"No, he didn't know them either!"

"How many people did you meet?"

"Only two that I saw?"

"So you think there were more?"

Shane shrugged his shoulders. "I don't know, maybe."

Niigata stepped forward quickly, leaning over so his mouth was beside Shane's ear. "It only gets worse from here." He snatched the remnants of Shane's underwear out from under him.

Shane yelped as a cruel smile spread across Niigata's face.

Chapter 5

Thad and I were sitting in camp chairs by the fire. He was stirring the pot of slurry. After the wood ash soaked in water, the lye was leached out. Now it had to be reduced.

"How do you know when it's done?" I asked.

"There's a test for it we can do in a few minutes," Thad replied.

Jeff and Danny walked up carrying fishing rods. "We're going fishing while you Girl Scouts make your soap," Danny said. Jeff started to laugh.

Thad looked up and shook his head. Rolling my eyes, I said, "Go ahead, yuk it up. But when we're done, I'll know how to make soap *and* I can catch fish."

"Good, then there will be twice as many people around here who can make soap," Jeff replied, laughing.

I looked at the pot bubbling on the fire. "Thad, would that stuff burn your skin?"

He lifted the stick he was stirring with, the thick slurry sloughed off in thick strings. "It might"—he raised it back as if to swing it—"let's see."

Danny and Jeff looked like two of the three stooges as they pushed and shoved one another and ran away.

Thad looked up, laughing. "Serves 'em right."

"Damn straight! Shoulda slung it at them. I would have," I said with a chuckle.

Taylor and Lee Ann walked over.

"Dad, can we take a walk in the woods?" Taylor asked.

Without looking up, I replied, "Not right now. You guys need to hang out around here. I'll go with you later."

"Come on, Dad, we've got our guns. There's no one around here," Taylor protested. Lee Ann shifted her weight from foot to foot.

"You don't know that," Thad said.

I nodded at him and stood up. "I know you guys are bored, but we can't chance it. Just because you have guns doesn't mean you're protected, as we have already seen." I felt kind of bad adding that last line, but it was true, and I hoped they took it for how it was meant. The last thing I wanted was for one of them to get shot again. "Look, why don't you two go work on the garden plot over there? We've got to get those plants in the ground soon."

The girls looked at one another. It was obvious they weren't impressed by the suggestion.

"A little hard work never hurt anyone," Thad said with a grin.

"If we do that, will you *promise* to take us for a walk later?" Lee Ann asked. The past few weeks, she had been staying inside the cabin, sleeping late into the afternoon. A little bit of fresh air would do her good.

With a smile, I replied, "Sure."

They turned and headed for the small plot. We watched as they took up the rake and hoe and set about chopping at the ground. I looked at Thad. "Why is it you can get them to do chores with a little suggestion, but I can't pay them to do it for me?"

"It's that third-party thing. You know, other people can get kids to do things they won't do for their parents. I read about it somewhere."

"Well, third party, I hope you stick around for about ten years."

Thad's head rocked back as he started to laugh.

Little Bit came over and wanted to help the girls, but it was quickly obvious that none of them were very interested in what they were doing.

"I'm bored," Little Bit said.

Taylor leaned against the hoe she was using. "Yeah, this sucks."

My head popped up. "It *what*?"

She gave me an innocent smile. "Can we do this later?"

I sighed. "Yeah, go see if your mom needs anything first, though."

I looked at Thad. "So much for that."

He laughed. "Yeah, didn't last long, did it?"

The sound of a motor at the river snapped us back to reality. Instinctively I reached for my rifle, which was leaned against the picnic table. We both looked downriver for the source of the sound. It wasn't long before Danny's boat came into view. We walked down to the river as it eased into the mud.

"Back so soon?" I crowed.

I shook Mike's and Ted's hands as they got out of the boat, followed by three others I didn't know.

"Morgan, Thad, this is Ian, Jamie, and Perez," Mike said, introducing them.

Thad and I both shook hands with them as Doc got out of the boat.

"Well, to what do we owe the pleasure of this little visit?" I asked. Looking at the boat and the load it was carrying, I added, "Looks like you guys are about to stir some shit somewhere." I pointed at the pile of packs, ammo cans, and other gear. "Y'all bring enough party favors?"

"Yeah, we got a little sneaking around to do," Ted said.

Mike smiled. "What's a party without some noisemakers?"

"Better not be any noise, that is not the point of this mission, peckerwood. You better keep your noisemaker in its holster," Ted said.

Mike rocked his boonie hat forward on his head, put his hands on his hips, and leaned back at the waist, pushing his hips out, "You mean my noisemaker, or my *noisemaker*?" He was smiling and bouncing his eyebrows up and down, looking at Jamie.

Jamie cracked her knuckles. "I see your *noisemaker* and I'll fieldstrip it." Her statement got a round of laughter.

Thad looked at Doc. "You gonna take care of these guys?"

"Nah, I'm not going. I just delivered 'em here." He looked at Ted. "If they do this right, they won't need my skills. They're just supposed to do some surveillance on the camp so we don't go in there blind."

"Holy crap, they're going out without adult supervision?" I asked, with a laugh.

"That's what she's here for," Ian said, nodding over to Jamie.

Jamie snorted. "If you're counting on me to be the positive influence, you're in trouble."

Perez snorted. "There's an understatement." We all started to chuckle. It was clear that Jamie was a rough-and-tumble girl.

"Hey, Morg, I need some pipe. I know you guys brought a bunch. Do you have any to spare?" Doc said.

"Yeah, Danny's piled it up somewhere."

"Where is he?"

"He and Jeff went off fishing somewhere. What sort of plumbing you doing?"

Doc rolled his eyes. "You don't want to know, really." He

looked down the river. "I'll go find them as soon as we get the boat unloaded."

"I'll go get the war wagon," Mike said and headed off toward where they were parked.

We all pitched in and started to unload the boat. There was a mountain of ammo and supplies piled up in it: some for us and some for their mission.

Mike soon rolled up in Sarge's wagon and started setting it out it so it could be organized with the supplies. Once the boat was emptied, Doc got in and started it up.

"Which way did they go?" Doc asked.

I pointed upriver. "Last I saw them, that way."

Doc nodded and eased the boat out into the river. "I'll be back," he said.

Mike was bent over at the side of the buggy pinning a SAW to the hard mount. I kicked the back of his knee, buckling it. "When are you guys heading out?"

He looked back with an expression that said *asshole*. "After dark. And actually, we need your help. We want to go over the drawing of the camp with you. You know this location way better than any of us. We need all the details you can remember about the landscape."

"Sure thing. Let me see the drawing. When you guys are done sorting out your crap, come over to the picnic table."

Ted handed me the drawing and Thad and I walked over to the table. I sat down while Thad took a seat in the camp chair and went back to stirring his slurry. The crew came over to the table and sat down. Mike looked over in the pot. "I was going to ask what's for dinner, but I'm afraid to ask now. That looks like shit"—he sniffed the air—"and smells worse. What the hell is that?"

Thad chuckled. "It's soap, or it will be."

"Damn, you wash with that, and you'll smell worse than before you started," Mike said, scrunching his nose. Thad and I both laughed.

"Hey, Thad, we got a couple of hours before dark, and it looks like this soap project isn't going anywhere fast. You think we could grill up a piece of that hog for these guys?"

"Sounds good to me. Let me get some more wood and some meat," Thad said as he stood up.

"Great. And if you don't mind, tell Mel we're going to have company for supper."

He nodded and headed for the woodpile.

"You guys have fresh pork?" Perez asked.

"Yeah, we've got a few hogs. Butchered one recently."

"Damn, fresh pig meat! I haven't had that in forever."

"Thad's great on the grill too," I said with a smile. Mike and Ted both nodded their agreement.

Ted tapped the drawing. "So, what can you tell us about this place?"

I spun the drawing around and started making some marks. I indicated where the antenna where we had met Calvin was, then marked the approximate location of the rear gate. I drew in the roads to the best of my memory. As we were discussing the access to the camp, the boat came back into view with Danny and Jeff on board. They climbed off and Danny and Doc headed for Danny's cabin. Jeff came up and flopped onto the bench beside Jamie, looking at her with a big grin. "Hello, I don't think we've had the pleasure of meeting," he said with a wink.

Jamie cut her eyes at him, then scooted away. Ted rolled his eyes and smiled. "Jeff, this is Jamie, Perez, and Ian."

Still smiling, Jeff grabbed Jamie's hand. "Really nice to meet you." He looked back and gave the others a curt nod.

Ian couldn't help himself and started to laugh. Jamie couldn't take it anymore. She was a redneck girl, and so she was used to speaking her mind.

"Fuck you, Ian!" she shouted across the table and kicked at his knees under it.

Still laughing, Ian jumped. "What'd I do?"

Jeff was resting his head on one hand, the elbow propped up on the table, still grinning like a mule eating briars. Being a single man, Jeff enjoyed the company of beautiful women, and we all knew from tales of his conquests that one in uniform with weapons was a real turn-on for him. This was classic Jeff flirtation style—embarrass the girl a bit, hoping that his charm would win her over.

For her part, Jamie wouldn't turn her head in his direction. The look on her face told everyone she wasn't happy. Ian was enjoying it more than Jeff—you couldn't have smacked the smile off his face if you'd tried. While all this was going on, I was still trying to make notes on the map. Once I had given them all I could remember, I dropped the pen and stood up just as Mel and Bobbie walked over with the two older girls.

As they were introducing themselves I checked on Thad and the soap, which he was tending to in between getting the cooking prepared. The pot of lye had cooked down considerably.

"How much longer till we can get clean?" I asked.

Thad lifted the stick he'd been stirring with, looking at the liquid as it ran off. "Might be there," he said.

"How will you know?"

He smiled and plucked a chicken feather from the cupholder in the arm of the chair he was sitting in. Dropping it into the pot, he explained, "This is a little test you can do to see if the lye is strong enough."

The feather hit the lye and the fine edges of it dissolved nearly immediately, then the quill slowly dissolved. After less than a minute there was nothing left of it.

"Holy shit! It just dissolved the entire thing!" I exclaimed.

Thad smiled. "Yeah, it's some rough stuff, ain't nothing to play with. But now we know it's ready."

"What do we do next?" The process was fascinating to me, way more than I'd expected.

"Now we add the fat and mix it up."

"I'll go get it," I said and headed for the cabin. We had rendered a bunch of it and kept it in a five-gallon bucket with a lid hammered down on it.

As I headed for the cabin I looked around. Everyone was down at the picnic table talking. The older girls had made their way over to where Thad was. He was showing them the feather trick again. *Little Bit would like that*, I thought and looked for her. She wasn't in the cabin either. I looked around the grounds for her as I carried the bucket back over to Thad.

"Hey, have you two seen your little sister?"

"Earlier. She was playing with the dogs," Taylor said as she watched the feather melt. "That's cool," she said, looking up at Thad.

"Hey, Mel, where's Ashley?" I called to her.

She and Bobbie both turned around. "Lee Ann, you were supposed to be watching her. Where is she?" she said as she looked around.

"I don't know, she was running around with the dogs and I didn't feel like following her," Lee Ann said.

"Well, I don't see her, and I don't see the dogs either," I said as I walked out toward the dirt road in front of the cabins. I looked back at Lee Ann. "You shouldn't have left her alone."

Quickly everyone was up and looking for her. With so

many people in our group, we covered the area around the cabins in just a few minutes. She wasn't anywhere, and neither were the dogs. Panic was quickly beginning to overtake me as my heart began to race.

"Where could she have gone?" Mel shouted as she ran from cabin to cabin.

"It's not my fault!" Lee Ann cried.

"We'll go check the road, you stay right here," Ted said as he and Mike passed me.

I nodded at them and headed for the woods on the east side of the cabins, behind the chicken coop. The chickens were back there browsing through the scrub, but no Ashley. Hearing my name being called, I ran out of the woods.

"Go out to the road," Mike said, pointing.

I turned and headed for the road as he ran past me. Ted was knelt down, looking at the dirt track.

"What is it?"

He was holding a small stick and began to describe what he saw, "Here's her print, and the dogs', of course." Pointing with the stick, he rose up and moved in a crouch. "Then there is this," he said, pointing to a much larger track from what appeared to be a full-grown man.

My heart sank.

Mike came wheeling up in the buggy with Jamie, Perez, and Mel. Danny was right behind them on his Polaris with Doc.

Ted looked at me. "Notice how it's only this track that leaves, plus the dogs'?"

I nodded and said barely above a whisper, "He must have carried her off."

Ted nodded. Then Mel shouted, "Morg? What's the matter? Where is she?"

I stood up as she ran up. "Someone took her. All we have are tracks."

"What do you mean someone took her?" she screamed. "How could someone take her from right here with everyone around?"

"I don't know," I said, fear gnawing the pit of my stomach.

"But we're going to find out, Mel," Ted said.

I climbed into the buggy with Ted and Mike. Mel jumped in too. "Make room for me."

Danny and Doc pulled up beside us. "We'll follow you guys. The girls are staying here with Thad," Danny said.

Mike drove down the road as Ted hung out the side watching the tracks. From the ATV, Doc was also tracking as Danny drove. They were going to the north, toward the paved road. If they got to the paved road it would be nearly impossible to find them. My head was spinning as I thought of Ashley's smiling face. She was so little, so sweet. The thought of what could be happening to her made me sick. Tears began to run down my cheeks.

I looked at Mel. She was a total mess. I wiped my face to try and give the appearance of certainty that we would find her. I put an arm around her and she laid her head on my shoulder.

"We're going to find her," she said, more to herself than to me.

"Don't worry, babe, we will."

Several times we had to stop and get out to look for the tracks. For whatever reason, they wandered off the dirt road from time to time. At one of these spots, Ted found the tracks heading off the road. Ted, Mike, Mel, and I followed them off the road for about fifteen feet. We could clearly see Little Bit's footprints in the sand, then a wet spot.

"Looks like someone took a leak," Ted said.

Mel started to cry again. "She's afraid to pee in the woods." She looked at me. "You know she doesn't like to do it when we go camping."

Little Ashley had a thing about it, often requiring a detour to a real bathroom somewhere. The thought of her being forced to relieve herself out here in front of a stranger, a malicious one at that, sickened me. I wrapped my arms around her. "We'll find her, babe, don't worry."

But even as I said it, a part of me feared the worst.

Chapter 6

Shane's face and chest hurt. Niigata had been repeatedly slapping them in turn. The skin on his chest was now bright red, as was his face. Niigata had paused the assault. One of his gloves had ripped.

"You can't do this shit to me. I'm an American citizen!" Shane shouted, his face stinging as he yelled.

Niigata turned, smiling. "So you are, but you are also now classified as an enemy combatant, which means I can do what I want to you."

"Enemy combatant?! We were defending ourselves! Your people opened fire on us without warning!"

"Let's not quibble over the details," Niigata said, delivering a savage slap to the right side of Shane's head. He slowly turned back to face Niigata. "Fuck you."

In his pain, Shane hadn't noticed the object in Niigata's right hand. Niigata brought the stun baton up quickly, jamming it into Shane's neck and triggering it. The hundred thousand volts caused his body to convulse and jerk in the chair as a long, loud moan escaped him. When Niigata finally let off, Shane's body went limp, his head hung on his chest.

"Now, where were we? Ah yes, your meeting—what was the purpose of it?"

Shane's head rocked back and forth. "I told you, we were just riding around and ran into them."

Niigata stuck the end of the baton under Shane's chin and raised his face. "No one just *goes out for a ride* these days. Fuel is precious, and the fact alone that you have a running vehicle and fuel says a lot about you. Now, who did you meet with?"

"There's nothing to tell!" Shane yelled.

"If you were just out for a ride, as you say, then why were you armed? Under martial law you are not supposed to have weapons."

"Come on, everyone's armed!" Shane exclaimed.

"I can see this is going to require a little more effort. You may be telling the truth, or you may not, but we'll find out." Niigata took the gloves off and tossed them on the table.

Shane heard the door open. Niigata spoke to someone then returned with two other men. The hood was once again pulled over his head, and the two men set about removing the restraints that secured him to the chair and reapplying the ones he'd worn coming into this torture session. Once he was secured, the men pulled him to his feet and led him toward the door. Shane was thankful to be getting away from Niigata, though he didn't know what would happen next.

Once outside, the sun's rays warmed his entire body. This reminded him that he was still naked, being trotted around the camp with just a hood. He was led back into the building containing the cells—he could tell it was the same one from the smell. A cell door was opened and he was led in. The cuffs were disconnected from the waist chain and his arms lifted over his head as a clicking sound filled the room. Before he realized what was going on, his arms were pulled high over his head, then the clicking changed in pitch as he was lifted to the balls of his feet. He was barely supporting any of his weight with his legs, and his wrists ached.

"What the fuck?" Shane shouted.

"Here, this'll make you feel better," a voice said, a second before he was hit with a bucket of water.

The water was so cold, it caused Shane to yelp. Reflexively, he tried to turn his body, but before he could even react, he was hit with more water. The door was slammed shut, and one of the men said, "We'll be back."

Shane pictured how he must look: cold, wet, naked, hanging like a side of beef. He began to shiver. The building was cold to begin with, but now that he was naked and wet, Shane knew he was about to experience a level of cold he'd never known existed.

Kay was busy in the kitchen, humming to herself. The next lunch service would start in twenty minutes. She was stirring a large pot of red beans and rice and thinking of the girls. She was worried about them, and whatever cruel fate they were experiencing in detention. She had heard rumors about what happened there, but she didn't even want to think of what those three were going through given the crime they'd committed. She smiled, thinking about how they would banter in the kitchen. Those girls had been different from most of the other women who worked for her, and she really cared for them. But there was nothing she could do for them now. Any attempt to help would land her in detention with them. Kay tilted the big pot and started raking the beans and rice out into a serving pan. As she carried the pan to the dining area she was greeted by the usual racket from the crowd.

Kay set the pan in the warmer and turned back to the kitchen. Before she made it through the door, someone called out to her.

"Hey, Kay!"

She stopped with one hand on the door to the kitchen and looked back. "Oh, hi, Aric."

Aric approached and nodded for her to go into the kitchen. He followed her in then motioned for her to go to the dry storage room. Kay led the way. He took a look around the kitchen and closed the door behind them.

"Is everything all right?" Kay asked with concern in her voice.

Aric turned to face her. "Oh yeah, everything is okay. I just wanted to talk to you in private."

"About what?"

"Fred and the other girls. Have you heard anything about them?"

"Oh no, I'm the last person who would find out about them. You'd probably know something before I would," Kay said.

"Well, you know how it is. Everyone around here seems to have a source of their own. I was just hoping you'd heard something."

"No, I'm sorry," Kay said, lowering her eyes to the floor. "I wish I knew something. I'm so worried about them."

"Tell me about it. I know they did what they're accused of, but I also know he deserved it," Aric said, running a hand through his hair.

Kay looked up at him and grabbed his arm. Her eyes were pleading. "Then why don't you say something? They'll believe you! You're one of them."

"Pfff, they wouldn't listen to me. If I said anything, it'd go badly for me, and I don't want to end up where they are. It wouldn't help at all."

"They wouldn't do that to you!" Kay protested.

Aric shook his head. "You're right, they might just kill me."

Aric could tell from the look in her eyes that Kay didn't believe that. "These people don't play around, Kay, believe me."

Kay nodded in understanding, thinking about some of the cruelty she had witnessed. "You're probably right."

Without thinking about it, Aric reached out and hugged the old woman. It surprised him nearly as much as it did her. After a pause, Kay wrapped her arms around him. Aside from the girls, Kay hadn't hugged anyone since her husband had died. And in the Before, her husband was one of few people she ever showed affection to, for that matter. Aric was the same way. He'd never been a very affectionate person. Hugs and saying *I love you* were not very common in his house growing up. But in this moment, they needed each other's comfort.

"Thanks, Kay," Aric said as he turned to leave.

"Thank you," Kay said. "I knew you weren't like the others."

Aric gave her a weak smile then left the kitchen. He was going to find a way to get to Fred, he decided. He knew what her future held and, in that moment, he decided he was going to do something about it.

Calvin listened as Shane was brought in. While he couldn't see him, hearing him yelp confirmed it. It was the same cry he'd made many times as a kid when Calvin would prank him. Calvin would creep into the bathroom quietly and stand there for a moment, then he would dump a glass of ice water over the top of the shower curtain. While that was a fond memory of Shane as he grew up, when he heard that splash he knew they'd just soaked his son. He also knew that the cold in the building would certainly lead to hypothermia. He waited for the men to leave. Once he heard the door close he called out. "Shane? Is that you, son?" The effort required to call out was incredibly painful. Calvin slumped back against the wall holding his side.

Shane's arms were already burning and his teeth chattered uncontrollably. "Y-yeah, I'm h-here."

"You okay, son?"

"I'm c-cold. They t-took m-my clothes and threw water o-on me."

"Bastards," Calvin moaned. "Let your body shiver, don't try and stop it. It's generating heat."

"N-not enough."

"Jess, hey, Jess!" Fred called in a loud whisper.

Jess whispered back, "What?"

"Is it day or night?"

"How should I know? It's always dark."

"Yeah, tell me about it. I get dizzy if I stand up too long," Fred said, leaning against the wall.

"That's why I spend so much time on my ass," Jess replied. It was a weak joke, but the first joke heard in a while. Fred's laugh echoed through the building.

"I-it's daylight out," Shane said.

Fred looked in the direction his voice came from. "I'm so sorry they did that to you. I wish I could help."

"M-me too."

Mary was lying on the floor of her cell in a fetal position. She didn't hear the whispers of those down the hall from her. Her head was filled with voices. Despite her best efforts she couldn't stop them and they were driving her mad. Curled up like she was, she was able to get her hands over her ears. She clasped them tightly and rocked back and forth. In an effort to drive the voices out of her mind, she started to hum.

"Mary, is that you?" Jess called out.

There was no reply, and after a moment Fred called out, "I think it is. It sounds like she's humming."

A key sliding into a door caused everyone to stop talking. Fred moved along the wall away from her door. The sounds of boots scuffing and grinding the concrete filled the air. At least two people were there, the faint sounds of their voices echoing down the halls.

A key sliding into the lock of his cell caused Shane to look up. When the door opened he was immediately blinded with the light again. Closing his eyes, he tried to turn his head away. Once again, he was doused with cold water. He let out a howl as the water hit him.

"How you holding up there, sport?" one of the guards asked, moving into the cell. "We've got a little something here for you, to take your mind off the cold and all. That is, unless you want to go back and talk to Niigata?"

"F-f-fuck you."

"Gonna play tough, huh? That's all right, I like it better this way."

Shane heard the man step toward him, but he couldn't anticipate what would happen next. The man delivered a forceful slap to the bottom of his scrotum, causing his stomach to instantly knot. What little weight his legs had been supporting was now entirely on his shoulders as his knees buckled.

The guard laughed. "Looks like it's cold in here." He laughed again. "That thing ready?" he asked.

"Yeah, you ready? I don't want to be in here when this shit starts up," another guard said. Jess's mind raced, trying to anticipate what torture they were going to inflict next—and on who.

"Just a sec," the guard said, fiddling with something. "All

right, you fuckers, we're going to play you a little music!" he shouted.

Before the words stopped echoing off the concrete, music began to blare. The sound was so loud it took a minute for it to even register what it was that was assaulting their ears.

Fred immediately sat down to cover her ears. "Fucking polka music!" she screamed. Even if someone had been in the cell with her, they couldn't have heard her.

Though it was torturous for all, the music was even more torturous for Shane. The speakers were facing his cell and the sound bore into his head. He was freezing and his shoulders and arms were now numb—for that at least he was thankful. The music, if you could call it that, was so loud that it overwhelmed all other senses. He couldn't believe that just a day ago, he was out roaming free, and now he was hanging like a sack of meat, beaten, bruised, and defeated.

Chapter 7

We bounced down the road in the buggy, following the tracks to a paved road. Mike stopped and got out to inspect the tracks.

At the paved road we got out again. "Which way did they go?" Mel asked.

"Hard to say," Ted said as he circled the sand at the edge of the pavement.

Mike pointed to the east. "What's that way?"

"Nothing for a long ways. The river is over there, then several miles of open forest," Danny said.

"Let's start out this way," Ted said, pointing to the west.

"How are we going to find them?" Mel asked, her voice cracking.

"They couldn't have been too far if they were on foot. You take the left and we'll take the right," Danny said.

Mike nodded and we got back in the buggy. Perez was on the left side, scanning the edge of the road as we drove. Seeing the M4 in his lap made me realize that I'd left mine by the fire pit. Here I was, out looking for someone who'd taken Little Bit, and I didn't even have my rifle. At least I had my pistol.

Mike was driving slowly and everyone, except for Mel, was looking at the side of the road.

"Morg! Are those your dogs?" Mike said, pointing in the distance. I looked up to see Meathead and Little Girl standing on the right side of the road. Meathead's ears were up and he was looking right at us, his tongue hanging out the side of his mouth. Relief flooded me, just for a moment.

"Yeah, that's them," I said excitedly. If the dogs were here, that meant Little Bit couldn't be too far away.

Mike sped up as the dogs darted off into the woods. As we got closer to where they disappeared, I realized we were almost at the entrance to Alexander Springs.

The dogs were nowhere to be seen, but I started to have a feeling that I knew who we were looking for. The realization hit me like a ton of bricks.

"Remember that guy who was living back in here?" I asked Ted.

"Yeah, weird little dude," Ted replied, then rubbed his chin. "Didn't he shoot at us when we were coming back from our meeting that day those guys gave us the map?"

"That's the one," I said. I remembered how dirty he was, with that disgusting tangled beard. And he had a dog—Drake was its name, if I remembered correctly. *He probably lured Little Bit over with him*, I thought angrily.

"I'm not going to look for the dogs—screw it. I remember where that guy was staying," Mike said as he sped up through the parking lot, heading for the snack bar.

I jumped out of the buggy as Mike slowed to a stop, leaving Mel in her seat. Ted was right behind me, along with Jamie and Perez. Danny and Doc rode past us and up toward the small building. Rounding the building, I was both enraged and relieved. The hermit weirdo was sitting in front of a smoky fire under the canopy of old oaks with Ashley on his lap. He looked up as we ran toward him, a crooked smile on his face. I drew my pistol and started yelling.

"Let her go! Let her go you sick fuck!" The filter in my

brain for my choice of words around the kids was not functional at the moment.

"She's my friend," he replied, grabbing her tighter. It was then that I actually looked at Little Bit. She was crying, obviously scared.

"She's not your friend!" Mel screamed as she ran past me and everyone else, not even considering whether or not he was armed.

Ashley reached out, crying and screaming for Mel. The man stood and started to turn, to block Mel. Mike, Ted, Danny, and I were moving in an instant. Mike and Ted were screaming at him to put her down, to show his hands. When Mel got close, the man pushed her aside, yelling something about how she wanted to visit him, to play together. Danny made it to him just before I did and grabbed Ashley. Her eyes were wide in terror as she reached out for him. As Danny started to pull her away, the guy fought back. It was like a tug-of-war, with my daughter in the middle.

Coming in between the two at a run, I brought my right leg up hard and fast and kicked the bastard in the balls as hard as I could. He let out a loud groan as he started to fall. Danny scooped Ashley up and moved her out of the way, and Mel quickly intercepted her. Doc shielded Mel and Ashley and pushed them out toward the buggy, sheltering the two as he quickly guided them down the walkway to the parking lot. Mike and Ted moved in and pinned the creep to the ground, searching him for weapons. Seeing he was under control, I went to Mel and Ashley.

They were sitting in the buggy in the leaf-littered parking area, on the other side of the concession stand. I walked toward them, my mind racing a mile a minute. I was thankful we'd found her and yet was worried about what we didn't yet know. Ashley had her face buried in her mom's neck. I tried to lift her head to look at her, but she was clinging on with surprising strength. Her little form was racked with sobs, as was Mel. I patted Ashley on the back as Mel looked up, tears soaking her face.

I leaned in and kissed Ash's head, then Mel, and looked back toward the concession stand. I could hear the guys shouting at that son of a bitch. Without hesitation, I headed back toward them.

When I returned, the guys had him sitting in the chair. Stings of spittle stretched from his beard to his shirt, and he'd vomited on himself. He was obviously in a lot of pain, clenching his eyes shut, leaning forward at the waist with his knees together. Mike stood behind him, one hand on his shoulder. They'd bound his hands with a set of cuffs. Ted was in front of him, pacing and asking questions.

Between gulps of air he spoke. "I told you, she came to visit me."

Ted knelt down and looked at his face. The man's eyes were closed, so Ted slapped him in the side of the head. "Look at me." He half opened his eyes at the command, his mouth hanging open. "You took her from by the river, didn't you?"

He shook his head, the strings of spit swinging as he did. "No, I didn't take her! She wanted to come. We're friends."

I stepped toward him. "She's eight years old, you sick fuck. She's not your friend."

Leaning forward he looked up, a disturbing smile on his face. "She *is* my friend."

"This guy's lost his fucking mind," Ted announced as he stood up.

"What are you going to do with him?" Jamie asked.

The man laughed. "She'll come back, you'll see. Next time you won't find us."

Hearing those words, I lost it. I put the muzzle of my pistol an inch from his head, just above his ear, and fired. His body fell out of the chair as the .45 bullet tore the top of his head off.

"Oh my God!" Jamie screamed.

"Shit, Morgan!" Mike yelled as he stepped back. "Give me a frickin' warning next time. Look at my pants!" Mike was looking down at the specks of blood, tissue, and small shards of bone that covered his left leg. "Oh, for fuck's sake!" he shouted as he knelt down and grabbed a handful of leaves to wipe it off.

Jamie had her hand over her mouth, her eyes wide. She was looking at the corpse, smoke still coming from the side of the head. Perez simply stood there, no expression on his face whatsoever.

"Well, so much for that," Ted said as he knelt down and took the cuffs off.

"I can't believe you did that," Jamie said.

"Yeah, Jamie, Morgan's a little . . . different," Mike said.

I spit on the body and went back to the buggy. Danny was sitting beside Mel in the backseat, rubbing Ashley's back while Mel rocked her from side to side. Doc was trying his best to examine Little Bit, but she was really clinging to Mel. Danny climbed out and stopped beside me.

"Has she said anything?" I asked.

He shook his head and nodded toward the snack bar. "That taken care of?"

Doc climbed out. "Morg, she looks all right, but I'll really need to do a more thorough exam when we get back."

"Thanks Doc," I said, looking at her and Mel. "I hope you're right."

Danny patted me on the back and walked toward the other vehicle. The dogs came trotting up, tongues still lolling out of their mouths. I smiled at Meathead and thought to myself, *Thanks, ole buddy.* Mike started up the buggy as Danny pulled up beside us. It was a quiet ride back to the cabins, the few miles seeming like many more. No one said anything during the trip. Gone now were the sobs and tears. A tempered sense of relief filled me—tempered because there was still one question to answer.

Pulling up to the cabins, we were met by Thad, Ian, and Jeff, whose looks of relief reminded me how good of friends they are. Mel quickly got out and headed for the cabin with Ashley. I caught up to her and grabbed her arm.

"When you go in and clean her up, check her clothes . . ." I didn't know exactly how to say what needed said. ". . . for, you know." I left the terrible thought unsaid.

Mel stared at me blankly, spun on her heels, and went into the cabin. Bobbie was right behind her.

"I'll go check her out," Doc said quietly.

Taylor and Lee Ann were sitting by the fire. It was clear that both of them had been crying.

"Is she all right?" Taylor asked.

I nodded. "She's going to be okay."

Lee Ann looked up. "I'm so sorry. I didn't mean it. I didn't mean for it to happen."

"I know, no one's blaming you," I said.

She started to cry and quickly stood up and ran off.

"Hey! Lee Ann, come back!" I called to her, then looked at her sister. "Go keep an eye on her."

"She shouldn't have left her alone."

"True, but it's not her fault—and you better not be saying it is."

Taylor walked off after her sister, passing Thad on her way. He put his hands in his pockets and leaned back on his heels. "Lee Ann is pretty upset. She's blaming herself."

"She shouldn't have left her little sister alone, but it's not her fault," I replied, still looking at Taylor.

"You'll need to talk to her. Taylor gave her some trouble about it, which didn't help."

I shook my head. "I'll talk to both of them."

Thad nodded and went over to the fire pit and sat down. I followed him. Everyone was gathered there and I could feel them looking at me, though no one said anything. I'm sure the word had already spread and they all knew. On the table was a muffin pan full of soap. Thad had finished his project while we were gone. People started talking, but my attention was focused on the pan. I watched the soap as it began to harden before my eyes. It was a necessary distraction for my mind at the moment.

Taylor and Lee Ann had come back and were sitting in chairs by the fire. Danny was knelt down between them, talking in a low voice. I was thankful Danny was there. He was offering the comfort I couldn't at the moment. He and Bobbie were so close to us, part of our family. I couldn't imagine not having them.

Doc sat down beside me as Danny propped a foot up on the bench across from me. I looked at Danny, then at Doc, hoping beyond hope.

"We looked at her clothes." He paused for a moment. "We didn't see anything, you know, that would show—" I raised a hand to stop him. I'd heard what I needed to and didn't want that thought to enter my head again, ever.

Doc left and Danny sat down. "As bad as it is, it could have been worse. Thankfully, she's okay."

I nodded. "Thanks, Doc."

Danny folded his hands, laying them on the table in front of him. "Between you, me, and the other guys, nothing will ever happen to one of them again."

I'd been staring off at the tree line across the river. I looked him in the eye. "I hope not."

"You gonna be all right?"

I nodded. "Yeah, I'm gonna go check on her," I said and stood up.

No one in the group stopped me, which was good. I appreciated the concern and the help, but I didn't want to keep hearing their sympathy. Thad was standing at the fire, eyes locked on mine. Several large pieces of pork were sitting on the grill, the fat snapping and popping as it dripped into the flames. He gave a quick knowing nod, then went back to tending his meat. I smiled at him. The circumstances that had brought the two of us together were certainly interesting, and I was incredibly thankful to have him in my life as well. Besides Danny, there was no friend I trusted more in this world.

I stopped by the fire for a moment and knelt down between the girls, asking if they were all right. They said they were and asked about their little sister again. I told them they needed to be especially nice to her and to look out for her. I also told them she probably wouldn't want to be alone and they would have to tolerate her hanging around with them. She was surely about to become their ever-present shadow. They nodded silently, agreeing with me. When I got to the cabin, I found Mel lying with Ashley, who was asleep. Mel was running her fingers through her hair, watching her.

"How is she?" I asked.

"She's fine now," Mel said without looking up.

Ashley's eyes opened. "Daddy?" she said, reaching a small hand out.

I grabbed her hand. "Right here, Little Bit, right here." She wrapped her hand around my thumb and closed her eyes. Soon her breathing settled into a slow rhythm. I rubbed her hand and settled in beside Mel. Soon we were all asleep.

When I woke up, it was dark. Little Bit was sitting up. "I'm hungry, Daddy."

Mel sat up and looked around. "How long did we sleep?"

"I don't know, but she's hungry. Let's go get her something to eat."

Little Bit walked between us, holding our hands. Everyone was out at the table with a couple of kerosene lanterns set out for light. They were talking and laughing.

As we came into the light Mike called out, "Hey, glad to see you're up, there, Sleeping Beauty. Enjoy your nap?"

Little Bit smiled. "I did. I'm hungry."

Mike smiled back. "I bet you are, Ashley, but I was talking to your daddy."

She laughed. "He's not Sleeping Beauty."

"You're right, no beauty there," Danny said.

Room was made for us and we sat together on one end. "What's for supper there, Grandpa?" I asked Thad.

He laughed. "Grandpa?"

"Yeah, remember the old show *Hee Haw*? *What's fer supper, Grandpa?*"

"Oh damn, you're really dating yourself now, Morg," Ted said with a chuckle.

"What's *Hee Haws*?" Little Bit asked.

"Just an old show," Mel said, then, looking at me, added, "a really bad one." This got a laugh out of everyone.

"Well, tonight we're having some roast pig and fried rice," Thad said as he prepared plates for the three of us. Lee Ann and Taylor carried them over.

When I got my plate, I looked at the rice. "Fried rice, huh? Who pulled this off?" It actually looked like fried rice from the Before, with carrots and peas in it. It even had the egg.

"I did!" Mike said, waving a hand. "Y'all didn't know I could cook, did you? More than a pretty face here, boys and girls."

Ted was picking through the rice with a fork. "I'm still not sure you can."

"Pfft, hater," Mike said with a dismissive wave.

Little Bit seemed surprisingly normal during dinner. Danny was sitting across from her, making faces at her and chewing up mouthfuls of food and sticking out his tongue to reveal them, which had her rolling. Jamie was talking to her and Mel, as was Bobbie. It was as if it never happened, which was good. I just hoped it stayed that way.

"Ian, Jamie, Perez, you guys get enough to eat?" Ted asked.

Perez sat back and patted his stomach. "I haven't had anything that good in a long time."

Jamie looked at Thad. "It was wonderful, really good," she said, looking around the table. "Thank you all for sharing with us."

"I've never had *enough*, but I'm good. Thanks, guys," Ian said with a smile.

Mike raised his hand. "I'm good too, in case anyone's wondering."

Ted leaned back and folded his arms over his chest, looking sideways at Mike. "We're not."

"You guys about to head out?" Danny asked.

"Yeah, back to the real world," Ted answered.

"Interesting choice of words," Jamie remarked.

"Thad, since you made dinner, I'll take care of cleaning up," Jeff said.

"I'll help you," Bobbie offered.

The two began collecting the plates and bowls as Ted and company started getting their things together.

Before they left, I thanked everyone for their help with Ashley, though it went without saying.

"Don't sweat it, man, there was no way we wouldn't have," Mike said.

"Morgan, thanks for the hospitality," Ian said. He looked as though he wanted to say more, but instead he stuck out his hand.

We all shook hands, telling each other that if anything was needed to call. The guys said they would stop by on the way back. We watched as they got in the buggy and drove away. Once even the sound of it was gone we finally started back toward the fire.

"You going back tonight, Doc?" Thad asked.

"Nah, it's dark. I'll wait till morning. That damn latrine ain't going anywhere."

"Piss tubes?" I said in the dark.

Doc laughed. "Yeah, that's what I'm doing, you'd think they didn't know shit about sanitation over there."

"Well, Doc, if you need any help—" I was saying, until he cut me off.

"Don't worry about it, but thanks."

"I was going to say, *Don't call me!*" I said with a laugh.

Doc laughed. "Thanks, Morg, nice to know who your friends are."

"Yeah, movin', roofin', and plumbin' will sort your friends out quick," Thad said.

We all laughed. It was a good way to end a rough day.

As we walked back to the cabin I put my arm around Lee Ann's shoulder. She hadn't said anything all evening.

"You know what happened wasn't your fault, right?"

She stared at the ground and shrugged her shoulders.

"It's not your fault. There's only one person to blame, and he's been taken care of," Mel said.

Without looking up, Lee Ann spoke. "If I hadn't left her alone it wouldn't have happened."

I was surprised when Little Bit spoke up. "I'm sorry I didn't listen to you, Lee Ann."

I gave her a little smile, then rubbed Lee Ann's head. "See, she doesn't blame you." But even with that, Lee Ann kept her eyes glued to the ground.

Chapter 8

Mike was at the wheel, driving the buggy through the forest, while Ted was navigating for him using the updated map for guidance. After a short security check, they crossed Highway 19. They decided that they would start on the south side of the camp to find an observation spot.

They looked for a place to set up in a small bayhead, which was thick with cabbage palms, small oaks, gum trees and other brush. Mike drove in from the south, keeping their entrance and escape on the opposite side of the swamp from the camp. Once in, the small group set about camouflaging their location. Great effort was taken to cover their tracks and hide where they had driven off the road. An inspection of the road revealed that there hadn't been any traffic in some time, foot or wheeled.

"I wish we could get this damn wagon closer," Ted said.

"Me too. I'd like for a quick exfil should we need it," Ian said.

"I'm not worried about that. I want to use the cameras on the battle wagon. They'll keep us from having to get too close," Ted replied.

"We'll just have to do it the old-fashioned way," Ian said.

"Yeah, all right. Now, let's talk assignments," Ted said, taking the lead. "Jamie, you and Perez are going to stay here as our security."

"Why, 'cause I'm a woman?" Jamie asked as she crossed her arms.

"No, it's because Ian said you're a really good shooter." Jamie's expression changed slightly. Ted continued, "And I don't need shooters right now, I need people trained as observers. Have you been to sniper school?"

Jamie snorted. "No, but I can still handle the job."

"Not saying you can't, but this is just the way it's gonna be," Ted said, making it clear the issue was closed. He looked at Perez, waiting for him to protest too.

Perez raised his hands. "I'm good. I'm in no hurry to die."

"Good, me neither," Ted replied with a smile.

Once the security team was chosen, they went through radio procedures. The observation team would call in three times a day. Just in case there was trouble and the group was discovered, they covered the planned exfil route and rendezvous points, of which there were several.

"If we get found," Ted said as he dug into his pack, "throw these into the woods." He handed Jamie two white phosphorus hand grenades.

Ted went on to show them the possible locations for the incendiaries to be used, giving each location a letter code. These incendiaries would set fire to the forest, creating a diversion for the guys inside the fence to escape. It was a drastic measure that everyone hoped wouldn't be necessary.

"You know if we set these off, it will start one hell of a wildfire," Perez said. He was right—the area was dry, and there hadn't been rain in weeks.

Ted nodded. "I know, but when it comes to it, I'd rather burn the woods down than die." He looked back at Mike and Ian. "You guys ready?"

Both men nodded, and they headed out, leaving Perez and

Jamie to get settled into their new home. Ian took point, carrying a SAW. Ted had Sarge's M1A, and Mike was carrying the 203. While contact wasn't the point of the mission, they wanted enough firepower to break it if it happened. They moved very slowly through the bush, taking a step and listening, then taking another. It took them hours to reach the road that ran around the perimeter of the camp.

They crawled up a small hill that had cabbage palms on it. From there, they could see the road.

"How the hell are we going to cross that without leaving any tracks?" Mike asked.

"I don't know," Ted replied, "but we got to figure it out. From the looks of all those tire tracks, the Feds must patrol this regularly." He pulled out a set of binoculars to take a better look, then pointed east. "Let's move that way."

The guys nodded and Ian took the point again, first moving back into the woods for cover and then turning parallel to the road. The ground was a steady, slow slope down, and they continued to follow the contour. After a few hours of this movement, Ian held up a fist and slowly dropped to his knee. Ted slipped up beside him. Ian pointed out in front of him. There was a small branch of flowing water crossing their path. Ted patted him on the shoulder and moved past him.

The water was flowing across the road from the direction of the camp. Ted surveyed the situation. There was a culvert running under the road, but a lack of maintenance had allowed sand to fill it, so now the small flow of water was washing over the road itself. Satisfied that the flowing water would help cover their tracks, he decided this was the best place for them to cross. Ted moved back to the other two men.

"Here's where we'll set up and watch the road. We need to figure out their patrol routine before we cross."

Mike and Ian nodded, then began to look for hides to observe the road from. The men positioned themselves close enough to be able to speak in whispers. Once they were settled in, Ian said he would take the first watch. Mike told Ted to get some rest and he would pull security. Ted didn't argue—he could use a nap, he said. He looked at his watch. It was three twenty-five.

Even if asleep, men conditioned to combat can wake up nearly instantly. A low whistle caused Ted's eyes to snap open what seemed like minutes later. Instead of jumping at the sound, Ted took in the scene for a moment, then looked at Mike. He was pointing at the road. Ted looked up to see a Hummer slowly rolling by. There were two men in the front and two in the back along with a gunner in the turret. The truck was black with the DHS logo on the door. Ted shook his head, looking at the gunner. *What in the hell does a law enforcement agency need an M240 Bravo for?*

The gunner in the turret sat behind a heavy machine gun. In the Before, there was much talk about the amount of equipment the DHS was buying, things like MRAP vehicles (or Mine-Resistant Armored Patrol Vehicles), billions of rounds of ammo, MREs, everything an army preparing for war would need. It was now rather obvious what it was all for.

They watched as the truck rolled out of sight. As soon as it was gone, Mike whistled again. He pointed at the road with an arching motion. "Let's cross now!" he said in a loud whisper.

Ted looked at the road hesitantly, then back at Mike and Ian. They both nodded. The three men jumped to their feet and cautiously but quickly made their way across the road, walking in the small flow of water. Mike crossed first, taking up a position to provide security for the other two. Once across the road, Ted looked back at the track, watching as the water cascading over the road washed away the mud stirred by their crossing. It wasn't long before it was back to a clear flow again and the tracks left by their boots were nearly imperceptible.

The fence was their next obstacle. Cutting it was out of the question, so Mike climbed to the top and straddled it. All the packs were handed up to him, and he tossed them over one at a time, then climbed down inside. Ted quickly followed, with Ian right behind him. The last real obstacle behind them, they took a short break.

Over sips of water, Mike asked, "Which way you want to go?"

Ted looked around, trying to determine the best way to cut through the brush. They couldn't see the camp from where they were. It was still at least a mile off.

"Let's make our way north, till we can get it in our sights. Then we'll figure out a place to watch from."

"Sounds good to me. Let's get going. We aren't getting anywhere sitting here," Ian said.

The three men quietly strapped on their packs and headed toward the camp.

Jamie sat under a piece of camo net concealing her hide. She wasn't happy about it either.

"Jamie, you stay here" . . . what a bunch of BS. They think since I'm a woman I can't pull my own weight, assholes. She looked over at Perez who was stretched out with his hat pulled down over his eyes. *Look at him, just lying there. Typical. They'll see, I can do my part.*

To occupy her time, Jamie sorted through her pack. She knew everything that was there and exactly where it was—it was just something to do. She laid out her poncho and arranged the belts of ammo for the SAW. At the sound of an engine drifting through the trees, Jamie's head snapped around, trying to pinpoint its location. She quickly settled in behind the SAW, scanning the area to her north. It sounded like a slow-moving Hummer. *I wonder if they found the guys' tracks*, she thought.

The engine continued on. She tracked it as it passed, never seeing it through the thick brush. Perez sat up. "What's going on?"

"There's a Hummer out there."

Perez scrambled around, grabbing his weapon. "Why the hell didn't you say something?" He barked in a harsh whisper.

Jamie glanced over. "I had it under control."

Perez crawled up beside her. "Next time you better wake me up. This isn't some game! This shit is for real!"

"What, you're like them, don't think I can handle myself?" Jamie asked without looking over.

Perez grabbed her shoulder, Jamie twisted her head to look at his hand, then at him. "Jamie, this isn't about whether you can do this or not. You're here, aren't you? Out of all the people at the camp, they brought you, and you're sitting here thinking they don't trust you?"

"Yeah, whole lot of good I'm doing, babysitting this damn go-kart."

"You are fucking hardheaded, aren't you? What we are doing is every bit as important as what they are doing. This isn't some kind of competition. Trust me, you'll get your chance to kill." Perez gave her a hard look. "I hope it's everything you expect it to be," he added.

Jamie didn't say anything as she adjusted the SAW on her shoulder and peered down the barrel.

It was nearly dark when the camp came into view. Using the terrain to their advantage, they came upon it while in a draw between two small hills. Ted was on point. Raising a fist, he slowly lowered to one knee. Ian and Mike did the same. Whether stalking game or men, they knew it was always best to be slow.

"We need to find a place to hide," Ted said, looking at the edge of the camp. "Mike, you go to the left and I'll go to the right. No more than a hundred yards, and then we'll meet back here. Ian, you're on security."

Mike nodded, dropping his pack so he could move with more stealth, then began easing through the woods. Ian came up and to the edge of the woods and set up his SAW as Ted moved in the opposite direction. Ian pulled a small monocular out of his blouse pocket and looked out across the camp. With all the brush, he could only see the tops of the numerous tents and structures. What was most shocking, though, were the camp's use of things from the Before. Lights illuminated the camp, casting an eerie glow, and he could hear the hum of generators. Diesel exhaust rose up through the light towers. He shook his head at the sight.

It wasn't long before Ted gave a low whistle to let Ian know he was back. "Hope Mikey finds something, 'cause there's nothing that way, at least not without having to go halfway around the camp." He flopped down beside Ian. "What's it look like out there?"

"Lotsa lights. Look at that place," Ian said with the monocular still held to his eye.

Ted pulled his pack over and pulled out a spotting scope. Surveying the site, he was blown away by how large the camp was. "It's fucking huge."

"Yeah, and we can only see part of it from here."

Ted continued to examine the camp, sweeping the big glass back and forth. After a few minutes, he looked off in the direction that Mike went. "Dammit, Mike, where the hell are you?"

Ian looked over. "You think something happened to him?"

Ted shook his head. "Nah, not likely. The kid's scary good, actually, despite his mouth."

Ted turned back to the spotting scope. A low whistle told him Mike was on his way in. Ted looked at Ian. "Here he comes."

Mike crawled up from behind, lying beside Ted.

Still looking through the scope, Ted asked, "Well, what'd you find?"

"There's a little hill about hundred fifty yards over there. The ground in front of it falls off and there is a slash pile on top. Perfect place to make a hide."

"Sounds good to me. How far is it from the camp?"

"'Bout three hundred meters."

"That'll work. Let's move out," Ted said as he stuffed the scope back into his pack. "Lead the way, Mikey."

Mike led them back toward the fence, making a wide loop so that they arrived at the hide spot from the rear. It took most of the night to get the hide set up properly. They had to dig into the pile to maintain cover over them and provide plenty in the front as well. A secondary hide was prepared behind the first for whoever was pulling the security duty.

"The sun's going to be coming up soon. Who wants the first watch?" Ted asked.

"I haven't had this kind of fun in a long time. I'll take it," Ian said.

"Sounds good to me. I'm tired," Ted replied.

Ian crawled into the hide and Ted unrolled his sleeping bag beside Ian.

"I'll go back to the security hide. I'll be up for a while," Mike said, then looked toward the camp. "What's that fucking noise?"

"Sounds like music," Ian said.

"Not any music I've ever heard. It's frickin' loud too," Mike replied.

"Well, hopefully it won't keep you from your rest, Sleeping Beauty. Get some sleep," Ted said as he pulled his bag up over his head.

"It's definitely coming from that building there," Ian said, trying to get a better view through the scope.

Examining the sketch Ted had been working on, Mike asked, "Building number seven?"

"Yeah, it's got that fence around it. Kinda weird it's sitting apart from all the others."

Mike looked through his binoculars. "Think it's a segregation unit or something?"

"Be my bet. Remember Abu Ghraib? They played Eminem real loud to loosen up the detainees."

"Yeah, I ever tell you I was there once?" Mike asked.

"You and your stories. Thought you were going to security position," Ted said.

"This is more fun."

"Fine, then I'll put you to work. Call the other team and let them know we're in position."

"Ten-four. On it."

After Mike called, they spent the next couple of hours

marking up the drawing of the camp. All of the structures inside the camp were given numbers and approximate ranges. From their hide location they could see the rear gate, so they also spent time tracking the camp employees and counting their vehicles.

"Got to love the fact the government puts numbers on everything," Mike said, adding a hash mark to a column on the list before him.

"Sure makes counting a lot easier," Ted said as he swiveled the scope. "Hey, check out building seven."

Mike picked up his binoculars and scanned the building. "Looks like someone's going to work."

They watched as a group of four people approached the building. One went in, while the rest waited outside.

"Is one of them wearing scrubs?" Mike asked.

"Yes, she is—looks like a nurse or something," Ted replied.

"She? What's she look like? I can't tell with these."

Ted clicked his tongue. "Now's not the time, Mikey."

"Can't blame me, though, can ya? Oh hey, listen. The music stopped."

With the music now off, the individuals waiting outside opened the door and disappeared.

"Let's see what happens here," Ted said.

Chapter 9

After the events of yesterday, I figured now was as good a time as any to make pancakes for breakfast. Everyone was sitting around the fire or at the picnic table. Even the dogs were lying in the sun, all three of them. That's right—three. The creep's dog followed us home, and we decided to let him stay. Little Bit was sitting close to Mel. She hadn't ventured very far from us since she returned.

I felt like one of those hibachi chefs, with everyone sitting around watching me mix up a bowl of pancake batter. I used the pancake batter we had left and cut it with about one-third cattail starch. I had the stove set up with two cast iron skillets heating up some of the rendered pig fat. I scooped up a spoon of batter and let it run out into the bowl.

"How's that look?" I asked.

"Looks good to me," Mel said.

"Looks yummy!" Little Bit said, bouncing up and down in her seat.

"Get to cookin', man!" Jeff shouted as he banged a fork on the table.

"All right, all right, if you guys just can't wait," I said as I turned to the skillets.

"We can't! Now get crackin'!" Danny said.

I spooned the batter out into the skillets, making cakes nearly the size of the pan.

"All right, who gets the first one?" I asked.

I was showered with shouts from everyone at the table. I laughed and watched for telltale bubbles to form in the batter in the pan.

"Daddy, can I flip them?" Little Bit asked.

"Sure, come on over here."

I helped her get the spatula under the cake and she flipped it successfully, then did the next one. When the other side was browned, I had her take them out and put them on a plate as I quickly poured in more batter. I then took the plate from Little Bit and set it on a grate near the fire to stay warm.

"We'll wait till there's enough for everyone," I said. Naturally I was met with a chorus of jeers.

In about ten minutes there was quite the stack of cakes. Jeff reached for the first plate, a huge smile on his face. I slapped his knuckles with the spatula. "Ladies first, you damn Neanderthal."

He jerked his hand back, shaking it. "Damn, that hurt!"

I set the first plate in front of Mel, then another in front of Bobbie.

"Lee Ann, how many you want?" I asked.

She didn't look up, just shrugged her shoulders.

"Come on now. One or two? How many?"

"I don't care," she replied.

I slipped two onto a plate and set it in front of her, then served her sisters. Once all the ladies had their breakfast, I passed a plate to Thad. He quickly poured syrup on them. Taking a big bite, he looked at Jeff and smiled as he chewed. "*Mmmm, mmmmm,*" he moaned.

Jeff sat there shaking his head. "Y'all ain't right."

With a big smile I set a plate in front of him. "Here ya go, princess."

Once everyone had a plate I sat down with one. "Well, how are they?"

"These are just like the ones you used to make, Dad," Taylor said.

"They're great!" Little Bit shouted.

"Yeah, these are really good," Danny said.

It was universally agreed that they were a hit. It didn't take long for the table to be littered with empty plates, except for Lee Ann's. She had barely touched her food. I looked over at Mel and nodded toward Lee Ann. She put her hands up in the air as if to say, *I don't know*.

After finishing up the meal, Doc took off, thanking me for the breakfast. We said our good-byes and the rest of us sat around the table a bit longer, full from the pancakes.

"Guys, we got to get serious about hunting. We're almost out of meat and the other stuff is nearly gone too. We need to focus on getting some protein," I said as I stirred the fire with a stick.

"I'm up for some hunting," Jeff said.

"Me too," Danny added. "I want to go get a gator."

Jeff's head jerked around. "A gator? Hey, that'd be fun. I'm in."

"I'll cook it if you kill it," Thad said, shaking his head.

Looking at Thad, I said, "We'll let them go lizard hunting. You want to help me rig up some limb rat snares?"

"Sounds good to me."

"Let's go get the canoe," Danny told Jeff.

Jeff jumped off the picnic table. "Let's do it!"

I got up to go get some snare wire from the cabin. After finding the wire, I dug around the bottom of my pack, pulled out a small package of MRE peanut butter, and headed back to the picnic table, where Taylor and Lee Ann were chatting with Thad.

"Morg, I've never rigged up a squirrel snare. How do you do it?" Thad asked.

Before I could answer, the girls piped up. "Can we help, Dad?"

"Sure. I'll show you how to do the first one, and then you guys can make the rest. First, we have to make some loops out of this wire."

Using my Leatherman tool, I cut a piece of wire about two feet long, then folded it in half.

"Hey, Taylor, can you go get me a couple of nails, big ones?"

Taylor nodded and left to go find some as I continued cutting pieces of wire and folding them in half. When she returned, I took one of the nails and laid the fold of wire over it. Holding out the two tag ends, I told Lee Ann to take them, one in each hand.

"Now, while you hold it I'm going to twist the nail, so the two pieces of wire are twisted together."

Thad and the girls looked on as I twisted the wire up. When it was finished, it was nice and uniform, leaving a small loop in the one end and about two inches of untwisted wire on the other.

"Now we pull the nail out and feed the other end through the loop." I slid the tag end through the loop, making the snare, and held it up, sticking two fingers in the big loop. "See, with the wire twisted, when a squirrel gets in it and the snare closes"—I pulled the snare around my finger—"the twists act like locks and hold it in place."

"That's pretty neat," Thad said. "Let me see it."

I handed him the snare and told the girls to get started twisting the wire up. "Just be sure not to twist it too tight. Hey, Thad, let's go get a piece of wood."

Thad nodded and followed me out toward the woods. I

was looking for a limb, not too big in diameter. Seeing a possible contender, I picked it up and waved it around. "We need some limbs like this."

We looked around and found four of them and carried them back to the table.

"Now wrap the loose end around the limb like this." I showed Thad how to secure the snare to the limb and how to space them and position the open snare on it so the squirrel would go through it. "We'll lean these against trees at an angle"—I put one end on the ground and leaned it against the trunk of one of the nearby trees—"and when they run up it they'll get trapped."

"Why don't you just shoot them?" Taylor asked. "You used to go hunting for them."

"Because this way, we can 'hunt' while doing other things. It will work for us all day long." She nodded.

Once everything was ready, we took the snares out into the woods near the camp. The place was full of limb rats, and Thad and I agreed it would be a productive spot. I looked for trees that showed signs of feeding. Piles of cut shells of hickory nuts and acorns were a dead giveaway. We leaned the limbs against these trees and put a dab of peanut butter between the snares.

"Will this actually work?" Lee Ann asked.

"Sure, squirrels love peanut butter. If they come from either the top or the bottom of the tree to get the peanut butter, they'll have to pass through the snares."

"Will the snares kill them?"

"They can. Sometimes they will, sometimes they'll be alive."

"Sounds kind of mean."

"Well, we have to eat, and they aren't just going to climb up on the table and lie down for us."

"I'm not going to eat them," Taylor said.

I looked at her with my eyebrows raised. "It's just *meat*, Taylor. And if you get hungry enough, you will. You've had it before anyway."

She looked at me and scowled. "Yeah, but you didn't tell us until after we ate it."

"I remember that," Lee Ann said.

"Me too, and as I remember it, you guys liked it till I told you what it was."

Thad laughed. "Yeah, funny how that works out."

When we got back to the cabin, Mel was in the garden plot plucking the weeds that were beginning to sprout. The small plants that were transplanted were precious to us, and it was very important that all of them survive. This was no hobby garden.

"I'm gonna go check on the hogs. Thanks for the lesson, Morg," Thad said as he walked off.

Little Bit held up a tiny seedling. "Look, Daddy, it's a baby." She had a big smile on her face.

"Yep, but it's the wrong kind. Let's get this garden cleaned up."

"We're going to go look for eggs," Taylor said.

I nodded at them and they turned to leave. Little Bit jumped up. "I want to help!"

The girls ran off, leaving me and Mel sitting in the garden. Mel crawled out of the garden and spread out on the grass. I lay down beside her, propped up on an elbow.

"It's nice out. The sun feels good," she said.

"It does," I said, looking upward. "I think it's going to start warming up."

"That'd be nice," she said. Her eyes were closed, and she was resting her head on her hands.

"Yeah, but that means it's going to get hot soon."

"And that means there'll be mosquitoes. Don't forget about them."

"Oh yeah, a shitload of them!" I said with a chuckle.

The weather had been warm for several days, probably in the upper sixties. One thing I wish I had was a weather station with a thermometer, barometer, and hygrometer for humidity. That would be handy now that the Weather Channel was no longer on the air. My grandfather had one hanging on the wall in his living room back in the day, a nice brass instrument on a teak plank.

The girls came running back over. "Mom, look at all the eggs we got today!" Taylor hollered as she came up. All three of them had their hands full.

"Wow, that's a lot of eggs. Good work, girls," Mel said, sitting up and brushing the grass off her hands.

"We should make something with them," Taylor said.

"Yeah, Mommy, what can we make?" Little Bit asked.

"It depends. What do you want?"

"Something sweet!"

"You could make that custard that you've made before," I said.

"Yeah! Can we make custard, Mom?" Lee Ann asked. "Please? It reminds me of when we made it with Grandma last Christmas." She looked down at the ground and muttered, "I miss Grandma."

Mel got up and patted Lee Ann on the shoulder. "Oh, I remember—your grandma sure is good in the kitchen. Let's see if we can make it as good as she did. You guys want to help?"

All the girls nodded, and she led them toward the cabin. I got up and went over to the picnic table. Thad was coming from the pigpen and met me there.

"We may have a problem," he said.

"Oh yeah? What's up?"

"Someone's been snooping around the pigpen."

That got my attention. "Really? You sure?"

"Yeah, come on, I'll show you."

I followed Thad back to the pen. On the far side of the pen he stopped and pointed at the ground. "See the tracks?"

"I do. It's kinda hard to tell how many people there were, or what they were doing."

"That's what's interesting," he said. "The tracks go all the way to the creek." I followed Thad as he pointed out the tracks leading down to the creek, north of the cabins. "Looks like they crossed here," he said.

I knelt down and looked closer at the bank. "Yeah, I don't see where a boat was pulled up. They must have waded across."

"That's what I thought too. Kinda strange to come over and not take anything." Thad jerked his chin toward the other side of the river. "What's back there?"

"Nothing for a long, long ways."

"We may need to keep an eye on things for a couple of days. You still got that night vision?"

"Yeah, I got something else we can put over here too that will help out. Let's go back to the cabin. You're gonna love this."

Back at our cabin, I started digging around in the ammo cans, looking for a silver package. When I pulled it out, I called over to Thad, "Look at this. They're trip flares—not real big, but at night they'll give off plenty of light, enough to get our attention." Tearing open the package, I pulled out a box, opened it, and removed a smaller box about three inches long and an inch square.

The small box contained a small white flare, some nails and

fence staples, a spring, and a roll of trip wire. Thad looked at the instructions and then at the parts lying on the table. "That's pretty neat. How bright is it?"

"It's about as bright as a small road flare."

Thad nodded and put the paper back on the table. "We'll set it up after dark, so no one sees us."

Somewhere down the river a shot rang out. Thad and I both looked up, anticipating more. The echo faded down the river and it was quiet again. Mel stepped out of the cabin and shouted, "What was that?"

"Jeff and Danny are out hunting gators—maybe they got one," I called back.

She looked off down the river for a moment, then went back inside.

"Maybe we'll be having gator for supper tonight," Thad said with a grin.

The faint sound of banging and some shouts drifted up the river. "Sounds like they're trying to get it in the canoe," I said.

"Sounds to me like they already got it in and it's trying to get out!" Thad said with a laugh.

I started to laugh at that mental image. "Yeah, I can just see them trying to fight a gator they thought was dead!"

"Yeah, up in the boat with 'em and it wakes up. *Oh shit, it's still alive!*" Thad said, doubling over.

We were both laughing so hard we had to sit down. We sat watching the river expectantly, waiting to see the canoe come into view.

"How do you like it cooked?" Thad asked.

"I've only had it fried, to be honest."

"If we have the stuff, I got something I'd like to make: a gator piquante."

I looked over, eyebrows raised. "What's in it?"

"Just peppers, onions, canned tomatoes, and seasoning, poured over a bowl of rice."

"Sounds good to me. I know we still have dehydrated peppers and onions, canned tomatoes too."

"I'll use the Dutch oven. Should be real good, cook it slow."

I could see Thad was already imagining it in a bowl. His dreams of gator piquante were soon interrupted as the canoe came into view. I was surprised to see a not-so-happy Bobbie sitting in the middle seat.

Thad gave a low whistle. "She looks pissed."

"I didn't know she went with them," I said as I started walking toward the creek.

Jeff was sitting in the bow of the canoe, a huge smile on his face. Danny was grinning as well. Quite the contrast between those two and Bobbie. Thad called out, "How big is it?"

"It's at least a nine-footer!" Jeff called back.

As soon as the bow of the boat ground to a halt in the mud, Bobbie launched herself out, and, without saying a word, headed for the cabin. As she passed, I noticed how wet she was. Looking back at Jeff and Danny, it was evident that they'd gone for a little swim themselves.

"What happened, turn the boat over?" I asked.

Jeff was pulling the canoe up. "Yeah, getting one of these in the boat ain't as easy as it looks on TV."

"That why your wife is so pissed, Danny?"

"Yeah, it wasn't the getting wet part as much as the fact she thought the blood from the gator would draw others in, like sharks. You should have seen her—kinda funny, actually."

Once the boat was pulled up onto the shore, we looked at the big-ass lizard. It was lying in a dark pink soup, grass and debris floating around it. There was one bullet wound in the back of its head.

"Got it with one shot?" Thad asked.

Jeff smiled and held up his peasant rifle. "Yep, one of these was all it took."

"One of those is all it *should* take!" I laughed.

"Oh, let's see you do it, Morg." He laughed. "Well, let's get to work, I want to eat this sucker for dinner tonight," Danny said.

It took all four of us to drag it out of the boat.

"Where are we going to clean it?" Jeff asked.

"Let's turn the canoe over and use that as a platform," Danny replied.

"Good idea," I chimed in.

Once the gator was laid out, everyone grabbed a knife and went to work. The dogs were very interested in the beast. They kept getting in our way, smelling and barking at it. Every time it moved as we worked on it, they would jump and bark more. Meathead grabbed it by the tail once and tugged. Thad had to kick him away, but it got a laugh out of all of us.

We salvaged every piece of meat we could from the carcass. The tail and jowls of a gator are the main sources of meat, but the ribs and legs also can be edible. Legs generally aren't used because they are very sinewy, but that can be overcome by grinding or cubing them. Fortunately, Danny had his manual grinder, which meant we would have plenty to last us.

While I generally keep some of the internal organs, nobody else was too keen on keeping them for our use. But they wouldn't go to waste. The heart, liver, and kidneys would be cooked and fed to the dogs, and the rest of the guts would be fed to the hogs.

When we were done, we ended up with around seventy pounds of meat.

"I want the skull," Danny said as we were finishing up.

Jeff looked up. "What for?"

"I'm going to strip it to bone." He shrugged his shoulders. "You know, something to do."

"How are you going to do that? Sounds like a tough job."

"Not really. I'll boil it for a while, then set it out on an ant mound. They'll take care of the rest."

Jeff's eyebrows went up. "Sounds interesting, I'll help."

"Cool," Danny said as he ran a blade around the base of the skull, separating the head from what was left of the body.

Thad picked up the bucket with the hog feed in it. "I'm gonna go give this to the pigs real quick."

"Hey, how we cooking this up tonight?" Jeff asked me.

"Thad's got something planned for it," I replied.

Jeff smiled and patted his stomach. "Can't wait. Thad's a master chef."

Mel and Bobbie were washing the meat off and putting it in buckets, when Mel gave me one of her famous looks of *You need to help out and you need to help out now.*

"We have a problem," Mel said flatly.

I looked up, "What is it?"

"We're almost out of toilet paper."

I stood up, "Ooh, that's not good. How much do we have left?"

"Maybe a dozen or so rolls," Bobbie said.

"I was worried that this day would come. Unfortunately, ladies, there's not much we can do. We're going to have to stop using the TP."

"Stop using it?! We need to figure out how to get more!

What are we going to use if we stop using it? Leaves? I'm not using leaves!" Mel said, her voice getting increasingly frantic.

"Calm down, Mel. I have a plan for this."

"I hope so, 'cause I ain't using leaves either," Thad said with a chuckle.

"I'll be right back," I said, heading off to the cabin.

Back in the day I'd read about this very issue. At the time I was studying up on various alternative methods for the issue at hand, as well as many other things, just to prepare for whatever may come. Not that I ever thought anything of this magnitude would ever occur, but I'm thankful now for all those hours of reading and research.

Most publications talked about using a bidet: not only did that not sound appealing, but under our current situation it was completely out of the question. I knew that what I came up with—something used in many other countries—was probably going to be met with some resistance. I prepared myself for the blowback.

As I was returning, everyone, including the girls, was at the picnic table. All eyes were on me and what I was carrying. I set everything down on the table for everyone to see.

"Okay, now I'm worried," Danny said, picking up one of the long rubber gloves.

"All right, boys and girls, the only option for this situation is to use a personal cloth," I said as I picked up a washcloth. "This does a better job if you wet it first." I took in the shocked faces of my oldest daughters. "This is done all over the world," I said, as if that would make any difference to them.

"Okay, but we don't have enough washcloths saved up. They'll be gone in the first day," Mel said.

I laughed. "We'll reuse them."

That got a look of surprise from everyone.

"And, uh, how exactly do we do that?" Jeff asked.

"I'm not reusing one of those! That's just gross," Lee Ann added. The rest of the girls, her mom and Bobbie included, agreed with her.

"Look, I know you guys aren't thrilled about this—frankly, neither am I, but we don't have a choice. We will reuse them. You just have to wash it after use."

That statement was met with a chorus of complaints.

"Calm down, calm down," I said, motioning with my hands for everyone to quiet down. "We need to save what TP we have left in case someone gets really sick. Everyone else will use the cloth, and you ladies will have two, one for number one and one for number two. When you are done with it, you'll wash it out. There will be a bucket with a solution of this"—I held up a bag of pool shock, calcium hypochlorite—"you'll use this with these"—I picked up one of the gloves—"to wash your cloth. There will be a second bucket of clean water to rinse with, then you hang it up to dry. This powder is essentially bleach. We'll mix a solution of it with water, not too strong, to sanitize the cloths."

For a moment no one said anything, they just looked at the stuff on the table. The two girls were shaking their heads. "This is bull," Lee Ann muttered.

I shot her a look. "We don't have a choice, guys, it's what we have to do. And it's important to clean your cloth thoroughly. We don't want anyone to get sick," I added.

Again, I was met with silent stares. Thad was the one to first come to my side.

"Beats using leaves," he said, shrugging his shoulders.

I smiled, "The only other option is to use the Seminole Indian method."

"The *what*?" Mel asked flatly, narrowing her eyes.

"Hang on," I said and jogged off toward the woods.

I was smiling as I came back with my hands concealed behind my back. I rocked back and forth on my heels.

"All right, what is it?" Mel asked as she crossed her arms over her chest.

"The Seminoles used this for a number of things: wound dressings, TP, several things." As I said the last word I revealed what I'd been hiding: it was a piece of the inner fiber of the sable palm. It has an open weave and is a great source of dry tinder when nothing else can be found. It forms at the base of the fronds on the tree.

Mel and Bobbie both immediately scowled, shaking their heads. "I'm not using that," Bobbie quickly said.

"Nope, me neither," Mel added.

"Looks like it would hurt," Taylor said.

Lee Ann scowled. "I'm not about to wipe my butt with that, no way."

I picked up one of the cloths. "Doesn't look so bad now, does it?"

Little Bit was standing beside me now. She picked one of the cloths up and looked at Mel. "Mommy, I have to go now. Can I try it?"

I looked at her, then at Mel, and smiled. "Our first customer."

Mel rolled her eyes and took her by the hand, headed for the outhouse.

"I'll get the bleach mixed up, and bring it and the rinse water over," I said.

"Well, I'm going to start dinner," Thad said. He was met with a chorus of agreement. "Miss Bobbie, can you get a pot of rice ready and show me where the dehydrated stuff is?" Bobbie nodded and led Thad off.

I opened the bag of shock and went to the cabin for a couple of buckets. With the buckets filled from the creek, I added the shock in the appropriate ratio, then took them, a Solo cup, and the gloves over to the outhouse. Mel was leaning on the side of the structure, cloth in hand.

"Here you go," I said, setting the buckets down. She did not look enthused.

Mel dipped the cloth in some of the clean water, wrung it out, and then handed it inside to Ashley.

"Thanks, Mom," she called out.

For a moment she was quiet, then the door swung open and she came out, hitching up her pants. The cloth was folded in her hand and she held it out to Mel. Mel put on the gloves and dipped a cup in the bleach solution, pouring it over the soiled cloth and agitating it. After rinsing it and wringing it out, she looked up at me.

"Where do I put it?" she asked.

"Just hang it on a limb," I said.

"All right," she sighed. "This isn't *too* bad."

"And it feels good too!" Little Bit shouted, jumping up and down.

Chapter 10

When the music stopped, it took a moment for Jess and Fred to register it. Their ears were ringing badly, and everything sounded as if their heads were packed with cotton. Jess rolled onto her back, reveling in the silence. She fell asleep a few moments later, exhausted from the evening's events. Fred lay there trying to ignore the ringing in her ears. Her head hurt so badly that, for once, she was thankful it was dark. She had never experienced pain like this—her body was on the brink of collapse. She could only imagine how Shane or the old man were faring in their respective cells.

As if on cue, the door to Shane's cell was opened. Fred braced herself for the sound of water splashing, but she couldn't hear anything. Shane was so weak that he didn't even respond to the noise. His body hung limply from the restraints. A nurse entered the cell and checked him, running a digital thermometer across his forehead.

"He's hypothermic. You need to warm him quickly or he's gonna die, and soon."

"Well, shit! I told you we should have checked on him last night," one officer said to another.

"So what if he dies? Gonna happen sooner or later."

"Yeah, well, Niigata wants it to be later."

"Come on, let's take him down."

Shane was lowered to the floor and old wool Red Cross blankets were brought in. The nurse laid a few on the floor then covered him with the rest.

"This isn't going to do it," she said, looking at the guard.

"What else do you want us to do? How can you warm him up?"

"Ideally, another person. Skin-to-skin contact is the best way."

"What? Someone wrapped up with him in the blankets?"

"Mmhmm, that's the best way."

The guard smiled and motioned for the other officer to follow him.

"Where are you going?" the nurse asked.

"To get you a warm body," he called over his shoulder as he twirled the keys on his finger.

Jess was barely able to open her eyes before she was grabbed by the guard and pulled to her feet.

"Get up, we've got a treat for you," a man's voice said.

"No, no . . ." She tried to protest, but she was so exhausted from the previous night, it was futile.

"Come on," one of the men said as they dragged her down the corridor and into another cell.

Jess could make out what seemed like a body under a pile of blankets. The officers pulled her to her feet and removed her restraints, then issued a command that terrified her.

"Strip."

Adrenaline shot through her body, horrible memories flooding her. Jess tried to bolt for the door, but she was still weak and feeble. One of the guards easily grabbed her arm and stopped her. She fought back and screamed.

"You do it or we'll do it for you!" one of the men shouted as she was thrown back into the cell.

"Get away from me! Don't come near me!" Jess screamed as she backed away from the two men.

Fred was lying on the floor of her cell when she heard Jess scream. She quickly got up and moved to the door.

"Jess, Jess! You all right?" she shouted. Before Jess could respond, the nurse grabbed Jess by the shoulder and looked her square in the eyes.

"Look, we need you to warm him up. Get under the blankets with him. Skin-to-skin contact is the fastest way to warm someone up. He isn't going to hurt you, look at him," she said, pointing to the motionless form under the blankets.

Jess looked at the mound under the blankets, then at the nurse, and last, the guards.

"It's going to happen one way or another, sweetheart," one of the officers said.

"Fuck you! Don't call me that!" Jess shouted. She then looked back at the nurse, begging her with her eyes. "Tell them to leave and I'll do it."

The nurse turned to the officers. "Would you two get out of here? I'll make sure she gets undressed and show her how to lie with him."

The two men stood their ground for a moment, eyeing Jess. Then one of them gave a dismissive wave. "Fuck it, let's go," he said and stepped out of the cell.

Jess watched the men leave, then looked at the nurse, twirling her finger to tell her to turn around. Jess took off the jumpsuit and laid it aside, then carefully lifted up the blankets to reveal a nude man. He was rather young and appeared to be totally unconscious. She lay down beside him, flinching when she first touched his skin.

"You sure he's not dead?" she said as she pulled the blanket over herself.

The nurse turned around. "Not yet. That's why you're here with him—to keep that from happening."

"My God, he's so cold. What'd they do to him?" Jess said as she stretched out alongside him.

"I don't know, but just stay there with him. I'll be back in an hour to check on you."

Jess moved around to get comfortable. Despite the circumstances, lying on a blanket seemed heavenly after spending so much time on the bare concrete. Once she was somewhat comfortable, she thought about the man. *This must be Shane. You better not get any bright ideas when you wake up, buddy.*

After it was clear that the guards and nurse had left the building, Fred called out to her. "Jess! Jess, you all right?"

"Yeah, I'm fine."

"What's going on? Why were you screaming?"

"I'll explain when I can. I'm in here with Shane, I think."

Fred was surprised. "You're *in there* with him?"

Jess pulled the blanket up over her head. "Yes! I'll tell you later. Now, *shhh*! I don't want to get us in trouble." The reply came out muffled.

Shocked, Fred fell back against the wall. *What the hell is going on?*

"We're going to have to move tonight," Mike said as he looked across the camp.

"Yeah, we've seen everything there is to see on this side," Ian replied. "Wonder if the music is going to start up again," he murmured, looking through the spotting scope.

Mike looked toward the small rectangular building, "I don't know, but it's obvious they are working someone over in there."

"Think we should make that a priority when we hit it? See who's in there?"

"I'd say so, but that's up to the old man and your officers to decide," Mike replied, adjusting the binoculars.

Ian laughed. "Let's be real, it's totally up to Sarge. Don't get me wrong, my officers are nice guys, but even they admitted it."

Mike looked over. "Admitted what?"

"That they're scared shitless of going in there. They're National Guard, not Special Forces."

Mike clicked his tongue. "Well, he told 'em they'd have to earn their money."

"Well, that's one thing about them, whatever has to be done, they'll do their best. There was a lot of discussion after you guys left the first time, lots of talk about what might happen. No one knows other than me and the brass, but everyone suspects they are going to be pushed into action."

"The captain hasn't said anything to the troopers about what they're going to have to do?" Mike asked.

"Not yet, but these guys are smart. Seeing you guys in the camp, they've caught on that something's coming. They think you guys are like Delta Force or something."

Mike started to laugh. "Delta Force, that's funny as hell!" He dropped his face into his hands and laughed even harder. When he looked up he had tears in his eyes. Wiping them away, he said, "Delta Force, that's rich."

Ian shrugged. "Just telling you what they're sayin'."

Mike nodded and went back to observing the camp, still chuckling from time to time.

Throughout the day, they watched the small building with special attention, making notes any time it was approached by the staff. It was during one of these times that Ian called Mike's attention to it.

"Hey, man, check out seven. Looks like they might be bringing in food."

Mike was on the spotting scope this time and swung it quickly over to the building. There were three individuals approaching the building, carrying what appeared to be trays.

"Looks like food trays. Let me try and get a count," Mike said as he focused the scope. "It looks like five trays, could be six."

Ian made a note. "All right, possibly six, no less than five."

"Yeah, that's as best as I can see. Go wake Teddy up. We should relocate soon."

Ian nodded and slowly backed out of the hide. As soon as he was outside he gave a low whistle. Ted turned around and nodded, then turned back and scanned the area in front of him. Ian started packing up his gear. It wasn't long before Ted crawled up, cradling the SAW on his elbows.

"You guys ready to move?" he asked.

"Yeah, I figure we'll get packed up, grab some grub, and move out after dark."

"Cool. See anything new?"

"They brought what looked like food trays into the building—five, maybe six of them."

Ted nodded and then looked up through the trees. The tops were gently swaying in the breeze and for a moment he was mesmerized by them. Ian glanced at him, then looked up to see what he was staring at. Not seeing anything of note, he waved a hand in front of Ted's face.

"Earth to Teddy. Mike thinks we should make that building a priority when we hit the camp," Ian said.

"Sorry. Yeah, probably," Ted replied as he pulled an MRE out of his pack.

Ian looked at him for a moment. "You all right?"

"I'm good, just need a vacation," Ted said with a laugh.

"Me too. Somewhere with a beach and topless chicks."

Ted dumped out the contents of his MRE pouch. "Ugh, don't even get started on women."

Mike crawled up. "Women? What women?"

"That's the problem. There ain't none," Ted said with a laugh.

While they ate, the three traded locker room stories, in whispers, of their various escapades. When the meal was done they packed all of their trash, stuffing everything back into their packs. When all their gear was packed, they did a very careful check of the hide to make sure nothing was left behind.

"Mike, you want to call in to the old man real quick?" Ted asked.

Mike nodded and sat down beside the radio. Putting on the headset, he made the call.

"Stump Knocker Stump Knocker, Cracker One."

The reply came immediately. *"Send it, Cracker One."*

"Moving to next, all's quiet."

"Roger that. Cracker Two, report."

Perez picked up the handset. "Cracker Two, all's quiet."

"Roger that, Cracker Two. Stump Knocker out."

Livingston looked at Sarge. "Well, sounds like your boys are doing all right. Wonder how long they'll be out."

Sarge rubbed the stubble on his chin. "Hard to say. They'll stay out as long as they need to. Them two are nuttier than squirrel shit, but they are good at what they do." He paused and nodded respectfully. "Sounds like your crew is all right too."

"Perez is an old salt. He's got several tours under his belt.

When he was younger, he was one of those guys that always looked for a deployment. He liked it better when bullets were flying past him. As he got older, he came over to the Guard to finish off his retirement. He's not as gung ho as he used to be, but he's still a dangerous old bastard."

Sarge nodded. "That's good, we'll need some dangerous ole bastards. And some young ones too."

"We've got plenty of young ones, problem is most of them haven't been deployed before. We had a pretty big turnover right before the shit hit the fan, lost a lot of seasoned guys. I'm worried how they'll react when the lead starts to fly."

Sarge spit into the dirt. "I'm hoping to come up with a way to get into the camp without a lot of shooting."

"How the hell do you expect to do that?" Livingston asked. "It's not like they're just going to let us walk through the gate."

Sarge shrugged. "They might, if they don't know any better." He stood up. "All right, we'll discuss more later. I'm gonna go talk to Doc and see how everything is going."

Sarge left the command tent and wandered through the camp, observing the people as he went. Soldiers and civilians alike had weapons on them. Good for the safety of the settlement, he thought. They would probably need some of the civilians to assist in the assault. The camp was large and was going to be a hell of a job to take down.

Doc and several others were tossing the last of the dirt into the pit. Sarge stood at the edge of the pit, examining the scene. Several pipes were sticking out of the ground with tar paper cones on top.

"Nice piss tubes, Doc," Sarge said.

Doc looked up, shovel in hand. "Gee, thanks."

Sarge pointed at the pit. "What's in there?"

Harmon looked up from where he was throwing dirt. "Ole Doc there is pretty smart. We crushed a ton of cans with a truck, used it to line the pit about three-quarters"—he pointed at the fresh dirt— "and now we're filling in the rest with dirt."

Sarge looked confused. "Cans? What the hell for?"

"It acts as a drain field. This will last a lot longer than just digging a pit." Doc pointed at one of the tubes. "They travel all the way down to the cans. It's the best we could do."

"Well, glad someone knows something about this." Sarge stepped up to one of the tubes. "Allow me to break it in for you."

Doc shook his head but couldn't help himself and smiled.

As Sarge was taking care of business he asked, "What about the ladies?"

Doc pointed off to the east. "We made a couple of slit trenches for them over there. There are also some fresh slit trenches for defecating in. They're deeper, and we have barrels of wood ash for people to pour in after use. Lime would be better, but we don't have any."

Sarge had finished up and asked, "Where do we shit?"

Doc pointed at a tarp strung up between two poles as a screen. "Back there's our slit trenches. You gonna break that in too?" he asked with a grin.

Sarge patted his belly. "Nah, not yet. The crap we're eating has me bound up tighter than Dick's hatband."

"Haven't had your prune juice in a few days, huh?"

"Fuck you, Doc," Sarge said with a smile.

Doc smiled back. "Love you too."

Sarge shook his head and spun on his heels.

"I'll take point," Ted said as he flipped his NVGs down over his eyes. They were slowly heading east to scope out the front gate. As the sun had set, a breeze had picked up. In the green glow of the optics each man wore, they could see the trees swaying back and forth.

The three men stayed about fifteen feet apart, moving in a staggering pace. Ted was in the lead. He would take five or six steps and pause, then Ian would walk up and stop, then Mike would follow. This way, there was always at least one person looking and listening. As they made their way around the camp, the artificial light from the towers helped so they could clearly see their way.

Hearing vehicles outside the perimeter, they halted and took a knee. The times and direction of travel were noted. Ted made sure they were at the tree line but checked his compass—they were now on a northerly track, with the main gate in sight. It was time to start looking for a hide.

Through the NVGs, Ted could see light off to his right. It was in the opposite direction of the camp, which was puzzling. He halted and whispered to Ian that he wanted to check it out. The group moved slowly toward the lights. As they got closer, they could hear people shouting, then the sound of an engine revving up.

Kneeling down, they tried to get a view of the activity, but there was too much brush. "Let's see what's up. We may need to find another way," Ted whispered.

The men dropped their packs and began to crawl toward the voices. After a few hundred yards, Ted stopped, and Mike and Ian came up on either side of him. In front of them was a bus and several Hummers. A group of people sat on the ground with armed men standing over them. Two of the Hummers were chained together, and they were trying to pull the bus out of the deep sand in the road with no apparent luck.

"Looks like they were bringing people in," Ian said, looking at the group.

"Yeah, I don't think those two trucks are going to get that thing out either," Mike whispered.

"Yeah, good luck with that," Ted whispered back.

The three men stayed in their positions, watching the futile efforts to get the bus out. After an hour or so, the crew working on it gave up. The guards ordered the group to their feet and began leading them toward the camp. The guys waited until the group was down the road, and then began to follow them while staying inside the tree line.

When the main gate finally came into view, the three stopped and took up a position to observe. The gate was a fortified area with sandbag emplacements and a bunker on either side. On the inside of the gate, a large diesel-powered light tower with four bright heads illuminated the area.

The group was led through the gate and disappeared into the camp. Once they were out of sight, Ted tried to get a count on the number of personnel stationed at the gate.

"I got five, how many you see?" Mike whispered.

"That's what I got," Ted replied.

"Me too," Ian confirmed.

"This gate would be a breeze to take down," Ted said.

"I only see one machine gun, in the bunker on the left," Ian said.

"Let's see what their response is like. Ian, you stay here.

Mike, come with me. Ian, keep an eye on the these guys and see what they do. I've got an idea."

"What do you want to do?" Mike asked as he knelt down behind a tree.

Ted scoped out the area, then nodded toward the bus. "I want to do something to get their attention."

Mike rooted around in a pouch on his plate carrier. "I got a thermite grenade," he said, holding it up.

Ted scowled at him. "No, dickhead, I don't want to burn it! They'd figure out something was up and start looking."

Mike shrugged and put the grenade away.

"I'm gonna run out and turn all the lights on and honk the horn. Then I'll run back and we'll see what these guys do."

"That's stupid! They'll know someone's around then. I say burn it. Put that thermite on the engine and it'll look like an engine fire. Think about it. Plus, we'll take out one of their busses," Mike said.

Ted clicked his tongue, thinking about what Mike said. "You're smarter than you look, kid. All right, go burn it, let's see what they do."

Mike giggled like a little kid as he headed for the bus. Once he was behind it, he knelt down and looked around. Confident the area was secure, he quietly opened the engine compartment and took out the grenade, pulled the pin, and wedged it in behind the air cleaner with the spoon up. As soon as he let go of it, the spoon flew off with a pop and a hiss; the fuse lit. He quickly closed the lid and made his way back to the side of the road. As he entered the woods, the grenade went off.

Thermite grenades don't explode like a typical hand grenade—they simply ignite and begin to burn, turning into a fountain of molten metal as the iron and aluminum burn.

Because of this, the engine compartment was quickly engulfed in flames. The fire spread throughout the bus within moments, flames leaping high into the night's sky.

"Burn, baby, burn!" Mike whispered.

Ted was watching the road. "You're a pyro, aren't ya?"

"There's nothing wrong with having a little fun with incendiaries," Mike replied with a grin.

"Hey, here they come," Ted said as he elbowed Mike.

Headlights were coming down the road, and soon two Hummers came into view. The trucks stopped short of the bus and men got out. For a moment they ran around, but without a fire truck, they were helpless. They settled for leaning on the hoods of their trucks and watching it burn.

"I count six. They must be the reaction force," Ted said.

"Yeah, did ya see how they ran around? What the hell did they think that was going to do?"

One of the men was talking into a radio and, soon, a UTV side by side pulled up and two more men got out. They stood with the others as the bus burned, gesturing at the inferno. After a few minutes of conversation, the two in what could be assumed were command-like positions got back into the UTV and left, the others staying behind.

It took over an hour for the bus to burn itself out. Once the flames had died down, the six men who had been watching it moved in for a closer look. Now that the sound of the crackling fire had dissipated, Ted could just make out what the men were saying.

"Huh, they bought it! They think it's an engine fire," Ted said.

"Told you it would work," Mike replied.

"Whatever, it's like seeing Bigfoot. Anyone who wasn't here won't believe it."

After making their way back, the three regrouped. Ted moved them farther back into the bush to compare notes.

"That was a hell of a fire," Ian said, wiping his nose. "I could feel the heat over here."

Ted jutted his thumb at Mike. "Yeah, he likes to burn shit."

Mike smiled. "Now, *that's* a fire."

"What'd they do when they saw it?" Ted asked.

"They started jumping and hopping around, then called for backup, I guess. Two Hummers came running out of the camp."

"How long did it take them to respond?" Mike asked.

"'Bout five minutes. Longer than I would have thought."

Ted nodded. "All right, let's go find us a place to set up a hide."

They settled for a high spot covered in palmettos. Ian set a security position about thirty feet behind the first. The guys worked on camouflaging the hides, finishing around two in the morning.

"Why don't you both get some sleep and I'll keep the first watch?" Ian said as he crawled into the hide.

Mike yawned. "Don't have to ask me twice."

Jamie pulled her bag up tighter around her. She wanted to sleep, but she couldn't.

"Hey, Perez, you think the guys started that fire?" she asked.

Perez was lying behind the SAW, giving his eyes a break from the NVGs. He hated wearing the things—they always gave him a headache. He sighed. He was looking forward to Jamie going to sleep. When she was awake, she yammered on incessantly, and that wasn't helping his headache any.

Perez sighed, "I doubt it. The object is to not be seen, not go starting a damn inferno. Besides, there wasn't any shooting. If they were involved, I'm sure we would've known."

Jamie thought for a minute, then closed her eyes. If it wasn't for Perez, she would have run over there to back them up, but he made her stay. *Oh well, maybe tomorrow we'll find out*, she thought to herself.

Perez was thankful for the silence. He listened to the breeze as it sighed through the trees above. Periodically, he would hold the NVG up to an eye and scan the area. He liked it out here, no one around—well, almost no one. Of all the things he missed, it was his solitude. He lived alone and liked it that way. During the day he drove his truck, a terminal freight, around town. Even with this he didn't have to talk to too many people, just back up and get loaded or unloaded, then back on the road.

Perez was twisting a strip of palmetto frond around his finger when he heard something. He paused and waited to see if he'd hear it again. Again, he heard it. He quietly picked up the NVG and peered through. About five yards out, at his eleven o'clock, a skunk was nosing around the scrub. Perez's eyes went wide. *That thing better not come over here*, he thought. He watched as the rodent searched for its dinner, the white stripe running down its back glowing in the goggles. After a while the animal wandered off, leaving Perez with his thoughts and, finally, some quiet.

Chapter 11

It was getting late in the day and the sun was beginning to wane. We started smoking the gator we weren't going to use for tonight's meal, knowing it would probably take a couple of days to finish it. Danny, Jeff, and I were cutting the rest of the meat into strips while Thad tended the smoker. Taylor and Little Bit were sitting around the fire. It was then I heard the first buzz, that high-pitched annoyance that can only mean one thing: mosquitoes.

"Well, it had to happen eventually," I said.

Danny looked up. "What?"

"You heard any skeeters yet?"

"No, you?"

"Just did, first one."

"What are we going to do about them?" Jeff asked. "Out here, they'll probably carry you away."

"Oh yeah, in the summer, they can be a bitch," Danny said.

Jeff stopped cutting. "Damn! First bite of the season! Man, I would give my left nut for a can of Off."

"There's a couple of natural remedies, not as great as Off, but better than nothing," I said.

"What's better than nothing?" Thad asked as he came for more meat.

"A cure for the skeeters," Jeff said.

Thad looked around. "Yeah, it's 'bout that time of year. What kind of ideas you got, Morg?"

"We need to get some myrtle berries and leaves, boil them up, and use the extract. It's a technique the Seminoles used."

"Nice. I think we should build a cover over the table too. The rainy season's gonna start soon," Thad said.

I nodded. "Excellent plan, my brotha."

Jeff smirked. "Well, aren't you two just the nature nuts."

Mel came out of the cabin with some bags for the dried meat. "Hey, hon. Where's Lee Ann been? I haven't seen her all day," I said.

"She's lying in her bed," she said, nodding toward the cabin.

I looked back at the cabin. "Is she feeling okay?"

"She's on her period. She was complaining earlier."

"Is that all it is? She seemed a little off this morning."

"She's been acting a little weird lately," Mel said as she tucked dry gator into a bag.

"Weird in what way?"

"Have you talked to her much recently? She's been awfully mopey."

I thought about it for a minute. "I guess I haven't, not much anyway, not since the whole thing with Ashley went down. I'll go talk to her later. The girls wanted to go for a walk the other day. Maybe I'll just ask her to go."

Mel smiled. "That'd be a good idea." She took the bags of meat and headed back for the cabin.

"Kids, what can you do?" Thad said.

"No, Thad. Girls. Whole different universe," I replied, causing Thad to laugh.

"Better you than me," Danny said.

"Shit, those girls are as much yours as they are mine. Little Bit already calls you her other daddy." I turned to where she was sitting by the fire. "Isn't that right?"

She was poking at the fire with a stick and looked up. "What?"

"Isn't Danny your other daddy?"

She sat back in her chair and smiled. "Yep, I got two daddies!"

I looked back at him and smiled. "Ha, by the way, you owe me about four years' worth of raising our kid."

Thad laughed, slapping the table. Danny laughed too. "More like three, maybe two, as much time as she spends at my house."

"Okay, you got me there."

"You guys ready for some of this for dinner?" Thad asked, holding up a piece of the tail.

He was met with a chorus of *Hell yeahs!* Thad smiled and took the meat to the smoker. With it, we were going to have a pot of watercress. Mel and Bobbie were going to take care of the veggies. They had gotten pretty good at steaming the tender leaves on the fire.

"Hey, Danny, you want to come give me a hand real quick?" I asked.

"Sure, what's up?"

"We need to set up a warning system out by the pigs. Someone's been sniffing around over there."

Danny's head snapped around. "Who? What?"

"Thad saw some tracks over there. I've got a little something to give us notice if they come back."

"Hold on. Tracks, like people tracks?" Jeff asked.

As I started toward the pigpen, I looked back over my shoulder. "Yeah."

Danny and Jeff both caught up quickly. At the pen I showed them the tracks, which were faded now. I took out the kit I had and explained what it did.

"That's not going to do much," Jeff replied with a frown.

"No, but whoever is keeping watch will see it, plus whoever trips it will know that we're watching and probably haul ass," I replied.

It was nearly dark when we set the flare up and ran the wire. The trigger for the simulator was a spring held under tension. If the wire was tripped, the spring would release, pulling the igniter and lighting the flare.

"We need to pay special attention to this area," Danny said. "Some fucker thinks he's going to come in here and steal our hogs." His voice grew increasingly irate. "I'll kill his ass. I'm taking the first watch tonight."

"Calm down, man, we don't know if they were after the hogs. We don't know what they were after."

"That's what I'm worried about—they may see the pigs as a bonus," Jeff said.

"We need to make sure the girls know someone is poking around," Danny said. I nodded my agreement.

Later, as we ate the delicious gator dinner that Thad had prepared, I cleared my throat.

"All right, everyone. We noticed some tracks down by the pigpens. We need to be cautious and watch out for any possible intruders," I said.

I went on to stress that everyone needed to keep their weapons handy, just in case. Of everyone, it was Little Bit that was the most bothered by the news. She was scared the hermit was coming back to get her, she told me, burying her face in Mel's side.

"He's not coming back, baby," I said.

"Are you sure?"

Without telling why I was so sure, I replied, "Positive, he's never coming back."

"Don't worry, Ashley. We'll protect you," Taylor said. I smiled at her—I was happy she was being a good big sister.

Her other sister, though, kept silent during this whole exchange. Lee Ann was picking at her plate and didn't even look up during the discussion. I imagined that dealing with her period under the current circumstances wasn't pleasant, and I hoped that was all that was wrong, but I couldn't be sure.

"Dad, can I stand watch too?" Taylor asked.

I didn't answer right away, as there was a lot to consider in response to her question. She had a weapon and knew how to use it, but the biggest question was if the time came, could she shoot, and would she do it fast enough.

Before I could answer, Danny looked up from his plate. "If it's okay with your mom and dad, you can hang out with me tonight when I'm on watch. I can show you what to do."

She looked over at me and Mel. "Please?" she asked, drawing out the word.

I glanced at Mel, who said, "As long as Danny's there, then yes." Taylor smiled and went back to eating. I looked at Danny with a grin, he nodded his head slightly and returned to his dinner as well.

"Thad, this lizard is good," Jeff said.

"Thanks! Did what I could with it. A little salt and pepper go a long way. Wish the old man was here: he'd love this."

"Yeah, he'd been aching to shoot one," I said with a smile.

Chewing a bite of the watercress, I looked at Mel. "What'd you guys do to this? It's good too, even better than the last time."

"We spiced it up a bit, added some garlic and butter powder," Bobbie replied.

"It's damn good," Thad added, and pointed across the table at Little Bit. "Even she likes it."

Little Bit scrunched her nose. "It's okay."

I laughed. "Yeah, she's just hungry."

"I hear you guys are going to build something over these tables," Bobbie said.

"Yeah, we're going to use some of the river cane and build a canopy," Thad said.

Mel looked up, her eyes bright. "Oh, like a tiki hut? I've always wanted a tiki hut."

Thad laughed. "Somehow I don't think whatever we come up with will look much like a tiki hut."

"Sure it will. If you make it from that bamboo-type stuff, with a thatched roof, it will look just like one."

"We aren't going to be thatching the roof. We're going to use plastic sheeting. Sorry, ladies," Danny said.

"That's going to be ugly as sin," Bobbie said.

"I think you should use palmettos or something and make it look like a tiki hut," Mel added.

Danny, Thad, and I were laughing. "This isn't a design contest, it's just to provide some shelter over the tables. With the weather warming up, it's going to start raining a lot soon, and we need somewhere to get out of it besides the cabins," I said.

Mel looked at Bobbie. "Don't worry, they'll thatch it." Bobbie nodded her agreement, leaving us menfolk to stare at one another. Jeff was the only one laughing now.

"Lee Ann, can you and Taylor clean up the dinner dishes?" Mel asked.

Lee Ann leaned forward. "Mom, I don't feel good. I want to go to bed."

Mel looked at her closely. "Lee Ann, you just came from

bed. Are you sure you're okay? Is it just cramps or . . ." She trailed off.

Lee Ann replied with an edge in her voice that I had never heard before. "Jeez, Mom, I'm *fine*. I just don't feel good, that's all."

Mel opened her mouth to say something, but Jeff interrupted.

"Don't worry, Mel, I'll help," Jeff said as he stood up and started collecting plates.

"Can I go, please?" Lee Ann asked.

"All right. Go to bed. But I don't like that attitude you just gave me."

Lee Ann walked away toward the cabin, shoulders slumped. "Whatever," she muttered.

"I heard that! Lee Ann Carter, you don't *whatever* your mother!" Mel yelled after her.

"I'm SORRY," Lee Ann yelled back, slamming the door to the cabin.

Taylor and Jeff looked at each other, eyebrows raised.

"Mel, I'm worried about her," I said.

"She has been acting strange," Bobbie said.

"I just don't know what to do. She won't get out of bed, now she's giving me attitude," Mel said. "I don't think it's just her period."

I nodded, but couldn't think of any solution. "Maybe she just needs some alone time. We're all in close quarters," I offered.

"I guess," Mel said, not looking convinced.

Taylor walked back up with Jeff, so we stopped our conversation. I didn't want her to hear us talking about her sister.

She slung her MP5 and sat on the table. It was obvious she was excited to be standing watch. I just hoped she was ready for it. Danny came over and took a seat by the fire, laying his carbine across his lap.

"All right, Ashley, time for bed," Mel said.

"Ah, come on, Mom! I want to sit by the fire for a while."

Mel pointed toward the cabin. "Nope, time for bed, let's go."

Little Bit put on her best pout. I nodded toward the cabin. Very reluctantly, she walked over to me, falling face-first into my lap. I gave her a hug and told her good night. She mumbled a muffled good night into my lap and stood up.

"Good night, Little Bit," Danny said.

She went over and hugged him around the shoulders. "Good night, Danny."

With shoulders slumped, a very sad Ashley trudged up toward the cabin.

"She's such a little character," Danny said with a smile.

"Yeah, she's the littlest of the prettiest," I said.

Taylor's head popped up. "Hey!"

I laughed. "I said *the littlest* of the prettiest. You're the biggest of the prettiest, and Lee Ann is the middlest of the prettiest. See how that works?"

She smiled. "Oh, now I see. You're funny, Dad. Hey, Danny, when are we going to start our watch?"

Danny let out a loud burp. "We already have."

Thad came from behind Danny with some wood for the fire. "That was a nice one."

Danny smiled. "Thanks."

"What do you mean we've already started? I thought we would go hide or something."

Thad tossed a piece of wood onto the fire, causing a shower of red sparks to rise up into the air.

"Nope, this is pretty much it. We just sit around and keep an eye on things."

It was clear that standing watch didn't seem so much fun to her anymore. "Oh," was all she replied.

Jeff reappeared with his AK in hand and took a seat by the fire as well.

"Man, I wish we had some coffee," Jeff said as he plopped down.

"Me too, I'd kill for a cup right now," Thad said.

Suddenly, I had an idea. "Danny, you still got all that stuff you used to steal from hotels?"

Danny stared into the fire for a moment. "Ha! I forgot all about that. I think I do," he said, hopping up.

"Never pegged Danny as a thief. What sort of stuff did you steal from hotels?" Jeff asked.

"You know, the coffee, the tea bags, the stuff they leave out for you."

Thad's head snapped up. "You think he's actually got some coffee?"

"I'll bet on it. I just can't believe I didn't remember he had it till now."

Danny came back carrying two-gallon Ziploc bags, stuffed full. He opened one and dumped its contents onto the table. Packs of coffee, sugar, and creamer spilled across the table. Thad smiled and jumped up, grabbing a pot and filling it from the bucket filter at the end of the table.

Danny was picking through the pile. "Here you go, boys."

Taylor cleared her throat.

"Sorry, boys and girl. Man! I can't believe I'd forgotten all about this stuff," he said as he sorted the items into piles. When he finished sorting, he counted out twelve packs of coffee.

Jeff stood over the loot, rubbing his hands together. "Ooh, we're gonna make some coffee."

"Let me see three or four of them bags," Thad said, a giant smile on his face. Danny tossed them over.

"Thad, I haven't seen you this happy in a *long* while," I said.

"Well, Morg, it's been a *long* while since I had a decent cup of coffee. I figured we were out forever."

"I want some too," Taylor said.

"You'll get the first cup," Thad said.

Mel and Bobbie walked back out. "Get her to sleep?" I asked.

"Yeah, only took two stories, and some groaning from Lee Ann. What are you guys doing?" Mel said.

"Makin' coffee!" Jeff said excitedly.

"Oh nice! I want some too," Mel said.

"You can have mine," Bobbie said.

"What? You don't like coffee, Bobbie?" Thad asked.

"Nope, never have. Now, if we had some beers . . . that'd be a different story." We all laughed.

The coffee began to bubble and Thad pulled it off the fire and set it on the table. Cups were quickly produced and sugar and creamer packs were passed out to those that wanted it.

"Oh my God, that's good," Jeff said as he stretched out in his chair and rocked his head back.

"Yeah, after going awhile without it, it's really nice," Thad said, holding the cup between his hands.

I was sipping on my own cup and started to giggle. "Ain't none of us going to be able to sleep tonight."

Bobbie laughed. "That's why I don't drink the stuff."

"Yeah, guess it was a bad idea to drink it right before bedtime," Jeff said.

"Not me. If I don't sleep a wink it was worth it," I said. After finishing our coffee, Mel and I were ready for bed. Jeff and Thad said they were going to hang out a little longer.

"Someone wake me up when I need to take watch," I said as we turned to head for the cabin.

Everyone said their good nights and we left. After so long without caffeine, I was really feeling it. There was no way in hell I was going to be able to sleep. To my surprise, Mel passed out right away. I grabbed the NVGs and carried them back to Danny, then came back to the cabin. It was nice to just lie there. I could hear the guys talking out at the fire, their voices were faint and seemed to drift on the wind. I closed my eyes, trying to clear my mind, and eventually drifted off.

At the sound of a shot, I was confused. *Did I hear that or was it a dream?* The follow-up shots told me it wasn't a dream. I jumped to my feet as rifle fire filled the air.

"What's going on?" Mel asked as she sat up. Fear was in her eyes. "Where's Tay?"

"I don't know, I don't know. You got your pistol?"

She leaned over and picked it up. "Yeah."

"Let me see what's going on," I said.

Little Bit got out of her bag and came running over to Mel. I was stuffing my feet into my boots when there was a long, subdued burst, like something ripping. I ran out the door with my carbine in my hands to see brass flying out of Taylor's H&K. It spun through the air twinkling in the moonlight before bouncing off the aluminum table.

She held the trigger for the entire magazine. When the weapon stopped firing, she looked at it, unsure of why it had stopped. Danny was still firing upriver. I ran and looked toward the river, searching for the muzzle flashes of the incoming fire. But the river was dark.

When Danny stopped firing I ran to him. "What is it? What happened?"

He pointed down the bank. I followed his arm and could see a small flame from the flare.

"The flares went off. Someone was running across the river."

"Did they shoot?" I asked.

"No, but when I heard them hit the river I started shooting."

"Did you hit any of them?"

"I didn't hear anyone yell."

Taylor came over with the H&K slung over her shoulder. I looked at her with raised eyebrows. "Full auto, huh?"

"I didn't mean to. It was an accident," she said.

"Well, make sure it doesn't happen again. Go on and go to bed," I told her.

She turned to leave, looking a little hurt and embarrassed.

"Hey," I called out. She turned to look at me. "It was fun, though, wasn't it?"

A big smile spread over her face and she nodded.

"Good night, kiddo."

"Night, Dad."

Jeff and Thad came up together. Thad clutched the old coach gun hanging from one hand.

"What the hell happened?" Jeff asked, looking around.

"Someone tripped the flare," Danny said, nodding upriver.

"We'll have to try and figure out where these people are coming from," I replied. "I don't want any more late-night shoot-outs."

We all nodded in agreement. The guys and I discussed the matter a bit further, and then I was overwhelmed with exhaustion.

"Guys, I gotta hit the hay. Jeff, mind taking over for Danny? You look wiped, man."

"Too much excitement for me," Danny said. "I'm going to bed too."

"Yeah, yeah, I'll watch out for your asses. Thad, want to keep me company?"

Thad nodded. "Can't promise there's gonna be any coffee left by the time you two wake up for breakfast," he said, looking over at me and Danny with a grin.

"Hey! Don't you go wastin' my coffee!" Danny said, punching him in the shoulder.

"Night, fellas," I called out, heading back to the cabin.

Once everyone was awake, we ate a quick breakfast of boiled eggs and smoked fish while discussing today's activity: working on the tables. We all headed off to a stand of cane just downriver. Everyone worked together, the girls included, to cut and drag the canes back. We piled them up by the tables and trimmed them. To tie it all together, we used a roll of twisted rope I'd brought.

It was great to have everyone working together, chattering as they did. The smell of smoke from the fire, the warm sun, and the clear morning made for a great day. Lee Ann and Little Bit sat in chairs by the fire and trimmed the small shoots from the canes, putting them in a pile. We collected these and bundled three or four together and used them as posts. The corners were made from four canes lashed together and buried about a foot in the ground.

Initially we wanted to make a peaked roof, but after some back-and-forth, we decided it was too difficult and settled on a pitched roof. We worked all day to get the frame up, and, satisfied with our work, we decided that tomorrow we would put the plastic on.

Once we finished for the day, I sat by the fire, cutting a piece of cane with my knife. Suddenly, I had an idea of another way to pass the time. I grabbed a full-length piece and began to split one end, cutting it into eight sections. Then I found a stick slightly larger in diameter and whittled it into a cone shape. I forced it down inside the cane, which spread the sections nicely. I then sharpened the ends of the sections.

"Aren't you tired of working?" Danny joked. "What is that, a gig?"

"Yup. I'm thinking of trying to get some frogs tonight."

"Oh, hell yeah! Let me make one too."

Soon everyone was sitting around the fire making their own spears—well, almost everyone. Mel and Bobbie made it clear they weren't going to be gigging any frogs and Thad said he'd be happy to cook them, but he wasn't one for boats. Lee Ann also opted out, and just sat by the fire, looking unenthused.

"Hey, kiddo, you want to go with us later?" I asked her.

She didn't look up from her slouched position in the chair. All she did was shake her head.

"You all right?"

She nodded and stood up. "I'm going to go lie down." I watched her as she walked back to the cabin. Her shoulders were sagging and she looked miserable.

I frowned. Something was definitely up.

Even after the gigs were done, there was still a lot of the afternoon left. The warm day was energizing, and I didn't want to just sit around.

Looking at Taylor, I asked, "You wanna go for a walk?"

She smiled and nodded, and Little Bit said she wanted to go as well. "Let me go get your sister and we'll head out."

Lee Ann was lying in her sleeping bag. I kicked her feet. "Hey, let's go for a walk."

Her reply came back muffled. "I don't want to."

"Yeah, you do. Get up. Let's take a walk." She didn't respond, so I grabbed the bottom of her sleeping bag and pulled it up, half dumping her out of the bag.

"Dad! Leave me alone!"

"No, get up. Quit feeling sorry for yourself. We're going for a walk."

She tried to pull the bag around herself.

"All right, I'll get a bucket of water. You're coming out of that bag one way or another," I said and turned for the door.

"All right, jeez! I'll get up." She got up and put on her shoes in silence.

I waited for her by the door. She came past me and thumped down the steps, sitting on the last one. I called for the other two girls and they came running up. Mel also walked over. "What are you guys up to?"

"We're going for a little stroll. Wanna come?" I asked.

"Sure."

We started up the trail that led to the dirt road. I was holding Mel's hand while Little Bit ran ahead with Taylor. Lee Ann was behind us, shoulders slumped and looking at the ground. I laughed as Taylor tried to pull palmetto hearts out for Little Bit. It never failed that if we walked in the woods she'd want one of these treats.

Mel shielded her eyes with her hand, looking up at the sun. "It's really nice out today."

"It is. It's so weird that it's always so quiet here," I replied.

"Not around camp."

I laughed. "Guess you're right."

We walked for some time through the sugar sand, listening to grasshoppers as they took to the wing at our advance. Taylor and Little Bit stayed out in front of us, leaving a trail of nibbled palmetto shoots in their wake. I looked back at Lee Ann and tugged on Mel's hand. We slowed, allowing her to catch up to us. As she came up I wrapped my arm around her.

"Hey, buster, how you feelin'?" I asked. She shrugged.

We continued walking in silence. After a bit I said, "You know what happened with Ash wasn't your fault, don't you?"

She didn't reply immediately. Finally she said, "Taylor said it is. She says it's all my fault."

"But it's not. I'll talk to her, but you shouldn't blame yourself." She nodded.

"What else is bothering you, hon? You don't seem yourself," Mel said. Lee Ann answered with her ever-present shrug, but Mel pressed on. "Is there something you want to talk about?"

"No. I'm just tired of being here. I want to see my friends, I want to go home, I'm just tired."

"Cheer up, it's not the end of the world. We're still here. Besides, we may be going home sooner than you know it," I said.

I'd hoped the thought of going home soon would cheer her up, but it appeared to have little effect. At the crest of the small rise in the road, I called the other girls back, telling them we needed to head home. Lee Ann immediately spun on her heels and headed back for the house, not waiting for the rest of us.

Chapter 12

After dinner, Danny, Jeff, me, Taylor, and Little Bit went out on the river with our gigs in hand. I wished we had a spotlight, but all we had were our flashlights. They proved to be sufficient if not ideal. We took opposite sides of the creek, moving slowly and shining the water's edge. Taylor was holding the light for me as I poled down the bank, scanning slowly. On the opposite bank, Jeff held the light for Danny. Danny was standing up in the bow of the boat as they glided along.

"Got one!" I called out as I speared a frog. Little Bit giggled.

Danny looked over and smiled, holding his spear. I pulled the frog off and dropped it in a bucket with three others. I had just turned back to spear at another when there was a thundering boom, followed by a scream and a splash. I immediately turned to see Danny in the water. Jeff was flailing around in the boat, then he began firing his AK into the trees.

"Little Bit, get down, lie down!" I shouted as I sat down and grabbed a paddle. "Taylor, paddle over there! Danny! Danny!"

There was another boom and I heard the shot as they peppered the aluminum canoe. This time though, I saw the muzzle flash. Picking up my AR, I began to fire in that direction. Danny's head popped out of the water, and he held on to the side of the canoe. As we got closer I took up my paddle again and steered toward Danny. We hit a small sandbar and ground to a stop. Suddenly all the shooting stopped, and I heard Jeff yell, "Shit!" I looked up to see Jeff changing mags frantically.

"Taylor, shoot into the trees, no full auto!"

She nodded and picked up her H&K and started to fire, the suppressor making a spitting sound. Little Bit was lying in the bottom of the boat, wailing. Throwing the sling of my rifle around my neck, I jumped into the water just as Jeff started to fire again. I grabbed Danny under his arms and lifted him up, trying to push him into the boat. He was obviously in pain.

"Get back to the cabin!" I shouted at Jeff. He nodded and grabbed his paddle and began to back-paddle toward the camp.

I shoved our canoe off the bar and climbed in. "Taylor, you paddle, paddle fast!" I said, then started firing into the trees again. There was no more return fire and after a few minutes, I started paddling too. It was only then that I noticed Taylor's arms were shaking. "Good job, Tay, good job," I said.

When we got to the camp Danny was already out of the boat, bent over at the waist. Thad and Jeff were on either side of him, helping him walk. I grabbed Little Bit and set her out as Mel ran up.

"What happened?" Mel asked, on the verge of tears. "Where was all that shooting from?"

"Someone started shooting. Danny's been hit," I said as I ran off. "Watch the girls."

Danny was sitting in a chair by the fire, Bobbie beside him, looking nervous and holding a flashlight. Thad and Jeff were pulling his shirt off when I ran up. His left side was covered in little red spots, some bleeding, some like welts. They extended from just under his arm to his hip. It was strange to see where his belt had stopped the shot, leaving a strip of untouched flesh.

"You're lucky, Danny. Looks like it was just bird shot," Thad said as he dabbed at one of the bleeding spots.

Jeff held up two fingers, a small bead pinched between them. "Nope, looks like number four."

"I don't know about lucky, it burns like hell," Danny said through gritted teeth.

Using flashlights, we went over Danny's wounds. There were a few that looked like they may have actually penetrated into him. They weren't life-threatening by any means, but they would have to be checked carefully so we could prevent infection. That was the last thing we needed.

"Tomorrow morning, I'll call Doc to get down here and look you over," I said.

"Let's get you into bed," Bobbie said, helping him get up.

"Bobbie, you want someone to stay with you?" Thad asked.

"No thanks, Thad, we'll be all right. I got it from here." She headed off toward their cabin as the rest of us made our way toward the fire pit.

"What the hell happened?" Thad asked.

"He was standing up and someone in the trees took a shot," Jeff said.

"I heard the shot, then heard him scream and hit the water all at the same time," I said.

"Did you ever see them?" Thad asked.

"No, I just started shooting, hoping to make them duck," Jeff said.

"I saw the muzzle flash from the second shot and fired at it, for what good it did," I said.

"Yeah, that second one almost got me."

"You were pretty lucky," I said.

"Yeah, if it had been any higher it'd have got me too," Jeff said. "Let's go look at the boat and see where it was hit."

As the beam of the flashlight swept the length of the boat, the light illuminated the spots of raw metal where the shot had raked the side.

"Wonder why they did it," Thad said.

"I'll bet it was whoever he shot at last night. They probably came for some payback," I said.

Thad nodded. "Could be." Then he reached in for the bucket sitting in the bottom of the boat. "No sense in wasting these."

"You're right. I've some in my boat too. I'll get them," I said.

I dumped my frogs into the other bucket and Thad carried them up to the fire. Mel and the girls were gone. I told the guys I'd take over on the watch. I needed some time to think.

The fire was burning low, so I added a couple of pieces to it. While I was up, I made my way over to the bags of Danny's hotel loot. I rifled through one and picked out a bag of Earl Grey, deciding to make myself a cup.

It was cool and quiet. The cloudless sky above was full of brilliant stars, too many to count. Looking through the NVGs, even more appeared. I continued staring at them when something caught my eye. A small light traced a line across the sky. I'd seen this very thing countless times in the Before, now I was struck by it. A small satellite drifting across the sky above me. I wondered what kind it was, whether it worked or if it was just slowly making its way back down to earth.

Turning off the NVGs, I thought about the satellite for a minute. The fact that it was still up there was very reassuring. Maybe things weren't as bad as we thought. Maybe there were more working systems out there. Or, worse, maybe this whole situation was an illusion. That was a horrible thought—to think that someone would let people suffer when something could be done about it. But right now, right here, I guessed it didn't really matter.

Sometime just before dawn Jeff wandered up. I smiled. "You my relief?"

He yawned as he sat down, leaning his AK on one of the other chairs. "Yep. When you going to call Doc?"

"Right now," I said, getting up. "Be right back." I went to where the radio was stored. After checking our codebook, I set the frequency and made the call.

"Stump Knocker, Walker." I repeated the call and waited.

After a moment there was a reply. *"Go for Stump Knocker."* But it wasn't Sarge's voice.

"Is the old man around?" I asked.

"Hold," came the terse reply.

I waited for what seemed like an eternity. Finally Sarge's gravelly voice came over the radio.

"Go for Stump Knocker."

"Can you get that witch doctor down here this morning?"

After a brief pause he replied, *"Roger that, what's the SITREP?"*

I thought about how to reply. "Brief contact last night, one GSW."

"How serious?"

"Serious enough that I'm calling you."

"Roger that, we're on our way. Stump Knocker out."

I laid the handset down and crept out of the cabin back to the fire. Jeff looked at me expectantly. "They coming down here?"

"Mmhmm. Sarge said they were on their way, so I imagine they'll be here soon."

"Hey," Jeff said as he jumped up, "let's surprise the old man with a cup of coffee." He pulled out a couple of coffee packets, then filled the pot and set it on the fire.

We sat around the fire shooting the shit until we heard the sound of the outboard downriver. Jeff grabbed a cup and filled it with the steaming brew and we walked down to the river.

As the bow ground into the mud, Doc cut the engine. Sarge hopped out, followed by two others I didn't know. Doc hopped out last, shouldering his bag.

"Who's been shot, Morgan?" Sarge asked as he stuck his hand out.

I grabbed it and we shook. "Danny. Someone hit him with a scatter gun."

"What kind of shot?" Doc asked.

"It was small, like number four or something. Not buck, thank God," I said.

Doc started up the bank. "He in his cabin?" I nodded and he and one of the other guys trotted off.

"Morgan, Jeff, this is Martin," Sarge said.

We shook hands with him. "Nice to meet you. Thanks for coming up," I said.

"No sweat. That's Jeremy over there with Doc. He's the closest thing we have to a medic," Martin said.

Jeff and I relayed the events of the previous two nights. I told him I thought it could have been someone trying to snatch a hog that came back for a little get-even after Danny shot at them.

"Let's go check on Danny," Sarge said, then looked at the cup in Jeff's hand. Pointing, he asked, "What's in there?"

Jeff smiled broadly as he raised the cup to his lips. "Coffee."

Sarge jerked around to face me. "You got coffee? You holding out on me?"

I smiled "Yeah, we got a pot on the fire. Why, you want some?"

"What do you think, dipshit?" Sarge shouted as he pushed past me and stomped off toward the fire pit.

"Hey, weren't we going to check on Danny?" I called after him.

The old man waved me off. "He's in good hands, there's more important things at the moment."

Jeff was cracking up. "Man, look at him go."

"Yeah, you'd think we told him we had a pot of gold or something," I said, shaking my head.

"At the moment, it is, a pot of black gold," Jeff said with a grin, slapping me on the shoulder as he started toward the fire pit.

I shook my head and followed him. Sarge was holding the pot in one hand and drinking coffee with the other. As we walked up, he said, "This is some crap coffee." Then a broad smile spread across his face. "But it's wonderful."

"We thought you'd like it," I said.

As he poured another cup he said, "I do. All right, now let's go check on Danny."

Danny was sitting up, leaning forward. Doc was checking his breathing, having him take deep breaths. Satisfied Danny's lungs were all right, Doc had him lie down so he could start examining the wounds where it looked like actual penetration could have occurred. Doc held a gloved finger against one of them, rolling it around.

"That hurt?"

"Hell yes. Feels like you're sticking a poker in my side."

"Yeah, I think there's a piece of shot in there. Jeremy, get that instrument kit out for me."

Jeremy dug into the pack and produced a small OD kit. He

took a bottle of alcohol out and cleaned a pair of large tweezers before handing them to Doc.

"All right, Danny, this is going to hurt. I'm about to stick a poker in your side now for real."

Bobbie grabbed Danny's hand as Doc gently probed the wound. "There it is," he whispered. Danny grimaced, and from the look on Bobbie's face, he must've clamped down on her hand something good. "Got it!" Doc exclaimed as he held up a small piece of shot.

Danny exhaled loudly and looked over. "It sure felt bigger than that."

"Let's see how many more there are," Doc said.

He pulled three more pieces out before starting to clean all the wounds.

"Hell, Danny, next time, duck," Sarge said.

"Yeah, you should've heard him squeal when he was hit," Jeff said, trying to get a laugh.

Danny raised his head. "Let me shoot your ass once," he said with a chuckle.

"I think you'll be all right. Just keep the wounds clean. I'm not going to give you any antibiotics, just keep them clean and dry and you should be all right," Doc said as he put away his stuff.

"You sure he doesn't need any antibiotics?" Bobbie asked.

"Nope. Too often when people went to their doctors for any number of things they'd get an antibiotic as a precaution. It was one of the worst practices conducted in the medical field. Sure, for some things you need them, but the 'just in case' excuse shouldn't be used. Just keep an eye on them, and if they start to look inflamed, red, swollen, and painful, let me know and I'll give him something. You guys are pretty healthy, though, so his immune system should handle it fine. Just take it easy for a few days, Danny. No strenuous activities. Try not to get all sweaty—keep it clean and dry."

Danny nodded as he pulled his shirt back on. "Thanks for coming out, Doc, I really appreciate it." Doc and Jeremy collected their things and headed out.

I walked with Sarge back to the boat, the dogs running beside us, tongues lolling and tails wagging. Sarge looked at the black dog.

"Get another dog?"

"Yeah, I guess you heard about the guy who grabbed Little Bit."

"Yeah, I heard. You did the right thing." He pointed at Drake. "That one was his?"

"I guess. Can't blame the dog for him being nuts."

Sarge smiled and rubbed Drake's head. "Guess you can't."

At the riverbank, Sarge stuck out his hand. "If you guys need us, give me a call," Sarge said.

"Thanks for coming down, really appreciate it," I said.

"No problem, you guys just try and stay outta trouble."

I stood on the bank and watched as Doc backed the boat out into the current. They all waved and I waved back as he opened the throttle and the boat took off downriver. Thad walked up and handed me a frog leg he'd grilled on the fire.

"Breakfast?"

I took it and smiled. "Thanks." I sucked all the meat off the bones and said, "We need to get more of these. That was too good."

"Got another on the fire for you. Better hurry up before someone else snaps it up," Thad said, waving over his shoulder.

Chapter 13

Sarge leaned back in his chair, his hands behind his head. Livingston and Sheffield were staring at one another.

"Of course, we'll have to see what the guys get out of the recon, but I think it will work."

Sheffield looked baffled. "You really expect to just drive up to the gate and they'll let us in?"

"Sure. If we roll up looking like a government unit and tell them we're there to add to their security, they'll let us in."

"Hm. I like giving them the drawing the guys are working on as 'evidence.' Telling them that we have intel that they're being scouted and we're there to bolster their defenses is very plausible," Livingston said.

"I don't know. It sounds like a hell of a way to get killed, and fast," Sheffield said, shaking his head.

"Look, there is a lot of confusion right now in the camps and the government. These guys aren't going to know what's up. They'll probably make some calls, but we will hopefully be inside the camp by then," Sarge said.

"Hopefully?" Sheffield asked. "Once we're in, then what? Start shooting?"

"No, Sheffield. We'll meet with their CO, tell him we need to have a meeting with his security personnel ASAP. Once we get as many of them rounded up as we can, we'll just politely disarm them. This could be done without firing a shot," Sarge said with a smile.

"I'll meet with their CO?" Sheffield shouted. "Why me? Why don't you do it if you're the one with this scheme?"

Sarge pointed at his collar. "'Cause you're wearing them oak leaves, not me. Don't worry, I'll be there as well. But you need to take the lead if we're going to pull this off."

"You think we should have some men out at the gate on the back side just in case?" Livingston asked.

"I do, plus another squad hidden out front to take down that gate when the time comes."

Sheffield let out a long sigh. "All right, I'm in. If we can do it without having to kill anyone or, more important, getting any of my people killed, I'm all for it."

Sarge smiled. "I knew you would be. Now there's just one more thing we need." Sarge walked over to the radio and picked up the handset.

"Cracker One, Cracker One, Stump Knocker."

After a moment there was a whispered reply: *"Go for Cracker One."*

"Cracker One, I need you to bring me back a body, the walking, talking kind."

There was a long pause. *"Ah, say again, Stump Knocker."*

"Bring back one of them black-clad ninjas, alive."

Ian crawled out of the security position and up to the new hide. They'd moved to get eyes on the rear gate. Ted and Mike were observing the new target. Ian crawled up and grabbed Ted's leg, giving it a shake.

"What's up, you got contact?" Ted asked, looking around.

"No, just got a call from the old man." Ian paused.

"And, what's he want?"

"He wants us to snatch one of these guys and bring him back with us."

Ted was dumbfounded. "He wants what? Has he finally lost his feeble grip on reality?"

"I don't know, he's your daddy."

Mike crawled out of the hide. "What the hell's going on?"

"That crazy ole bastard wants us to snatch one of these guys and bring him back with us," Ted said as he dropped his face into his hands.

"Yeah, so?"

"*So?* How do you think we'll pull that off? They never go anywhere alone! Hell, they never come outside the wire unless they're in a vehicle. How do you think we'll be able to grab one?"

Mike smiled. "Easy, we'll take one of them back there." He jutted his thumb over his shoulder toward the gate they'd been observing.

"There's three men there, Mike," Ted said.

"No, you're looking at it all wrong. There's *only* three of them."

Ted was struck by the comment and thought about it, slowly starting to nod his head. "Yeah, you're right, there's only three of them."

Ian smiled. "And there's three of us."

"Wrong, there's five of us," Ted said with a devilish grin, "and, not for nothing, but one of us has a set of tits. Could be a handy distraction . . ."

Ian started to giggle. "There is no way in hell she'll go for that."

"She doesn't have to sleep with them or anything! Just get them outside their bunker. Then we can take care of them."

Ian nodded. "So long as she gets to hit one of them, she'll probably do it."

"She can beat the shit out of them for all I care. Sarge said alive, not perfectly healthy," Mike said.

"All right, let's break this down and call to tell them we're heading in their direction," Ted said.

"There is no fucking way I'm doing that!" Jamie practically shouted.

Mike held his finger to his lips. "Shhhh, keep it down."

"Just 'cause I'm a woman I have to be the bait? That's bull!"

"You're looking at this all wrong! Yes, you're a woman, and a damn attractive one too." Mike's comment caught Jamie off guard, softening her attitude ever so slightly. He continued, "If you walk out and act like you need help, those goobers will be falling all over themselves to get to you."

"What about my uniform, idiots? They're going to see that."

"I've got a T-shirt under my blouse that I got at a Hooters in Tampa. You can wear that," Ian said.

Jamie rolled her eyes. "Oh, that's just fucking *perfect*."

Mike smiled. "Actually it is! Wear that, and act like you're cold."

Jamie pursed her lips together as she thought it over. "Ugh, *fine*. What happens next?"

"This is the important part. When all three of them approach, jump the one closest to you, and take him to the ground. We'll come out and take the rest of them down," Ted said.

She looked skeptical. "All right, whatever, I'll do it. As long as I can kick somebody's ass."

Perez nodded. "Let's get this show on the road."

They used the buggy to get as close to the gate as possible. It was still going to be a bit of a walk to get there.

"It's going to be a long walk dragging one of these guys back with us," Ian said.

Ted laughed. "One? Hell, if this works, we're taking all three. We can't have the other two going back and blabbing about the plan, now, can we?"

Mike started to laugh. "The old guy's gonna shit."

"We need someone to stay here and bring the buggy up so we can load up and haul ass as soon as this is over. I, for one, want to be long gone before they realize their boys are missing," Perez said.

"Good idea. You wanna hang back?" Ted asked.

Perez shrugged. "Guess so."

"All right, Perez stays here, we go in. Soon as we get them trussed up, we'll call him on the radio. He rolls up, and we load up, and get out of Dodge quickly," Ted said. "Sound good?"

They all nodded. Ian then took off his BDU top and stripped off his T-shirt. "Here, Jamie, put this on," he said as he tossed it to her.

She caught the shirt right before it hit her in the face, immediately turning her head. "Jesus, Ian, take a freaking bath!"

Ian laughed as he put his top back on. Jamie took off her body armor. She was holding the shirt and looking at everyone with raised eyebrows. The guys were oblivious, just looking back at her. When she started to strip off her shirt in front of them, all four men were embarrassed and quickly turned away.

"What's the matter, boys, never seen a woman's body before?" Now that they were uncomfortable, she was loving it. Jamie couldn't help but grin from ear to ear.

Everyone carried the most basic of gear, leaving all the packs and SAWs with Perez. The four began their stalk, moving quietly and slowly. It took several hours in dark to get within thirty meters of the bunker. A light tower sat behind it, which demanded even more caution.

Once they were within ten yards, Ted nodded to Jamie. She got up from the palmetto scrub and whispered, "You better be there."

"We will, don't worry," he whispered back.

Jamie took a deep breath. Mike grabbed her leg and motioned for her to wait. He pulled her pants out of her boots. Bloused boots were a dead giveaway. Once he finished, he slapped her thigh and winked at her. She stuck her tongue out at him and quickly stepped onto the trail.

Jamie stood in the trail, shielding her eyes from the lights. She expected someone to come running out, yelling and shouting, but to her surprise nothing happened. She took a couple of steps, then called out, "Hello!" After a moment a face appeared in the bunker opening—and a very surprised face at that. Then three figures came running out from behind it.

Jamie was standing with her arms wrapped around herself, like she was cold.

"Show me your hands!" a man's voice shouted.

Jamie held her hands up. "Please don't shoot! Can you help me? I'm lost!"

The three figures discussed the situation for a moment, then started to move toward her.

"Keep your hands up!"

As the figures got closer they blocked some of the light. It was then Jamie realized one of them was a woman. *Well, shit*, she thought.

"What are you doing here?" the woman asked.

"I was hoping you could help me. I'm cold and hungry."

The woman stepped forward. "Where'd you come from?"

"I've been wandering around the woods for days. I'm lost."

The woman looked her up and down. "I think you're full of shit." She pulled a set of cuffs from her belt and stepped toward Jamie. "Turn around and put your hands behind your back."

As she moved to cuff her, Jamie jumped on the woman, knocking her to the ground. The woman recovered rather quickly and punched Jamie in the jaw, but it was a glancing blow. Jamie grabbed her by the collar and jerked her head off the ground, at the same time she tucked her chin and brought the top of her forehead down onto the woman's nose. There was a satisfying crunching sound and the woman under her went limp.

She looked up to see the other two men rushing toward her. *Oh shit,* she thought as they closed in. Suddenly there were two small pops. Both men went rigid and fell face-first into the sand, twitching as the Tasers pumped voltage into them. Ian moved in and quickly cuffed one of the men, stripping his weapons and tossing them aside. Ted held the Taser on the second one while Mike restrained him.

Once both were secured, the guys quickly began getting them ready to move.

"Do you know who you're messing with?" one of the men snarled.

"Shut up," Ted said, kicking his boots.

"Damn, Jamie," Ian crowed.

Jamie stood up, blowing her hair out of her face. "You got a little something right there," Ted said, touching his forehead.

Jamie wiped at it and realized it was blood. "Bitch is a bleeder," she said, then spit at her.

The other two men were face down on the ground, Taser wires trailing from their bodies. Ian leaned down and put duct tape over their mouths. The one who'd spoken jerked his head, trying to prevent being gagged. Ted hit the trigger on the Taser and the man went rigid, allowing Ian to easily slap the tape over his mouth. Looking up at Ted, Ian smirked. "Thanks."

Ted smiled. "What are friends for?"

Jamie looked at Mike. "Cuffs," she said, holding her hand out.

Mike pulled a flex cuff from his cargo pocket and tossed it to her. Jamie rolled the woman over, securing her hands. She rolled her back over and sat on her chest. "Tape."

Ian looked at Mike, laughing quietly. Mike gestured with his chin in a "you better hurry the fuck up" manner. Ian tore off a piece of tape and laid it in her palm. With the tape in one hand Jamie slapped the woman's face on both sides. When her eyes began to open, Jamie smiled and slapped the tape over her mouth.

Jamie leaned down close to her. "Take that, *bitch*!"

Mike laughed and parroted her comment. "Take that, bitch!" Jamie looked up at him. "That's hawt," Mike said.

"You want some?" Jamie asked with a sneer.

"The tape, or you sitting on my chest?"

Jamie stood up and stepped toward him. In a seductive voice she said, "I'll sit on your chest"—her voice quickly changed—"right after I break your fucking nose." She finished her statement with a coy smile.

"You're a rough girl," Mike said and smiled. "I like it."

Jamie gave him a dismissive wave and turned her attention back to the woman on the ground.

"On your feet."

Seconds later, Perez arrived. The three prisoners were

rapidly loaded up and soon they were off and racing down the trails. With the three prisoners there wasn't room inside for everyone, so Ian was standing on the rear platform, manning the top-mounted SAW. Ted and Mike were sitting in the back with the prisoners piled between them.

Mike looked over at Ted, grinning. "I can't believe that worked!"

Ted was smiling from ear to ear, "Me neither. The old man's gonna piss himself!" They both started laughing.

"You boys are welcome," Jamie said.

The guys all looked at her, and she briefly made eye contact with each of them. "Now that we've established that I can take care of myself, there'll be no more guarding the camp. Agreed?"

"All right, all right, I think you've proved yourself," Ted said.

"That's what I thought," she said with a smirk.

Aric's friendship with Kay had blossomed. He looked at her as a motherly figure, and she enjoyed talking to him because he wasn't like the other officers in the camp. So many others had let their positions become their identity, and consume their lives. Kay was grateful that Aric provided her with some company, as he was this afternoon.

"Doesn't seem like much food, Kay. You skimping out?" Aric asked, pointing to the trays.

Kay looked over her shoulder. "These are for the people in detainment."

"Really? Jeez, there's so little food."

"I'm just doing what they tell me."

"Just doesn't seem like enough food. The girls are over

there. How are they supposed to hang on with no more food than this?" Aric asked.

"The food is the least of the problems." Kay picked up a sixteen-ounce bottle of water. "We only send one of these a day over there. I don't know if they get any more."

"Bunch of bastards," Aric said, shaking his head. "Is someone coming to get these?" he asked, gesturing toward the trays.

"Mmhmm. They should be here soon."

Aric nodded and plucked a French fry from one of the serving trays. It wasn't long before two men came into the kitchen.

"Hey, Kay, these for us?" one of them asked.

"Yep, they're all yours."

"Hey, Cortez, what's up?" Aric asked.

"Hey, Vonasek, SOS, how 'bout you?"

"You called it, just waiting for the next mission outside the wire."

"Dude, you're so lucky, getting to leave here," the other man said.

"It ain't all that much fun, Hamner," Aric said.

"Yeah, well, it's better than dealing with that shit over there."

Aric saw his chance to ask some questions and pounced on it. "How many you got locked up over there?" he asked casually.

"There's five in there right now, those murdering bitches and a couple of guys they caught with weapons outside."

"Oh yeah, those girls who killed what's-his-name?"

"Yep, that's them."

He was afraid to ask the next question, but knew he had to. "What are they going to do to them?"

"I don't know, they haven't said yet, said there's some *mitigating circumstances.* Might just leave them in there to rot for all I know."

Aric felt his pulse rising, but he knew he had to play it cool.

"Hey, man, can I go with you and check out the place?" Aric asked.

"Sure, we could use the help," Cortez said, shoving a couple of trays into Aric's hands and picking up the others. "Follow me."

Jess was sitting with her back against the wall. She'd been dreading the moment when Shane woke up, but it was a moot point—it was so dark he couldn't see her anyway. When he started to come around, she slipped out from under the blankets and put her jumpsuit back on. He reached out to her.

"Hello?"

"Hey, I'm Jess. They put me in here to warm you up. You were pretty close to being hypothermic."

"Oh. Um, hi. Thanks. Where are my clothes?" he replied.

"I don't know, they brought you in here without them," she said.

Shane was embarrassed at the thought of being naked with her. "Oh, sorry about that."

"No problem. Wasn't your fault. So . . . why are you and your dad in here, anyway?"

"The DHS jumped us out on the road, shot up our truck. Pretty sure they killed some of my friends and then brought us here."

"What'd you do wrong? I mean, why'd they start shooting?" Jess asked into the dark.

"Wrong? You don't have to do anything wrong these days, all you have to do is be seen by DHS. That's all we're guilty of."

"Where did they take you the other day?"

"I got . . . interrogated," Shane said. He shivered at the thought of what was awaiting him the next time.

"Oh wow, I'm sorry. We haven't experienced anything like that yet."

"Pray you don't. I have a feeling things are going to get worse the next time I see him." Shane pulled the blankets tighter around himself.

Hearing voices outside, Jess said, "Shhhh." Shane closed his eyes. Fear swelled in his throat. The door opened and the voices got louder and closer to them. Jess's stomach dropped as the key slid into their cell door. Jess quickly lowered her eyes to avoid the light that was surely coming. Shane pulled the blankets up over his head.

The door opened and the light poured in. "How're our lovebirds today?" Cortez asked.

"Is he still alive?" Hamner asked.

Jess kept her head down, but nodded to the affirmative.

"Why are they in here together?" Aric asked.

Cortez pointed to the lump under the blankets. "He had hypothermia, 'bout froze to death. The nurse put her in here to keep him warm, said body heat was the best thing."

"Yeah, I see she's got her clothes back on now. Too bad," Hamner said.

Aric looked at him. "You made her take her clothes off?"

"Yeah, nurse said it was the best way." He looked in at Jess and grinned, the light illuminating his face like a jack-o-lantern. "*Skin-to-skin contact* is how she put it." He laughed, then looked back at Jess. "You get yourself some skin, darlin'?"

Aric set two trays down in the cell, resisting his urge to snap the guy's neck. Cortez threw two water bottles in and quickly turned off the light. "Have fun finding those," he said as he slammed the door.

Fred listened to the exchange and knew there was someone else with them today. Hearing the key slide into her door, she hid her face in her knees. The cell was soon flooded with light.

"This one here is a little firecracker," Cortez said.

Aric's heart stopped when he saw Fred. *She at least looks okay*, he thought. As Cortez and Hamner were talking about getting the nurse back in for Shane, Aric knelt down and slid a tray toward her.

"Hang on, Fred," he said, barely a whisper.

Fred thought it sounded like Aric, but she wasn't sure, and she couldn't risk looking into the light. Trusting it was someone friendly, she gave a quick thumbs-up with her left hand. Aric saw it and smiled to himself. Cortez threw a bottle of water in, bouncing it off Fred's head.

"There's some water, sweetheart," he said with a laugh.

Aric sucked in his breath. They moved on to Mary's cell. Opening the door they found her lying on the floor in a fetal position.

"This one is a fucking *wreck*," Cortez said.

Aric slid a tray in. Mary made no movements. There was no indication that she was even alive.

"Is she dead?" Aric asked when he stood up.

Cortez snorted. "Not yet."

Calvin didn't bother to cover his face when they shone the light into his cell.

"How're them ribs today, Grandpa?" Cortez asked.

Hamner looked at Aric. "Yeah, he wanted to play tough guy. Had to take a beatin'."

Aric slid a tray toward him. Cortez stepped into the doorway and tossed the water bottle into the far corner of the cell, then slammed the door shut.

"What's he in here for?" Aric asked as they moved down the hallway.

"I don't know. He was caught outside the wire somewhere," Cortez said.

Aric nodded, and they headed for the door. "Well, thanks for the tour. I'll see you guys later—"

He was cut off by the camp siren going off.

All three men took off running toward their respective assigned posts. Aric ran toward the motor pool where all the vehicles were kept. A Hummer pulled through the gate as he was going through it.

"Vonasek! Get in!" his supervisor shouted, jutting a thumb over his shoulder.

Aric climbed into the still-moving vehicle. "What's going on?"

"Get up in the turret! Someone's hit the rear gate!"

Aric got up into the web straps for the turret gunner and checked the weapon. *I didn't hear any shots*, he thought to himself as the truck bounced across the camp. It took several minutes for them to get to the gate. Several others were already there when they arrived. It was obvious there wasn't any kind of a fight, as people were just milling about. Pulling to a stop, they jumped out.

"What the hell happened?" his supervisor asked.

"They're gone. All the guards on duty. They've disappeared," one of them answered.

"How many were on duty?" another asked.

An agent came up to Aric as he walked around, checking the trail by the gate. "All three of them are just . . . gone."

"A vehicle must've come in here and loaded them up. See all these tracks?" Aric said, pointing at the ground.

Soon there were a number of people in the trail, walking over the only evidence they had of what happened. Aric shook his head and walked back toward his truck. It seemed impossible: someone was able to come in and snatch three of their people and get away, without a shot being fired. *How in the hell did they do that?*

Chapter 14

Thad, Jeff, and I worked together to get the plastic on for the roof. We'd made two ladders out of cane that may have looked like crap but actually worked very well. After getting the second layer of plastic on, we took a break from the action. The past few days had been filled with projects for making this camp more like home, and man, was it hard work.

"Daddy, can we check the squirrel traps?!" Little Bit shouted as she jumped out of her chair. I sighed, having just sat down after being on my feet all afternoon.

"They were empty yesterday," I said.

"Maybe we'll get lucky today," Danny said. I shot him a look.

"How're the spots, man?"

He ran a hand over his side. "Not as bad as you'd think. There's only a couple that actually bother me."

I looked over and grinned. "The ones Doc picked at?"

He laughed. "Yeah, the ones he made *better.*"

"You got polka dots!" Little Bit said, giggling.

I rubbed her head. "Maybe we should start calling him Spot, what do you think?"

"Yeah!" she shouted and pointed at Danny. "Your new name is Spot!"

He grabbed her up real quick, swinging her up onto his shoulders. "I got your spots, you little booger!" She squealed with delight as she feigned fighting him off. Seeing her smile melted my heart, especially considering what she had been through the past few days.

"All right, Ashley, we can check the traps."

"Yay!" she shouted.

The first trap we came to had a squirrel hanging from one of the snares. It was still alive and was doing its best to get free.

"We got one!" Little Bit shouted. She looked at the rodent for a second then asked with wide eyes, "Are you going to shoot it?"

"Naw, shooting it would be a waste," I said as I looked around for a stick.

Walking over to the set, I grabbed the squirrel quickly by the tail and pulled it tight against the wire, then delivered a swift hard blow to its head.

"Eeww! Poor little squirrel," Little Bit said, a frown creasing her face.

"It's the fastest way, dear," Danny said as he removed it from the snare.

We checked the rest of the snares, finding five more.

"It's weird, nothing yesterday and six today," I said.

Danny nodded. "Yeah, kinda strange. Maybe they needed a day to get used to it."

"Good as any reason. I'll go with it," I said with a smile.

Little Bit was skipping along in front of us, holding a squirrel by the tail in each hand. I was shaking my head and smiling at the scene before me. An eight-year-old girl a hundred and fifty years ago would do this. An eight-year-old girl of this generation would run away screaming. Hell, most boys would too. For some reason society has been bent on destroying the idea of anything masculine or self-reliant. The effects were really starting to show before things changed like they did.

I wondered for a moment how the urbanites fared, the ones that never left the city. I mean, during normal times, everything you need is nearby: grocery stores, transportation, all that. But when the world changed, what did they do now? Did they possess the skills to provide for themselves? As hard as this all was on me, I can only imagine what it was like for them.

Back at the camp we cleaned the rats. It was a simple process, but some of us had never done it before, so I took the position as teacher again.

"All right, first you pinch the skin on the back and make a cut across it. Stick a finger in either side and pull. The skin comes off easily. Then it's like taking off his furry little pants and shirt. Pull the skin down to the feet and cut them off. Then push the skin down the tail and cut it off. See! Now his pants are gone. Push the skin up toward the head and cut the head off behind it, his furry shirt is gone."

There was very little blood during this. Once they were skinned, we gutted them by making small slits in their bellies and scooping their innards out. We took out the meat and saved the entrails for the dogs, who were happy to get them.

"I'll cook these in some water. Maybe we can mix 'em with some rice later," Thad said as he picked up the cleaned carcasses.

Jeff and I spent the rest of the afternoon cutting wood. It was a never-ending process that was now requiring us to venture farther and farther into the woods. Keeping a fire burning all the time was nice and convenient, but it was starting to become a chore to make it happen. Taylor, Mel, and Bobbie all helped with the wood. While we needed nice pieces of split wood, we needed smaller stuff as well. This was where

Little Bit really helped. She was a pro at finding kindling-sized pieces.

Danny spent his time by the fire—doctor's orders, of course. I was splitting wood when I noticed Lee Ann had joined us. She had her feet up in the chair and her head resting on her knees. I was getting worried. She wasn't interacting with any of us. Laying down the maul I was splitting with, I went over to her and knelt down. I put a hand on her head and ran my fingers through her hair.

"Hey, kiddo, are you all right?"

She wouldn't lift her head. All I got in return was a nod. I tried to raise her head. "Hey, look at me."

She resisted at first then finally looked up. What I saw scared me more than I could have imagined. Her face was blank, completely devoid of any expression. It was hard to witness. The face I was looking at was not the same beautiful girl I loved. It was truly disturbing.

It was obvious I was surprised, so I tried to play it off. "Hey, what's the matter? You've been acting funny the last few days."

With that same expressionless face she replied, "Nothing, I'm fine."

I looked straight into her eyes. "Bullshit," I said. I knew it would shock her and let her know I was being serious.

She suddenly dissolved into tears. She was trying to say something but I couldn't make it out. She was completely unintelligible. I wrapped my arms around her and whispered in her ear, "It's okay, whatever's wrong, it's going to be okay." I leaned back and wiped her face. "Hey, calm down, just try and calm down."

Finally, through her sobs, she said, "It's not okay. It'll never be okay."

I stood up. "Come on, let's go to the cabin." I grabbed her hand and led her back to the cabin and to her bed. She lay down and I lay beside her, rubbing her hair.

"Look, I know you think it's the end of the world, but it's not. It's really not." She didn't respond, and she was lying facing away from me so I couldn't see her expression.

"It'll all come back someday. It may take a long time, but it will come back."

"No, it won't. It's all gone, and it'll never be back," she said in a soft voice.

This is what I was afraid of: she thought the life she knew was gone forever. It was gone for now, but to dwell on that fact could eat you alive. I hoped someday everything would come back, and, of course, I didn't know whether it would. But I wanted to express a hopeful opinion. Being stuck in a mind-set like Lee Ann's would only bring more trouble.

"Hey, I haven't told anyone yet, but I saw a satellite the other night when I was out sitting by the fire." I paused. "You know, if there's still satellites, then everything isn't gone. Maybe it's just around here that people are experiencing this. Maybe there are places where things are normal."

She shrugged her shoulders. "Doesn't matter, we couldn't get there anyway."

I rubbed her head again. "I know it sucks and I know you think life is over, but it isn't, I promise you that."

In a robotic voice, she replied, "I want to go to sleep."

I lay there looking at the back of her head, then leaned over and kissed her. "Okay, I love you, know that. And it will be all right."

I got up and walked toward the door. We'd taken to keeping all the guns by the door, because it was easier to pick them up as you left. I paused by Lee Ann's H&K and picked it up. As I came back to the fire, Mel was sitting in a chair.

"What's going on?" she asked as I laid the H&K on the table.

Sitting down I told her, "She's depressed. I'm worried about her."

She pointed at the weapon. "Why'd you bring that out?"

"I don't want her to be left alone with a gun."

Danny looked up from the fire. "Whoa. It's that bad, you think?"

Mel looked at him, then back to me. "What? She's not going to do anything like that." It sounded like she was trying to convince herself more than anything else.

"Well, I don't want to give her an opportunity," I said as I kicked at a log.

"If you're that worried, you better keep an eye on her, Morg," Thad said.

"I think so too. She has been acting a little weird, withdrawn," Bobbie said.

"What's the matter with Lee Ann?" Little Bit asked.

I looked at her and smiled. "She's just sad."

"Is she going to be okay?"

"Yeah, she'll be fine."

"She isn't talking to me either," Taylor said.

"I think everyone just needs to help keep an eye on her," Danny said.

At dinner, Lee Ann didn't come out, despite Mel and me both trying to get her out of bed. It reinforced our fears. The rest of us sat around the tables in the light of a lamp and had our dinner, but conversation was slow and Mel and I were both clearly distracted.

After dinner, we cleaned up and sat around the fire a bit longer. Danny was antsy after sitting around so much and offered to take the first watch. I lay down but had trouble falling asleep, my mind busy thinking about how to deal with Lee Ann.

Danny woke me up around midnight and I went out to the fire as usual. I'd been out there for a couple of hours when a sound caught my ears. After so much time without man-made noises, I was acutely aware when they were present. This one was certainly an engine. I listened to it for a while until I was able to determine that it was getting closer. In fact, it sounded as if it was heading straight for our little camp. I jumped up and ran over to Thad and Jeff's cabin, knocking on the side.

"Hey, get up! Someone's heading this way."

I heard them both scuffing around, and Jeff yelled out, "We're coming!"

I ran over to Danny's cabin and did the same thing, then headed back to my cabin.

I opened the door and stuck my head in. "Mel, wake up."

"What is it?" she asked as she sat up.

"There's a vehicle headed this way. Get your weapons and be ready just in case. Stay here unless you hear me call for you."

"All right," she said as everyone, Lee Ann included, woke up.

As I ran up to the guys I asked, "Do you guys hear it?"

"Yeah, we hear it," Jeff said.

"Sounds like it's going to come right down the road there," Danny said.

"Let's take up some positions where we can see them if they come in here," Thad said.

"Good idea. Let's break up in pairs," I said.

"Me and Jeff will go out by where the driveway cuts off the road," Thad said.

"All right, Danny, let's go behind the chicken coop."

As we split up the dogs started barking, announcing that whatever it was was a lot closer now. They ran toward the road, tails up.

"What do you think it is?" I asked Danny as I looked for lights.

"Sounds like a four-wheeler or something."

"That's what I thought. And whoever it is, is riding blacked out. There's no lights."

"Yeah, I'm trying to get my eyes," Danny said as his head bobbed and weaved, looking through the brush and trees.

As the sound grew closer, I tensed up, my carbine at low ready. I had my thumb on the safety, ready to flip it off and start shooting. We both had lights mounted to our rifles. They used the CR123 batteries, so we seldom used them, as there were no replacements.

"It just turned off the road," Danny said as he gripped his rifle a little tighter.

I looked through the NVGs and could see a large UTV pulling in.

As it pulled in past my cabin, I nudged Danny and we both stepped out, turning on the lights and illuminating the buggy. At the same moment, Thad and Jeff jumped out.

"Stop right there!" Danny shouted.

I followed. "Show me your hands! Hands up, all of you!"

A light way brighter than the ones on our rifles lit up on the buggy. "Morgan, it's us," a voice called out.

I shielded my eyes and could see Ted standing up in the rear of the buggy. "Holy shit, man! You guys scared the shit out of us."

The buggy shut down and they started getting out as we gathered around it.

"Yeah, looks like you guys were ready," Mike said.

"Almost, I didn't see Ted up there! He would've cut us in half," I said.

"No, he wouldn't have. Ole Thad was about to blast him with that scatter gun of his," Jeff said.

Ted turned to look at Thad. "I'm hurt."

Thad smiled. "Not as bad as you woulda been."

Ted and Mike both laughed. Danny peered into the back of the buggy. "What's with them? Are they DHS?" he asked, pointing, shock apparent on his face.

"Oh, they're a surprise for the old man," Ted said.

"Let's get 'em out," Mike said to Jamie and Perez.

They pulled three people out. I was surprised to see one of them was a woman. She was trying to mumble through the tape over her mouth. The two men stood there looking around, then looked at each other with a quick glance. Suddenly they bolted for the trees. With their hands cuffed behind their backs they weren't exactly making a graceful escape.

The one in the lead almost made it to the tree line. Jeff was closest to them and he swung his AK like a bat, clipping the guy in the back of the head. It was a perfect hit, knocking the guy unconscious. He fell like a sack of bricks. The second one was caught by Mike, who grabbed the guy's cuffed hands from behind. His feet went out from under him and he crashed to the ground as well.

"Nice try, boys, nice try," Mike said as he rolled the one he had ahold of onto his stomach. Ted had forced the woman to the ground too, in case she tried to make a run for it. She was still running her mouth through the tape.

Ted leaned down and pulled the tape back. "What the hell do you want?"

"You dumbasses have no idea the trouble you're—" She was cut off when Ted slapped the tape back onto her mouth. He was laughing and said, "No, you have no idea who *you're* messing with and what sort of trouble *you're* in! I suggest you shut up."

I pointed at the woman. "What happened to her?"

Ian grinned and pointed at Jamie. "*That* happened to her."

"Yeah, she took a swing at Jamie, so Jamie delivered a beautiful head butt back to her," Mike added.

Jamie looked down at the woman as she glared up at her. "Bitch hit me. Bit off more than you could chew, didn't ya?"

This started another muffled tirade through the tape.

Another motorized sound drifted up through the night. Mike smiled. "Looks like the party is about to start."

"Is that Sarge?" Danny asked.

"Yeah, he's on the way in."

Mel and the girls came out, standing by the door of the cabin with Bobbie. Mel called me over.

"What's going on?"

"They're done with their little sneak and peek, and picked up some prisoners."

She looked at them, eyebrows raised. "A woman?"

"Yeah, she's got a lot to say too."

"What are they going to do with them?" Taylor asked.

"Sarge is on his way to get them."

Moments later, the boat came around the bend in the river and glided up to the bank. Sarge hopped off before it even stopped and came stomping up the hill. Mike and Ted were standing there smiling like the cats that ate the canary.

Sarge stopped in front of the three prisoners, his hands on his hips.

"I said bring me *one*," he barked, shaking his head.

"Ah hell, we figured three would give you three times as much fun," Ted said.

Sarge shook his head. "Fuckin' overachievers."

Mike was leaning against the buggy. "You ungrateful ole prick!" he said with a smile.

Sarge smiled. "Let's get 'em loaded up. One of you will come back with me, then we'll send the boat back for the rest of you."

They led their captives down to the boat, the woman still being difficult. As Sarge was getting her into the boat he looked at her. "Don't worry, missy, you'll have plenty of time to talk." She stopped her mumbling for a moment, then, with her brows furrowed, she started with renewed vigor. Sarge laughed and pushed her into the boat. The other two were loaded up and Mike jumped in with them.

Mike waved at Ted with a big grin. "See you guys later."

As the boat pulled away, we drifted back to the fire pit. Danny tossed a couple more logs on the fire. Thad brought out the pot with our dinner leftovers and set it on the fire. Mel and the girls came out and sat by the fire too. All the activity ensured no one was going to sleep anytime soon.

"Y'all hungry? We got a little left here," Thad said.

"Hell yeah. Anything is better than those MREs," Perez said.

"How was the camping trip?" Jeff asked.

"It was an interesting time," Ian said.

"So how'd you guys end up with them?" I asked.

Ted pointed at Jamie. "She did it, did a damn fine job too."

"I don't know about all that," Jamie said, waving her hand dismissively.

Ian cackled. "You should have seen her tackle that broad."

"Ooh, catfight!" Jeff said. Jamie shot him a look.

There wasn't much of the rice and squirrel left, but each of them managed to scrape together a bowl. Perez was munching away when he asked, "What kind of meat is this?"

"It's squirrel!" Little Bit shouted.

Jamie looked at her bowl, picking at the meat. "Really? I'd have never guessed."

"Thad is a magician with meat in all forms," Danny said.

"Apparently so! It's really good," Jamie said as she scraped the last few grains of rice from her bowl. After she was done, Jamie stood up from the table. "I don't know about you guys, but I'm beat. I'm going to sack out until they come for us."

"Go to our cabin, you can use it," Jeff said as he stood up.

Jamie eyed him with suspicion. Jeff held up his hands. "I won't be in there, I'll be out here. Promise."

Jamie looked around at everyone. "Well, all right, thanks." She went to the buggy and dragged her pack out, taking it to the cabin with her.

"Any of you guys want to get some sleep?" I asked.

They all shook their heads. "Nah, I want to sit by the fire and warm up," Ian said. The rest of the guys nodded their heads in agreement, so we spent the rest of the night sitting out by the fire. There wasn't much talk. We just sat watching the flames dance.

Mel woke me up just before dawn. I'd fallen asleep in my chair. I looked around. Thad was still there tending the fire. I was wet from the dew and felt cruddy.

"Why don't you go in and get some sleep?" Mel asked.

"Nah, I'll wait. How many eggs do we have?"

"A bunch. They are really starting to lay now. Why? You want to make breakfast?"

"Yeah, I'm going to make some tortillas and scramble up some eggs. Maybe throw in a little pork."

"I'll make the eggs if you want to do the tortillas," Thad offered.

"Deal," I said.

Thad whipped up the eggs using some of the rendered fat and diced pork. I mixed up the tortilla batter and rolled it into balls, then pressed them out. Using a hot skillet with just a little oil in it I quickly cooked them, turning out about two dozen. Thad had used the big Dutch oven and it was about half-full of fluffy eggs. My mouth watered at the thought of the breakfast burritos. When we set them out, everyone jumped up to make theirs. Even Lee Ann was eager to have some.

"This is *so* good," Jamie said. "Thanks, guys."

"Yeah, Dad, thanks," said Taylor.

Everyone else nodded appreciatively, expressing thanks between bites.

At about eight, we heard the boat coming up the river. Thad looked into the pot—there was just enough for one more burrito. He rolled up the last of the eggs and set it back in the oven to keep warm. We all sat facing the river and watched as the boat glided to a stop at the river's edge. Mike hopped out and came up to the group.

He stood there with his hands on his hips, looking at everyone. "Look at this bunch of frickin' nuts."

"Well, good morning to you too, Sunshine," Ted said as he stuffed the last bite of burrito in his mouth."

"Oh, that's nice, rub it in, dickhead," Mike said, then looked over and saw the girls. Looking at Mel, he mouthed a silent *sorry.*

"What, you hungry? Don't they make breakfast over there?" Thad asked.

"Not like this!" Perez barked.

"No, I didn't eat that sh—stuff this morning," Mike replied, looking at Mel. She couldn't help but smile at him.

Thad lifted the lid from the Dutch oven and handed Mike the burrito. Mike flashed a huge smile. Taking a bite he held it up. "Thanks, man. I miss the food here."

"Miss the food here?" I asked. "We don't have too much to brag about."

"I know, but you still manage to make something that tastes good with what you don't have. Believe me, you don't want to eat the stuff they serve down the river." He shoved the rest in his mouth.

Ted stood up. "Well, as great as this was, I think we need to be getting back. Let's get everything loaded up." He looked at Mike. "What's the old man doing with those poor souls?"

Mike grinned. "Oh, he let 'em stew all night. He's going to question them today. Wait till you hear his plan." Mike started to laugh. "You're going to love it."

"Really, do tell," Ted said, crossing his arms over his chest.

Mike wagged a finger at him. "No, no, you'll have to wait. I want him to tell you. It's priceless."

"All right then, let's get our stuff." Ted turned to Thad. "Thanks for breakfast, I appreciate it." Then he looked at Mel. "Thanks, Mel."

Jamie, Perez, and Ian thanked us all as well. They quickly loaded their gear into the boat. Danny, Jeff, Thad, and I went to see them off.

I waved at them. "Come back when you can't stay so long."

Ted gave me the finger, getting a laugh out of everyone.

"Yeah, bring some groceries back when you come," Thad said.

"Sure, we'll swing by Publix," Ian said as the boat began to back away from the bank.

We laughed and waved. But in the back of my head, I wondered if things would always be so happy. Sarge's plan to invade was going to happen soon, and even though I didn't know too many details, the sheer size of the operation told me it was going to be dangerous. We could only hope that they all stayed safe.

Chapter 15

The three prisoners sat on the ground, hands tied behind their backs. Sarge sat on a bucket in front of them, staring at each in turn. The woman's face was covered in blood that ran from her nose down to her shirt. Both of her eyes were now black from the head butt Jamie had delivered. Her hat was gone now and her red hair hung down over her face in strings. She looked, in a word, miserable.

Sarge stared at her, then looked at the tag on her shirt.

"All right, there, Singer, I'm going to remove the tape from your mouth so we can talk," Sarge said as he pulled it off with a satisfying rip.

Once the tape was removed it left a clean rectangle on her face, giving her a comical look. Singer blew some hair out of her face, then looked at Sarge. "Do you know who you're fucking with?"

Sarge looked up at the people gathered behind him. "Do *we* know who *we're* fucking with?"

Mike and Ted laughed, and Ian had a big smile on his face. Sheffield and Livingston both were expressionless. Jamie had a sly grin on her face, remembering the sound Singer's nose made when she crushed it.

Sarge looked back at Singer. "Yeah, I think we do. Do you have any idea who we are?"

Singer glanced around the assembly of people. "A bunch of dead men"—she looked at Jamie—"and one dead bitch."

Jamie's grin grew into a smile and she winked at Singer. Naturally, this sent Singer off on a tirade of cussing. Sarge snapped his fingers in front of her face to get her attention.

"Look, we're here to help with the security of the camp. I just need a little info."

The two men tied beside Singer shared a look, then motioned that they wanted to speak. Sarge pulled the tape from one of them.

"If you guys are here to help with the security of the camp, why are we tied up?"

"We have intelligence that the camp has been infiltrated. We have to be cautious."

"Bullshit!" Singer shouted. "Don't tell these assholes a damn thing!"

Sarge looked over at her. "I'm not talking to you. *You* need to keep quiet."

"We're DHS . . . you, you, you bunch of *idiots* are under our authority right now! You answer to us, we don't answer to you!" Singer screamed, then added, "Now untie me!"

Sarge smiled and got up, going inside the command tent. He returned with a pair of socks. Singer looked at them, then back at him. "Don't even think about it!"

Sarge sat back down on the bucket and smiled. "What? I need to change my socks. You know how your feet get when you've been wearing the same socks for four or five days. My dogs are barkin'."

Sarge looked back at the man he spoke to moments ago while he unlaced his boots. "Like I said, we have to be careful. Now we're going to see if you're one of the ones who snuck in. What's the name of your CO?" Sarge pulled one of his socks off and wiggled his toes. "Ahh, damn, that feels good."

"Don't tell him. He's fishing. They aren't here to help us!" Singer shouted.

Sarge had his foot pulled up, picking at his toes. Sheffield and Livingston both looked on, uncomfortable with where the situation was.

Singer looked at Sarge as he dug between his toes.

"What the hell's wrong with you, you nasty son of a bitch," she asked.

With more speed than anyone thought the old soldier possessed, Sarge reached out, quickly grabbing her bottom jaw and forcing her mouth open. He then forcefully crammed a rolled-up sock into her mouth. Singer gagged and choked as Sarge smiled and ran his finger underneath her nose. Her face turned a bright red, almost purple, veins bulging in her neck.

Almost immediately, Mike shouted, "Holy shit! That's the nastiest thing I've ever seen!" Jamie too was sickened by what she saw. With her hand cupped over her mouth she said, "Oh my God, I think I'm going to be sick." She turned away from the scene and quickly walked toward the brush. Mike started retching too. Ted shook his head. He knew the old man was capable of doing almost anything, but this pushed the limits.

Sheffield grabbed Sarge's arm. "What the hell are you doing?"

"Shutting her up. She isn't hurt, she'll live."

The two men sitting beside Singer were clearly horrified. There was one more sock sitting there and neither of them had any desire in their souls to find out what it tasted like.

"Mitchell, take that out of her mouth," Sheffield said.

Sarge swiveled around. "She ain't hurt," he said, then looked back at Singer, "but she did shut up."

Sarge moved in closer to Singer, who was now a real mess. Drool ran down her chin and with every breath through her broken nose snot flowed back and forth.

"All right, missy, I'm going to take this out now. You say one damn word and it'll be my drawers in your mouth next." Singer looked up and nodded weakly. "And that applies to you too, gentleman."

Sarge pulled the sock out. It was followed by an impressive amount of saliva that rolled onto her shirt. Singer spit repeatedly into the dirt. She hung her head and didn't look up. Sarge looked at the other two men and smiled.

"Gentlemen, I guess it's up to you."

"If you guys are here to help, why'd you do this?" one of the men asked.

Sarge looked at his name tag. "Well, Dunlap, it's like this. We have intelligence that suggests there are elements inside the camp that may be planning to take it over. We don't know why they want to do this or who they are, so we are a little suspicious."

Behind Sarge, Sheffield and Livingston shared a look.

"What? Take it over? Who the hell would want to do that, and why?"

The man sitting beside him began to mumble through his tape. Sarge reached over and pulled it off, then looked at his name tag. "What'cha got to say there, Wallace?"

"I can believe there are some that would want to. There's a lot of people in there that are unhappy."

"So you understand our need for security, then?" Sarge asked. Wallace nodded. "With that in mind, then, can you help us out?"

"Sure, I'll do whatever I can to help out."

"I'll help too," Dunlap said.

"Out-fucking-standing, gentlemen!" Sarge said as he stood up. "Let's get these guys some grub, maybe a drink of water."

"What about her?" Ted asked, nodding at Singer.

"Leave her ass right where she is, but someone bring her a drink of water."

"Or some gasoline to wash that funk out of her mouth," Mike said.

"Ted, can you guys build us a sand table model of the camp?" Sarge asked.

"Sure. Ian, you want to give us a hand? Jamie, you too," Ted replied.

The four headed off to start building the model. Before Dunlap and Wallace were cut loose, Sarge asked them a few more questions.

"What's your CO's name?"

"Charles Tabor, but I don't think he wants to take over the camp. Hell, he already runs it," Wallace said.

"I agree, just wanted to make sure my info was accurate," Sarge said, then waved them off. "Go with these fellas. They'll get you some grub and water."

Sheffield motioned for Sarge to follow him into the CP. Once inside, Sheffield fell into a chair, running his hand through the stubble on his head.

"What the hell? Are you just making this shit up as you go?"

"Yeah, that's not what you told us you were planning," Livingston said.

"It's called improvisation. Look, we have very little intel to work on here. But think about it: we roll up and tell old Charles Tabor that we've intel saying some of his people are trying to take over the camp and we're there to help him. Do you think he's gonna question it?"

"Why in the hell would he believe that?" Sheffield asked.

"We've got the map the guys made—it's very good, like someone inside drew it up. Plus," Sarge pointed out the tent flap, "those two are going to give us even more info, so we'll be able to label everything on it. And, I'm going to take their IDs with me, to show him."

"What the hell is that supposed to prove?" Livingston asked.

Sarge shrugged his shoulders. "We'll have to see how he reacts to it. It'll lend credence to the story that there are people inside the camp looking to overthrow his command."

"I don't know, this just seems like a cluster fuck in the making," Sheffield said.

"You got a better idea, Captain? I'm all ears," Sarge said as he sat back in one of the chairs.

"No, not really. It just seems kinda sketchy."

"You want to try a frontal assault, maybe a classic pincer movement? We need at least five to one to pull that off and there aren't nearly that many people here. If this works, they're going to open the front door and invite us in. I'm going to get ole Charlie to assemble his people and surrender their weapons."

"How the hell do you expect to do that?" Livingston practically shouted.

"'Cause I'm going to tell him some of them want to put a bullet in his head and we're there to find them. They'll lay down their weapons and then we'll tell him that we're interviewing the staff. Once we've got all the weapons, we own the place. This takeover can be done without firing a shot."

"You know, Captain, as crazy as this sounds, it may just work. I mean, it really could work," Livingston said.

"I just don't want to get any of my soldiers or these civilians killed," Sheffield said.

Sarge stood up. "Captain, I don't know what you did in your civilian life, but you are in the army, now more than ever. You're a commissioned officer at that, you're going to have to make decisions that *will*"—Sarge emphasized the last word—"get people killed, whether it's your enemy or some of those under your command. All we can do is plan the best we can to minimize the latter."

Sheffield nodded his head. "I know, it's just life is hard enough right now. Adding casualties to the mix will make things that much worse. I just want to anticipate that scenario."

"You're right. Life is tough right now, but you're out here and those poor people are trapped in there. Some of them may want to be there, and that's fine, but if there's even one person in there being held against their will, then it's got to be dealt with," Sarge said.

Sheffield thought about that for a minute. "How many of my people's lives is that one person worth? What's a fair trade?"

Sarge wagged his finger at him. "What's that you're wearing there?"

Sheffield looked down. "What? My uniform?"

"Exactly—a uniform, and not a mailman's or basketball player's, you're wearing the uniform of the United States Army. Keeping that in mind, you're not in a position to decide which missions you will and won't take. You have no politics. It is up to us to go into harm's way on behalf of those who cannot defend themselves."

Sheffield let out a long breath and nodded. "You're right. Let's get to it, then. What do we need to do now?"

"Assemble your NCOs. When the sand table is done, we'll go over it. Then we need to get everyone organized. Everyone needs to be in clean uniforms, as sharp as possible. They have to look the part. Get all your trucks cleaned out and ready too. How are you on fuel?"

Sheffield looked at Livingston. "Low, very low. We have enough to put some in every truck, but not much beyond that," Livingston said.

"That's fine, this is a one-way trip. They got fuel there. And we need to make sure we've got an NCO in each truck. I don't want anyone getting trigger-happy," Sarge said.

"We've got that covered. We'll split the squads up and stick a couple of the civilians in to supplement the ones that are short. I've scrounged up enough uniforms for them as well," Livingston said.

"How about weapons and ammo?" Sarge asked.

"Oh yeah, with that delivery there's plenty."

"Good, then let's get to work on the model so we can get everyone up to speed. Have you picked out your civilians yet?"

"I've got a list of volunteers. We picked out a dozen that we feel are up to the task," Sheffield said.

"I'll round up the noncoms," Livingston said.

"Good. I'm going to check on the boys working on the sand table."

Sarge found the guys out on the road. They had a large area swept clean and were laying out leaves, sticks and rocks to indicate structures inside the camp. Ted was holding the drawing and pointing out where the various things were to be placed. Ian and Mike were arguing over the materials they were using. Jamie was knelt on the opposite side of the area they were working on, shaking her head.

"No, use these magnolia leaves for the tents. They're bigger," Mike said.

"What's the difference? A leaf is a leaf," Ian said.

Mike snatched up a smaller leaf. "No, it's not—use the bigger ones!" he snapped as he threw the leaf.

"You two are idiots," Jamie said.

Mike and Ian both looked up. Mike asked, "What, you got a better idea?"

"Just pick one, jeez!"

"Teddy, you got this under control?" Sarge asked.

Ted looked up. "Yeah, I got it, if these two will stop arguing."

"Hey! We're not arguing, we've got creative differences," Mike said as he knelt at the edge of the model.

Sarge chuckled. "Yeah, that's what you got. Hurry up and get this done." Looking at his watch, he added, "You got an hour." Shaking his head, he spun on his heels and walked off.

Charles Tabor sat behind his desk looking at the stack of paper in front of him. His deputy, Ed Mooreland, sat in a chair on the other side of the desk. He was holding a file and tossed it onto Charlie's desk.

"What do you want to do with those girls?" Ed asked.

Charlie picked up the file and flipped it open. "Well, they admitted to it. The rules say they have to be executed."

"What about the claims he raped one of them?"

Charlie looked up. "He's dead, so we can't ask him, now,

can we? Do it tomorrow afternoon in front of a full assembly so they know what happens if they get any ideas." He tossed the file onto his desk and picked up another from the pile. "We get anything out of those two we brought in?"

"Not yet, the guys roughed the old man up pretty bad, so he hasn't been questioned yet, and the kid's been interrogated once. But they strung him up overnight and he got hypothermia, nearly died. I'll have Niigata take another shot at him once his condition improves."

Charlie tossed the file onto his desk with the others. "All right, any word on the three we're missing?"

Ed shook his head. "Nope, they just disappeared."

"Did they disappear or were they taken?"

"It's unclear. There wasn't any call from them, no spent brass. There were obvious signs of struggle. I'd say someone snatched them."

"Well, keep your ears open." He picked yet another sheaf of papers. "Okay, how about the comm link to the new camp in Apopka?"

"Word is it will be up tomorrow." Ed shifted in his chair. "You know, there's some folks here who said the state spent millions buying that land up just so they could shut those farms down. Now we're going to put it back into production again."

"Well, it isn't going to be farmed like it was back then, that's for sure. Besides, all they grew was sweet corn and sod. Sweet corn would be nice, but no one needs sod now."

Ed chuckled. "Yeah, I don't see anyone wanting to purposefully plant any grass anytime soon. What are they going to be growing anyway? I mean, if they can keep the lake from flooding, that is. Bet no one's going to care about all that fertilizer dumped out there now."

"I have no idea, Ed. I manage refugees, not crops. Those farms were a mess, but you could grow golf balls in that muck. Got anything else?"

"We also got a call from Frost Proof wanting to know if we could send some of our people to their camp. They say they're going to be ready down there soon and they'll need labor."

Tabor rocked back in his chair. "What the hell? Their camp is bigger than ours, and they don't have enough people there?"

Ed shrugged. "Just relaying the message, boss."

"Tell 'em we'll send what we can, but they'll have to provide transport."

"Already did."

"I would imagine we'll start getting more and more requests along these lines as spring gets closer. There's going to be lots to plant and those fields will need tending," Tabor said.

"There's going to be a bunch of really unhappy people soon. Going from doing software programming to running a hoe on a farm is gonna be a shock," Ed said with a chuckle.

"They want to eat, they got to work. That's the way it is." He waved his hand. "All right, I got work to do."

"Niigata's outside."

Tabor rolled his eyes. "What does he want?"

Ed shrugged. "I don't know."

Tabor exhaled dramatically. "Send him in on your way out."

Ed smiled and left the office. After a moment Niigata was standing at attention in the doorway.

"Come on in, Niigata, take a seat."

Niigata nodded and stepped in, not taking a seat. "Thank you, sir."

Tabor sat back in his seat, folding his hands across his chest. "What can I do for you?"

"I wanted to give you a report on the interrogations to this point," Niigata said.

Tabor sat up in his chair. "What have you learned?"

"Nothing of substance. No more than you already knew."

A look of annoyance spread across Tabor's face. "Then why are you here if you have nothing to tell me?"

"I simply wanted to keep you apprised of the situation," Niigata said, smiling.

"Look, let me make this clear, I don't want to be kept *apprised*. I only want the end result with no details of the trip it took to get there." Now Tabor smiled. "Unlike you, my interest is in the destination, not the journey."

Niigata nodded. "I see, I'll report to you once I reach the destination. If you'll excuse me," Niigata said as he turned for the door.

Tabor looked down at his papers and shook his head. "Where do they get these people?"

Dunlap knelt in front of the model of the camp. "Wow, looks really good."

Sarge nodded. "What can you tell me? Our intel didn't provide too much detail."

He pointed at the rows of magnolia leaves. "These are the tents for the detainees. They are brought in here"—he pointed to a couple of leaves near the front of the camp—"and processed, then moved here." He went on to point out the medical, mess, and latrine facilities, as well as fuel storage, motor pool, and equipment storage.

"Where's the armory?" Ted asked.

"It's inside of this connex here, underground. There's a set of steps that take you underground once you're inside. All weapons and ammo are stored there."

"What sort of weapons do you guys have? What could we be facing if these rogues get to them?" Sarge asked, keeping up the lie.

Dunlap looked at Wallace. "You know better than me."

Wallace cleared his throat. "M4s, SAWs, a couple of Browning .50s—"

He was cut off by Mike. "Why the fuck does a law enforcement agency need .50s?"

Wallace smiled. "Just as strong, just as well equipped, remember that speech?"

Sarge bit his tongue. "I remember, what else?"

"Let's see, everyone carries a Glock. There's a few .300 Win mag scoped rifles and a few M320 launchers."

"Jesus, 320s?" Mike blurted out. Sarge shot him a look telling him to rein it in.

"We mainly use them for less than lethal, they're for gas and stuff like that," Dunlap said.

"Do you have any lethal for them?" Sarge asked.

"Oh yeah, we got that too," Wallace said.

"Where's the CP?" Sarge asked. Wallace pointed it out.

Ted knelt down and pointed at a rifle magazine with sticks arrayed in a square around it. "What's this?"

"That's the detainment facility," Dunlap said.

"Who's held there?" Sarge asked.

"You know, troublemakers, people caught committing crimes. Sometimes they take people straight there from reception. I don't know why. I'm not part of that."

"Anything else we need to know?"

"Not really. It's basically run like a big jail. People come in and they go out."

"Is that how they operate, like a jail?" Ted asked. "What I mean is, that's how the security is set up, looking in?"

"Yeah, for the most part. They do fence-line patrols, drag the roads, that sort of thing. Other than the gates, everything is focused in."

"Thanks for the input, gentlemen. Why don't you guys go get some rest while we get ready to move," Sarge said.

Jess was moved back to her cell once they realized Shane's hypothermia was no longer an issue. What she'd initially thought was going to be a horrible experience had turned out to be an almost enjoyable break from the monotony of isolation.

Shane stayed under the blankets. He expected they would take them and was surprised when they didn't. Any time he was not under them he would start to catch a chill. Now his thoughts focused around when he would have to face Niigata again as that was surely in his future.

The door to the unit opened, and Shane listened as footsteps grew nearer. The sound of his cell unlocking was accompanied by the usual light washing in. He hid under the blankets to avoid it. Then the nurse pulled his blankets back and began to check him out: taking his temperature, checking his pulse, the usual routine. What she did not do, unlike any other health care professional, was ask him how he felt. That was irrelevant.

"How does he look?" a man's voice asked.

"He's getting better. Probably one more day and he'll be back to normal. Well, nearly normal," she said.

"You got one more day, there, sport, then you've got a date with your favorite person," the man laughed. "You and him will have all kinds of fun."

When the door closed, relief washed over Shane. Sure he had to meet Niigata again, but at least it wasn't today. He wasn't sure he could take it right now.

The men went to Calvin's cell where the nurse checked him over as well. The diagnosis for him was not as positive as Shane's.

"His ribs are healing slowly. He's old, and old people just don't heal that fast," the nurse said.

"Well, how long will it take him to get healed up?" the man asked.

"It could take weeks."

"You better hurry up, old man. They aren't going to feed your worthless ass forever."

Calvin didn't respond from the floor where he was lying with his arms over his eyes. There was a lot he wanted to say, but he was in no shape to deal with the consequences.

The men continued down the row of cells. As they passed Jess's cell, one of them banged on her door.

"Wake up!" he shouted.

The other banged on Fred's and Mary's cells.

"Tomorrow is the day, ladies! You're finally going to get what's coming to you!" the man said, then began to laugh.

"Yep, tomorrow's your big day!" the other shouted.

Jess was immediately terrified. She tried to convince herself that she didn't know what that statement meant, but deep down she knew. She sank against the wall.

Fred took the statement without any emotion. She'd already accepted the fact. There was no escaping from her current situation and she knew it. It'd taken time to come to the conclusion and it was hard to accept. But now that she had accepted it, there was nothing more that could affect her. She didn't want to give the bastards the satisfaction of ruining her last hours.

Aric sat on an empty fuel drum, staring at the detention facility. He was thinking of ways to get Fred out of there—and fast. But then what? Where would they go? They'd have to leave the grounds, with no place to stay, without any food. *Wait a second*, he thought to himself. Looking back at the motor pool, he started to develop a plan. Kay would probably give him food, or at least turn a blind eye if he took some. He could stash it in a truck along with weapons and extra ammo. The hard part would be getting out of the camp. He'd never get through the gates with Fred in tow. He thought about how he could pull that off when an idea struck him. Right before the breakout, he would cut through both fences, opening a path. He could move a truck over to the fence, cut it open, and head to the detention center. The fence line was only about a hundred yards past the detention facility.

When Cortez and the other idiot showed up to deliver food, he'd go inside with them, as he had the other day, and shoot them both. Once they were down, he'd take the keys and get Fred out. Then he thought about the other girls. If they wanted to come, they could. If not, they were on their own. Aric hopped off the barrel and headed for the kitchen. It was still a rough plan, but it was the best one he could think of. He decided to run parts of it past Kay.

As it was between services, Aric found Kay in the dry

goods storage doing an inventory. The shelves weren't exactly overflowing.

"Hey, Kay, whatcha doing?" Aric said as he came up behind the older woman.

Kay yelled and jumped, turning around with a hand over her chest. "Aric! You scared the life out of me!"

"Oh, I'm sorry, wasn't trying to."

Kay smoothed her hair, composing herself. "I'm inventorying our supplies."

Aric looked at the shelves. "Doesn't look like there's much here."

"There's supposed to be a delivery tomorrow. I was just trying to see what we have on hand."

"Well, that's *kinda* what I wanted to talk to you about."

Kay laid her clipboard on a shelf. "What do you mean?"

Aric looked around, then quietly asked, "Is there anyone else in here?"

"No, what's going on?" Kay asked, concern in her voice.

"Look, this needs to stay between you and me. Can you promise me that?"

"What is it? What are you talking about?"

"Will you promise me that you won't say anything to anyone about what I'm going to tell you?"

"All right, Aric, I promise. What's wrong?"

Aric took a deep breath. "I'm going to get Fred out."

Kay's eyes went wide. "What? How are you going to do that?"

"The less you know, the better for you."

"Then why are you even telling me? I don't understand."

"Because I need your help. When I get her out, we're leaving here, and we need food."

Kay slowly nodded her head. "I see."

"You don't have to give me anything. Just let me, you know, take some."

Kay looked upset by what she was hearing. "I don't know, I don't want to end up over there too."

Without even thinking, Aric blurted out, "Then come with us."

Kay was shocked. "What? Come with you? Where are you going?"

Aric looked at the floor and shrugged his shoulders. "I don't know yet. I'll have to figure that out. But anywhere is better than here."

Kay looked around the kitchen. "How do you plan on getting out of here? You're going to just try and run? They'll catch you in no time. You need to be smart about this, Aric."

"Well, I'm going to take a truck, so we'll have transportation. I'm taking weapons and ammo too."

Kay started thinking it over. The idea of getting out of camp was intriguing, but the uncertainty of what lay outside the camp's fence was scary.

"I—I don't know if I could, Aric. I mean, where do you plan to go? Hell, how are we going to get out of here?"

"I can get us out, I think."

"You think! This isn't the sort of thing we're going to do on a hunch—either you can or can't. Do you want to end up dead?" Kay was incredulous.

"Look, I want to get her out of there, and I've decided I want out of here too, and I'll do whatever it takes to get out."

"When are you going to do this?"

"Soon. There isn't much time before the"—Aric swallowed hard—"execution."

Kay thought about the situation for a minute. She'd like to be in charge of her own life too. But it was scary to think about having to try to survive without the camp. She'd been there long enough that it was the only life she knew now.

"Let me know when you're going to do it. I've got to think about it."

"What about the food?" Aric asked.

"You can take what you want. If I don't go, I'll just say it was stolen. If I do come, it won't matter, will it?"

Aric smiled. "I guess not." He wrapped his arms around the older woman. "Thanks, Kay."

Kay patted his back. "No problem, just think it through. I don't want you winding up dead over this."

"Me neither, me neither." They released their embrace and Aric added, "I gotta go, got things I need to check out, so that this is a smart plan."

Kay nodded and Aric quickly left. Kay stood there thinking about what he'd said for a long time. It was both petrifying and exhilarating, the thought of getting out of the camp. Even though she wouldn't admit it at the moment, she knew in her gut that she didn't want to be here forever.

Aric went back to the motor pool to look for a truck. The Hummers were fuel thirsty, but not nearly as bad as the other options, so one would have to do. At the pool he started checking the truck, and headed to the mechanics office. He knew they kept a roster of all the vehicles and their statuses in there. While he was going through the log, he remembered something that would really help: the locker for the scavenging crew.

The locker was literally a one-stop shop for what he was planning. *Why didn't I think of this before?* he thought to himself, as he surveyed the SAWs, ammo, batteries, body armor, first aid supplies, and stack of MREs inside of it. He took a quick inventory. Everything he needed was there—it would just be a matter of loading it quickly when the time came.

Returning his attention to the log, he read that one of the Hummers had recently been serviced and went to look for it in the rows of vehicles. After he found the truck, he started it up. It seemed to run just fine. Now he needed to make sure it was still there when they made the escape. There was only one way to take a truck out of service, and that was to red tag it, but he needed a reason. *That's all I need, a reason—doesn't have to be legit,* Aric thought. Going back to the mechanics desk, he looked around for anyone who might snitch on him being there. Seeing no one, he grabbed a red tag and took it back out to the truck.

Filling out the tag, he listed the default as electrical short. In the description box he wrote, *shocked driver when attempting to start.* Anyone other than the mechanic that saw the ticket would just move on to the next. And if the mechanic saw it, he would have to find Aric to find out what happened. Either way the truck would be there until he needed it.

With the transportation element sorted out, he breathed a tiny sigh of relief. His mission was going to be easier than he'd first anticipated. He smiled to himself and headed back toward the kitchen to reassure Kay. It was there that he realized his timetable had just become a hell of a lot shorter.

Aric arrived back at the kitchen to find Cortez there, collecting meals for the prisoners in the detention center.

"'Sup, Vonasek?" Cortez asked.

"Same old shit, man, what are you up to?"

"Getting ready for the big day!" he said with a smile.

Kay and Aric both looked at him. "What big day?" Aric asked.

"Oh, you haven't heard?"

"No, heard what?" Kay asked.

"There's gonna be an execution tomorrow."

"Execution? Who's being executed?" Aric asked, playing dumb.

"Those three murdering bitches are going to be shot in front of a full assembly of the camp tomorrow."

Aric's head started to spin. It took considerable effort to remain on his feet, as his knees wanted to buckle. Kay was just as stunned. Her mouth was hanging open.

"Hey, man, you all right?" Cortez asked, squinting at Aric.

Aric placed a hand on the counter to steady himself. "Oh yeah, just tired. When are they going to do it?" Aric's mind was racing, trying to figure out a way to get Fred out in the shortened timeframe.

"Tomorrow afternoon. Gonna be a firing squad, and I asked to be on it," Cortez said as he tossed a freeze-dried pea in his mouth, smiling as he crunched it up.

Aric wanted to beat the man to death where he stood. Not shoot him, but use his own hands to inflict pain. It took every bit of restraint he possessed to stand there and look at him.

"Well, I guess I'll see you then," Aric said.

Cortez picked up the meals. "Get there early so you can get a front-row seat."

Kay and Aric watched as Cortez walked out. As soon as the door shut Aric looked at Kay, tears were running down her face.

"Oh my God, what are we going to do?" Kay asked as she fought back sobs.

"I'm going to kill that bastard," Aric said through gritted teeth.

"I can't believe they're going to do that." Kay shook her head. "I just can't believe it."

"We have to get her out before tomorrow afternoon. Kay, please say you'll come."

Kay nodded her head, wiping away tears. "Yes, yes, I'll come with you. If this is how they are going to act, I don't want to be here. Jess was raped. He deserved it. What those girls did was right. We are going to get them all, aren't we?"

"Of course we are. I'm not leaving any of them behind. Get ready. I'll let you know when I am."

She gave him another quick hug. Aric left the kitchen and headed for his room. It was time for action.

Chapter 16

We were running low on meat again. The fastest way to get some was to use the gill net in the creek to catch mullet, so we used the kayak to get the net across the river just as we did last time. The difference now was that there just didn't seem to be any mullet in the river. We watched the creek for hours, even going up and down the river to look for them, but we came up empty.

"I guess we need to let the net sit for a while," Thad said.

"Yeah, let's leave it out for the rest of the day and see if it catches anything. No use waiting here," Danny said.

"Well, in that case, I'm going to go over to Chase's place. I want to see if he knows of anyone around who might have taken the shots at us," I said.

Danny adjusted his hat. "You think he'll know?"

I shrugged. "Can't hurt to ask. Plus, we can get out of here for a little."

"I'm going to stay here. I don't think I need a change of scenery," Thad said.

"Me too, I'll hang out with him," Jeff said.

"You want to see if Mel and Bobbie want to go?" Danny asked.

"Sure, we'll take the girls too. Getting out of here would be nice for everyone. We'll take Sarge's big buggy so we can all fit."

Danny gave me a look. "You think he'll care?"

"Hell no, he wouldn't care. Plus, he ain't here to say anything about it," I said with a grin.

"Cool, let's get everyone rounded up and take a ride."

Everyone was excited to leave the camp, even if it was just for a short trip up the road. After making sure we all had our weapons, Danny and I tossed our packs into the back. I got in behind the wheel with Mel beside me and we headed out.

"This is fun!" Little Bit said, holding her hand outside the buggy.

"It *is* nice to get out," Bobbie agreed.

Mel nodded her agreement. Taylor sat in the back with her face to the sky. "The sun feels good."

Even Lee Ann seemed to be enjoying the ride. She was at least looking around, not sitting with her face buried in her arms.

The road was windswept, the only tracks on it from deer and other critters.

"We need to come hunt out here. The deer are obviously using the road a lot," Danny said.

"Can I go hunting with you?" Taylor asked.

"We'll see," I replied.

"Come on, Dad, I wanna go."

"You ever been hunting?" Danny asked.

She shook her head. "No, but I want to try it."

Danny looked at me. "You never took her hunting?"

I laughed. "She never wanted to get up early enough to go. Plus, she's been fishing with us before, and we know how that goes."

"Hey! What do you mean?" Taylor shouted, half smiling.

I did my best to mimic a teenage girl voice. "I gotta pee, can we go to the boat ramp?"

Danny started to laugh. "Yeah, she never would use the can in the boat. But you're one to talk, you can't piss out of the boat either!"

"Hey. That's not from lack of effort, it's the whole bobbing-up-and-down thing," I said.

Taylor rolled her eyes and Mel hit me in the arm playfully.

"Ew, Dad. But yeah, I still want to go hunting, though," Taylor said.

"You're quick to volunteer for things that involve guns," Danny said.

"She does like her some shootin' irons," I said. Taylor smiled. "You know you can't use that machine gun to deer hunt."

"I know, I know, I just want to go."

"I think we can work it out," Danny said.

We drove on, chatting. About a half mile down the road, I pointed out a large patch of leafy greens.

"Ooh, we gotta stop here on the way back and pick that," I said, pointing to it.

"What is it?" Danny asked. "Mustard?"

"It's in the same family and tastes a lot like it. It's called winter cress."

"Yuck, mustard greens are gross," Taylor said.

I looked back at her. "Shoot, when you were a baby you would sit in my lap and eat them as long as I would feed them to you." I knocked on the window, gesturing toward the greens. "You ate that very type all the time."

"I remember that! You were so cute, Tay," Mel said.

"Well, I ain't a baby anymore," Taylor replied.

Chase's place wasn't that far from our camp, so it didn't take long to get there. As we got closer, Danny told me to slow down.

"Let's see if anyone is around before we go running up in there."

I stopped and we watched the place, looking for any sign of life. After a few minutes I honked the horn. The front door opened slowly and Chase stepped out holding his turkey gun.

"Hey, Chase. It's me, Morgan!" I called out. "Can we come up?"

Chase looked around, then waved us up.

"Hey, Chase, how you been?" I asked as I got out.

"We're doin'," he replied.

Seeing it was safe, his wife and daughter came outside as well. The ladies started to chat while Danny and me talked to Chase.

Looking around, I asked, "Where are the boys?"

"They set out on their own."

"Really, just left?" Danny asked.

"Yeah, 'bout a week ago. Said it was boring around here."

"Where'd they go?" I asked.

Chase shrugged. "Got no idea, haven't seen hide nor hair since they left. Andy's momma's a little worried about him, told him it was a bad idea, but he's pert near growed and left anyway."

"How have you guys been here?" Danny asked.

Chase scratched at what was now a very full beard. "We're all right. I manage to get enough out of the woods to feed us. Sure could use some vegetables, though."

"You see them patches of winter cress down the road?" I asked, pointing back the way we came.

"What? That green stuff on the west side?"

"Yeah, they're kind of like mustard greens."

"Good to know. I thought it looked like mustard greens but wasn't sure and didn't want to get anyone sick," he said.

"It's good to eat. We're going to pick some on the way back," I said.

"Some fresh greens would be good. I found a lemon tree and we been eating them—sour as all get out, but we need it."

"Wow, a lemon tree, that'd be nice," Danny said.

"It has been. I'd trade you some but we've 'bout cleaned it out now."

"Thanks anyway," Danny said with a smile.

"How's your daughter been feeling?" I asked.

Chase looked over at her. He wasn't the type of man to show emotion, from what I gathered, but I'm sure he was smiling on the inside.

"She's been real good. Boiling the water really helps and that bleach idea y'all had really helped out too."

"Good, glad to hear it," I said.

"Hey, Chase, you seen anyone around lately?" Danny asked.

"'Bout a week ago a couple of fellers come through here. Said they was from Orlando, had to get out 'cause it got so bad there."

"Did they say where they were heading?" I asked.

"Naw, just said they was passing through."

"Did they have any guns?" Danny asked.

"One of 'em had an old H&R single-shot shotgun. Why? They give y'all some trouble?"

"Someone was sneaking around our place at night, then the next day they took a shot at Danny with some sort of shotgun." I left out the part about Danny shooting up the creek.

"I think I heard that, heard a whole bunch of shooting one night not long ago."

"Yeah, that was probably it. I was just curious if you'd seen anyone around," Danny replied.

"Not since them two fellers, but they came through 'bout a week before I heard the shooting, so I don't think they're your guys," Chase said.

We talked a little more about what each of us was doing to get by. I told Chase about the squirrel snares and explained the concept to him. He said he'd give it a try. He'd been concentrating on hunting, shooting deer and even a turkey.

"Bet that was nice," Danny said.

"Yeah, it was. I cooked it on the grill, best meal we've had in a while."

"We haven't seen any turkeys yet. I'd like to, though," I said.

"I'd like to see more of 'em myself. I'll fight you for it," he said with a chuckle.

"How are you fixed for ammo?" Danny asked.

"Been doing most of my hunting with my .22, trying to save the shotgun and rifle ammo. I still got a couple hundred .22s and a couple boxes of birdshot, some turkey loads and slugs and buck."

"If you get to where you need some, come by. Ammo is something we've got," I said.

Chase smiled. "I figured you for the type to hoard ammo." He nodded at the carbine slung across my chest.

After talking a little longer, we said our good-byes and got back in the buggy. Everyone wanted to ride a bit longer. They weren't ready to go home yet. I told them we could for a little while and we continued on the road away from the camp. There were several houses in the area, though none of them seemed occupied. All the homes showed the lack of human attention, leaves piled up all over the yards and roofs, lawns composed almost solely of weeds. The dirt road met a paved road at the transfer station in Paisley. As we passed the site, Danny suggested we ride over to Clear Lake Campground. As soon as he suggested it, there was no getting out of it, as it was met by cheers from all the girls.

We rolled down Highway 42 at a good clip. The ride was so smooth that I was soon going seventy without even realizing it. Just as I started to slow down, the sign for the campground came into view.

The campground was much like I remembered it, just with an air of neglect about it. The small shack at the entry was actually lying on its side. All the windows had been knocked out and shards of glass littered the ground. I stopped beside it.

"You think it's a good idea to be here?" I asked as I looked at the broken glass.

"Yeah, it doesn't look like there has been anyone through here in a long time," Danny said.

"Let's ride through, just check it out," Bobbie said.

We drove past the gate and down the narrow paved track that was now covered in leaves and other natural debris. The namesake for the park, Clear Lake, sat on the west side of the campground. On our way there, Bobbie suddenly shouted, "Stop!"

I slammed on the brakes, looking for whatever she saw. Bobbie was pointing to a small building.

"A bathroom!"

Bobbie's idea was immediately seized on by the rest of the girls, so I pulled up to it and everyone got out.

Danny and I cleared it, then waited by the buggy.

"Wonder how the fishing is in the lake now?" Danny asked as he leaned over the front end of the buggy.

"You'd think it'd be better with fewer people around now," I replied.

A breeze picked up, blowing through the trees and dropping even more leaves down on us. It carried with it the very familiar smell of woodsmoke.

"You smell that?" I asked.

Danny stood up and looked around. "Yeah, I do. Wonder where it's coming from."

We looked around for the source, but couldn't get a visual on anything or anyone.

"Someone's out here," I said.

"Yeah, let's keep our eyes open."

"You still want to go through or do you want to leave?" I asked.

"Naw, I don't want to leave yet. Let's just see who's here."

When all the girls finished using the facilities, we loaded up. I told them about the smoke and asked them to keep their eyes peeled.

"I can smell it too," Taylor said as she adjusted the sling on her H&K. She had the slightest bit of worry on her face.

I pulled back out onto the road and continued to follow the loop around toward the lake. I was driving slowly, not wanting to run into an ambush, which was a strange thought in itself. A few months ago I would never consider an ambush a potential road hazard, but that was the reality in this new life.

"There! There," Mel said, pointing to a campsite just beyond the woods.

I stopped the buggy and Danny and I got out to look the camp over. There were two tents as well as a lean-to-style structure that appeared to be used for cooking. It was then that Danny noticed four people down at the lake—a man, a woman, and two children, from the looks of it.

"Let's go say hi," Danny said.

"I don't want to get shot. You and me coming up to them

like this through the woods isn't going to look very friendly. Why don't you get Bobbie and you two walk out and call to them? I'll cover you from over here," I replied.

"They've got kids. I don't think they're a threat."

"Yeah, well, better safe than sorry."

"All right, all right, let me get her," Danny said.

Danny and Bobbie walked out through the campsite while I took up a position where I could cover them but hopefully not be seen. They held hands as they walked. Danny had his carbine slung behind his back to look less threatening. When they got to the edge of the campsite, Danny called out, "Hello!" and waved.

The people at the water's edge immediately looked up. The woman grabbed the two kids and pulled them behind her, while the man moved to pick up a rifle leaning against a chair. I raised my carbine and drew a bead on him. If he shouldered it, I would have to shoot him, not something I wanted to do in front of his kids.

"Can we come down?" Bobbie called out.

The two exchanged words for a moment, then the man said something I couldn't hear. Danny and Bobbie started walking toward them as the man walked to meet them, still clutching his rifle. They stopped a short distance from each other and talked, Danny gesturing toward the campsite. After another minute of talking, the man called to the woman and motioned for her to meet them. Holding the kids' hands, she cautiously made her way toward Danny and Bobbie.

When I saw Danny and Bobbie start back up toward the camp, I headed over toward the buggy.

"What's going on?" Mel asked.

"I think they're coming up here."

"Is everything going to be all right?" Little Bit asked.

"I think so, don't worry," I said to her as I rubbed her head. She smiled but didn't really look like she believed it.

Danny and Bobbie came up. "Are they friendly? What are they doing?" I asked.

"They're coming up to meet everyone."

"What'd he say?" I asked.

"Not much, just that we scared the hell out of him."

"Good thing he didn't know I was watching, or he would have really been scared."

The couple came to the edge of their campsite and stopped. They were looking us over when a little girl about Ashley's age grabbed her mother's hand. "Mommy, can I play with her?" she asked, pointing at Little Bit.

Her mother looked at Ash, then at us. "Uh, I don't know."

Mel looked up. "Oh, they can play. They both could probably use some time around other kids."

The woman smiled. "Okay"—she looked down at her daughter—"go ahead."

The little girl ran up to the buggy. "You wanna play with me?"

Little Bit looked up at Mel, who nodded at her. She smiled and jumped out of the buggy and they ran back toward the tents.

I smiled at them. "We should all be more like kids."

"Kids are lucky, they still retain a little of their innocence," the man said, sticking his hand out. "I'm Tyler, and this is my wife, Brandy."

We did a quick round of introductions and they invited us into their camp. We took seats on a couple of logs they'd dragged around the pit. Brandy was very obviously uncomfortable with the amount of weaponry sitting across the fire from her. Everyone except Lee Ann and Little Bit had at least one firearm, and Danny and I each had two. I couldn't blame her: I'd be nervous too.

"Where are you guys from?" Mel asked Brandy.

"Daytona, not too far from the beach."

"Did it get bad there?" Danny asked.

"Yes and no. It was weird. The beach always draws a lot of transient types, so that became an even more serious problem. But the biggest issue was resources. There were so many people there, and not enough to go around," Tyler said.

"What about you guys, where are you from?" Brandy asked.

"We live nearby," Mel said.

"Must be nice not to have to leave home," Brandy said.

"It hasn't been easy. We've had our fair share of problems too," Danny said.

"That's a nice Ruger, Tyler," I said, pointing to the rifle in his lap.

"Yeah, she wasn't real happy when I bought it"—he smiled at her—"but it was worth it in the end."

"Yeah, sadly, guns are necessary tools these days."

"Mom, sorry to interrupt, but I have to use the bathroom," Taylor said.

"Oh, use the one right over there," Brandy said, pointing to a nearby restroom. "It's the one we use. It's pretty clean."

"Lee Ann, go with her," Mel said. Lee Ann didn't reply, but did get up and walk away with her sister. As they walked, they came across the two younger girls, squealing and running. Ashley and Tyler's daughter came running through the center of the camp, being chased by a little boy.

"What's your daughter's name?" Mel asked.

"Her name's Edie, and her brother, the monster over there, is Jace," Brandy answered.

"They look like a handful. How old are they?"

"Edie is seven and Jace is six."

This got raised eyebrows from Mel and Bobbie. "Wow, you're brave," Mel said with a laugh.

"Yeah, well"—Brandy looked at Tyler—"it wasn't supposed to be like that, but it happened."

Tyler laughed. "It's always my fault. If I remember right, you were there too."

Now I laughed. "Amen, brother, amen!"

We talked for some time about what's happened since that fateful day. They told us about their time in Daytona, of people taking over resources that should have been available to all and demanding payment in exchange for drawing water from a lake. There were also gang fights, wars as they called them, to control such resources. I asked about the beach, if they ever tried to get there to fish, but Tyler said it was impossible to get on the beach, even as a local. As we grew more comfortable, I told them of my trip home and about the raiders.

"I've heard of the camp. We traveled with some people who were trying to get there. They said it was the answer to all of the problems they were dealing with," Tyler said.

"Yeah, I don't think it lives up to the advertising," Danny said.

"That's why we're here and not there. I'd rather take care of my family myself."

"What'd you guys do for work before all this went down?" I asked.

"I worked for the county in maintenance and Brandy was an elementary school teacher."

Bobbie looked at Brandy. "Oh my. What was it like in the school?"

"Horrible. Despite all the preparedness crap they talked

about, all the drills they did, they were totally unprepared. Even if it'd only been a couple of days, they weren't prepared."

"What'd they do with all the kids?" Mel asked.

"That whole shelter-in-place thing is such a joke. The first day there was nearly a riot because the administration wouldn't release kids to their parents. We had used an electronic system for ID verification, and since it didn't work they didn't know what to do, and, of course, there was no backup. The water went out way faster than I would have thought, and things just got worse from there."

"Where were your kids?"

"They were in day care. I managed to get home and then went to pick them up on an old two-stroke motorcycle I had. It wasn't an easy trip, but we did it," Tyler said.

"What happened to all of your students?" Bobbie asked.

"Tyler came to the school to let me know he had the kids. Once I knew they were all right, I stayed to try and help in the classrooms. They finally started letting kids go when their parents showed up with guns. I mean, I can't blame them, I would have too. But when I left, there were still six of my students there." Her voice grew softer. "I don't know where their parents were. It was really sad. I hated to leave them."

"Wow, I can't imagine how horrible it must have been to leave those kids behind," Mel said.

"It was awful. But I had my own kids to think of."

"It became clear the situation was only going to get worse. I went there every day to bring stuff to Brandy. After a few weeks, I knew we had to go. It just wasn't safe," Tyler said.

"How'd you guys get out of Daytona? I mean, you couldn't all ride on that motorcycle," Bobbie said.

"I traded the Suzuki for that cart and some other stuff,"

Tyler said, pointing to a two-wheeled cart attached to a mountain bike. "Between that one and the kids' cart we were able to get out of town pretty quickly."

"If it wasn't for that cart, I don't know how we would have hauled everything. We already had the kids' trailer, which made life easier," Brandy said.

"So you guys ride from place to place on those?" Danny asked.

"Yeah, we're looking for a place to call home, so to speak. But it's hard, because every time we find a nice place, there is either someone already there or people show up and we leave because they put off a bad vibe," Tyler said, then jutted a thumb over his shoulder. "Where'd you guys get that rig out there? Looks pretty sweet."

"It's not ours, belongs to a friend," I said.

"Looks military."

"It is."

"Man, that'd be nice, but I guess gas would be an issue." Tyler stared thoughtfully into the coals of the fire then looked up. "You guys remember that show *Doomsday Preppers*? I used to watch that and laugh at those people. I thought they were all so crazy. But they were right. Everyone called them crazy, but they're probably the best off out of any of us."

"A lot of them were nuts," Danny said.

"Not just them, but all those people, they called them Preppers, Survivalists, or nut cases, but they were on to something. I wish I'd have been one of them."

"Hey, man, you've done a pretty damn good job so far from the looks of it. You're here, your family is healthy. It isn't about what you've got, but what you're capable of," I said.

"I'd be capable of a lot more if I had more, though," Tyler said with a laugh.

"Wouldn't we all." I chuckled. "How long have you guys been here?"

"Four days so far."

"You plan on staying put?"

"As long as we can. There's water, fish in the lake, and plenty of firewood," Tyler said, waving toward the tree line.

"How is the fishing in the lake? We were talking about that when we were driving in," Danny remarked.

"Great so far."

"Are you guys hunting at all?" I asked.

"A little, but I don't have much ammo left. I'm down to ten rounds for the Mini 14. I have a little .22 too but only a few rounds left for it."

I looked at Danny, who gave a knowing nod. I pulled a mag from my vest and started to strip rounds from it. Tyler looked on, unsure of what I was doing at first.

"Here, Tyler, take these for now," I said, holding the rounds out.

Tyler looked at Brandy, then back at me. "I can't take these. I have nothing to offer in exchange."

"This isn't a trade, man, you've got a family to protect." I gestured toward my family. "I can relate."

Tyler stuck out his hand. "Thanks, Morgan, I really appreciate it."

"We'll be by in the next day or so with some .22 ammo too," Danny said.

"Wow, I don't know what to say."

"It's uncommon today to see someone willing to do anything for someone else," Brandy said.

"We don't have much ourselves, but we can spare a little ammo. Nowadays, you need it to feed and defend yourself. It's a modern necessity," Danny said.

Tyler nodded. "Sad but true."

"It's starting to get late. We're going to head home," I said as I stood up.

"It was nice to meet y'all," Mel said with a smile.

Danny and Bobbie said the same, and Brandy shared her sentiments as well.

"Come on, Ashley, we have to go now," Mel called out.

The kids were sitting together stacking sticks like a log cabin. "Aw, come on, Mom, can't we stay a little longer?"

"No, it's time to go."

She pouted and stomped her way over, then ran back and hugged her new friend.

After rounding her up, we headed back to the buggy, where the older girls were hanging out. Tyler and Brandy came over to say good-bye.

"Thanks again for the ammo. I really appreciate it."

"Yes, thank you," Brandy added.

"No problem. You guys be safe," Danny said.

They waved as we pulled out. Mel leaned forward and commented, "They seemed pretty nice."

Bobbie agreed with her. "I hope they're going to be all right."

"That's why I gave them the ammo. I hope it wasn't a mistake," I said.

"What do you mean?" Mel asked.

"You know, people aren't always what they appear, but since they don't know where we live I'm not worried about them."

She looked at me like I was nuts. "They're just a couple with two kids. They aren't going to hurt you."

"I guess you forgot the story I told you about my trip home, when that couple with kids nearly killed me."

She didn't say anything, turning instead to look out the side of the buggy. I stopped on the way back to pick up the greens I had pointed out to Chase. They'd make a nice addition to dinner.

We made it back to the camp without seeing anyone on the road. Pulling up to the camp, I saw Jeff sitting by the fire, poking at something inside of a pot.

"What's in the pot?" I asked Jeff as we all sat down.

"Some more limb rats. Thad and I went out to check the snares. We took .22s with us and managed to shoot a bunch, so we got a good dinner going for tonight."

Cool," I said, then looked around. "Where's Thad?"

Jeff jerked his head toward the pigpen. "He's back there. We cut up a cabbage palm and he's throwing it to the hogs. He brought in the net earlier. There weren't many fish."

A few minutes later, Thad walked up, carrying something.

"Hey, Little Bit, come see what I got," he said. As he got closer I could see what it was—a tiny piglet.

"It's a baby piggy!" she shouted when he knelt down. "It's so cute! Are there more?"

Thad was smiling. "There's six more with the momma. You want to come see them? We need to get him back so he can eat."

Little Bit started hopping up and down. "Yes, yes, yes, I want to go see them."

We all walked over to the pen to find the momma pig lying under a small tree nursing her brood. The piglets were a mass of tiny bodies all trying to get to a teat. The girls were gushing over them. Little Bit wanted to get in the pen. As Thad leaned over and gently laid the piglet on its momma's side, he said she needed to wait a few more days. She frowned but was quickly transfixed.

"I didn't even know she was pregnant," Danny said.

"Me neither," Thad said with a smile, "but I'm glad she was. In a couple of months we'll have a bunch of pork."

"Yeah, we could butcher one of the others now that we have more," I said.

"Yeah, it'll be nice when they get a little bigger. Maybe barter with someone," Danny said.

I laughed. "Barter for what?"

He shrugged. "Dunno. Guess we'd have to find someone to barter with first."

"How was the drive?" Thad asked.

"Good, Chase is still hanging in there. Those boys all left, though," I said.

Thad raised his eyebrows. "Really? Wonder where they went."

"No idea. He doesn't have any idea either," I said.

"We went over to Clear Lake and met a couple over there with two little kids," Danny said.

Thad nodded. "Where'd they come from?"

"Daytona. They rode bikes all the way here," I said.

"Pretty long ride, especially with two kids."

"They had a couple of cool little trailers, one for the kids and one for all their gear."

"That's a good idea." Thad nudged me and smiled. "Bikes would have been nice on our trip home, wouldn't they?"

I laughed. "You ain't lying, brother. I would have given almost anything for a bike back then."

"What's in the pot on the fire, Thad?" Mel asked as she walked over.

"Just boiling some squirrels. Tonight we'll have squirrel and grits," Thad said with a smile.

"That should be interesting. But I'll trust your instincts, chef," Mel said with a wink.

We went back over to the fire over Little Bit's protests. Soon, everyone gathered around the tables for dinner, the light of the oil lamps illuminating our surprisingly delicious meal. This was a nice habit we'd gotten into—everyone coming together to eat and talk. The real reason for it was that we had to prepare communal meals and that forced everyone to eat at the same time, but it developed into something that we all looked forward to. It was a very happy circumstance, something that was needed in these unsure times.

Chapter 17

Sarge stood before the assembled noncommissioned officers. "Everyone clear on their assignments?" He was answered by a row of a half-dozen nodding heads.

"Remember, we want to do this without firing a shot. Shooting is the last thing we want to do, but if it comes to it, pour it to them and attain fire superiority quickly. We want to avoid civilian casualties—that's a priority. It won't do us any good to free the camp if we're killing the very people we're there to help. We roll out at 0600 tomorrow morning, any questions?"

He was met with silence.

"All right, then get your trucks in order. Make sure your squads are squared away and be ready in the morning."

As the crowd broke up, Sarge joined Sheffield and Livingston.

"I hope this works," Sheffield said.

"It will if everyone does their jobs right, especially you. They've got to buy into the fact that you're an army officer sent to assist them."

As Sheffield was thinking that over, Vance walked up. "Captain, what do you want me to do tomorrow?"

"You stay here and keep an eye on the folks we're leaving behind. Once we take the camp down, we'll send someone back. We'll move everyone over there, where we can have shelter and access to supplies."

Vance looked unhappy. "What, just 'cause I don't have a black rifle, I can't go?"

"The army hasn't carried lever actions for some time now," Sarge said with grin, looking at Vance's .357 lever gun.

Vance laughed. "I guess not. Fine, I don't mind sticking around here."

"Besides, you gotta keep an eye on them three we got trussed up over there," Sarge said.

Vance looked in the direction where the prisoners were being kept. "No problem, me and a couple of the guys will keep watch. I've already talked with them, and we'll split it up into shifts."

"Good, be careful with 'em, don't take any guff from 'em."

Vance smiled. "Oh, we won't," he said as he headed off toward the camp.

"All right, let's make sure everyone has their shit together," Sarge said, then looked at Ted and Mike. "You two make sure all the trucks are ready to go in the morning." The guys nodded and headed off to where the trucks were being staged.

Sarge went off to get his own gear ready. He would be riding in one of the lead Hummers with the officers. The rest of day was a flurry of activity with everyone getting ready to move. It wasn't until late in the evening, when things finally started to wind down, that the camp got quiet. The NCOs broke up with their respective squads to go over the plan again. Sarge stood in front of the CP tent looking out over the numerous small fires that were burning, each one representing a squad.

The Guard unit was made up of engineers. While they

were trained for combat, it was never their primary mission, though the combat requirements of the various Gulf wars and Afghanistan meant that nearly all of them had seen combat. For many of them, their orders were to act as if they belonged there, which wasn't hard in theory. But the idea of rolling into a FEMA facility and facing the unknown kept many of them awake that night.

Sarge was up at 0400. After dressing and putting his gear on, he headed out to look over the convoy. For the most part the camp was still asleep. Only the sentries were up and moving. Sarge nodded as he passed them. Each of them had a hard look about them, trying to steel their nerves for what lay ahead.

A little after 0500, Ted and Mike found Sarge leaning on the hood of the Hummer he would be riding in. They joined him and stood together as the camp began to come alive, silently observing the activity in front of them. The air was heavy with morning dew, giving everything a clammy feel. By 0530 the camp was fully awake, with people moving all over. Wives were hugging their husbands, who were about to leave on the mission, and in a few cases, those roles were reversed.

At 0600, Sarge stood at the door of his Hummer, looking back along the column. It wasn't very long—eight large trucks and five Hummers—but it looked impressive enough. Diesel exhaust hung low around the line of vehicles. With everyone loaded, it was time to move out. Mike, Ian, Jamie, and Perez were in the lead Hummer, while Sarge, Sheffield, and Ted were in the number two truck. After performing a quick radio check with each truck, they started to move out.

Five miles of dirt roads took them from the highland pines down into low oak hammocks and swamp lands before reaching the paved road. The route had been memorized by every member of the unit: one left turn and one right turn, then the camp would be on the left several miles down the road. Sarge watched the scenery as it passed by, smiling to himself. Unlike many of the others, he was at ease and not even thinking of what lay ahead.

At Highway 19, they turned right for the last leg of the ride.

"You ready, Captain?" Sarge asked Sheffield.

"Ready as I'll ever be."

"Just remember, for the purposes of this mission, we're on the same side as they are. Don't look at them as the opposition—at least not yet."

Sheffield nodded and pulled out the drawing the guys had made of the camp. It was going to be one of the best pieces of evidence they'd offer to Mr. Tabor to prove their "allegiance." Despite his efforts to remain calm, Sheffield's stomach was in knots. He wasn't certain this was going to work, and they'd be inside the perimeter of the camp with nowhere to maneuver if it didn't.

As they approached the sign that read NAVAL BOMBING RANGE OCALA, Sarge slipped his Kevlar helmet on. This too was part of the ruse—they had to look the part of an army unit, and his old ratty 101st Airborne hat wasn't exactly regulation.

"All right, Ian, nice and slow till you see their gate," Sarge said into his mic.

Ian turned onto the access road to the range, slowing down so those behind him could catch up. As they eased down the road, the burned-out bus came into view.

"That your doing?" Sarge shouted up to Ted, who was manning the SAW in the turret.

Ted smiled and nodded back. Sarge shook his head but couldn't help but smile. Shortly after the gate came into view, three men in front of the bunker became visible.

Sarge looked at Sheffield and clapped his hands. "It's game time! You ready?"

Looking quite the opposite, he nodded.

They halted the trucks and Sheffield, Livingston, Sarge, and Ted all got out and approached the now six men gathered at the bunker. They were carrying on a lively conversation amongst themselves. Ted kept a close eye on them as they were all armed, though none of them attempted to raise a weapon. In the lead Hummer, Mike kept the SAW pointed in their general direction, though not directly at them as he didn't want to instill fear. Upon reaching the men, Sarge waited for Sheffield to speak first. It was important that the ranking officer be the first to say anything.

Sheffield nodded at the men, who simply stared back. "Gentlemen, I'm Captain Sheffield. I need to talk to your CO, Tabor."

The six men looked at one another, unsure of how to respond. They had clearly never been told what to do if the military rolled up and started talking. In fact, the only thing they'd been told of the army was that they would attack—this soft approach completely threw them.

Sarge, being the diplomat he was, was growing impatient with their bewildered silence.

"Get on the horn to your CO now, dammit! It wasn't a fucking request!" Sarge shouted. The sudden outburst startled the men, causing some of them to visibly jump. Two of them quickly disappeared into the bunker.

Tabor was at his desk going through the reams of paperwork piled on it. Even after the world ended, paperwork continued.

"Main gate to Alpha One."

Tabor looked at the radio. *Why in the hell are they calling me?* He picked up the handset on his desk and punched a couple of buttons. "Ed, see what those idiots at the gate want, would ya?" Then he picked up the mic to his radio. "Stand by."

"Sure thing," Ed said. He left his office and climbed on an ATV and headed for the gate. As the gate came into view, he was shocked at what he saw: a line of Hummers and trucks and several men standing at the gate in army uniforms.

He quickly dismounted and stepped up to the group. "What's going on?" he asked.

"You Tabor?" Sheffield asked.

"No, I'm his deputy commander, Ed Mooreland."

Sheffield took a step forward. "I'm Captain Sheffield. I need to speak with Tabor immediately."

Ed, just like the men at the gate, was unsure of how to respond. "Uh, what's this in reference to?"

Sheffield looked at the black-clad men beside Ed. "It's a private security matter of utmost urgency."

Ed looked around nervously. "Uh, all right, you guys follow me in. Just leave the rest of your people here."

Sheffield nodded and they got back in the Hummer. Ted was up in the turret and got a bird's-eye view of the camp as they drove through. They drew a number of looks from the surprised camp staff, who stopped and gawked at the passing truck.

Ted surveyed the camp as they passed through it, paying particular attention to the detainees. Groups of detainees were doing physical labor, everything from filling sandbags to erecting additional tents. The scene was always the same: black-clad men watching over them with guns at their side. *Hu, field boss*, Ted thought. As they passed through, the detainees glanced at the vehicle sideways, not rising from their toil. The DHS troopers, on the other hand, gawked, pointing and gesturing amongst themselves.

"Well, we're in," Livingston muttered.

"Yeah, went better than I thought," Sheffield said.

"Remember, Captain, just like we discussed: these guys are clueless for the most part. If we convince Tabor, the rest will fall in line," Sarge said.

"Right. Have you noticed all the people working?" Sheffield asked.

"Yeah, seems like everyone's busy," Livingston replied.

"Yeah, they're busy all right. Hard not to be when there's a man with a gun standing over you," Sarge remarked.

Sheffield looked out the window. "I noticed that every group has more than one guard standing over them."

"You think those folks are out there working like that by choice? Did you see the water jugs?" Sarge asked.

"And a cup tied to it. I'm sure they're having to ask for a drink of water. Probably gotta ask for permission to piss too," Sarge said.

"That just ain't right. Grown men having to ask for permission to take a piss," Livingston said.

"Or women." Sarge waved a hand at the window. "I've seen plenty women out there working as well."

"I understand now why this needs to be done. There is no liberty. What they're doing here is obviously a forced labor situation. I can't even imagine what the rest of their day-to-day is like," Sheffield said.

"Well, if all goes well, soon we'll find out," Sarge said.

The ATV stopped in front of a line of shipping containers converted into offices. Ed climbed off and waited as Sarge and his crew exited the Hummer. He looked at them, wanting to tell them to leave their weapons in the truck, but glanced up at Ted on the SAW and changed his mind.

Ed stepped up to an office and rapped on the door frame. "Hey, Chuck, you need to come out here."

Tabor looked up from the reports he was reading on his desk. "What is it, Ed? I'm busy."

"No, you really need to come to the conference room," Ed said, stepping aside so Tabor could see the men in ACU uniforms.

Tabor practically leapt from his chair and came around his desk.

"Captain Sheffield, this is Charles Tabor, our camp commander," Ed said.

"Mr. Tabor, good to meet you. You got somewhere we can talk in private?" Sheffield said as he offered his hand.

Tabor shook his hand, uncertain of what was going on. "Uh, sure, over here," he said, gesturing to the conference room, then looked at Ed with a "WTF" look. Ed shrugged, as he was just as confused by the appearance of the United States Army as Tabor was.

Sheffield glanced at Sarge, who nodded. They filed in and sat down.

"What can we do for you, Captain?" Tabor asked.

"We've got intel that indicates there are elements of your security force plotting to overthrow the camp. These elements may be aligned with guerrilla forces outside the camp." Sheffield delivered the comment exactly as they'd rehearsed.

Tabor and Ed were clearly shocked by the information and sat in silence.

"My security force, Captain?" Tabor finally said.

"Yes, sir," Sarge said as he unfolded the drawing of the

camp. "We captured some individuals and found this on them. Through interrogations, we learned of the plot, but we don't know how many of your people are involved in the plan." He slid the drawing across the table to Tabor.

Tabor picked it up and he and Ed examined it as Sarge continued, "As you can see, there are facilities noted there that could only come from someone with inside information."

Tabor looked at Ed, then laid the drawing on the table. "Captain, you will forgive me for being skeptical. But as you know there are some, how should I put it, *issues* between the armed forces and the DHS."

"I understand that, and I assure you, this is real. Some of us are still patriots. We're here to help you put this down before it gets out of hand. We're not sure if this is an attempt on just your camp or if it's part of a larger plan to take down other camps as well. That's why we need to identify the actors and interrogate them for additional information," Sheffield said.

Inwardly Sarge smiled. *Damn fine acting, Captain, damn fine.*

"Have you had any issues with any of your people lately?" Sarge asked, baiting them in to bringing up the three missing people currently being held back at the Guard camp.

Ed looked over at Tabor. "Might explain those missing personnel."

Sarge seized the moment. "You got missing people?"

"Yeah, we had three go missing recently. They were on the rear gate and just disappeared," Tabor said.

"That's not good. Were there any known issues with them?" Livingston asked.

"For the most part, no, though we had some behavioral issues with one of them, a woman," Ed said.

Sarge fought back a smile again. *I knew that bitch was trouble.*

"Then, as you can see, we're not here by accident," Sarge said.

"How big of a threat do you think this is?" Tabor asked.

"You've got several hundred civilians in here, and you've also got an armory full of weapons. We do not want those two things to mix. Let's just say that," Sheffield said.

Tabor let out a long breath. "All right, what do you propose we do?"

"I seriously doubt that there are too many of your people involved in this plot, as it would be hard to keep something like this a secret for long. But we can't take any chances until we sort out who is and who isn't a threat. I would suggest that you assemble your security people and have them turn in their weapons. Then we—you and my intel team—will interview them. As they are either cleared or identified as conspirators, they will be either detained or released to return to their duties," Sheffield said. This was the moment that would determine if the plan would succeed or not, and he could hardly keep from tapping his foot nervously.

Tabor sat back in his chair. "Who were these people you captured? Where were they caught?"

"As far as we know they are civilians. One claimed to have escaped from here. He's the one that had the map. They thought we would assist in their plan and gave the info up freely at first," Sarge said.

Tabor looked at Ed. "How many people have gotten out?"

Ed thought for a minute. "Six, not including the guards."

"How'd you bag these folks?" Tabor asked.

"Like I said, at first they approached us. Once they figured out we weren't who they thought we were, they clammed up. But the cat was outta the bag by then, and with a little encouragement, we were able to get more info out of them," Sarge said.

Ed smiled. "What sort of *encouragement*?"

"I believe the proper term is *enhanced interrogation techniques*," Livingston said.

Ed smiled and looked at Tabor. "They should meet Niigata." Tabor rolled his eyes.

"What's that now?" Sarge asked.

Tabor waved his hand dismissively. "Back to your prisoners, where are they now?"

"In a secure location for the moment," Sheffield said.

"Why didn't you bring them here? They could help point out who's involved."

"We thought about that, and will bring them in later. But if we paraded them through here now and the people involved saw them with us we'd lose the element of surprise, making this a hell of a lot harder," Sarge said.

"Did they have any ID on them?" Tabor asked.

Sarge laughed. "No, not like anyone carries a wallet these days."

"I'd like to ID the one who said he escaped from here."

"If you issue photo IDs to your detainees, when we bring him in you can go through your files and find out who he is. We might be able to connect him to some of the other conspirators that way," Sarge said.

Ed looked at Tabor. "We do issue photo IDs. That'd be easy enough to do. We'll know where he was housed and what details he was on. It might shed some light on the people in here who are in on it."

Tabor sat staring at the map. It was obvious he was conflicted. To help make his decision easier, Sarge decided to make another play.

"Mr. Tabor, part of the plot called for the torture and execution of the camp administration. Now I don't know how many people that is here, maybe it's just you and Ed, maybe more. But we take this kind of thing seriously in the armed forces and I suggest you do the same."

"Who's going to take care of security when we call everyone in? These people will take advantage of the situation if given half a chance," Ed said.

"We'll handle that. Our people will take over their positions and run your camp during the vetting process. As your people are cleared, they can return to their posts and our people will pull out. I don't think it will even be noticed by the majority of your detainees," Livingston said.

Ed looked at Tabor. "What are we going to tell them we're bringing them in for?"

Tabor was overwhelmed and shook his head. "I don't know."

"Why don't you tell them we're here to inventory weapons? Say we've got armorers with us and they will go through them and make sure they're all up to speed," Sarge said.

"That could work. That'd explain why they're turning in their weapons," Ed said.

"We really do have armorers, and they'll check out the weapons. We can also do an inventory for you to make sure everyone has the correct weapon too."

"That's a good idea. We've been meaning to do that, but it's been quite a trial to figure out how to do that without compromising the safety of the camp," Tabor said.

"Sounds like we're in agreement, then. Can my people come on up?" Sarge asked.

"Sure," Tabor said, then looked at Ed. "Go ahead and call the gate. Tell 'em to let them through."

"I'll go call my folks," Sarge said as he stood up.

As Sarge headed for the door, he was stopped by Ed. "Hey, First Sergeant, want some coffee?"

Sarge smiled. "Damn right I do! Let me make this call and I'll be right back."

Ed started to pour him a cup as Sarge stepped out. Ted looked over as Sarge came out. "What's the word?"

"It's showtime," Sarge said. "Call 'em in, Teddy."

"Roger that," Ted said as he climbed into the turret.

"I want the last Hummer to stay at the gate. Let me know when they get here. Soon as that's done, you and Mikey get over to their comm shack and shut it down," Sarge said quietly as he spun around and headed back inside. Ted gave him a thumbs-up and Sarge headed back in, eager for that cup of coffee.

It was still dark when Aric snuck out to the fence behind the detention facility. He looked around to make sure no one saw him and pulled the small bolt cutters out of his pocket. His plan was to cut the fence at one of the poles, then cut the ties holding the top to the crossbar all the way across to the next pole. He hoped that by loosening the foundations, the Hummer could break through the fence. He snipped the first wire, and it gave with a snap loud enough to wake the dead. He froze where he was and checked around again. At this rate, it was going to take forever.

The sun was already above the horizon as he finished the second fence. He'd worked up quite a sweat and as he walked back toward the motor pool, a chill crept into him. He quickly put the bolt cutters back and was on his way to his room when someone tapped him on the shoulder.

"Hey, Vonasek, grab your weapons and go to the mess hall. They're doing an inventory today. Tell everyone you see. I've got to go get Cortez and what's-his-name from the detention center then wake up last night's shift." It was Nelson, his supervisor.

Hearing Cortez's name, he reacted quickly. "You get the rest of the guys up. I'll get Cortez for you."

Nelson gave him a thumbs-up. "Thanks."

It was now or never. With everyone lining up for the inventory, it was the perfect opportunity to enact the plan. He ran into his room and grabbed the pack that was sitting on his bunk and headed back to the motor pool. The place was deserted. He tossed his pack into the truck and went to the locker and began moving supplies. He took all the MREs that were there, as well as a SAW and several cans of ammo. Ammo for the carbine came next, then the first aid bag, sleeping bags, and a small tent.

He went around to the rest of the trucks and pulled the fuel cans off them, tossing them into the back of his truck. The Hummer was filling up fast. Deciding he had enough, he got behind the wheel of the truck, pulled the red tag off the dashboard, and started it, heading for the kitchen.

He saw Kay inside when he stuck his head through the door. Taking a quick look around to make sure no one was there, he called out, "Kay!" in a loud whisper. When she looked over, he said, "It's time." Kay nodded and picked up a small blue duffel bag, quickly making her way outside and into the passenger side of the truck. Neither of them said anything as Aric steered the truck toward the detention center.

"Hop out here. If this doesn't work, I don't want you sitting in this thing if other people show up. Just watch the door. I'll come out and wave when we're ready."

Kay nodded and got out of the truck. "Good luck, hon," she whispered.

Fred didn't pay any attention when the door to the cell block opened. She didn't even take much notice when her cell door opened. It was what *didn't* happen that caught her attention—no jingling keys, no blinding light. Fred opened her eyes and could make out two men standing in the door. One of the men stepped in and grabbed her arm, pulling her to her feet. He led her out of the cell and up to the small desk that sat in the front of the block. The other man threw something at her. She made no attempt to catch it, letting it hit her and fall to the floor. Looking down she saw it was clothes—her clothes. The ones she had on when she arrived at the camp.

"Put 'em on. No sense in ruining our stuff," one of them said.

Fred looked around for a place to change. "Don't worry about that, just do it here," the man said.

Fred had accepted her fate. There was nothing she could do at this point, so the request had little effect on her. She took off the smock and slipped the pants off. She was wearing the underwear and bra issued by the camp and knelt down to pick up her clothes.

"No, no, sweetheart, all of it," the man said.

It was then she knew what would happen next. A tear began to roll down her cheek as she pulled the bra over her head.

"Damn, they look better without anything covering them up," one of them said.

As Fred pulled the underwear off one of the men stepped forward, and as they slipped off her foot he grabbed her arm.

"No sense in letting something that looks this good go to waste."

"Put her on the desk," the other man said as he unbuckled his belt.

Thoughts of what happened to Jess flooded through Fred's mind. *This is it, this is how it's going to end, this can't be happening, this can't be real.* As one of the men pushed her toward the desk, her mind began to race. *How can I get out of here?*

Chapter 18

I took the first watch after dinner and brought my RWS air rifle out with me, hoping to see a rabbit. I remember when I was young my dad, uncle, and I would hunt them at night with a light. This wasn't sport hunting—we needed it. There were times those rabbits made a difference. So tonight, I'd use the same tactic to try and bag a bunny.

I kept the fire low and sat on the top of the picnic table, periodically shining my light around the open area between the cabins and the river. At about ten, I saw the first set of eyes. Raising the rifle while holding the light on it, I looked through the scope. I could clearly see it and centered the crosshairs on one of the eyes and pulled the trigger. The rabbit flipped and hit the ground.

There are two kinds of rabbits in Florida, cottontail, which I had gotten here, and what we call swamp rabbits. Taking this cottontail back over to the table, I quickly skinned it out and gutted it, saving the entrails for the dogs and tossing the hide into the woods.

With one in the bag, I was now motivated to find another and started actively looking. Slipping around the perimeter of the camp, I kept close watch on the area where the clearing met the brush. By midnight, I'd bagged two more and decided I'd had enough. I went over and woke up Danny to take his turn and told him about the rabbits.

"Nice, man," Danny said looking at the three skinned bunnies lying on the table.

"Yeah, they'll be good for breakfast," I said.

"Sure will. Go on, dude, I've got this."

I slapped him on the back and headed for my cabin. I managed to find my way in without a light and was quickly in my bag. Sleep came almost instantly, a heavy dreamless sleep. In the Before I often joked about this kind of sleep, calling it the darted-rhino sleep. I got it from one of those wildlife shows where they were darting white rhinos in Africa. Seeing how they acted as the drug took hold, I remembered thinking, *I've felt like that before.* It became a running joke in my family.

What seemed like moments later, I was awakened by little feet dancing around my sleeping bag. "Wake up, rhino!" Little Bit said, giggling. "Breakfast is ready!"

I headed out for breakfast and joined the others. As we ate the rabbits, I was deep in thought, remembering what Chase had said about the lemon tree. It would be great to have citrus, but I didn't know of any lemon trees around here. Everyone thinks Florida is covered in citrus trees, but that's not the case. The area we lived in was in the northern limit of their range. Suddenly, something hit me.

"There's a tangerine tree upriver," I said, out of nowhere.

Everyone stopped eating and stared at me.

Looking at Danny, I said, "Remember that tangerine tree we found on the opposite side of the river up there?"

Danny chewed his grits for a moment. "Oh yeah! Had those sour tangerines."

"Yeah, that's the one. I want to go find it today. I totally forgot about it."

"Sounds good to me," Danny said, then, looking around the table, added, "Anyone else want to go?"

"What are we going to do with sour tangerines?" Jeff asked.

"Don't knock it, we could use the vitamins," I said.

"We could make jelly," Bobbie said.

"I know how to make marmalade," Thad said.

Everyone now looked at Thad.

"You are just full of surprises," Mel said.

Thad smiled. "I know a thing or two."

"I want some marblade," Little Bit said, doing her best to say the word. "Can I go with you, Daddy?"

"Sure, I don't mind, we're going to take a canoe."

"I'm not going in any canoe. I'll take a kayak," Mel said.

"Yeah, I wouldn't want you in one either, it's still too cold to go swimming," I said with a laugh. Mel was famous for her ability to turn over a canoe. I couldn't even count the number of times she's turned one over at the launch, before we'd even begun a trip.

"I'll kayak too," Bobbie said.

"Aw, I wanted to take a kayak," Taylor said.

"Sorry, kid, you're riding with us," I told her, then looked at Lee Ann. "You want to go?"

She was picking at her grits with a spoon and barely looked up. To my surprise, this time she actually answered me. "No, I'll stay here." Mel shot me a look, but I shrugged. We couldn't force her to go.

Noticing there was a bit of tension in the air, Jeff jumped in. "I'll stay here, got a couple of things I want to work on today. Plus, you know how I am with canoes," he said, getting a chuckle from us.

"I'll stay too. I'm going to get some more swamp cabbage for the pigs. I want to make sure all them little ones will make it," Thad said.

"Well, when are we going?" Bobbie asked.

"As soon as I finish this rabbit," I said.

"Yeah, it's good, nice job," Thad said, holding up a leg.

"I haven't had rabbit in a long time. I don't remember it being this good," Bobbie said.

"Hunger has a way of changing your perspective on food, doesn't it? We need to keep our eyes open for them from now on," I said.

"Absolutely," Danny said as he sucked on a bone.

After we finished up, those who were going on the tangerine hunt headed for the boats. Mel and Bobbie got in the kayaks while Danny, Taylor, Little Bit, and I got in the canoe. I took the bow seat and Danny got in the stern.

The morning was cool and the water like glass. I watched the eel grass sway in the current as we passed over it. Red-eared slider turtles sunned themselves on downed trees, looking comical with their feet held up in the air.

Mel and Bobbie were on the opposite side of the river, gliding past the low-hanging oaks on that side. It brought a smile to my face. It seemed just like a normal paddle down the river. Little Bit was hanging over the side, grabbing at the passing lilies. She latched on to something and I felt the boat tug.

"Hey, let go—don't do that, or you'll get pulled out of the boat," I warned.

There was a little pop and she pulled a slender green stem into the boat. "Look, Dad."

She was holding a seed head of the yellow pond lily. It was a small bell-shaped pod containing a number of seeds. I was surprised to see it this early in the season.

"Can we take them back and pop them?" Little Bit asked.

I smiled. That was something we did for fun in the Before. We'd strip the flesh off and separate the seeds and put them in a hot skillet. They'd pop, and though they weren't as good as popcorn, they had an interesting likeness to them.

"Keep your eyes open for more," I told her. She smiled and looked back to the river for the next one.

We maneuvered the canoe over to the edge of the river to get into a patch of lilies. Feeling the canoe tip, I looked back to see Danny pulling something out of the water. He held up a large apple snail. "Check it out."

"Oh, let me have it!" Little Bit said, holding her hand out.

I looked over into the water. "See any more?"

"Yeah, I do."

"Hey, me too. Let's collect them," I said.

We spent the next fifteen or so minutes collecting snails. Little Bit piled them all in the bottom of the boat. Even Taylor helped, plucking several from the weeds in the slow-moving water.

"What are you going to do with these?" Taylor asked.

"Eat 'em," I said.

"Eew, I'm not going to," Little Bit said.

"Are they good?" Taylor asked.

"I don't know, never had them, but I know they're edible. We'll have to try them out," I said.

"We're getting all kinds of stuff!" Little Bit exclaimed, holding a handful of snails and seed pods.

"Let's see what else we can find," I said as I pushed the bow of the boat out into the current.

Mel and Bobbie were ahead of us, in the middle of the river, where it opened up and the current slowed. They were sitting there talking, waiting on us. As we glided up, Mel pointed toward the trees.

"Is that your tangerine tree?" she asked.

We moved the boat toward them. From there, we could see the top of the tree, its orange fruits shining in the sun.

"Yep, that's it. It's late in the season for them, but let's go see what they look like," I said as we paddled.

It was a bit of an event getting everyone out of their boats. We had to pull the kayaks up onto the bank so the girls could get out of them without tipping. Once everyone was on dry land, we checked out the tree. The only fruit still on it was high up in the top. Naturally, Little Bit volunteered to climb up.

"No, you stay here. Dad will figure something out," Mel said.

I looked at her. "Let her climb it—it's a tree! She's a kid. That's what kids do."

While not thrilled with the idea, she relented and Danny helped Ashley into the tree. Of course, as soon as she was in it, she got scared.

"Go on up and pick some, kiddo," I said.

"I can't, Daddy! Can I come down?" she asked, panicked.

"Yeah, come on," I said as I reached for her and set her on the ground.

"Now what? How are you going to get them down?" Bobbie asked.

"Let's see what we can find," Danny said, scanning the woods.

I moved off the shoreline to look as well. There was a decent trail and I started walking down it, looking for something long to reach up into the top of the tree.

"Hey, Morg," Danny called.

I walked back down the trail toward him, and saw him waving a long limb. As I got closer, he held out a handful of tangerine peels.

"How was it?" I asked.

"Don't know because I didn't eat any. I found these peels on the ground."

"Hmm, that may not be a good sign."

"Yeah, well, look at this," he said as he turned and started to walk. He stopped at a wide portion of the trail that was littered with an assortment of trash.

"Looks like someone's been camping here," I said.

"Yeah, and I found this." He handed me a spent shotgun shell.

"Someone must be moving up and down this side of the river. Could be our friends who visited the other day," I said.

"Looks that way. Let's go get some fruit and get out of here."

"All right, don't say anything to the girls right now. They'll probably get scared and want to leave. You go after the fruit and I'll keep an eye out," I said.

Little Bit and Taylor occupied their time collecting more snails in the slack currents by the bank. Mel and Bobbie were sitting in the sun, relaxing and chatting. It almost felt like normal times, for a moment. Meanwhile, Danny went to work with the limb he found. It was a comedy of errors of sorts, watching him try to piñata tangerines out of the tree, but after a bit he got the hang of it and actually managed to get quite a few to fall. I picked up one. It was on the dry side, but they weren't as sour as I remembered. Overall, I'd call it a success.

Thad pulled the axe out of the splitting stump, putting it over his shoulder. Jeff followed behind him as they headed into the woods in search of another swamp cabbage. Jeff was plodding along behind Thad when Thad stopped short, causing Jeff to walk into him. He was just about to go off on him when he looked out past Thad to see a doe standing not twenty yards away. Jeff knelt down and took aim with his AK.

Wonder if I can hit her? he thought as he squeezed the trigger, causing Thad to jump. The doe jumped as well and ran off.

"Shit, guess I missed her."

"I was hoping you'd take a shot, but a little warning next time might be nice. You scared the hell out of me. Let's go take a look. Maybe you hit her."

They both searched the area, looking for blood or any other indication that she had been hit. Moving in the direction the doe ran, Jeff called out, "Over here."

Thad came over to see a thick, dark blood clot. "That's good. Let's see if we can follow the trail."

The trail wasn't hard to follow, and they soon found her lying under a palm tree. The round had entered her right shoulder and exited on the left side, taking a substantial piece of rib with it. Thad rolled the deer over, examining the wounds. "Good shot. For a full metal jacket round, it did a good job."

"I was wondering what it would do. I thought the wound would be a lot smaller."

Thad pointed at the missing section of rib. "Hitting that bone there really did a number. Let's take her back to the cabin and get her cleaned up."

They each grabbed a front leg and dragged her back to the cabin. Dropping her near the tree line, Thad went to get his knives. On his way back, he asked, "You ever dress a deer before?"

Jeff shook his head. "No, never was much of a hunter. I've been missing out. It's fun."

"Well, the real fun's about to start," Thad said as he lifted one of the front legs. "Hold that."

With Jeff holding the leg, Thad slit the belly and set about gutting the deer. He removed the organs, setting the heart and liver aside. Next, he made a cut behind the tendons on the rear legs and stuck a sharpened stick in both sides. He then tied a length of rope to it, and together, he and Jeff hoisted it up into a tree.

"It's a lot easier to work on it this way," Thad said as he hung it.

"I've seen pictures, you know, but it's really neat to see in person."

Thad smiled. "First time for everything." He went on to explain to Jeff how to skin the deer. He wanted to save the hide and talked about the process of removing it properly. Thad then discussed the quartering process, showing Jeff how to remove the backstrap and tenderloins.

"This here is some of the best meat on a deer," Thad said, holding up a tenderloin.

"I didn't even know that was there."

"You sure don't want to leave it behind. It's really good."

Once the deer was quartered, they moved over to the table and started to cut the meat from the bone, removing every usable piece of meat and dropping it into a clean bucket. When they were done, all that was left was a pile of bones and the spine. The dogs had sat patiently watching the process and were finally rewarded when Thad took an axe and cut the spine into three pieces, tossing one to each of the dogs.

"What about these bones?" Jeff asked.

"We'll save them. I'll boil some of them to make broth and I'll smoke some, for the dogs later."

Jeff looked around. "Damn, the only thing you threw away is the head."

"We can't afford to waste anything right now. Can you find something to cover the bucket of meat with? I'm going to go throw this to the hogs," Thad said as he picked up the bucket of guts.

Jeff nodded and headed for the cabin as Thad moved off toward the pigpen. When he got to the pen he went to turn off the solar hot wire, but it was already off. Curious, he rounded the corner with cautious steps. He was surprised to find Lee Ann sitting in the pen, holding a piglet on her lap. She held a pistol in her other hand, and was staring at it.

"Hey, girl, what'cha doing out here?"

She looked up, startled, and dropped the piglet, quickly raising the pistol toward Thad. "Don't come near me!"

Thad set the bucket down and raised his hands. "Whoa, whoa, I'm not coming any closer. I'm right here. What're you doing with that pistol?"

Lee Ann was shaking, still pointing the pistol. "You can't stop me! Leave me alone!"

"You're right, I can't stop you, but you can't make me leave either." Thad lowered his hands and slowly knelt down. "I'm gonna sit down here."

"No! Just leave. Leave me alone!"

"No, I'm not going to leave you alone. I can't stop you from doing whatever you're gonna do, but you're going to listen to me in the meantime," Thad said as he sat down.

Lee Ann kept the pistol on him, but said nothing. Tears ran down her face. For a long time, it was quiet, save for the sound of Lee Ann sniffling.

Thad cleared his throat. "I know you're upset, and I understand—"

Lee Ann cut him off. "How can you understand? What do you know?" She practically spit the words at him.

"Little girl, I know more than you can imagine. Your dad told me you were upset, that you think life as you knew it is gone." He paused for a moment. "You don't see any reason to keep going, do you?"

"Why should I? No one cares. Everything is gone forever."

"You think no one cares? You know how much your momma and daddy talk about you?"

She didn't say anything, so Thad continued. "You don't think I can relate? Let me tell you how I can, and how I do. Did you know I had a wife and young son?"

She didn't say anything but lowered the gun into her lap.

"You know why they aren't here with me?" Lee Ann slowly shook her head. "'Cause they're dead." Thad let that sink in for a minute. "They were killed by some government men. Some sick, sick men killed my beautiful wife and my son, my baby." Now tears began to roll down Thad's face. "I had to dig them out of the house. I found them together, holding on to one another. I had to dig a grave for them. I buried them like I found them: holding each other."

Thad paused to regain his composure as Lee Ann started to cry even harder.

"After that happened, I was thinking the same thing that you are now: that my life was over, that there was no sense in going on. I wanted to end it." Thad paused again.

After a long silence, Lee Ann wiped her nose and asked in a quiet voice, "Why didn't you?"

"Because of them. Because I knew deep down that they wouldn't want me to. I live for them even though they are dead. You think your life is over, but it's just the silly little things from the Before you're thinking of—cell phones, the Internet. You're right, those things are not worth living for." The last part got her attention, and she looked up at Thad. "It's your momma and daddy, your sisters—that's what you have to live for. You have any idea what your daddy went through to get home? I mean, really?"

Lee Ann gave a little shrug. Thad continued, "You know he almost died, that he was shot in the head?" She looked stunned. "There was nothing in this world that could've kept your daddy from getting back to you. He talked about you girls and your momma. He loves you more than you know."

She started to sob. "But it's so different now. I want to go to school, I want my friends back."

"And it will all come back. The world didn't end, it"—Thad looked for the right words—"it's just on pause. Everything is still here. It'll get fixed."

Wiping her nose again, she replied, "That's what Dad says."

"Of course he does, and he's right. Now think about it for a minute: you do what you're thinking about doing and you'll never see it. How do you think your parents would feel if you did this? How do you think it would affect them? What about your sisters? You really think no one would care, no one would miss you?" Thad paused again, letting the words sink in, then added, "I know I would." Lee Ann looked up at him. "Little Tony and Anita are gone, but I'm here with you and your family now. And you, all of you, *are* my family now."

Lee Ann laid the pistol on the ground and picked at the grass. "Tony and Anita . . . those were their names?" she asked, looking up. Thad nodded.

They sat quietly for some time, neither one saying anything. Thad would sit there all day if it came to it—he was determined to get her back to the cabins safely. After some more time Lee Ann asked, "Do you really think it will all come back?"

"I do."

She reached and picked up one of the piglets that had finished nursing. It squealed in complaint, causing the momma pig to look up. Lee Ann sighed. "I just want to go home."

"And you will be able to soon. There's things happening right now that will probably let you go home. I know your mom and dad want to take you back to your old neighborhood when things settle down."

She rubbed the piglet for a minute. "They're going to be mad at me."

"Baby girl, the last thing they are going to be is mad." Thad looked at her intensely. "But I'll make you a promise." Lee Ann looked up. "This will be our secret. You get to feeling better, don't try this foolishness again, and I won't say nuthin'."

Again they sat in silence, then the tears returned to trace paths down her cheeks. "I don't want to do it, Thad. I want to live. I just get so sad."

"You need to stop sittin' around thinking about it. There's lots to do. Get involved! That's why I always like to keep busy . . . it keeps the sadness away." He smiled.

Setting the piglet down, Lee Ann sat up straight and wiped her face. She let out a loud breath and stood up. Thad rose as well. Lee Ann looked at the pistol, then at Thad. "You want me to leave it here?"

"No, let me have it."

She bent over and picked up the pistol. When he took it, he grabbed her hand in his.

"Thank you, Lee Ann. You're savin' me too," he said and smiled. Lee Ann began to cry again and wrapped her arms around his big waist. Thad bent down a bit and picked her up, giving her a hug.

"If you ever need to talk to someone, I'm here. You come to me anytime," Thad said as he set her down.

For the first time in a long time, Lee Ann smiled. She reached out and took his hand. "Thanks, Thad."

They walked back to the cabins like that, hand in hand.

Chapter 19

Sheffield and Livingston milled about the command center, coffee cups in hand. Sarge was getting his people into place, relieving the DHS personnel. Tabor and his deputy were outside giving orders to their people to assemble. After he was done assigning his men and had checked the situation with Tabor's team, Sarge hopped in the Hummer and drove up to the gate, trying not to spill his coffee. As he pulled up to it, a couple of the Guardsmen waved at him.

"Everything all right?" Sarge called out.

One of the Guardsmen gave him a thumbs-up. Satisfied that was taken care of, he turned back toward the camp to check on Ted and Mike.

He found them sitting inside the camp's comm shack. Ted had a headset on, listening to the traffic on the DHS net. Ian was standing outside, making sure no one tried to come in.

"Where are the DHS boys?" Sarge asked.

"We sent them to get their weapons," Mike said.

"They didn't get anything out, did they?"

Ted shook his head. "Not that we know of. Hell, they were relieved for the help. Gave us their call sign and everything. They bought it. I'm more worried about the civilians. They know something is up, and some of them are causing some trouble."

"What kind of trouble?"

Ted tossed a handheld radio to Sarge. "Listen in. They're asking questions and some of the DHS boys are gettin' rough with 'em."

Sarge nodded. "I will, Mike. You stay here. Ted, you come with me."

Sarge and Ted left in the Hummer, leaving Mike and Ian to watch the store.

They rode to one of the mess halls, where the security personnel were being grouped. Several of the Guardsmen were playing the part of armorers, taking in the weapons that were being checked against an equipment list by one of the DHS supervisors. After the weapons were turned in, they were taken to an empty tent to be disassembled, out of the view of the DHS crew. What they were really doing was removing the firing pins from the weapons to render them all inoperable. Jamie, Doc, and Perez were at the head of the line, taking the weapons in.

Sarge dropped Ted off there, instructing him to call him on their secure radio when all had been disarmed. He then headed back to the command center. Sheffield and Livingston were sitting at a conference table with Tabor and Ed.

When Sarge came through the door, Sheffield asked, "How's it going, First Sergeant?"

Sarge smiled. "Good, good, they've almost got all your people together." Then he looked at Tabor. "Who do you have that you trust to do the interviews?"

Tabor looked at Ed and asked, "What do you think?"

Ed rubbed his temples and replied, "Right now the only people I trust are sitting in this room."

Tabor and Ed didn't see the look Sheffield and Livingston

shared. Sarge smiled to himself. "Well, we don't know your people, but I've got a couple of intel folks who will help you two."

Tabor nodded. "I appreciate it. We'll take any help you can offer."

"I'll get them rounded up. As soon as your folks are disarmed we'll start bringing in a few at a time. Let them wait out there and you can talk to them one at a time."

"Who's going to handle detentions?" Ed asked.

"I'll have a couple of my guys here for security," Livingston said. He was really starting to warm up to the part he was playing.

"What do y'all do with the detainees brought in here?" Sarge asked.

"We have first contact with refugees. We bring them in and process them into the system, then they are moved on to other facilities based on their skills and the needs of those facilities," Tabor said.

"We also sort out those who may pose a problem," Ed added.

Sarge cocked his head to the side. "What do you mean?"

"You know, the sort who resist going along with the program," Tabor said.

"One of our primary missions is to identify those that are deemed a threat to the resurrection of the state. Many of these are the old survivalist types: Constitutionalists, libertarians, gun owners, anarchists, basically anyone that would resist the power of the federal government," Ed said.

"We have a country to rebuild. Everyone needs to be on the same page," Tabor said.

Sheffield and Livingston sat stunned from what they heard. These types of things had been rumored, but to hear it from the mouths of those tasked with doing it was something else entirely.

"Makes sense to me," Sarge said as he sipped his coffee.

"Glad we're on the same page. Most people have a hard time hearing that, but it's necessary if we're to bring this country back."

Ted's voice crackled in Sarge's ear telling him that all the security people were now contained in the mess hall. Sarge replied with a terse "Roger that," and stood up. "It looks like all of your people are in place. I'm going to go over and check on the detention facility so when we get these rogues identified, we can move them there."

Tabor nodded. "We only have two people on staff at detention. There are four prisoners in there right now," Ed said, then looked at Tabor. "That reminds me. We have that execution scheduled for this afternoon."

"Execution?" Sheffield asked.

"Yeah, we have three women in there who worked together to poison one of our people. One of them claimed he raped her, but instead of reporting it to us, they killed him. Since he isn't around to ask, we have to go on what we know: the three of them killed him," Tabor said.

"Plus, it's a pretty good message to the rest of the CIs here," Ed said.

"CI, what's that?" Sheffield asked.

"Civilian internees," Sarge said.

Tabor and Ed both looked up. "You been through training?" Tabor asked.

"Yes, I have. I know FM 3-39.40. Before my first deployment to Iraq, my command sent me. It was interesting," Sarge said with a smile.

"We sure could use someone with some experience like yours. You'd be a big help around here," Tabor said.

"We'll have to see what our mission is after this one is done," Sarge said.

"Well, you're welcome here, with open arms," Ed said with a smile.

Sarge smiled back. "I'll keep it in mind." He jumped in the Hummer and headed over to pick up Ted so they could see these prisoners.

.

Aric stopped with his hand on the door to the detention center and took a deep breath. He'd put on his body armor, just to be prepared, and run his head through the plan once more. But he could never have prepared himself for the scene he was met with when he opened the door. He threw the door open to see a bare ass, the owner of which was bent over, pulling his pants down. Two slender naked legs were on either side of him.

"Aric, shut the door, man!" Cortez shouted. He was holding a woman by the arms. It took Aric a moment to recognize who it was. Fred looked back at him with pleading eyes. Aric stepped forward, letting the door shut. In a flash, he drew his Glock and shot Hamner in the side of the head. He dropped like a stone.

"What the fuck!" Cortez shouted, letting go of Fred.

Fred jumped from the desk and grabbed a chair sitting in front of it, raising it quickly and smashing it over Cortez's head. The blow knocked him to the ground as the chair shattered. Still naked, Fred dropped on top of him and started beating his head in with a chair leg. Aric stood and watched. He'd wanted to do just what she was doing now, but he wasn't about to try and stop her.

The entire time she shouted unintelligibly, swinging the chair leg again and again. When it was obvious Cortez was dead, Aric finally moved to pull her off, grabbing her under her arms and dragging her away from him. She fought him, clawing and kicking at the body.

When Aric finally managed to pull her off, she collapsed into sobs. Covered in blood, she went limp in his arms and cried. Aric looked around for something to clean her off with and picked up the smock she'd been wearing. He wiped blood from her face and neck as tears rolled down her face. Aric wanted to say something but didn't have the words.

After cleaning her off, Fred pushed her hair from her face and got dressed. She looked at Aric. "Quick, let's find the keys so we can let the rest out."

"Are you all right?"

Fred was in shock, but functional for the moment. "Yeah, let's find those keys," she said, grabbing his hand. Fred inched forward, her body obviously in pain. "Keys, can we find the keys?"

"Fred! Fred, what's going on?" Jess shouted.

"I'm coming to get you, hang on!!"

Aric ran toward the door and flipped the light switch. Fred let out a cry.

"My eyes, oh my God! The light hurts, turn it off, turn it off!" Fred cried.

Aric flipped the lights off then fumbled though his pockets for his flashlight. Flashlight in hand, he ran back to Fred. "Are you all right?"

Fred was hunched over. "The light hurts so bad." Tears were running down her face.

"I'm so sorry, Fred, I'm sorry, I didn't even think about that," Aric said.

Fred wiped her face. "Let's get them out."

"What happened to the guards?" Calvin hollered, clutching his ribs in pain.

"They're dead," Fred said.

Calvin, Shane, and Jess all started to ask questions, frantically pleading for Aric and Fred to get them out, quickly. Shane and Jess were both at their doors, the thought of getting out almost too much to take. Aric found the keys on Cortez's belt and removed them. Fred quickly took them and the small flashlight and ran to Jess's cell, freeing her. Jess jumped out and wrapped Fred in a bear hug, eyes closed. She couldn't look in the direction of the entry—the light streaming through the open door burned her eyes.

"Come on, let's check on Mary," Fred said as she pulled away.

They ran to the last cell and opened the door. Mary was lying on the floor, motionless. They fell to their knees and turned her over, she didn't respond.

"Is she dead?" Fred asked.

Jess felt for a pulse. "She has a pulse. Let's get her out of here."

"Aric, come help us!" Fred called out.

"Let me out of this damn cell!" Shane screamed, banging on the door.

Aric ran into the cell and picked up the limp Mary, carrying her out to the desk, where there was only a small amount of light. After setting her down, he took the keys and went to the door. Sticking his head out, he saw Kay and waved at her to come. Ducking back in, Aric went to the cell where Shane was still shouting and kicking the door.

When the door swung open, Shane wasn't expecting what he saw. In the faint light coming through the entry door stood a DHS member in full uniform. . . . He froze, unsure of what to do next.

"It's all right, man, come on out," Aric said.

Shane stuck his head out of his cell and looked toward the entry, where he saw Jess and Fred kneeling over Mary. Taking a second glance at Aric, he slid out between him and the door, pressing himself flat so they didn't touch.

Shane pointed to Calvin's cell. "Open that one and help me get him out."

Aric quickly opened the door and Shane hobbled in, kneeling down beside his dad.

"Hey, old dude, how are you?"

"If they'd broken one more, it'd be just like I like it," Calvin said, forcing a smile as Shane and Aric helped him up.

"Can you move?"

"Depends, are we getting the hell out of here?"

Shane shook his head. "I don't know, come on." He helped his father to his feet and out of the cell. They stepped out into the corridor as Aric ran back to where the girls were.

Down the hall, Kay came through the door and immediately stopped. Before her were the bodies of Cortez and Hamner. Jess and Fred were kneeling beside Mary. Kay ran toward them and dropped to her knees, wrapping her arms around Jess.

"Oh, I'm so glad to see you girls!" she cried into Jess's hair.

Jess was surprised by the sudden appearance of Kay. "What are you doing here?" She looked at Aric. "And what is he doing here? What the hell is going on?"

Fred looked at Jess. "I told you he was a good guy."

"He's getting you out. We're gonna make a run for it," Kay said.

Jess and Fred both looked at her, but neither said anything.

Fred turned back to Mary and gently slapped the side of her face. "Mary, wake up, wake up, it's okay now, wake up."

"What's wrong with her?" Kay asked.

"It wasn't easy in here. We were kept in the dark the whole time. . . . They would shine bright lights in our faces and play music really loud for a long time," Jess said, sounding frantic.

"Oh," was all she could say in reply. She then quickly looked at Aric, "We need to get out of here. Now."

Sarge drove across the camp keeping an eye out for anyone in a DHS uniform. All he saw were Guardsmen in ACU digital, which was reassuring.

"These DHS idiots are out of their fucking minds," Sarge said.

Ted had his arm propped on the edge of the door. "Yeah, how so?"

Sarge looked over. "What they're doing here is fucking nuts. They're sorting people and using them for labor, and they also have categories of people they are segregating, basically saying they are undesirables."

Ted looked over with raised eyebrows. "Really? That's kind of crazy. What are they doing with them?"

As Sarge pulled up in front of the detention center, he shut the truck down. "I don't know, but I intend to find out."

Ted looked over as he opened his door. "Good idea. There's something suspicious going on here."

They walked to the door, Sarge in the lead. He stopped and asked, "You remember those speeches the president made before the election, about transforming the country?"

"You think it has something to do with the Oval Office?

He can't be reelected, though, so why do this, if he's the one behind it?"

"Maybe he likes the furniture in the White House and doesn't want to leave," Sarge said as he grabbed the doorknob.

What lay behind the door was totally confusing. Two cold bodies lay on the floor, one of which had its pants around its ankles. There were four women off to one side, one lying on the ground with the other three kneeling beside her. Sarge took the scene in in an instant, he also saw the other man in a DHS uniform, staring at Sarge with a look akin to someone who just saw an alien or Sasquatch.

"What the fuck is going on in here?" Sarge said in a tone only an army first sergeant could muster.

Every face swiveled toward him. Aric was petrified. Thinking he was caught in the act of killing two men, he quickly drew his pistol. Sarge saw the movement, but action is always faster than reaction. Jess caught the movement out of the corner of her eye and knew immediately what was about to happen. She started to rise and screamed, "No!"

Aric's pistol cracked, at the same instant, Sarge grunted and fell to the ground. Ted grabbed Sarge's shoulder and pulled him back out the door. At the same moment, he raised his carbine and flipping the selector switch to full auto.

Fred screeched, "Don't shoot," but it was too late. Ted fired a burst and Aric crumpled and collapsed. Ted stepped over the old man, gripping the fore grip of the rifle and moving quickly toward the downed man in the black uniform. Then something he hadn't expected happened.

"Ted! Ted! Don't shoot! Stop, stop!"

At the mention of his name, Ted swiveled around. It was then he realized who had called his name: Jess.

"Don't shoot him, Ted. He let us out. Don't shoot!" Jess shouted again.

Ted lowered the weapon. "Jess?"

"Yeah, it's me," she said as tears again began to run down her face. Ted looked back at Sarge. He was lying just outside the door, stuffing a dressing into his wound and cussing a storm. Jess and Ted both moved toward him. Ted fell to his knees. "How bad is it?" he asked frantically as he ripped open Sarge's IFAK.

Jess dropped to her knees and wrapped her arms around Sarge's neck. "Oh my God, oh my God, I can't believe you're here," she began to cry. "I thought about you all the time, I prayed you'd come and here you are." She was crying uncontrollably.

Sarge patted her on the head. "It's all right, Annie—you don't think I could leave you here, do you?" Jess smiled at the mention of the nickname he had given her what seemed like years ago.

"Jess, move out of the way, please. I need to wrap this up." Ted looked at Sarge. "How do you feel?"

Sarge was leaning on one elbow, gritting his teeth. "Well, it ain't good." Sarge looked over at Aric. "What about that little shit, is he dead?"

Jess looked over to see Fred kneeling beside Aric. Fred was crying and trying to stop the bleeding from Aric's right bicep. He was having a difficult time breathing, heaving slowly. Three of the four rounds hit the ceramic plate in his armor, and the fourth created a through-and-through wound in his arm.

"Aric, hang on!" Fred cried. "We'll get help for you."

Sarge groaned, and then cursed. The bullet had struck him in his left side where his leg met his hip. Ted helped him get the dressing on it and the bleeding under control.

"We're going to have to get you to a doctor,"Ted said.

"No shit! Don't look like it hit the artery, though," Sarge replied.

"Hopefully. Let's get you up and into the Hummer."

"Don't worry about me, check on his ass." Sarge jutted his chin toward Aric. "Jess said he was helping them?"

"Yeah, she said he let them out."

"Check on him, see if he's going to make it." Sarge looked down at his bloodstained pants, "Dammit, these were my best pants."

Ted chuckled. "Then quit leaking all over them. You're lucky he didn't shoot your dick off."

Ted moved over to Aric. When he knelt down Aric looked at him, unsure of what was going on. Ted glanced into his eyes for a moment, then picked up the Glock and shoved it into a cargo pocket.

"Do you have an IFAK?"Ted asked as he started to cut the sleeve of Aric's blouse.

Aric was going into shock. All he could manage was to shake his head no. Going against all the rules of using your personal first aid kit, Ted pulled a dressing from his own, wrapping it around Aric's arm.

"He's going to be all right. Elevate his feet to prevent shock. The dressing will stop the bleeding."

In a surreal moment, Fred grabbed Aric's legs, lifted them up and swung them over on top of Cortez's body, setting them on the dead man's chest.

Calvin and Shane were standing there, stunned as the scene unfolded before them. Shane helped his father over to where Sarge was now leaning against the door.

"I'd like to say I'm glad to see you, but this turned into a hell of a cluster fuck," Calvin said, shielding his eyes with his hands.

Sarge looked up. "I agree, Calvin, our first meeting was a little better. You look like shit."

"You don't look so good yourself." He laughed.

"So what happened? They put the boot to you?"

Calvin rubbed his side. "You could say that. They grabbed us right after our meeting with you."

Sarge nodded. "I know, we saw it. I'm sorry we couldn't help."

"I damn sure wish you had, but I understand why you didn't. What are you doing here?"

Sarge smiled. "We just took control of the camp."

Calvin let out a small laugh, then grimaced and grabbed his side. "Well, no shit."

"No shit," Sarge replied with a smile.

"I didn't hear any shooting," Shane said.

"We hadn't fired a shot till now."

Ted then appeared and helped Sarge up out of the building and toward the truck. Calvin and Shane also made their way out of the detention center behind them, moving slowly and methodically.

Just as Sarge sat down in the passenger seat, two Hummers came racing toward them.

"Dammit," Ted groaned. "What are we going to do about this?"

Sarge shifted in the seat, trying to raise the wounded leg. "Let's see who shows up."

The two trucks slid to a stop. Livingston, Sheffield, Ed, and Tabor stepped out of the lead truck. A group of Guardsmen piled out of the second.

"What the hell happened up here?" Tabor said.

Sarge saw an opportunity and quickly started to seize it. "I think we found some of your insurgents."

Tabor looked at the open door, then back at Sarge. "Are you all right?"

"They put up a little bit of a fight, but we took them out."

Sheffield and Livingston stepped forward. "How bad is it?" Livingston asked.

"Does it look any kind of good to you?" Sarge asked, the pain beginning to make him even more cantankerous.

Livingston looked at Tabor. "You got a clinic here?"

"We do. Let's get you over there," Ed said. He did a double take, noticing Calvin and Shane. "Why are these prisoners out of their cells?" he demanded.

"We took them out to interrogate them. They aren't going anywhere. Can you go see if you recognize the asshole who shot me?" Sarge asked, gesturing toward the door.

Ed and Tabor nodded and moved toward the door, and Sarge quickly motioned for Ted. He waited until the other two men stepped through the door. "Put those two in one of them cells. Take some of these guys with you and lock their asses up."

Ted nodded and waved at the Guardsmen, who ran over and followed Ted toward the door.

When Ed and Tabor stepped through the door they stopped in their tracks, shocked by the scene. Two of their men were dead, another was wounded, and the prisoners were all out of their cells.

"What the *hell's* going on in here?" Tabor yelled.

Fred and Jess both let out an audible gasp.

"Kay, what the hell are you doing in here?" Tabor asked. The look on her face was one of complete fright.

Ed stepped past Tabor and got in Ted's face. "What in the hell is going on in here? Why are these prisoners out?"

The four Guardsmen rushed by and took Tabor to the

ground, pushing him inside a cell. Then, Ted planted a knee into Ed's crotch, dropping the man. Ted bent over and stripped the pistol from Ed's belt, tucking it into a cargo pocket. Curled in a fetal position, holding on to his manhood, Ed looked up at Ted and moaned, "What the fuck was that for?"

Ted grabbed him by his shirt and pulled him up, pushing him through the cell door. Inside, Tabor was trying to fight the four Guardsmen holding him down.

One of the Guardsmen stood up and brought the butt of his rifle down on Tabor's sternum several times. "Go to sleep!" the Guardsman shouted. The blows knocked the air from Tabor's lungs. He immediately went limp, exhaling a forceful groan.

With Tabor subdued, the soldiers dragged him to the cell Ed was in. Ed looked down at his boss, then back at Ted. "What the fuck is this about? Why in the hell are you doing this?"

"You bastards are getting what you deserve, or at least you probably will, later," Ted spat.

"What we deserve—what the hell have we done? We run a refugee camp, for Pete's sake!"

Ted pointed at Ed's face. "That's the first time you've used the term *refugee*. They've always been *prisoners* or *detainees*, but now that your ass is in the fucking sling you're singing a different tune. *That's* why you're in here," Ted said, slamming the door.

He made his way to the door, ordering the Guardsmen to help assist the ladies out of the center. In their weakened condition, it was difficult for them to walk normally.

Outside Sheffield and Livingston were standing beside the Hummer, talking to Sarge.

"Just got word they've got the DHS boys all herded together and the situation has been explained to them. The jig is officially up now," Livingston said.

"Good. They got them all? Any trouble?" Sarge asked.

"Yeah, there was a little trouble, but they didn't have to shoot anyone. Couple of them took a bit of a beating, though. Guess some of the guys were a little wound up."

"A little beatin's good for 'em. God knows they've been inflicting it on others," Sarge said.

"We need to do something with the civilians. They're scared, now that they know there are no guards around. We need to make an announcement to let them know what's happening," Livingston said.

"I agree, but we also need to maintain the camp as it currently is until we can determine who's who. Then we can make an announcement," Sarge said. He groaned loudly and clutched his hip.

Sheffield shook his head. "We need to get you over to the infirmary."

"Teddy!" Sarge yelled.

"Yeah?"

"Hurry up! I've only got so much of this red shit in me!"

"Go ahead and take him, Ted. We'll take care of this situation and post a couple of our guys for security to deal with these bodies," Livingston said.

Ted looked back at Jess and Fred, who were still with Aric, eyes averted. "He needs to go to the infirmary too. So does that other woman." Livingston ordered the Guardsman to help Aric and Mary into the truck.

Ted helped the girls up, wedging them into the back of the Hummer.

"Ted, we need sunglasses or something. The light hurts our eyes," Jess said.

"We'll find something for you soon as we get to the infirmary. Speaking of which . . ." He keyed his mic. "Hey, Doc."

"Go ahead, Ted."

"Get to the infirmary. The old man's been hit."

Before Doc could reply, Mike broke in. *"Is he all right? How bad is it?"*

Doc came back. *"Ted, I'm on my way, is he stable?"*

"Yeah, he's stable and cantankerous as hell."

"Roger that, I'll be waiting."

"I'm on my way too," Mike said.

Sheffield and Livingston were discussing how many men to leave behind when they noticed that Shane and Calvin were staring at them.

"Sorry to interrupt, fellas. But what are we supposed to do now?" Calvin asked.

Livingston looked at the man, who was bent over and couldn't stand straight. "Who are you and what in the hell happened to you?"

Calvin stabbed a finger at the retreating Hummer. "We were captured right after meeting with them. My name's Calvin Long. This is my son, Shane."

"So what happened to you, Calvin?"

"We put up a fight, but there was too many of them. When we got here they put the boot leather to me"—Calvin looked at Shane—"and done worse to him."

"Why'd they come after you?" Sheffield asked.

Calvin thought about the answer. "We were in the wrong place at the wrong time. They saw us and started shooting when we pulled away from the meeting."

"You know the old saying, roads are for people who want to be ambushed," Livingston said.

"Truer now than ever before, I guess," Calvin said.

"Why were you out on the road?" Livingston asked.

"We found a guy who escaped from here, and from how he described it, the conditions were awful. I had a feeling that Sarge's crew was in the area for a reason, and this camp was the only reason I could think of. I reached out to them and we met up to give them some intel we had on the camp layout. Then we got ambushed," Calvin explained.

"So you guys were the source of the map?" Sheffield asked.

"The guy that we had found was the source. He was killed in the ambush," Shane replied.

Sheffield nodded. "I see."

"So, again, what do we do now? Can we go home?" Shane asked.

"Uh . . ." Livingston looked at Sheffield, then back at Calvin. "Yeah, I guess so. Where's home?"

Calvin chuckled. "You'll understand if I don't want to tell you that, won't you?"

"Oh sure, I understand," Livingston said.

"Hop in with us. Let's take you to the infirmary and get you checked out before you head home," Sheffield said.

"Thanks," Calvin said. The father and son supported one another as they walked toward the Hummer. Even though they were in rough shape, the fact that freedom was so close to being theirs again put a little pep in their step.

Chapter 20

The nose of the canoe ground into the bank. I hopped out, followed by Taylor, Little Bit, and the bucket of snails. Danny came out last with the tangerines. Mel and Bobbie came gliding up next. I grabbed the bow of Mel's boat and pulled her up. Danny did the same for Bobbie. Little Bit took my hand as we walked up toward the picnic tables. As we got closer I saw Lee Ann sitting by the fire, talking animatedly with Thad and Jeff. I was surprised to see her there and a smile crept across my face.

Mel caught up to me. "Look, Lee Ann's out here," she said. "And she looks happy. I wonder what's up?"

We all took chairs around the fire. I sat across from Lee Ann, who smiled at me. "Did you find the tree?"

"We did."

"Can I have one, please?"

"Sure," Danny said, tossing her a tangerine.

Before long we were all peeling and eating them.

"They're a little dry, but not that sour," Lee Ann said.

"Not as sour as I remember," I said, looking at Danny. "Remember when we found that thing?"

He was chewing on a section of the fruit and started laughing, revealing a mouth of tangerine guts. "Oh yeah, we were camping on that little island upstream."

I chuckled. "That's the night I caught that big-ass catfish."

Danny's head rocked back. "Yeah, and made that rice stuff with the summer sausage."

"Ooh, don't say *summer sausage*, gonna get me hungry," Thad said. "Speaking of meat, I've been thinking, we really wasted a lotta that that last hog we had. I want to do it right this time."

"What do you mean, do it right?" Danny asked.

"I want to butcher one, scald it, and use it all. Make bacon, crackling, and everything else we can."

Almost in unison, everyone shouted out, "Bacon?"

Thad was bombarded with questions about bacon. He started to laugh and held up a hand. "Yeah, I know how to make bacon, it's easier than you think."

"Then why, for God's sake, didn't we make it before?" I asked.

Thad shrugged. "We were kind of in a hurry last time."

"How do we make it?" Mel asked.

"All it takes is salt and sugar. We got both of those. I'll make a brine and soak it, then smoke it."

"How do we store it without keeping it cold?" Bobbie asked.

"You just hang it up. It'll keep. This isn't the kind of bacon you buy at the store, it's actually preserved meat as is," Thad said with a smile.

Mel and Bobbie looked at one another. "I don't know about that," Bobbie said.

"Back before refrigeration, this is how people did it."

"I'm all for some meat candy," Jeff said.

"Me too, I'm game," I said.

"I want bacon!" Little Bit shouted.

"It'll be a few days, Ashley," Thad said, patting her on the head.

Everyone's joy at the thought of bacon was short-lived, as it started to rain. The weather forced us under the small shelter we'd constructed over the picnic tables. What we discovered was that while it kept the tables dry, it was woefully inadequate in protecting all of the benches. We were forced to one side of the table, facing the river. Luckily we had enough bench space for everyone.

At first the rain was no big deal—it was almost welcomed—but after several hours of nonstop downpour, it dampened our spirits as much as it did the fire in the pit outside. That was another oversight. While the canopy covered the tables, it didn't cover the fire. I threw a piece of scrap plastic over the stack of firewood, and kept my fingers crossed that it wouldn't be too difficult to light after the storm.

"Daddy, I'm bored. How long is it going to rain?" Little Bit asked.

"I don't know, kiddo." I looked over at her older sisters. "Why don't you guys go into the cabin and play a game or something?"

Lee Ann spoke up. "Let's go play Monopoly."

Little Bit jumped up. "Yeah, yeah, let's go play!"

"I'll play," Taylor said.

"This is pretty miserable. I'll play too," Bobby said. "Mel, you want to?"

"Sure, you girls get it ready and we'll be there in a minute," Mel replied.

The girls jumped up from the table and ran off toward the cabin, splashing through the mud and laughing. Mel waited until the girls were gone, then looked at me. "What's happened to her? She seems like a different person."

I shook my head. "I have no idea. I was wondering the

same thing." Looking at Thad, I asked, "What happened while we were gone?"

Thad looked at both of us. "Nothing, we just talked a little. I think she'll be all right."

"What'd you talk about? I mean, it's a night-and-day difference," Mel said.

Thad rubbed the stubble on his head. "You know, she thought life was over. I just showed her what she had to live for." Thad stared off toward the river. "I told her what it's like to lose someone, what it's like to lose more than just the Internet and cell phones."

As Thad stared at the river, we sat quietly for a few seconds. "Thanks for sharing that with her, Thad. I know it was hard for you, but you may have saved her life," I said.

"Yes, thanks, Thad," Mel said.

Thad smiled. "Wasn't nothing. Like I told her, we're all family now. We got to look out for one another."

"This is one fucked-up family," Jeff said, causing everyone to break out laughing.

After we settled down, Danny asked about cooking the snails. "Since the fire's out, we need to get out a stove or something to cook them on. You got any ideas, Thad?"

"That's what I was thinking, use one of the camp stoves. We still have some lard from the hog and some seasonings. I'll sauté them up and make some grits."

"Snails and grits: doesn't have quite the same ring as shrimp and grits," I said, laughing.

"I'll go get a stove," Danny said, getting up. Mel and Bobbie got up too and headed toward the cabin. Unlike the girls, they tried to avoid the puddles.

"Man, this rain sucks," I said.

"Imagine how bad it'd be if we didn't have this little shelter," Thad said.

I looked up at the plastic over our heads. "You're right. Guess it could be worse."

Danny came trotting back with the stove, now wearing his rain jacket. As Thad was setting up the Coleman, he held the fuel tank up and shook it. He gave Danny a devilish grin. "Ain't no gas in it."

Danny looked up. "What?"

Jeff held his hand out, letting rain drops land in his palm. "Looks like you're going to get wet again."

Danny shook his head, muttering under his breath, and headed out for the fuel, though he wasn't running this time. When he finally got back and the stove was fueled, Thad set out a skillet and a pot of water to boil. We sat around the table chatting, waiting for the proverbial pot to boil.

After pulling the snail meat from the shells we cut off their hard little doors and their guts, leaving a small piece of meat. Fortunately, the girls had collected a little over three dozen. Thad made the grits and added the sautéed meats afterward. We called the girls out when it was ready, and they paused their game to have dinner. After cleaning up the dishes, everyone headed for their cabins, Thad taking the first watch. With no fire to sit around there wasn't any reason to hang out.

The cabin felt damp and musty, the rain was making it uncomfortable, but we couldn't do anything but make the best of it. The Monopoly championship was a great method of distraction.

Lee Ann laughed. "You landed on Boardwalk! You owe me rent big-time!"

"Why do you have two hotels there? That's ridiculous," Mel said as she started counting money.

"Well, you own all the utilities," Taylor chimed in.

"I wanna buy something!" Little Bit shouted.

I smiled at them. Even though they were in this miserable little cabin they were still having fun, seemingly oblivious to their surroundings. I fell asleep with a smile on my face.

Thad woke me up about ten, the rain still pounding. I collected my gear, threw a poncho on, and headed outside. This was going to be a long watch shift.

"See anything?" I asked as we walked back toward the canopy.

"No, even with the NVGs you can't really see anything. And with the rain, you can hear even less."

"Go on and get some sleep," I said, slapping Thad on the back.

He smiled and headed off into the downpour. I climbed up onto the table and sat with my feet on the bench, then pulled off the poncho and laid it aside on the table. I looked through the goggles, and like Thad said, they were useless. With vision completely impossible, I tried to focus on sound.

At about two a.m., I heard a pig squeal, and quickly, all of them started to make a racket. Slipping the poncho over my head, I headed for the pen. I was about to pass Thad's cabin, the closest to the pen, when the door flew open. Thad was standing there in a T-shirt and drawers. He was as surprised to see me as I was startled by the door opening.

"What're the pigs fussin' about?"

"Damn, you scared the shit out of me," I said, shaking my head. "I don't know, was about to go find out."

"Hang on, I'll go with you. Let me put on my pants." Thad

ducked back into the cabin and reemerged quickly, with Jeff in tow.

Thad was carrying the old coach gun and Jeff had his AK. We walked toward the pen in silence.

"I can't see anything," Jeff said.

"Me neither," Thad agreed.

We could hear splashing, like the pigs were running around.

"All right, keep your eyes open. I'm going to hit the light on my rifle," I said as I raised the carbine. As the light came on a voice in the dark said, "Oh shit!" We immediately moved toward the pen with weapons raised, I was sweeping the light from side to side trying to find whoever was out there.

We heard the zap from the electric fence, followed by someone screaming. Jeff started shouting, "Hey! Hey, stop!" We all ran for the fence and jumped it. For that brief moment when we were in the air, I saw Jeff disappear into the darkness. Thad scrambled up from the ground and kept running, while I shined my light, looking for Jeff. After a moment, I saw that he had landed facedown on the ground. If it wasn't such a serious situation, I would've started laughing, but in this moment, I just yanked him up and took off.

When I caught up to Thad, he was struggling with someone on the ground. I knelt down to help him as Jeff slogged up. Then from back at the cabins, Danny shouted, "They're in the chicken coop!"

"I'll go," Jeff said as he trotted back off for another attempt at jumping the fence.

I checked my pockets for my flashlight, not wanting to point my weapon at Thad. It seemed to take forever to find it. I turned it on just in time to see Thad land a crushing closed fisted blow to a young man's face. He went limp, all the fight leaving him. Thad patted the kid down, pulled a knife from its sheath and handed it to me, then rolled him over and checked him again.

A shot and shouts came from the other side of the camp. I looked back at Thad, "You got him?"

Thad nodded, and I started running toward the rising sounds of chaos. As I got closer I could hear a girl screaming and immediately thought it was one of my girls, which pushed me to run faster. The damn poncho was really getting in the way, so I worked at getting it off as I ran, which is much more difficult than one would think.

I found Jeff, Danny, Mel, and Bobbie at the coop with a young woman and man who were sitting in the mud, looking pitiful.

"They were trying to steal the chickens," Danny said.

"What was the shooting about?" I asked.

"I fired a warning shot," Jeff said.

"This one was fighting with me when he got here," Danny said, kicking the feet of the young man.

"What the hell are you doing?" I asked the kid.

Before he could answer Thad walked up and deposited the other one on the ground beside his friends.

"Well, what were you doing?" I asked again.

"We're hungry. We were just trying to get some food," the girl cried.

"And you never thought to ask?" Danny said.

"Ask? Like you would've given us anything. No one gives anything away," one of the young guys snarled.

"How many more of you are there?" I asked.

"You'll find out soon enough," the other said.

I shined my light into his face. "I hope for your sake we don't. I have no problem putting a bullet in your head. Are there others at your camp?" I took a good look at him. Even through the steady rainfall, I could see he was dirty. He had a patchy growth of beard and was wearing a faux-leather jacket with TRANS-AM on the sleeves.

The two men looked at one another, then dropped their faces to the ground.

The girl started to cry again. "Please don't kill us."

"What are we going to do with them?" Mel asked.

I looked at Danny, then at Thad. Both just shrugged. Jeff gave me the same response when I looked at him. Finally I said, "I don't know."

"We can't just let them go," Thad said.

"Yes, you can. We'll leave. You'll never see us again," the kid with the Trans-Am jacket said.

"Forgive me if I don't believe the words of a thief," I said.

"Let's tie them up for now," Jeff said.

We led them over to the canopy and sat them down on the bench. Once they were tied up, Thad and I sat down on the bench opposite them.

"You guys planned this pretty well. Good night for it. I guess you figured with all the rain no one would be out keeping an eye on things," I said.

None of them replied. Danny jumped in. "Were you the ones who shot at us the other night?"

The girl looked at the other two before answering, "We don't have any guns."

"Don't have any guns!" Jeff shouted.

"What're your names?" Thad asked.

They hesitated for a minute, seeming unsure. "I'm Julie, that's Brian," she said, pointing to the one with the Trans-Am jacket, "and that's Franco." She gestured to the kid Thad had captured.

"Where are you guys camped?" I asked.

The three glanced at each other.

"No sense in hiding. We've got you now."

Water and mud dripped from their faces onto the aluminum top of the table. Julie started to shake from the cold.

I looked at Jeff and pointed at my eyes, then to them. He nodded and I motioned for Thad and Danny to follow me. As soon as I came through the door of the cabin, Taylor was there with her H&K.

"What's going on?"

"Raiders. We've got them, though," I said, then looked at the group. "I say we load them into the Suburban and haul them out in the middle of nowhere and leave 'em."

"They could die out there," Bobbie said.

"That's their problem. They shouldn't have stolen," Danny said.

"All they wanted was some food. Why don't we just give them some and let them go? They're just kids," Mel said.

"If we give them food, they'll just come back. Or worse, they'll come back with others, now that they have an idea of what we have here. We aren't giving them a damn thing," Thad said with a tone of finality.

"I agree," Danny said.

"So do I," I said.

Mel and Bobbie didn't look too thrilled but didn't argue any further.

"You want to take them in the morning?" Danny asked.

"Yeah, I guess. We'll load them in the truck and have someone in Sarge's buggy, just in case," I said.

"Where are we going to take them?" Thad asked.

"Let's see if we can figure out where they came from. Then we'll take them in the opposite direction and dump them."

"We should blindfold them so they can't find their way back," Danny added.

"Good idea. Let's go see if we can find out where they came from in the meantime,"Thad said.

The three of us men slogged through the rain back to the canopy.

"All right, you guys needed food. You tell us where your camp is and we'll give you some, plus we'll take you there. But I'm warning you, if you try and come back again"—I paused and looked them each in the eye—"we will kill you."

The three shared looks and Brian nodded at Julie. "We're staying at the campground up the river."

"How'd you get down here?"Thad asked.

"We came down in a canoe," Brian said.

"How'd you guys find us?" I asked.

"We saw your camp one night when we were out on the river. We saw you had those pigs and the chickens running around."

"Why didn't you just come in during the day and ask, maybe try and trade or something?" Danny asked.

"Why? No one helps anyone today. It's every man for himself," Franco said.

"We're working together. We're not all family here," I said.

"Maybe you guys do, but it's not the way for most. Everyone wants to take advantage of you," Julie said in a small voice.

"Where are you guys from?" I asked.

"We're all students from Stetson. We stayed there as long as we could, but the good people of DeLand weren't too concerned about a bunch of out-of-town students," Julie said.

"You guys are law students?" I asked.

"We were," Brian said.

"You guys must be from good families. I mean, Stetson isn't a cheap school," Jeff said.

Franco looked up, a quizzical expression on his face. "What does that have to do with anything? Your net worth doesn't mean shit now. It's about survival."

"Well, the way you're going about it isn't going to work long," I said.

"It's worked so far," Brian said with a sneer.

"Till now," Thad said.

"You said you'd give us some food . . ." Julie said, her voice trailing off.

I looked at Danny. "Let's go check the campground and see if they really are staying there."

"Where's your camp?" Danny asked.

"It's on the first loop down the river," Franco said.

I motioned to Thad. "Make 'em a pot of plain grits. If they're hungry, they'll eat it."

Thad smiled. "Yeah, they better be real hungry."

Danny and I took one of the buggies and headed for the campground. As we bounced down the road Danny asked, "Think there's anyone else there?"

"I don't know, we'll see."

Pulling into the campground, I turned on every light on the buggy scanning the trails as we drove through. Finding their camp wasn't hard—it was a collection of a couple of tents and some other shelters constructed on site, with a fire burning in a pit.

"There's got to be someone else here. In this rain, the fire would've been out by now," Danny said.

"Yeah, someone's out there," I replied.

We scanned the area with the lights, looking for sign of anyone. "Hello!" Danny called out.

I looked at him like he was nuts. "What? Maybe they'll answer," he said.

"Let's pull up a little closer," I said as I eased the buggy forward.

At the edge of the camp we stepped out of the buggy, using our weapon lights to scan the area. "See anything?" Danny asked.

"No," Danny said, peering off into the gloom.

"I don't think anyone's here," I said as I reached down and pulled the rainfly up on one of the tents, looking in.

"Shit!" I yelled as I jumped back.

Danny swung around. "What?"

I had my weapon trained on the tent. "Come out! Hands first!"

"Someone in there?" Danny asked, raising his weapon.

I nodded. "Come out now!"

The zipper slowly opened. I stepped back a little, keeping the muzzle on the growing opening. After a moment a set of hands came out. "Don't shoot," someone said nonchalantly. A head followed the hands as a figure crawled out into the mud. As he finally stood up I was surprised to see it was Andy, Chase's son.

"What the hell are you doing here?" I asked.

He shrugged. "Gotta be somewhere."

"Why'd you leave your dad's?"

"Just wasn't big enough for both of us." He looked over his shoulder. "Come on out, Walt."

Another figure crawled out of the tent.

"What are you two doing with this group?" Danny asked.

Andy smiled, looking at Walt. "They got their uses."

"Like what?" Danny asked.

Andy nodded at him. "Jus' like you guys, it's easier to survive in a group."

"You guys got any guns?" I asked.

"Oh yeah, I got my shotgun."

"Them three said they didn't have any guns," Danny said.

Andy smiled again. "They don't."

"Which is why they're tied up over at our place right now. You sent them over there, didn't you?" I asked, my temper flaring.

"They go to do their part, we do ours," Andy said.

"And just what is your part?" Danny asked.

Andy spit into the mud. "Them yuppie kids don't know how to survive out here. They'd be dead if it wasn't for us. We keep them alive, show what they can eat and how to get it."

"Like stealing?" Danny asked.

Andy shrugged. "Ain't nuthin' personal. We gotta eat too. You got more of them hogs than you need, and more chickens than you can use too."

"So you showed them where our place was and sent them over to try and steal them," Danny said.

Andy crossed his arms. "We went with them the first time, but that little booby trap you set up got us."

"Not to mention you guys shootin' at us," Walt said.

"Was it you who shot us out on the creek?" Danny asked.

Andy smiled broadly, showing the plaque caked to his teeth. "Someone shot at you?" He looked at his buddy Walt. "Ain't that a shame."

Danny stared intently at the boy, and Andy returned his stare with empty eyes.

"Let's get your stuff loaded up," I said.

"Why? We ain't going anywhere."

"That's where you're wrong. You *are* going. One way or another," Danny said.

"What gives you the right to tell us that? You ain't shit. We ain't going anywhere," Walt said.

Danny raised the muzzle of his carbine so it was pointing at Walt's chest. "This gives me the right."

"I know you think you're King Shit on Turd Island, pushing those college kids around, but you aren't going to push us around. You're a liability to our security and you've gotta go," I said.

"Or what, you gonna shoot us up?" Andy asked.

"That is entirely up to you," Danny said.

"So where are we supposed to go?"

"We'll take you some place where you can set up a new camp, it'll just be far from here," I said.

"Wherever you take me, I'll find my way back," Andy said with a chuckle.

"Come back and we'll kill you. This is your only chance," Danny said.

"Now what?"

"Time to pack up. Where's your shotgun?"

"You ain't taking my shotgun, old man."

"We'll give it back to you later, but for now we'll hang on to it."

Andy glared at Danny. "If I'd known you assholes were gonna be like this, I'da shot your asses when you showed up."

"Yeah, well, you missed that opportunity. Now where is it?"

"I ain't tellin'!"

"Keep an eye on them. It's got to be in the tent," I said as I stepped toward it.

"You two get over here and sit on this log," Danny said, motioning with the barrel of his carbine. Neither of them moved. "Now!" Danny shouted.

Reluctantly, they moved to the log and sat down. I knelt down and stuck my head in the tent. Nearly gagging, I jerked my head back.

"Oh my God, that stinks." Looking back at the two on the log, I asked, "How in the hell can you guys sleep in there?"

Andy simply shook his head and shrugged.

Inhaling deeply, I stuck my head back into the tent, using the light on my carbine to search for the shotgun. My lungs quickly began to complain as I searched through the soiled, damp sleeping bags. Finally when I didn't think I could hold my breath another fraction of a second longer, I saw the muzzle under one of the bags and quickly pulled it out.

Letting out a huge breath, I stood up, shotgun in hand. "Got it."

"All right, you two pack this shit up," Danny said.

Walt and Andy went about packing up their soggy camp as Danny and I watched. Their idea of packing the camp consisted of taking the tents down and wadding them into a ball with their contents still inside. They collected their cooking equipment and tossed it on top of everything, not bothering to wash anything out.

"This place is a fucking mess," Danny said.

"Yeah, they live like damn animals."

"Sorry we don't meet your approval. We ain't got a nice cabin to live in," Walt said.

"Shut up," Danny snarled. Turning to me, he quietly asked, "Where are you thinking?"

"I'm thinking Salt Springs. I know a place up there we can take them, out in the middle of the woods."

"That's kinda close, isn't it?" Danny asked as we got in the buggy.

"A little, but I don't want to go far. It's too dangerous. I don't want to get myself killed over these losers."

As he started the buggy, he replied, "Yeah, I guess not."

"Now what?" Andy asked.

"Turn around," Danny said as he pulled a length of paracord from his pocket.

"Why, you tying us up?" Walt asked.

"Yep."

"This is bullshit!" Andy shouted.

"It is what it is, now turn around," I said. They tried to fight me a little, but some swift kicks to the shins made the process a lot easier.

Once they were tied up and loaded into the buggy, we headed back toward the cabins. By the time we got back to the camp, Thad had already cooked up the grits. He was standing with one foot up on the bench, resting his elbows on his knees, watching the three scrape the sides of their bowls. Thad looked up as we approached.

I looked at the nearly empty pot. "Guess you guys were hungry."

Brain looked up. "You have no idea—there's just nothing out there to eat."

"Did you find our camp?" Julie asked, hesitation in her voice.

"We found it," Danny said. "Your buddies too."

The three looked toward the buggy, where Andy and Walt were still sitting.

"Any grits left in that pot, Thad?" I asked.

Thad was looking at the buggy as well. "Yeah, how many are there?"

"Just two," Danny said as he walked off to get them.

He followed them back to the table, telling them to have a seat with their friends.

"Thanks for ratting us out," Walt said.

"Leave 'em be, Walt. We'll deal with this later," Andy said.

Thad slid bowls of grits in front of the two boys. Walt immediately started to eat the meager portion of grits while Andy eyed the bowl with suspicion. "What's this?"

"What's it look like?" Thad asked.

Andy took up a spoon and sampled a small bite. "These are the worst grits I've ever tasted!"

Thad reached over and grabbed the bowl. "Then don't eat 'em."

Andy reached out with his bound hands, grabbing the bowl. "Hang on, there, biggun, didn't say I wouldn't eat it, damn."

Thad let go and set the bowl in front of him. Despite them being the worst grits Andy ever tasted, he was soon scraping the sides of the bowl for every last piece.

"At daylight, we'll take you to your new home," I said.

Julie looked at the two guys. "Where are you taking us?"

"To a place much like this one, just farther away."

"And remember what we said, should you find your way back here it will not end well for you," Danny said, looking at Andy.

Julie looked at the carbine he cradled and nodded.

"Don't worry, there ain't that many places they can take us," Andy said, then looked at Danny. "I can find our way back."

"You're just too damn stupid for your own good, aren't you?" Danny asked.

"You think we should take him to his dad?" Thad asked.

I looked at Andy. "No, you heard what Chase said about him."

Andy's eyes narrowed. "What'd he say?"

We ignored him. "Let's build a fire and hang out till sunup now that the rain's stopped," Danny said.

"I could use a fire," Jeff said.

Instead of just building the fire on the wet ground, we laid several logs on the ground and started the fire on top of them.

By slowly building the fire up, we managed to get it going strong and hot in short order. Our guests were still sitting under the canopy, far from the warmth of the fire.

"Can we move closer to the fire? I'm cold," Julie said.

"Yeah, me too. I want to sit by the fire," Andy said.

"We'll let you sit by the fire, but if you try anything we'll be feeding your carcass to the gators in the creek," Danny said.

"We won't do anything, I promise," Brian said.

"I'm not into committing suicide yet," Franco said as Thad untied his hand.

"You ain't got to worry about me an' ole Walt," Andy said.

"You three sit in these chairs," I said, arranging three chairs with their backs to the creek. "Andy, you and Walt sit over here." I pointed to two chairs close to the picnic table.

"Why, so you can keep yer eye on us?"

Jeff walked around them and sat facing them across the fire with his AK in his lap. I sat down beside him and started thinking about the hog we were going to slaughter.

"What were you guys going to do with that hog if you got it? Do you know how to butcher one?" I asked.

"We'd have found a way," Brian said.

"Have you ever butchered anything, anything at all?"

"We've caught some fish," Julie said.

"A fish is a far cry from a hog," Thad said.

"Yeah, well, if you're hungry you'll do anything."

"I can butcher a hog. Like I said before, they do their part and I do mine," Andy said smugly.

"Doubtful. I don't know what's worse, the thought that you guys were going to steal one of our hogs or the fact that you would have wasted so much of it," Danny said.

Franco looked up. "Somehow it's a waste if we eat it, but it's not if you do?"

"It's our hog, so yes. And we know what to do with one, so nothing will go to waste."

"See, that's what I mean. No one wants to help. *It's our hog.* See how you think?"

"It's only yours if you can hang on to it." Andy smiled. "Possession is nine-tenths of the law."

"Something that belongs to us is ours, not yours to steal. Sure, you could ask for it, but we aren't obligated to give you a damn thing." The statement had pissed me off, so I continued, "Franco, how much charity did you do before? How much did you give away while you spent your daddy's money at that expensive-ass school? I bet I know. Not a fucking cent. It's funny how fast people want to share in what others have when they have nothing. Unlike you, we do believe in charity. But it's got to benefit those who deserve it."

"Doesn't do us any good," Brian muttered.

"So, you're pissed at us for looking out for ourselves when you're doing—trying to do—the same thing. You're worried about you and that's okay. We're worried about us, and somehow in your screwed-up mind it's wrong of us?" Danny asked.

"You people are fucked in the head," Jeff added. He always had a way with words.

"Their opinion isn't worth shit. They're gone tomorrow." I paused to look at them. "Be glad you're leaving here. I could just as easily shoot you."

"Yeah, big man with a gun. Is that how you solve your problems, shoot them?" Brian said.

"Like you said, it's about survival."

Andy sat back in his chair. "He wouldn't shoot anyone. He ain't got it in him."

I looked at Andy. "An' I suppose you have? You think you're some kind of badass? It's just big talk in front of your friends here. First, you're full of shit. Second, you don't know a damn thing about me."

Andy didn't respond. They didn't have anything else to say, so we all sat around the fire watching the flames. As the sky began to lighten I got up and went to the cabin. Inside, Mel and Bobbie were asleep. I tiptoed around the girls and gave Mel a shake. "Hey."

She sat up quickly, looking around the cabin. "What, what is it?"

"Nothing, I'm going to go take these people and get rid of them."

She looked shocked. "What do you mean, get rid of them?"

"I'm taking them up into the forest and dropping their asses off. They'll have a hard time finding their way back."

She nodded. "Oh."

"I'm going to wake up the girls. They need to keep an eye on things here. Three of us have to go."

She nodded and I gently shook Taylor and Lee Ann to wake them. "Hey, you two, you need to get up."

Taylor sat up. "What's going on?"

"I need you two to help keep an eye on things. Get dressed, get your guns, and come out."

Lee Ann rolled over. "Dad, where's my gun?"

I paused. Ever since Thad had spoken with her, her spirits were brightened. I did trust her with it again, I decided. "I'll get it. Now hurry up. Jeff is staying with you guys."

I got Lee Ann's H&K and set it by the door, then went back out to the fire pit.

"Let's get them tied up and into the wagon," I said.

"You don't need to tie us up. We're not going to do anything," Julie said.

Andy held his hands up. "You ain't no better'n us."

I looked at Julie blankly as I picked up a length of rope. "Get up."

Reluctantly, she held her hands out. "Behind your back," I said.

"Oh, come on, this is ridiculous!" Brian said as he jumped up.

Jeff raised the AK and flipped the safety off with a loud click. "I suggest you shut the fuck up and sit down. We'll decide what's ridiculous."

The kid stood there for a moment, glaring at us, before giving in. Thad then came jogging over. "Hey, don't forget these," he said, holding up a few bandannas.

"You're going to blindfold us?" Brian asked.

"Yeah, I'm not going to make it easy on you to find your way back."

"Are you kidding me?! What are you afraid of?" Franco said.

"I know what he's afraid of," Andy said. "You ain't putting that on me."

I smiled. "This isn't for me, it's for you. It's this or a plastic bag, which do you want?"

"How is blindfolding us good for us?" Julie asked.

With a straight face I said, "Because if you were to find your way back we'd have to kill you."

As we shoved them into the vehicles, I surveyed the scene around us. Fog was forming in pockets, appearing like a cloud clinging to the ground. The vapor swirled around our legs, giving everything the look of a low-grade horror movie. I guess, in some ways, this situation was like a horror movie. I could only hope we had a happy ending.

Chapter 21

Doc and Mike were standing in front of the infirmary when Ted skidded to a stop. They quickly opened Sarge's door and helped him out. The women in the back got out as well and started trying to drag Aric out. Doc looked at Aric. "Who the hell is that?"

"That's the fucker who shot me," Sarge said as he threw an arm over Doc's shoulder.

"You two get him inside. I'll help the girls get him," Ted said.

Mike and Doc helped get him inside, where the infirmary staff was waiting for him. A woman in scrubs pointed to a stretcher on wheels. "Get him up on here."

"Ted, can I borrow your sunglasses?" Jess asked. "We need to get Mary out, but the light hurts my eyes."

"I'll get her, then we'll see if we can find you guys something."

Ted pulled Mary out of the truck. He was surprised how light she was, it was like picking up a child. Jess had pulled another stretcher over by the door. He laid Mary out and Jess slowly wheeled her inside.

Before getting him on the table, Mike took Sarge's weapon while Doc and Ted helped him get his body armor off. A woman in scrubs began cutting his pants off.

"Don't cut my belt!" Sarge shouted as he started trying to get it off.

Mike slapped his hands away. "I'll get it."

Sarge laid his head back, a thin smile on his face. "You've always wanted to do that."

"Don't flatter yourself, old man."

Once the belt was off, the woman finished cutting the pants and removed the dressing.

Doc inspected the wound. "It didn't exit. It's still in there."

"We need to probe the wound and see if we can find the bullet," the woman replied.

"What've you got for pain?" Doc asked.

"We've got ketamine," the woman said as she pulled over a cart with several drawers in it.

"I don't need that shit," Sarge protested.

"Let's get a line started on him," Doc said as he tied a thick rubber band around Sarge's arm.

Once the IV was started, they injected the ketamine, which had the effect of making Sarge talkative. They probed the wound and succeeded in finding the bullet, extracting it one piece at a time, as he babbled on about completely random stuff. It wasn't long before they were bandaging him back up. Another small bag was connected to the IV line, which contained kanamycin, a broad-spectrum antibiotic.

Once Sarge was resting, Mike and Ted walked over to the nurse and Doc. "How is he?" Mike asked.

"He was lucky. The bullet hit his prosthetic implant," the woman said.

"His what?" Mike asked.

"His artificial hip," Doc said. "He's had an artificial hip replacement."

Mike looked down at Sarge. "No shit, I didn't know he'd had that done."

"Me neither. What's the prognosis?" Ted asked.

"We've got him on an antibiotic. The wound wasn't that bad, so he should heal up fine," Doc said.

"How long is he going to be laid up? He's not going to be happy to be out of the action," Mike said.

"It all depends on him. Some people heal faster than others," the nurse said.

"He'll heal fast. He's too damn mean to be laid up long." Mike laughed.

"Well, he needs to rest right now. He's lost some blood. He'll probably be down for a week or two," the nurse said.

Ted and Mike nodded and left the room. They made their way to the next one, where two attendants were working on Aric.

"How is he?" Ted asked.

"His arm has a lot of trauma. The bullet blew open the back of his bicep. It's going to take a long time to heal. The best thing for him is a delayed closure. We debrided the wound and left it open. It'll need to be cleaned and rebandaged every day," one of the attendants said.

"He's lucky that's all that happened to him," Ted said, then glanced at Fred.

Jess was sitting in a chair beside Mary, watching the goings on from across the hall. With Mary still passed out, Jess decided it would be okay to leave for a moment. She walked up beside Mike, who was still looking at Aric with suspicion.

"He let us out. He was helping us," she said, gently touching his shoulder.

Mike turned around. "Holy shit! I didn't see you. Where'd you come from?" He wrapped her up in a hug.

Jess wrapped her arms around him as well. "We were in the detention center. Aric helped us get out."

Mike nodded thoughtfully, reserving his judgment. The two of them then spent a few minutes catching up. Jess was glad for the company.

Kay walked into the building a few minutes later, eager to check on Aric and Mary. On her way to Aric's bed, she stopped by Sarge's bed, looking down at the old man, who was now asleep. Ted walked up beside her. "He's a good man."

"Friend of yours?" Kay asked.

Ted laughed. "I don't know if that's the right word, but he'd do anything for me and I would for him. I've trusted him with my life more times than I can count."

Kay smiled. After a moment, she walked over to where Aric was lying. Fred was still by his side. "How is he?" she asked her.

Fred was holding his good hand. "They say he'll be all right, but he's going to need a lot of care."

Kay looked at the IV tube in his arm and the two bags hanging over him. Like Sarge, he was on an IV antibiotic and oxygen.

"I hope so. I really like this boy. He's not like the others here. He's kind," Kay said.

Fred looked over and smiled. "He is, isn't he?" Kay smiled back and put her arm around Fred's shoulders.

"We'll take care of him," Kay said.

With Fred's head on her shoulder, Kay quietly asked, "Who are these guys?"

Fred straightened up. "I don't know for sure, but Jess is friendly with them. I think they're the ones who helped her get home."

Kay gave a knowing nod.

Once Aric was stable, the staff turned their attention to Mary. The ladies gathered around as she was examined.

"Is she going to be all right?" Jess asked.

The nurse stepped back. "I don't see anything wrong with her, to be frank. I mean, she's dehydrated and her blood pressure is a little low, but other than that I don't see anything physically wrong with her. I'll start an IV to get some fluids in her and put her on some oxygen."

Jess looked down at Mary, running a hand over her forehead. "Come on, Mary, wake up."

Kay tugged on the nurse's sleeve. When she looked over, Kay whispered, "These two need to be checked out too," pointing to Jess and Fred.

The nurse smiled at Jess. "Why don't you sit down here so I can check you out."

She performed quick exams on both Fred and Jess.

"What happened to you girls?"

"We've been locked in the detention center," Jess said.

"How long?" another one of the attendants asked, clearly alarmed.

"We don't know, because we were in the dark the whole time. But it was definitely a long time, more than a few days. They barely fed us and we had no water. It was really bad," Jess said, shuddering.

"Is that why you're squinting? Does the light bother you?"

"Yes, it does, a lot," Fred said.

"I think we have something that will help that," one of the attendants said as he walked off.

Once they were alone, Kay asked, "Jess, who are these guys?" pointing at Mike and Ted.

She smiled. "The one on the stretcher is Sarge, that one's

Mike, and the other guy is Ted. They helped us out on our way home."

"Us?" Kay asked.

"Yeah, remember me telling you about Morgan and Thad?"

Kay nodded. "Mmhmm."

"So these guys helped the group of us out," Fred said, looking at Ted and Mike.

Kay leaned in. "What are they doing here?"

In a whisper, Jess replied, "They took over the camp."

Surprised, Kay asked, "Just the three of them?"

Jess laughed. "No, there's more of them. Remember the other guys back at the jail? The ones with the army uniforms? They are all part of it, from what Mike told me."

"Oh wow. I wonder how many of them there are."

"Enough, I hope," Fred said.

Sheffield and Livingston came through the door, walking straight to Sarge's bed.

"How is he?" Livingston asked.

"He'll live, just gonna be out of action for a little," Ted said.

"We're getting ready to make an announcement to the camp, to let them know we're here now. Some of the civilians are getting a little antsy. For now we're keeping the DHS people where they are. Shortly, though, we're going to move them to a more secure place, probably that detention area back there," Sheffield said.

"Good idea. Anything going on out there?" Mike asked.

"Not yet, but if we don't get some info out to them soon, things could go to shit," Livingston said.

As if on cue, a sudden outburst of gunfire erupted, leading Mike, Ted, Sheffield, and Livingston to run for the door. Mike called into his mic, "What's going on? What's all the shooting about?"

"Captain, you and the lieutenant drive. Mike, get in the turret!" Ted shouted as he climbed up into the turret of the other Hummer.

The tempo of the shooting picked up. Ted keyed his mic. "Where's the shooting coming from?"

"By the armory. There's four or five people back there!" a voice replied.

Ted slapped the roof of the truck. "Go, go, go!"

As they bounced along, the radio filled with chatter. The Guardsmen were already trying to maneuver on the shooters. Ian's voice came over the radio just as a SAW opened up.

"Ted, come in from the south, there's cross fire on the east side!"

"Roger that! Captain, you get that?" Ted said into his radio.

He was answered by the truck swerving, forcing him to grab the SAW for support. *I guess so*, he thought as he righted himself in the turret. Livingston was behind them and followed the maneuver.

As they rounded the corner of the motor pool, the armory came into view. Ted could see three people on the side of the building, using it for cover. Slapping the top of the truck, he shouted, "Stop!" Sheffield locked up the brakes and the truck slid in the sand. Before it stopped, Ted went to work with the SAW. Soon, Mike's SAW was ripping away as well. Three figures besides the building were caught in the open, two of them went down immediately. The third ran around the corner of the connex. As soon as he cleared the corner, Ted watched him fall, cut down by fire from the Guardsmen.

"We've got two down on this side. Move up and clear the armory!" Ted called into his radio.

He could hear Ian shouting orders. Soon a line of Guardsmen with weapons shouldered appeared, moving toward the building. Again Ted beat on the roof of the truck, yelling, "Move up, move up!" Sheffield eased the truck forward. Ted kept the SAW to his shoulder as he bobbed around in the turret. Mike was likewise covering the building. The Guardsmen moved slowly toward the open door. Ted didn't like what he was seeing.

"Ian, stop them, we need to put some gas in there! Don't let them just walk through that fatal funnel!" Ted yelled. He was referring to the term used for a place that an assaulting force is made to enter one at a time with no idea what's on the other side.

Ted dropped out of the turret and grabbed his carbine. "Mike, stay here and provide cover."

Without raising his head from the SAW, Mike replied, "Roger!"

Sheffield and Livingston got out of their trucks and followed Ted as he moved toward the armory, running from one point of cover to the next. Ian came at the open door and launched a tear gas round from an M320 through it. When the round went off, white smoke began to pour out of the door.

"Ian, coming to you from your right," Ted said into his radio.

Ian flashed a thumbs-up in response. Ted ran toward him, keeping his weapon trained on the open door as he passed in front of it. Sheffield and Livingston were hot on his heels. Ted slid in the sand beside Ian. "We need to clear that thing."

"You got a gas mask?"

"No, let's just wait the gas out. Wish we had some flash bangs."

Ian smiled and held up two small black canisters. "We have these." He handed them to Ted.

Ted smiled. "Oh yeah, this will get their attention," he said, looking at the sting ball, a small grenade with a rubber base filled with weighted rubber balls. In the tight confines of the connex, its effects would be overwhelming to anyone inside. "Soon as that gas settles a bit, we'll put these two in at the same time."

Everyone waited outside while the tear gas dissipated. Ted called Mike and told him to come over. When he got there they went over their entry. It would be Ted, Mike, and Ian going in while Sheffield, Livingston, and their men provided security.

"We'll toss one of these"—Ted smiled as he held up the sting ball—"this little gem."

"Oh nice, I'll take point going in," Mike said.

They maneuvered themselves around to the side of the box. Mike was in the lead, with his weapon up, and Ted was behind him, a grenade in each hand. He tapped Mike on the shoulder with the base of the bang sting ball. Mike nodded and Ted tossed them in.

The bang from the sting ball was not very loud, but the sound of the rubber balls bouncing around inside made it clear that anyone in there was going to have a bad day. As soon as the grenades detonated, Mike, Ted, and Ian entered the building. They cleared it quickly. Ted then looked down and noticed a hatch in the floor.

"Got any more of those stingers?" Ted whispered to Ian.

Ian reached into his vest and pulled another one out, handing it to Ted.

"Ian, lift the lid a little and I'll drop it in. Slam it shut quick and don't stand in front of it," Ted said. Ian nodded.

"Soon as it goes off, snatch the door open and I'll drop in," Mike said.

"You sure?" Ted asked.

"Someone's got to go in there. It'd be best to drop in right after it goes off."

"You're right. I just hate the thought of it," Ted said.

Ted pulled the pin on the grenade and nodded at Ian. Ian reached down and grabbed the handle, then looked up at Ted and started to tick off his fingers while mouthing the words, *One, two, three.* On three, he raised the door and Ted dropped the device through it. Ian slammed the lid down and it went off. As soon as it detonated, Ian snatched the door open again and Mike dropped through the hole.

As quickly as he disappeared, Mike let out a howl. Ted and Ian looked down in the hole, Ted shining his weapon light down through the opening. They could see the light from Mike's weapon and hear him moving around. After a minute he called out, "Clear!"

"What's wrong with you?" Ted called through the hatch.

"I landed on some of those fucking balls and twisted my ankle," Mike yelled up.

"Can you get out of there?" Ian asked.

"Yeah, just give me a hand," Mike said as he started up the ladder. Ian reached down and grabbed Mike's extended hand and helped pull him up.

Ian and Ted helped him out the door. Ted shouted, "Coming out!" as they stepped through it.

"Anyone in there?" Sheffield asked.

"No, it was empty," Ted said, then looked at the bodies lying beside the connex. "Who the hell are they?"

"Civilian, I guess you'd call them employees."

"We should probably look at the CIs too, just to make sure none of them are of the same frame of mind," Ted said.

Sheffield looked over. "You think there could be issues with them as well?"

Ted shrugged. "We didn't think about the civilian workers. Who's to say there aren't folks out there who really like it here?"

"We'll check them out as well. I don't think any of them 'like it' here, but if some of them were put into positions of power by the goon squad, they may be resistant to change."

Ted nodded, then helped Mike over to the Hummer. "I'll get him over to Doc to look at his foot."

Sheffield nodded and turned to his men. "Let's get these bodies loaded up."

At the infirmary, Ted helped Mike inside. As he sat up on one of the stretchers, a familiar voice called out, "What happened, you get a boo-boo?"

Ted and Mike both looked up to see Sarge sitting up on his stretcher. Mike smiled. "Hey, you grumpy ole fuck, how you feeling?"

Still slightly slurring his words, he replied, "Like I been shot, how the hell you think I feel?"

Ted smiled. It was good to see Sarge back to his affectionate self. "They said you were lucky, said it hit your artificial hip."

"Yeah, when did you have that done? I didn't even know," Mike said.

"Of course you didn't know, dipshit, it's none of your damn business." Sarge looked down at the wound. "The VA did it after I got out. I'd taken a round"—Sarge jabbed a finger toward his hip—"in pert near the same damn spot in Iraq. Couldn't take it anymore and had it replaced."

"Huh, I thought it was just 'cause you're older than dirt," Mike said.

"You wait till I get out of this bed, I'll show you old. What the hell happened to you anyway? Why you gimpin' around?"

"I slipped on some sting balls and twisted my ankle."

Sarge made a face like he was about to cry. "Oh, you poor baby," then, pointing toward Aric, he said, "Least me and him have a real reason to here." Sarge looked over at Aric. "You know you're part of an exclusive club, don't ya?"

Aric was still pretty out of it and stared as a means of response. Sarge continued, "There's only one other person in the world who's shot me and lived to tell about it."

"Unlike the list of those who want to and haven't yet. That one's long as hell," Mike said as he tried to get his boot off.

Sarge's head snapped around. "Keep it up, smart-ass. You think 'cause I'm laid up, I can't get to you, but I ain't going to be in here forever."

Through his own pain, Mike smiled. Ted helped him get the boot off as one of the nurses came over and started checking the foot out. Mike winced as she tried to turn it. She asked him to pull his toes toward his knee, but he wasn't able to move them far.

"Yeah, it's a pretty bad sprain. You can already see bruising. All we can do is wrap it up. Unfortunately, there's not much else to help speed up the healing process," the nurse said.

"Okay, wrap it up, then. If you could just try to keep it small enough so I can get my boot on, that'd be great," Mike said.

Sarge looked across the room at Jess, who was sitting in a chair beside Mary. He motioned for her to come over. She smiled and walked to his side. Sarge had a sloppy grin on his face and held his hand out. Jess couldn't help but laugh at him, and took his hand.

"How are you doing, Annie?" Sarge asked.

"I'm good, now."

"I was worried about you, ever since we found out you were there."

Jess cocked her head to the side. "How'd you find out I was here?"

"We did a little sneakin' and peekin'. Morgan and Thad saw you."

A big smile spread across her face. "Where are they? I really want to see them."

"Teddy!" Sarge screamed. Jess jumped at the sudden outburst.

Ted looked up. "Damn, I'm right here. Whaddya want?"

"Get Morgan on the horn, tell him to get over here, and to bring that gentle giant with him."

Jess looked at Ted. "How are they going to get here? Is his house near here?"

"They're not at their house now. They had to leave, but he's got wheels." Ted looked at Sarge. "I'll call him."

Sarge nodded and looked back at Jess. "You're goin' ta be all right now." He was starting to slur his words more and seemed unable to keep his eyes open.

Jess leaned over and kissed him on the forehead, pushing him back onto the stretcher. "I know, now get some rest."

A small smile cracked his face. "I don't need no rest," he said as he drifted off.

Jess stared at him for a minute, then looked over at Ted and Mike. "You guys have no idea how much I prayed for y'all to come."

"You have no idea what it took to get here. As soon as Thad and Morgan saw you, they knew it was you. Sarge wanted to come back right then, but it wasn't possible," Ted said.

"How long ago was it?" Jess asked.

"Three weeks, I guess," Mike said.

Jess stared off into the distance and winced from the pain in her eyes. A few weeks seemed so long ago. "Can I have your sunglasses?" Ted pulled them off his hat and handed them to her. "What did you guys see? I mean, where was I?"

"Thad said it looked like you were cutting firewood," Ted said.

"Was it the day where there was all the shooting, I wonder? Was that you guys?"

"Ha, yep, that was us. Not what we intended to happen, which is part of the reason it took so long to get back here," Mike said.

"It doesn't matter, now that you're here," Jess said, then looked at the floor. Looking back up, she smiled brightly. "Now what?"

"What do you mean?" Ted asked.

"I mean, now what do I do?"

"Whatever you want. Everyone here is free to leave or stay. The camp is now under the control of the National Guard."

Jess stood there staring at them for a minute. "You all right?" Mike asked.

"Yeah, I . . . I just don't know where to go."

"Ah, don't worry about it, you've got time now to think about that," Mike said with a grin.

"Yeah, I guess." Jess looked back at Mary, laid out on a stretcher, then at Fred. "What are you going to do, Fred?"

Fred looked at Aric. He was out again. "I'll have to wait till he wakes up and see what he wants to do."

"He ain't going anywhere," Mike said, pointing at Aric, "at least not yet."

"Why not?" Fred asked. "It was an accident. He didn't know what was going on. What are you going to do to him?"

"He's DHS. We'll have to wait and see what the brass wants to do with him. Right now, he stays."

Fred looked down at Aric, then back at Mike. "But he saved us."

"And that'll be taken into consideration," Ted said. "Now, if you'll excuse me, I'm going to call Morgan."

Ted drove over to the comm shack, where two Guardsmen were stationed. "Anything come over the radio?" he asked as he went in.

"There's lots of traffic on their net. Sounds like the shit has hit the fan for them," one of them replied.

Ted looked at his name tag, it read BREWER. "Well, that's a good thing, now, isn't it, Brewer?"

"Yeah. It sounds like several of their camps are being hit."

"That was the plan," Ted said, connecting his radio to the power source. He unplugged the antenna from one of the other radios, connected it to his, and powered it up.

Forgoing the usual cloak-and-dagger radio protocols, Ted keyed the mic. "Hey, Morgan, you out there?"

"Yeah, who is this?"

"It's Ted, can you guys come to the camp?"

"It's a long ride out to your camp. It'll take a while."

"No, no, the DHS camp."

"Uh, yeah, are you guys there?"

"Yep, but it's no longer a DHS camp. We've got it under control."

Morgan whistled and laughed. *"Okay, we'll drop by later."*

"See you then, out."

Chapter 22

The ride to Salt Springs couldn't have been particularly comfortable for our passengers, who had their hands bound behind their backs and their eyes blindfolded. Luckily, I wasn't in the buggy with them to hear their complaints—Thad had offered to drive them in the lead buggy, while Danny and I traveled behind him.

We made our way west until we picked up one of the dirt forest roads and turned north. After several miles, we had to go cross country until we came to 445A, close to the intersection with Highway 19. As was our standard procedure on these rides, we stopped inside the tree line. Danny got out and walked up to check the road. He pulled his binoculars out and took a good look, checking both directions. I wanted him to hurry the hell up because the smell of their crap in the back of the buggy was choking me.

As he got back in I said, "Damn, man, you take long enough?"

"I don't want to just run out there."

I jabbed a thumb over my shoulder. "Yeah, but I had to sit here in this godforsaken stink."

Danny smiled. "That's why I went out to check the road."

"Asshole," I said, shaking my head.

"I'm going to keep us on this side of Grasshopper Lake," Danny said. I nodded and he called Thad on the radio, giving him instructions.

I smiled thinking of good times spent at the lake. Mel and I used to take the kids to swim there. It has crystal clear water and, the best part, no gators—at least, I've never seen one in it. The area to the west of the lake, the side we were on, was a sandy plain with pines and scrub oaks. It was a popular place in the Before for swimmers, campers, and partiers. The remains of bonfires gone by littered the area.

As we pulled up to the swimming area, Thad suddenly stopped. Danny called him on the radio. "Hey, what's up?"

Thad didn't respond. After a moment he got out, then we quickly got out and started moving toward him. He stood by the buggy, looking straight ahead. Danny and I were scanning the area as we moved up behind him.

"Hey, man, what's up?" I asked as I scanned the edges of the clearing.

Thad didn't reply. He simply raised a hand and pointed. I followed his arm to see a body hanging in a tree.

"Oh shit," Danny said.

"What the hell's going on out there?" Andy shouted.

We slowly walked toward the body. It hung there motionless, the head at a hideous angle. As we got closer, it became clear it was a young black man, probably in his twenties. He'd taken a hell of a beating. His hands were bound behind his back with wire that had cut into his wrists.

"He hasn't been here long," Danny said.

Thad moved toward the rope, which was tied off to the tree. Pulling out a big blade, he cut the rope. The body crashed to the ground. Looking back at me, he asked, "You got your Leatherman tool?"

I pulled it from its pocket on my vest and handed it over. He used it to cut the wire binding the wrists. As he handed it back, he said, "I'm going to bury him." Thad walked back to the buggy. Danny and I shared a concerned look and trailed after him.

Thad started digging around in the bed of the buggy. "Hey, what's going on?" Franco yelled. Thad didn't reply, eventually finding an e-tool. Taking the tool, he walked back over to the body and surveyed the area. Back from the water, toward the trees, was a low mound. An old downed tree on one side prevented anyone from driving over it. Thad walked over to it and knelt down. Unfolding the small shovel, he sunk the blade into the sand.

I was looking out across the flat expanse of the lake and thinking about the young man lying on the ground behind me. What was the reason for his death? Had he done something wrong—steal, murder, rape? Or, and this bothered me more than those possibilities, was he just in the wrong place at the wrong time? Or, worse still, just the wrong color? There is certainly an element in the backwoods of Lake County with openly racist views.

This led me to think of the many groups with these kinds of extreme views: white power groups, the Black Panthers, the Klan. It's hard to imagine that those sorts wouldn't seize the moment when there was no law to attempt to further their agendas. It was crazy that with all that was happening, people would think this would be the time to go forth and commit violence in the name of race, religion, or politics. But sadly, as is human nature, I was sure that was just what was happening. Reggie's niece was a prime example.

Thad was digging robotically. I went over and unslung my carbine. "Let me have a go at it. Take a break."

Thad rose to his feet and handed me the small spade. "I need a drink of water," he said, heading toward the buggy.

I dropped down to my knees and continued the digging. I worked for a while until Danny came over and relieved me. Thad was leaning against the front of the buggy, saying nothing as he cradled the old shotgun in his arms. The crew in the back of the buggy were starting to complain. Julie insisting that she had to pee.

"Keep an eye on 'em, Thad, I'm going to take her out," I said.

He nodded and turned to face them, gripping the shotgun. I got Julie out and pulled the blindfold from her face. "I'll untie you, just don't do anything stupid."

She squinted against the bright sun, shielding her eyes with her hand. "Where are we, and why are we stopped?" she asked as she looked around. Then she saw Danny working on the hole and a look of terror swept over her. "Oh my God, please don't kill us!" she cried out.

Her plea caused the other four to start asking questions. Andy was the loudest of them all.

"What the hell's going on? Untie me, dammit!" he shouted.

"We're not going to kill you. The hole's not for you guys," I said.

"Hole, what hole?" Andy shouted.

"They're digging a big hole," Julie said, sounding unconvinced.

Julie looked back toward Danny, then at me. I pointed to the body laid out on the ground. She gasped and covered her mouth. "Oh my, who is that?"

"We found him hanging from one of the trees," I said flatly.

Staring at the body, she asked, "Who would do something like that?"

"Who are you talking about? What's going on out there?" Andy asked, moving his head around.

"Shut up, Andy," I said. Looking at Julie, I asked, "Don't you have to pee?"

She nodded and I pointed toward some scrub on the edge of the lake. "Go in there, but I better be able to see the top of your head. Don't try to make a run for it."

Danny returned to the buggy and got a swig of water, and Thad took his place to finish digging.

"This is really fucked up," he said, looking at Thad's back.

Julie returned, looking at the water bottle Danny was holding. In a small voice, she asked, "Can we have some water?"

Danny handed her the bottle. "Don't take the blindfolds off the others."

She nodded and took a long drink before taking it to her friends. She handed the empty bottle back to Danny. "Thank you."

Danny twirled his finger in a motion for her to turn around. She did and he tied her hands again, then put the blindfold on before guiding her back to her seat. Once she was seated we walked over to the hole. It was four feet deep and about as wide.

"That's deep enough, don't you think?" Danny asked.

Thad stopped his work and surveyed the hole. "I reckon it is. Let's lay him to rest."

From my vest I produced two pairs of nitrile gloves. The body was a biohazard nightmare, and I didn't want to touch it. I handed the other pair to Thad.

"You don't want to get sick, man," I said as means of explanation. Thad nodded.

Together we carried the body down into the hole. Thad

laid the man's arms across his chest. Suddenly the sound of an engine straining in low gear drifted through the trees. Danny and I both looked up, rifles ready.

"Sounds like it's headed this way," Danny said.

"Is that a truck?" Andy called out. "Better hope it ain't no one I know."

Thad paid no attention to the sound. He was gently laying palmetto fronds out on the body, cutting them from a stand beside the hole. Danny and I stepped out toward the trail to get a better view down its length. Catching a glint of sunlight from a piece of chrome, we stepped back.

"Here it comes," I said.

It wasn't long before an old Dodge truck trundled down the trail. The driver pulled right past us but stopped when he saw the buggies. There were four people in the cab: two men and two women. The man driving quickly got out, as did the male passenger, both of them with rifles in hand.

Danny and I were walking toward the back of the truck when the passenger saw us and called to his friend, who quickly turned to face us. He looked at the two of us then to the tree where the body had been hanging, then back to us.

"What'd y'all do with our nigger?"

During all this Thad was busy filling the hole. He didn't bother stopping when the truck drove up. However, hearing that, he stopped.

"Your what?" Thad said as he slowly got up from the hole.

The driver looked at him and started shifting the rifle in his hands. Danny and I quickly brought up our carbines and began shouting.

"Don't even think about it! Raise that rifle and you're a dead man!" I shouted, drawing a bead on him.

Thad headed straight toward him, clutching the old coach gun by the grip in one hand. "Your what?!" he shouted.

"We was just coming out here to show our girlfriends that boy, is all!" one of the passengers cried out.

"And how'd you know about that *boy*?" Thad barked, adding a deliberate sneer to the last word.

"Lay the rifles down. Just set them in the bed of your truck," Danny said.

The passenger looked at the driver with wide eyes, and the driver looked at us, trying to figure out how to proceed. We had the drop on them, as our rifles were already shouldered and they were semiautos. He was still holding the lever gun by the receiver, but there was no chance in hell of him getting a shot off.

The driver raised his hands slightly. "Calm down, boys," he said as he stepped toward the bed of the truck and slowly lowered the gun in. The passenger did likewise.

Thad was nearly on top of the driver now. "How'd you know about this? Did you do it?" he shouted, pointing at the pit.

The driver licked his lips, looking from one of us to the other. "Naw, we didn't do it, just found him out here."

"An' you bring your girlfriends out to see a *man* hung in a tree."

The driver shrugged. "Not like he cares."

Thad looked at his hands. "Why your knuckles all busted up? Bust 'em up on that kid's face?"

The corners of the man's mouth pulled back ever so slightly. "Naw, wasn't us, told you that already." He looked over at the buggy with the crew sitting in the back and pointed. "An' what the hell are y'all up to? You got people over there blindfolded and tied up? What the hell are you doing out here?"

"They're thieves. We're just moving them to a place where they can't steal from us anymore," I said.

"Who's out there?" Andy asked.

The driver laughed. "Andy, is that you?"

"Yeah, who are you?"

"Looks like you finally are getting what you deserve, dumbass."

"Tommy Harrell, if I wasn't tied up I'd whoop your ass."

"If you wasn't tied up, I'd shoot your sorry ass."

"We don't have time for your foreplay. Knock it off," I said.

The driver looked back at Thad. "I don't know, you people seem like you're up to no good." He nodded his head toward the tree. "Who's to say you didn't do it?"

Thad was enraged. "Because I don't hang niggers, *boy*!"

Thad's outburst unnerved the man and he seemed to shrink a little. "Jus' sayin'."

I walked up to Thad and put my hand on his shoulder. "Let's just finish this and get out of here."

Thad's chest heaved with every breath. I could feel the anger coursing through him when I touched him.

Thad pointed at the man's face. "I know you did it. You're lucky they're here."

The guy shrugged and turned toward his truck. I called out, "Just stay where you are till we leave."

He looked back. "You can't tell me what to do. You ain't shit."

I brought my rifle up to my eye and looked down the barrel at him. "Right now I'm the shit pointing a weapon at you. Take another step and I'll drop you where you stand."

He squinted back at me. "Ain't no need to be like that, friend. We'll wait."

I grunted. "We aren't friends. You just stay where you are."

Thad finished filling the grave and returned with the e-tool, tossing it in the back of the buggy. Danny and I moved toward the buggies. "Go ahead and get in your truck," I said.

"I'll be seeing you, Andy, when you don't have anyone around to save your ass," the driver yelled out as he hopped in the cab.

"We'll see, asshole, we'll see."

Thad got behind the wheel of his buggy while Danny and I got into the other. We followed the Dodge out of the woods toward the road. They pulled out onto the blacktop and made a left, heading back toward Altoona. We stopped and watched them as they rolled away.

I looked at Thad. "You all right?"

"Yeah, I'm okay. I just know they did it."

"I know. Let's put this behind us, though, and get on the road. Now that the camp is secure we can use the road," I said.

"How far are we going?" Thad asked.

"It's about another ten miles."

"We going out to the paved road?"

"Yeah, follow this trail. It'll take you right to it." Thad put the buggy in gear and pulled out. He really pushed the vehicle. Looking over, I saw our speedometer was nearly pegged.

"Damn, he's in a hurry," I said.

We drove along for a bit without talking, then Danny looked over and said, "I can't believe they've already got the camp under control."

"I know. Wonder how many casualties they took."

"Yeah, I wonder. They sure did it fast, though. You think that girl you came home with is in there?"

"Jess? Thad's certain it was her."

"She'll be surprised to see you."

"I think all her surprise will be used up on Sarge and the guys. I bet she's relieved. They'll take care of her."

After crossing the Juniper Run, I called Thad and told him to hold up. He slowed and we pulled up beside him. "We're going to be turning off right up here. Follow us till we get there."

Thad nodded and fell in behind us. We continued a little farther up the road before turning off. Danny stopped and I got out, motioning for Thad to do so as well.

"What's up?" Thad asked.

"We're going to follow this trail. There's going to be a fork. Take it to the left. It'll head for a river. We'll let them out down there."

Thad nodded and went back to his buggy.

"Where the hell are we?" Andy asked.

"You'll see soon enough," I said.

"Well, hurry up. This shit is getting old."

Thad took off down the trail, much slower this time as it was rough. The trail ended short of the river, but we could see it through the trees. Danny pulled up beside Thad and we got out.

"All right gang, you're home," I said.

"About damn time," Andy said.

As we removed their blindfolds, they looked around.

"Do you know where we are?" Franco asked Andy.

"Sure do, know exactly where we are."

"Really, where are you, then?" I asked.

"We're in the fucking woods!" Andy shouted and started laughing.

"Nice, smart-ass. Let's get 'em untied so they can unload their stuff," Danny said.

"I'm going to untie you guys. Try any shit and it won't end well, I promise you," I said.

"We ain't going to do anything, just get these ropes off me," Andy said.

We untied them all. They stretched their arms, rubbing their wrists.

"Go ahead and get your crap out of there," Danny said.

Andy looked at the others. "You heard him, get to it."

Thad was leaning on the front of his buggy, and without turning around he shouted, "You too! You ain't no better than them."

"Hey, I loaded it, they can unload it."

Thad spun around and leveled his shotgun at Andy's head. "You better get your ass to work too!"

Andy raised his hands and turned to the mound of soggy gear in the bed of the buggy. Together the five of them unloaded it quickly. Once all their gear was out Andy looked through it quickly, then asked, "Where's my shotgun?"

"I got it," I said.

"What are you waiting on? Give it to me," Andy said holding his hand out.

"I don't think we should," Thad said.

"That's bull, you can't leave us out here without it!" Andy shouted.

"Yeah, come on, we need it," Brian said.

I grabbed the gun from the bed of the buggy. "All right, here." I tossed it to him.

Andy quickly pumped the action, looking into the empty chamber. "Where's my shells?"

"We didn't say we'd give you those," Danny said.

"Come on, man! Leave us the shells," Andy pleaded.

"We will, up the trail. You can walk up there and get them," I said, holding up the box of birdshot.

Andy glared at me as we got back into the buggies and started them up. A couple hundred yards up the trail I tossed the box of shells out of the buggy. "That ought to be a nice walk for him," I said, smiling at Danny.

"We going to the camp?" Thad asked over the radio.

"Yeah, you know where it is?" I replied.

"Straight down the road, ain't it?"

"Ten-four."

Chapter 23

It was kind of surreal to be hauling ass right down the middle of the road. Thad kicked up a cloud of dust and dry leaves and pine needles. We moved off to the side of Thad to keep from choking on it all. The ride was smooth, and it was kind of fun, compared to the damn dirt roads. I was curious to see what the camp looked like up close. The only view I'd ever had was from outside the fence, so I knew this would be interesting.

There were several uniformed men standing around in front of the gate. Ted walked out from the group, waving. Thad pulled up and stopped beside him.

"Hey, Thad," Ted said as he stuck his hand out. He waved at us. "Hey, fellas. Welcome to the newly run National Guard camp!"

Danny looked out at the camp. "Nice! So how'd it go?"

Ted glanced back. "Almost perfect. Just a couple little hiccups, but we've got it secured now."

"Where's Sarge?" I asked.

"He's one of the hiccups. He stopped a bullet."

"Is he all right?" Danny asked, looking alarmed.

"Oh yeah, he'll be all right. It wasn't too bad. He's already back to his jovial self."

"Good, that's good. Did you guys find Jess?" I asked.

"Yeah, she's back at the infirmary. I'll show you the way," Ted said.

"How is she?"

"She's had a rough time, but she'll be all right. Just needs some time."

"What happened to her?"

Ted hesitated. "I'll let her tell you about it." He hopped into Thad's ride. "Come on!"

As we followed them through the camp, Danny and I took in the surroundings. Being inside was strange—things looked very different from when we were spying from the outside. Being so close we could see the people's faces, see the hopelessness on so many of them, and the fear. Gone now were the DHS troopers, in their place were Guardsmen. I would have thought the folks inside would be relieved, happy even, but I wasn't seeing that.

"I figured these people would be happy to see the Guard here, but they look scared shitless," I said.

Danny glanced over. "I was thinking the same thing. There seems to be some tension hanging over the place."

As we weaved our way through the camp, every person we passed stared, and furtive whispers were exchanged. It was uncomfortable, to say the least. These people had lived under the boot of their oppressors for so long it appeared they didn't trust anyone.

Thad stopped in front of a large military-style tent, and Ted hopped out, gesturing for us to follow.

As we stepped out, the camp's PA system crackled to life:

"Attention, please—may I have your attention, please. This is Captain Sheffield of the Florida National Guard. I am sure you have a lot of questions about what's going on, and I'm here to answer them. Earlier this morning my unit took possession of the camp, and we are now in control if it."

To my surprise, there were no cheers. The address continued, "This is no longer a detainment camp: it is now a refugee camp. After we've stabilized the operation of the facility and interviewed each of you, you will be free to leave if you so choose. If you have nowhere to go, then you are also free to stay here. We will do our best to provide for your needs. I respectfully request your complete cooperation with my staff. Your security is our highest priority. If you see anything that you feel is a threat to the safe operation of the camp, please let one of the Guardsmen know and we will address it. They're easy to spot; they wear the same army uniform as me. In the meantime, I would appreciate your cooperation. Thank you."

I looked at Ted. "So how's it going?"

"It's been a cakewalk in terms of the takeover, but some of the civilians are getting nervous. Guess the captain is trying to relieve some of that."

"What are we doing at the infirmary?" I asked, pointing at the sign above the door.

"The old man's in here. So is Jess."

"How's he doing?"

"Cranky as ever. Come on, let's go in." We followed Ted through the door.

Once inside the tent, I immediately saw Sarge and Mike on stretchers and smiled.

"What happened to you?" I asked Mike.

"Ah, I twisted my ankle and fell."

"Graceful as a baby gazelle, aren't you?" Thad said, a smile finally showing on his face.

"Yeah, he is," Ted said.

"Well, look what the cat dragged in," Sarge said in a gravelly and somewhat weaker voice than normal.

"Lying down on the job?" I said with a smile.

"Let me poke a hole in you and see how you feel," he said.

"Looks like you managed to take this place without too much trouble," Thad said.

Sarge nodded. "It was almost perfect, almost."

Before Thad could say anything else, he was grabbed from behind. Jess wrapped her arms around him.

"You trying to break me in half?" he asked.

She finally released him, came around to his front, and once again wrapped her arms around him, burying her face in his chest. He looked down at her and smiled, patting her head.

"Nice to see you too," he said.

Jess pulled back and looked up at him with tears in her eyes. She was trying to smile, without much success.

"I'm just so glad to see you."

I couldn't help but smile broadly at the scene. "We're glad to see you too," I said.

She opened her arms, and we embraced in a heartfelt hug. I patted her back while she sniffled. I pulled away from her with concern. "You gonna be all right?"

She stepped back, wiping at her eyes. "Yeah, I've just thought about you two for so long." Her expression changed a little and she continued, "You left without saying good-bye, remember?"

I nodded. "I know, I felt bad about that, sorry. How are your mom and dad? Are they here?" She didn't answer me, and I could see it on her face. "Oh, I'm so sorry," I said.

She nodded and stared at the floor for a moment before quickly recovering. She grabbed Thad and me by the hands and started to pull us. "I want you guys to meet someone." She dragged us over to another stretcher with a girl standing beside it.

"This is Fred. Fred, this is Morgan and Thad," Jess said as an introduction.

Fred smiled and stuck out her hand. "I've heard a lot about you two."

"All good things, I hope," Thad said with a smile.

Fred winked at him. "Good enough."

"Who's this?" I asked, pointing to the man on the stretcher. "He looks like he's one of them."

Fred looked down at him. "He is, but he was helping us. He saved me more than once here."

"Sort of a sheep in wolves' clothing, huh?"

"More like a sheepdog in wolves' clothing."

They then introduced us to Kay and told us about her and what she'd done for them. We all chatted for a little while.

"Kay ran the food service here. We eventually were assigned to work for her." Jess smiled. "She took really good care of us."

"It's nice to meet you, Kay," I said.

"It's nicer to meet you. I'm so glad your friends showed up. It's been rough in here for"—Kay paused a moment—"some people." It was clear there was more she wanted to say, but she kept quiet.

"Who's this?" Thad asked, pointing to Mary.

Jess's face fell. "That's Mary. She's a really good friend of mine. She didn't do so well in the detention center."

"Why were you guys in there?" Thad asked softly.

Jess didn't respond. Fred looked at her and took the lead. "We killed a guard."

The answer shocked me. "You did what?"

"We had to. He did something horrible."

She didn't have to say it—I could tell from looking at Jess and the way her head was down what it must be. It was a horrible thing and it pained me to know. I stepped around to Jess's side and wrapped my arm around her. "It's okay now. With these guys here, you'll be safe."

Jess wiped tears from her face. She nodded and smiled but said nothing.

After a few minutes, I asked, "So now what? What are you guys going to do?"

"We don't know, we have nowhere to go," Jess said, then added, "Is there any chance we could come with you, to your house?"

I looked at Thad, then back at her. "I hate to say it, but where we are is a really tight fit . . ."

"We could make some room," Thad said.

"Yeah, we could." I looked at Danny. "Would you and Bobbie mind doubling up with us?"

"Sure. Whatever we need to do."

"Actually, let's think about this. Now that the camp is gone, we can go back to the old neighborhood. There are plenty of empty houses there. Maybe we can get one of them set up for you guys." I looked at Fred. "I assume you're coming too?" She nodded and smiled appreciatively.

"Wait—you're not at home? Where are you living now? I didn't think you'd ever leave," Jess said.

"Well, we were persuaded to do it, but it wasn't easy," I said.

From across the room, Sarge shouted, "Hell no, it wasn't, bunch of damn loggerheads."

Remembering those conversations, I said, "Yeah, he tried for a long time to get us to leave."

Sarge wagged a finger at me. "One of these days you'll learn to listen to me."

"Hey, we did eventually listen," Thad said.

"Pfft, eventually's ass," Sarge replied. His comment got a smile out of everyone.

I looked at Ted and Mike. "Glad to see he's still his same old self."

"Yeah, it'd take more than a bullet to get him down,"Ted replied.

"You need more than that to kill something that damn mean," Mike added.

Sarge looked over at Mike with one eye squinted. "You just wait, I'm gonna show your ass mean."

"Big talk from an old man lying on his back," Mike said with a laugh.

"Why, you rotten little shit!" Sarge shouted as he started to get up. "I ain't lyin' around now!" Before he could actually get up, Ted moved on him.

"No, no, lie down. There'll be plenty of time to whip his ass,"Ted said as he pushed Sarge back onto the stretcher, then he looked at Mike. "I'll even help you do it."

"Now, that's just uncalled for," Mike said, grinning like a Cheshire cat.

"I don't need no help to whip his sorry ass!"

Ted looked back at Sarge and patted his shoulder. "I know."

We were already laughing at the exchange going on, but what happened next put everyone in stiches: Sarge grabbed Ted's hand and rolled it over, twisting it. "Don't patronize me, Teddy. You're close enough for me to reach."

"Damn! I'm not. Let go of me, you old prick!"Ted shouted.

Sarge released him and Ted rubbed his wrist. "You're awful strong for an AARP member."

"Don't you forget it either!" Sarge barked.

Still laughing, I asked Ted, "So, with this place under the control of the National Guard, can we go home now? I mean . . . back to my *real* home?"

"I don't see any reason why not. Those DHS goons aren't going to be messing with you guys anymore."

"What about the storm troopers? What are you guys going to do with them?" I asked.

"They are going to be detained for a while. Once the interviews of the civilians here are done we'll have to address any abuses that come to light. Any of the staff that comes up clean will be paroled. They'll be allowed to leave, stripped of their uniforms, of course," Ted said.

"You're just going to let them go?" Thad asked.

"We can't keep them here. There's just not enough resources."

"What if they turn up later, causing trouble?" Danny asked.

"This camp has some nice equipment. We'll create a database, complete with photos and fingerprints. If they turn up later committing crimes against anyone, they will be executed. We'll make it clear to them before they go, so they'll know the risks," Ted said.

"How long before you start letting them go?" I asked.

"It's going to be a while. There's a lot that has to be done. It'll be a couple of weeks at best. They'll be under supervision of the Guards in the meantime."

I looked at Danny and Thad. "Looks like we can go home, then."

"Yes, Morgan, take the girls home! Get 'em out of that swamp," Sarge added from his stretcher.

Danny added, "They'd like that. Hell, *I'd* like that."

I looked at Thad. "You want to go home?"

Thad appeared deep in thought for a moment before answering, "I like it out there on the river, but them little cabins are kind of rough. I'm ready for a real bed again."

"What about us?" Jess asked, her voice small.

"You could come too. Like I said, there are houses there

I know no one is coming back to. You ladies could take one of those," I said.

"Really?" she asked.

"Really, Jess."

"Thank you so, so much. I don't even know . . ." She started to cry.

"Aww, dry up, Annie!" Sarge yelled.

I couldn't help but smile at the grumpy old bastard.

"What are you guys going to do?" Danny asked Ted.

He shrugged. "I don't know. I do know I'm ready for a break from the action for some time, though."

"Me too," Mike agreed.

"Morg, if you guys are leaving the cabins, we're going to go stay in them for a while. We could use a spot to take a break," Sarge said.

"Sure thing," I said. "Just wait for us to check out our neighborhood, and then you guys can take over."

"Perfect," Mike said. "Give the old man enough time to heal up."

"Speaking of healing, where's Doc?" Ted asked.

Mike looked around. "I don't know, wonder where he went."

Doc answered the question when he appeared from the back of the tent with an armload of medical supplies.

"Where the hell you been?" Ted asked.

Doc hefted the supplies in his arms. "Replenishing my stock."

"Hey, how long before we can move the old man?"

"Why, what's up?" Doc asked as he dumped his load on a table.

"Nothing, we're just talking about going out to the creek for a while. Taking a break from the action."

"Oh, I'd say two or three days at least," Doc said.

"I'm fine, I don't need to wait two or three days," Sarge barked.

"It's going to take us that long to get cleared out," Danny said.

"That works out, then, doesn't it?" Doc said.

"You wanna head back and let the ladies know the good news?" Thad asked.

"Yeah, let's go by the house on the way back and check it out before we make any promises," Danny said.

"Sounds like a plan to me," I said.

"Can we come?" Jess asked.

I looked at Danny and Thad, they both shrugged. "Sure. Just warning you, where we're staying now isn't exactly four-star," I said.

"I don't care, it's not here," Jess said, then looked at Fred. "You want to come too?"

Fred looked at Aric. He was still out cold. "Come on, we'll be back. Doc will take care of him. Let's get out of here for a little while," Jess said.

Fred looked at Doc. "You'll take care of him?"

Doc nodded, pointed to the caduceus on his sleeve, and said, "Do no harm. I'll take care of him."

"He'll be here when I get back?"

"He isn't going anywhere," Ted said.

Fred looked at Jess. "Okay, I'll go." Then she looked at Doc. "If he wakes up, tell him I'll be back, okay?"

Doc smiled and nodded. "Sure thing."

Jess looked at Thad. "When can we leave?"

Thad rocked back on his heels and started to laugh. "Calm down, little girl, we'll go in a minute."

It was good to see him laugh. I could tell that the incident earlier today had affected him, that he was shaken from it. Now he seemed to be back to our usual jovial Thad.

I walked over to Sarge. "You gonna be all right with these guys?" I asked.

"Yeah, they're idiots, but they know what they're doing. You go get them girls home."

"We'll start right away, but it's going to take a while. I've only got enough fuel in the old truck for one trip—the rest will have to be done on the four-wheelers."

"Don't worry about that. I'll take care of it. Just go get packed up."

"Will do. Now you get better. We still need you around here," I said with a smile.

Sarge smiled back and stuck out his hand. I clasped it in mine as he said, "I'm gonna be all right. I told Little Bit I'd be back to see her. Can't let her down."

It struck me that he was thinking of her, and I smiled. "No, you can't," I said.

Sarge gave my hand a squeeze then said, "Now go on, git."

"We'll see you soon," I said as I turned to leave.

Fred, Jess, and Kay were gathered on the other side of the tent talking quietly. It looked like they were scheming as they kept looking back in our direction.

Thad nodded his head in their direction. "Something's up."

We all turned to look. "Oh yeah, they're scheming," Danny said.

They concluded their skulduggery and headed our direction, Jess leading the pack.

"What's up? You ladies are obviously conspiring about something," I said.

Jess's eyes darted toward Sarge, then back to Kay. "Kay's going to stay here to help out. She runs the food service, and the captain will probably need her help."

Ted cleared his throat. "We'll need all the help we can get to keep order here. We'd be happy to have you on. I'll let Livingston know." Ted looked at Kay. "Are there other staff like you around?"

"Yes, there are other people in charge of some things—decent people. I can point them out," Kay said. "I really appreciate your men coming in and taking charge here. Jess has only said the best things about you all."

"They are some pretty good guys," Jess said. She waved over to Fred, then looked back at me. "We're going to grab a few things," Jess said.

"Hurry up," I said.

"You don't have to tell me twice," she said, skipping away.

Chapter 24

Danny stood in front of his shattered front door. Glass crunched under his feet as he stepped into his home. I was right behind him. We worked to clear the house, moving room to room, but it soon became clear that it was empty. The only room we didn't look in was the half bath downstairs. No one needed to see or smell that again.

It was obvious that more people had been through the house since we last were here. The house was a wreck. A lifetime of possessions were scattered everywhere. The only bright spot was that most of the windows were still intact. It looked as though the doors had taken the brunt of the DHS's frustrations. The front door lay in splinters in the entry. The two sets of French doors on the rear of the house were little more than kindling at this point.

Danny moved through the house, pausing occasionally to pick up something from the floor to brush away dust and debris and examine it. He was kneeling in the living room when he let out a sigh.

"Well, at least the house is in decent shape. The doors will have to be fixed, don't know how we're going to do that."

"We'll find a way, man. Let's go check out Thad's place and mine. I'll be outside when you're ready," I said.

I found Thad on the porch, leaning against a post. "It's nice to be back here. It feels like home," he said.

"A screwed-up version of home, though," I remarked.

"That can all be fixed. We'll get through it."

I gave a little laugh. "You are the most optimistic person I've ever met."

"My momma taught me a long time ago, you only get one turn on this ride. Don't worry about the things you can't control. Put everything into those that you can and live like you mean it."

I slapped him on the back. "I like that, *live like you mean it.* Wanna hear my take on life?"

A big smirk crossed his face. "Oh yeah, I got to hear this."

With a big smile I said, "Life is a sexually transmitted disease with a hundred-percent fatality rate."

Thad's chin dropped to his chest, a big smile on his face as he shook his head. "I've said it before and I'll say it again. Morgan Carter—you just ain't right."

We walked to the buggies together through the mess of pine needles and other debris covering the yard. Danny had always been so diligent about keeping it cleaned up, and I could tell the state of everything was just killing him. Jess and Fred were sitting on the bed of the buggy when we came up.

Fred looked around. "This is a nice place. I like it here. It reminds me of where I grew up."

"It used to be a lot nicer," Danny said as he made his way toward his barn.

"Where you going?" I asked.

"To see if my Kubota is still here."

Thad and I followed him. He slid the door open and he breathed a sigh of relief. The orange tractor was sitting there.

"Wonder why no one took it?" Thad asked.

"I pulled some parts to keep it from starting."

"Good idea. Wonder if Reggie's tractor is still around," I said.

"It should be. I did the same thing to his."

"Let's go check it out, then," Thad said as he moved back toward the vehicles.

We followed him to Reggie's old place. The front door was still locked, and it looked as though it hadn't been touched. But just to be safe we went in and cleared it room by room. It was empty. No one had even tried to enter it.

"I can't believe no one has tried to get in here," I said.

"Yeah, I don't understand it," Thad said. "But I am relieved."

Jess poked her head in the door. "Is this where you live, Thad?"

Thad spread his arms out. "Home sweet home."

She and Fred walked in and looked around.

"Could use a woman's touch," Fred said.

"You volunteering for the job?"

With a smile she replied, "Maybe. I think me and Jess could get this place in order."

Jess let out a little laugh. "I'd gladly clean this house. I used to hate chores, but now I'd do them with a smile on my face."

"Once we get moved back over here, there'll be plenty of time and opportunity to clean, don't you worry," I said.

Thad gave a nod of approval. "Let's go check your place out."

"Sounds good to me, let's go."

We got back in the buggies and headed up the road to my place. My stomach was in knots. Seeing what they'd done to Danny's place, I was certain mine was in just as bad a shape. Rolling to a stop in front, we could see the front door was gone. We worked together to clear it, then I started to survey the damage.

It was my worst fears come to life. Unlike Danny's place, nearly every window in the house was broken. Every piece of furniture was destroyed. The cushions on the sofa and love seat were shredded. With a heavy heart, I ran my hand over my leather chair, which had been slashed to pieces. Going into my bedroom, I was met by a foul odor. The mattress on the bed had also been cut up, all the furniture had been hacked at, and what clothes were there were scattered on the floor.

Danny came up behind me. "What's that smell?

"I have a feeling they pissed on my bed."

"Looks like they really did a number here."

"Yeah, I don't know where to begin to fix all this."

"Have you seen the bathroom yet?" Danny asked.

"No, I was afraid to look," I said as I walked to the bathroom off my bedroom. I let out a groan. "Why in the hell would they bust my toilets? I mean, really? What the fuck?"

Thad's voice came over my shoulder. "At least they didn't burn the place down. We can fix this. Remember what I said earlier."

I nodded. "Thanks, I'll need the help."

"Don't worry, I got your back."

"Me too, after my house is fixed up, of course," Danny added.

"Thanks for that, really. I appreciate it."

"Oh my God, Morgan, your house." Jess's voice came from the living room.

I stepped out. "Tell me about it. They really did a number on it."

"Who did this and why?"

"You must have really pissed in someone's Cheerios," Fred added.

"This is what the DHS does to people who don't go along with the program," I said.

"You have no idea what they'll do to you. I wish they'd just trashed my house," Fred said, with a blank expression. Jess nodded, with that same look on her face.

"Yes, it could be worse," I said, regretting my choice of words. Hearing them say that helped put this in perspective. Whatever the girls had gone through must make this seem like a cakewalk.

Fred waved around the room. "This, this can be fixed. We can handle this."

"I hope so. Mel and the girls are going to be pretty upset, but we'll explain that we can get this back toward normal."

"Bobbie's not going to be happy at all," Danny agreed.

"Let's get back and give them . . . I wouldn't call it good news, but the news," I said, heading for the doorway.

We loaded up and headed out, using the paved roads. Heading toward Altoona, I was curious to see if the market was still active. I slowed as we came up to it, taking a look. The parking lot was littered with trash, and the little tables used for wares were still there, but there were no traders in sight. Sitting on the walkway at the front of the store was a lone figure. I pulled in and Thad followed.

"Wonder where everyone is," Danny said.

"Let's see if we can find out."

The long figure turned out to be an old man with a full gray beard. Like many people now, his clothes were dirty and road-worn, though, surprisingly, he was smoking a cigarette.

"Howdy," I called out. With a nod, he raised his smoke at me, but that was it.

"Where is everyone?" Danny asked.

"Ain't no one 'round here."

"There used to be. Where's the old lady that ran the store?"

"She's dead. Ever'one else is gone. Reckon they went to that camp up there." He motioned up the road.

"You live around here?" I asked.

"I live wur ever, don't much matter."

"Have you seen anyone else around?" Danny asked.

He waved his hand. "Naw, ain't seen no one in some time now."

"All right. Well, then, take it easy," I said as I started the buggy up.

He nodded and flipped his hand. "Take it however I can get it."

As I pulled out, Danny said, "Let's stop by Clear Lake and see if that couple is still there."

I nodded. "Good idea."

Danny looked over. "You know, maybe they would want to move into our neighborhood. Another set of hands would be handy."

"I was thinking the same thing. Plus it would give Little Bit someone to play with."

Danny nodded. "Thought about that too."

We cruised down the road, kicking up leaves and trash in our wake. Seeing how the roads were a mess, I wondered what Orlando was like. I would imagine the destruction was enormous. With so many living in such a small area, the worst in people was sure to come out. I could picture the smashed windows, the looted stores, garbage piling up in the streets.

What would people do for food now? I shuddered at the thought. Orlando could be as bad off as a third-world country.

We pulled up to the camp and saw Tyler and Brandy sitting around a fire. They rose at the sound of the buggies. Seeing it was us, they smiled and waved. Tyler jogged out to where we parked.

"Hey, Morgan, Danny," Tyler said, then looked at the buggy with Thad and the girls.

"Hey, Tyler." I pointed to Thad. "This is Thad—he stayed behind on our last trip—and that's Jess and Fred."

"Hi, Thad, Jess, Fred," he said, shaking their hands in turn. "Glad to meet you guys! Come join us by the fire."

We followed him, waving hello to Brandy. She smiled and called out, "Hey, guys, nice to see you."

"Hi, Brandy, good to see you guys too," Danny replied.

We did another quick round of introductions for Brandy's benefit. The girls quickly got into a conversation. Tyler looked over and grinned, then back at us. "They don't waste any time, do they?"

"Nope, all's missing is a fence for them to lean over," Thad said, getting a laugh out of Tyler.

"How've you guys been out here, had any trouble?" I asked.

"We've been good. Haven't seen a soul."

"Glad to hear it," I replied.

"So to what do we owe the pleasure of your visit?" Tyler asked, sitting on a log.

"Well, we were talking and wanted to run something past you. We're about to move back to our old house in our old neighborhood, and there are plenty of empty houses over there. Would you guys be interested in taking one of those houses? You know, move over there with us?" I asked.

Brandy and Tyler looked at one another. It was obviously something they hadn't considered.

"That's a bit of a surprise," Tyler said. "We didn't even think about that, but it would be really nice."

Brandy looked at the tent they were using. "Right now, anything would be an improvement."

"It'll take us a couple of days to get things ready, but we'll come by when we get moved and bring you guys over if you're interested," I said.

"That'd be great," Brandy said, smiling. "We're interested, right, Tyler?" she asked eagerly, looking at her husband.

Tyler nodded. "We'd love to. Thank you so much. You guys have been more than kind to us."

"Yes, thank you so much. I can't express how nice it will be to live in a *house* again," Brandy said, smiling.

"How far is it from here?" Tyler asked.

"It's close, about ten minutes away," Danny said.

"Really? I haven't seen any houses nearby," Tyler said with surprise.

"Oh, I meant ten minutes by car. Guess I should have clarified that," I said.

Tyler and Thad started to laugh. "Yeah, that's a big distinction," Thad said.

Tyler was shaking his head. "Guess we don't really think in those terms anymore."

"Hopefully, we will again someday," I said.

"Hopefully. But I hope when it comes back, we do things a little differently. Sure, I miss having a car, house, and electricity. But this is a slower life. It's nice in a way," Tyler said.

Thad poked at the fire with a stick. "I think we needed to slow down. It was a hell of a way to do it, but it really emphasizes what's important in life."

"True. A lot of what we thought was so important disappeared and yet here we are," I said, standing up from the fire. "Well, I'm glad you guys are moving in. I think that'll be really nice to have you there. But for now, we got to get going."

"We'll come and get you guys when we get moved in. Just hold tight," Danny said.

Tyler looked at Brandy and smiled. "We'll be ready. I know I'm looking forward to it."

"Me too. A house! Wow, it's hard to believe." Brandy looked at Fred and Jess. "Are you two going to live there as well?"

Jess nodded. "Uh-huh"—she looked around—"but I could live here and be happy, anywhere other than where we were."

"That'll be great—you two, plus Mel and Bobbie. It'll be really nice."

I looked at Thad and Danny. "This is going to end badly for us guys, I can tell already."

Jess and Fred laughed. "Pfft, whatever," Jess said.

We said our good-byes and headed back. We didn't see a soul until we passed Chase's place. The big man was standing in his front yard, tending a tub sitting over a fire. We exchanged waves as we passed. Seeing him made me replay what we had done to his son and the rest of his crew. I didn't think it would be a good idea to tell him about the incident, though I thought he would agree that his son's behavior was terrible. From what I could tell about Chase, he was a man of principle.

As we pulled into the camp, we could see Mel, Bobbie, and the girls sitting around the fire in the late-afternoon sun.

Mel stood and hollered out, "Where have you guys been?"

I took a seat by the fire before answering, "Been busy! Lots going on."

Mel and Bobbie were eyeing Jess and Fred, so I made the introductions.

"You're *the* Jess, the one who . . ." Mel pointed to her head.

Jess blushed a little and nodded. "Yeah, that's me."

Mel gave her a hug. "It's nice to meet you. Thanks for taking care of him and helping him get home."

Jess smiled. "I don't know about that. He helped me more than I helped him. Nice to meet you, I've heard a lot about you."

Sitting in my chair, I rubbed my head dramatically. "You can say that again."

Thad started to laugh. "There ain't much you could do to make that punkin look any worse than it already does."

"Look who's talking! Cue ball doesn't cut it, that's a damn bowling ball sitting on your shoulders. Which reminds me, when you going to cut that shrubbery you got growing up there?"

Thad ran his hand through the nearly inch-long hair on his head. "Trust me, I want a haircut more than you even know."

"Once we get back home, we'll make that a priority," I said with a sly grin.

Mel and Bobbie both looked at me. "Get back home? Are we going home?" Mel asked excitedly.

"That's right, girls! Sarge and the boys joined with the National Guard and took over the camp. The DHS isn't a threat anymore . . . which means we're going home," Danny said.

Little Bit jumped up from her chair. "We're going home! When can we go, Daddy?"

"We have to start packing up and get everything loaded. We've only got enough fuel for one trip," I said.

"How are we going to move everything in one trip? It took way more than that to get it here," Bobbie said.

"I know, but we'll have to do the best we can." I looked around. "Where's Jeff?"

"He's in the reading room," Mel said. I nodded, but apparently the statement confused Fred.

"The reading room? What's that?"

I laughed. "The outhouse."

She too started to laugh, along with most everyone else. "Oh, I should have known."

"On a serious note," I said, looking at Mel, "the house is in rough shape. So is Danny's. It's going to take a lot of work to get it back to the way it was before."

"Did they tear it up?" Mel asked.

"Oh yeah, they did quite the job on them," Danny said.

"We may not even be able to live in ours," I admitted.

"Really? It's that bad?" Bobbie asked.

I nodded. "Yeah, they broke all the windows, the doors are gone, the furniture's all torn up."

"Well . . . it'll still be better than being here," Mel said cautiously.

"Wait a minute. Why don't you guys move into the empty house beside us?" Danny asked.

I hadn't even thought of that. "That's an idea. We'll have to look at it."

"Will we have our own rooms?" Taylor asked.

"I think it's a four-bedroom," Danny said.

"Good. I want my own room."

"Me too," Lee Ann said.

"One thing at a time, girls. Let's focus on the move first," I said.

Thad laughed. "Actually, let's focus on dinner first. What's in the pot?" he asked, motioning to the Dutch oven.

"Oh, Jeff got these," Bobbie said, opening the lid to reveal four medium-sized birds packed in.

"What are they?"

"They were some kind of a black bird with orange legs."

"Coots," I said.

"We'll pull all the meat off and mix it with some rice. Should be plenty for everyone," Mel said.

"Cool, so dinner's sorted out. Guess that leaves us nothing to do for the rest of the evening," Danny said.

Jeff came walking up. I smiled and greeted him with, "Hey there, Cooter." That got a laugh out of Danny and Thad.

He didn't catch the joke. "Huh?"

I kicked my foot out at the pot. "Coots, you got some coots today."

Mel rolled her eyes. "We're going to go get the rest of the dinner ready. Fred, Jess, you want to come help?" Mel asked.

"Sure," they said, jumping up.

We all gathered around the big table for dinner. There was a lot of chatter at the table, as everyone was excited at the thought of going home. Jess and Fred were really starting to open up, laughing and joking with Taylor and Lee Ann. Mel and Bobbie were also doing their best to make the two feel welcome, especially knowing that they had been in the detention center at the camp.

Thad carried the big Dutch oven around the table, placing a generous scoop on each plate.

When he got to Jess, she looked up and, in her best young-boy voice, said, "Please sir, I want some more." The table erupted into laughter.

Thad dumped another scoop onto her plate. "Sure thing, Oliver."

It was another of those precious moments we enjoy so much now: a moment of humor, a reason to smile and laugh, in these very uncertain times. Sitting under the plastic roof with my friends and family, I realized that it didn't really matter where we were as long as we were together.

After dinner we sat around the fire for a little while, but knowing that we had a busy day tomorrow, we all turned in early. Jess and Fred would sleep in Danny and Bobbie's cabin tonight, and Bobbie led them to get settled. I volunteered for the first watch and Mel sent the girls off to bed, staying behind.

"She's pretty," Mel said, once everyone was gone.

"Who?"

"Jess, she's pretty and young. And pretty. I see why you let her walk with you."

I laughed. "I guess, but when I met her, my first impression was that she was a pain in the ass."

"Hmm."

"What? You think there's something there?" I laughed. "She's like a little sister—a really annoying one at that."

"Mmhmm."

I laughed again. "Think what you want, but remember, I came home."

"I know, just making an observation." She sat there for a minute staring into the fire, then got up. "I'm going to bed."

"Okay, babe, I'll be there in a couple of hours."

She leaned over and kissed me. "Love you," I said as I grabbed her hand. "Hope you know that."

She smiled. "I do." Then she looked off toward Danny's cabin. "And I trust you too."

"Well, I should hope the hell so!" I said with a laugh.

She walked to the cabin, leaving me alone with my thoughts. The dogs came trotting up and lay by the fire. I was rubbing Meathead's head with my foot when I heard someone coming. I looked up to see Jess and Fred.

"What are you two doing up? I thought you'd want some sleep," I said as they sat down.

"I've gotten enough sleep for years," Fred said.

"Me too," Jess added.

We sat in silence for a few minutes. "So what was it like inside the camp?" I finally asked.

They both stared into the flames for a moment, then without looking up, Fred said, "It's not what's advertised."

Jess snorted. "To say the very least."

We sat talking for some time, each telling the story of how they met, in turns. They also took time to describe in considerable detail what life inside was like. They said something happened—something bad, but didn't elaborate—that led them to kill that guard. Jess sat quietly, letting Fred relay what little of the story they told. Then they both talked about how they were detained, the cruel methods used. Jess spoke up about their time in isolation.

"So what about Aric? What's his story?" I asked.

"He's a guard, but to him being part of DHS was a survival method," Fred explained.

"He was trying to bust you guys out?"

"Yeah, he actually had us out, but then Sarge showed up and it just went downhill from there."

"I'm surprised he's not dead," I said, then quickly thought about that statement. "Sorry Fred, I just know those guys and can imagine what they must've thought, you know."

"I understand. I don't know them like you all do, but I can

see where you're coming from. If it wasn't for Jess, he probably would be."

"I just hope Sarge is going to be okay," Jess said.

"Ah, don't worry about him, he'll be all right," I said.

"I know he's a tough guy, but he's getting older. My grandpa was a tough old guy too. He fell and broke his hip and never really recovered. He was never the same man again." She pushed at a log in the fire with her toe. "I just don't want to see that happen to Sarge."

"Well, let's just hope for the best," I said.

We sat and talked for a little while longer, than I looked at my watch. "Well, ladies, it's time for me to wake up Danny. I'm heading to bed. We've got a busy day tomorrow."

"I guess I'll turn in too," Jess said.

"Me too," Fred added.

As I stood up to leave, Jess caught me and hugged me. "You're helping save me again. Thanks."

"Aw, you say that to all the sailors," I said.

She laughed and she and Fred headed toward the cabin. I called after them, "Hey, wake Danny up for me, would ya?"

Jess gave me a thumbs-up over her shoulder.

Chapter 25

The next morning we were up early, buzzing around the grounds. We used the same method of prioritizing our load as we had before. The basics of living went in first—bedding, clothes, cooking gear, that sort of thing—and then other less important items were to be added later. Everyone was busy, loading and reconfiguring. Fred and Jess were pitching in wherever they were needed. The extra hands really helped out.

Sometime after noon, we were taking a break around the picnic tables when the familiar sound of an engine drifted through the camp. We quickly rose to our feet in uncertain expectation.

"Sounds like there's more than one," Jeff said.

"Yeah, diesels too," Thad added.

In short order a Hummer pulled down the drive, followed closely by a large military truck and another Hummer bringing up the rear. Mike was standing in the turret, grinning like the cat that ate the canary and waving like the homecoming queen.

"What the hell are they doing here?" I asked no one in particular.

"Maybe they're going back to the other camp downriver?" Danny posited.

Ted climbed out of the lead Hummer, a huge grin on his face.

"What's all this about?" Thad asked.

"The old man thought you guys could use some help," Ted said.

"No shit, that's cool," I said, then made a show of looking around. "So where's the help?"

With a grin he gave me the finger. "Hey, we can leave!"

"No, no, no, Morgan, shut up, we can use the help," Mel said, getting a laugh out of Mike and Ted. Six Guardsmen walked up behind them.

"Damn, you did bring some help, didn't you," Thad said.

"We'll help you guys get everything moved and back to your place. We brought you some fuel too," Ted said.

"Oh wow, thanks for that," I said.

"Thank the DHS. We figured they owed you guys anyway."

With the additional help, everything was loaded in no time. Everything except for one thing, that is: the pigs.

"With all these people here, we can get the hogs loaded up too," Thad said.

"Oh yeah, this should be fun," I said, rubbing my hands together.

"Hell yeah, let's go wrassle some pigs in the mud!" Mike shouted.

"Shit, you ain't going to be able to catch one, what with your bum foot and all," Ted said.

That statement started one hell of a challenge. Everyone moved to the pigpen, using MREs as bait to bring the hogs in close.

"All right, Mikey, there they are, go get 'em," Ted said with a grin.

Mike stepped over the wire, which he insisted on turning off personally. "Just remember I'm half-crippled."

Ted's head rocked back as he laughed. "Already trying to crawfish."

As soon as he stepped over the wire, the hogs knew something was up and started to scatter. Mike cornered one, moving on it in a crouch with his arms out. Deciding on his moment, he lunged for the pig. The porker had moves that any NFL scout would appreciate, and in a flash, Mike was lying facedown in the mud. A howl of laughter erupted from the spectators.

Little Bit was pointing and laughing. "He's got mud on his face!"

Thad leaned over and out of the corner of his mouth he said, "Wonder if he knows that's not just mud?"

I laughed. "Let's wait to tell him," I said, causing Thad to laugh.

The Guardsmen were quickly over the wire and stomping after the pigs in the mud. Even with seven men in the pen, it was Lee Ann who caught the first one, a piglet. This brought on a chorus of taunts aimed at Mike and his pig-chasing partners. With so many of them in the pen, though, it was just a matter of time, and they quickly had one of the boars trussed up.

It took three of us to pull the screaming porker out under the wire. Danny ran and brought one of the trucks over and we loaded it into the bed. Danny, me, Ted, Jeff, and Thad then managed to get the slippery critter up into the back and shut the gate. By the time we got back, they had another trussed up and we repeated the process. The girls, in the meantime, were steadily catching the piglets.

Once the last one was tied up, the guys came out of the

pen. They were covered nearly head to toe with mud and stunk to high heaven.

Ted looked at Mike, waving a hand in front of his face. "You're manning the turret on the way back for damn sure."

Once that was done, we took a quick look around, making sure we had everything. I walked out to the creek and knelt down beside the water. It wasn't the most comfortable place, these cabins, but it was beautiful here. The creek flowing by, the fog in the morning, they were constants in an ever-changing world. I was going to miss this place. We all had become so close since settling down here. But it wasn't the sort of life we wanted to live for the long run. Like any camping trip, it was always good to go home.

Thad and Danny walked up, and Danny patted me on the back. "I'm gonna miss it," Danny said.

I looked up and smiled. "Strange as it is, me too."

"Me too. But, man, I'm looking forward to living in a real house,"Thad said.

"It's time to move on, but we'll be back." I looked at Danny. "We always come back to the creek."

After a little shuffling of vehicles, we got everyone lined up on the road. It was quite the convoy: three Guard trucks, my truck with the trailer, the two buggies, Jeff on his hog, and the ATVs, manned by Lee Ann and Taylor.

Danny led the way in one of the buggies with Ted right behind him in a Hummer. As we approached Chase's place, I keyed the mic on my radio. "I'm going to stop in here real quick." It was weighing on my mind all night, and I decided that the best thing to do—the honest thing—would be to let him know about his son.

The other vehicles stopped in the road as I got out and waved to Chase. "Mornin', Chase."

He nodded. "Mornin'."

I stepped up on his porch. "I figure I owe it to you to give you some news."

"What's that?"

"We caught the kids who raided our place the other night. They were camped out over in Alexander Springs. Your boy, Andy, was one of them. The ringleader, as it was."

Chase rocked in his chair. "Is he dead?"

"No, nothing like that. We took them up and dropped them off on the side of Lake George with all their gear. I just figured you'd want to know."

Chase rocked for another moment. He was hard to read, but I assumed he was thinking. "Like I said before, he's grown. If that's how he's going to try and get by, he can deal with the consequences." He paused. "And thanks for letting me know. I appreciate your honesty." Chase looked out at the line of vehicles. "Where y'all headed?"

"Back home. The National Guard took over the DHS camp, so we don't have to worry about them trying to ruin our lives anymore."

"That's good to hear."

"Say, when we get things settled, I was thinking of having a cookout. Would you wanna come over?"

"That sounds nice. Don't know how we'd get there, though."

"We'll come get you. It'll be a few days."

Chase looked up and smiled. "That'd be real nice. I'd really like that."

"Till then," I said with a wave as I stepped off the porch.

The trip home was uneventful. I could tell that Mel was getting more and more excited the closer we got.

After we pulled in, I hopped out and said, "Home sweet

home!" I stopped Mel and the girls before they went in. "Look, guys, the house is really messed up. Let's go in and look and then go down to the house next door to Danny and Bobbie. We may want to stay there instead," I said gently.

Going in, there were a number of gasps. Little Bit was the first person to make a comment. She went into her room and came back out holding a large stuffed bear. "They cut Peanut Butter's head off." She had the bear's head in her other hand. Dropping them to the floor, she asked, "Can we go look at the other house?"

Mel didn't go very far into the house before she announced, "This is pretty bad."

"Holy shit, Morg, you must have really pissed them off," Mike said from the doorway.

"They do seem to have a way with destruction," I said. "Let's go check out the other house."

We went out and loaded into the truck for the short ride down the road.

"I hope that one is okay," Lee Ann said. "I don't want to come back here."

"I hope so too, sweetheart," I replied, looking at her in the rearview mirror.

We all mounted back up and headed down the road to the abandoned house.

Danny hopped out and opened the gate. As I pulled through, he said, "The gate being shut is a good sign."

"Let's hope," I muttered.

Stopping in front of the house, we all got out. Mel looked around. "This is kind of nice. I like all the trees."

Danny was already at the front door. "Is it locked?" I called up.

"Yeah, it's locked," he said as he jumped off the porch. He

knelt down and flipped over a large piece of limestone in what used to be a planter running the length of the porch. After digging around in the dirt for a minute or so, he triumphantly held up a key.

"How'd you know that was there?" I asked.

"Whenever Harry went out of town I'd keep an eye on his place. When he left for the last time, he hauled ass, so I figured he didn't remember to take it," he said as he opened the door.

The house smelled musty, but other than that, everything seemed fine. It was completely furnished, except for one bedroom where the bed had been removed. Mel and Bobbie were talking about the furniture in the living room, a sofa and love seat arranged in front of a large stone fireplace. Danny and I were more interested in looking for black mold or water damage. A quick check of all the bathrooms and kitchen showed no such issues.

"Well, what do you think?" I asked Mel when she came into the kitchen.

"I like it. It's pretty nice. I really like that fireplace."

"Yeah, it's going to be really nice on cold nights," Bobbie said.

The three girls came in. "What do you think, girls? Do you like it here?" I asked.

"I like it. It's got big bedrooms!" Little Bit shouted.

"I like it too. Can me and Taylor have the bedrooms with the bathroom between them?" Lee Ann asked.

"You like that Jack-and-Jill bathroom?" I asked.

"Hey, I want the bathroom too!" Little Bit shouted.

"Sorry, kiddo, your sisters get those rooms," Mel said.

"That's not fair." Little Bit sulked.

I laughed. "Life ain't fair, Miss Bit."

"All right, guys, it's settled. Welcome home. Now let's get to work," I said.

We had everything unloaded by early evening. Once they had stowed their stuff, Thad and Jeff came back over from their house and let us know that everyone was going to hang out around the fire pit in Danny's backyard.

"Damn, I'm hungry! What the hell are we going to do for dinner tonight?" Jeff asked, as we walked over.

No one had given it any thought. I looked at Thad. "You know if we have any dried meat left?"

"Don't worry, we got it covered," Ted said as he motioned for a couple of the Guardsmen to follow him. They returned a few minutes later with several cases of MREs and a stack of large foil trays.

"What are those?" Bobbie asked.

"These are called squad meals. We'll set them over the fire to heat," Ted said as he pried one corner of the top off one of the trays.

"Thanks, man, really appreciate it," I said.

"No worries, you've done a lot to help out with everything that's gone on here lately."

"We didn't really do much," I said.

"Yeah, you did," Mike said.

"When are you guys going to move out to the river camp?" Danny asked.

Ted spit into the fire before answering. "Soon as Doc clears Sarge. Hard to keep his old ass lying down."

"What are you guys going to do now? I mean, none of you are the type to just lie around," I remarked.

"We're going to run that camp now, and there's a lot to do

there to convert it back to a refugee camp and not a detainment facility," said one of the Guardsmen.

"Whatever it is, it's got to be better than that damn camp we were in before," another said. "And I feel confident that it will be. Livingston may not be great at battle tactics, but this type of restructuring task is right up his alley."

"As for our guys? We need a break. Well, I know *I* do. A lot has happened, and we haven't really had the chance for it to soak in," Mike said.

"I think everyone needs a break," Thad said. "I can use one too. You're right about a lot happening."

Danny was staring into the fire. "I haven't really thought about it much, I guess, but a lot *has* happened. There really hasn't been any downtime."

"I'm just happy to have a bathroom again," Taylor said, eliciting a chuckle from several people.

One of the Guardsmen spoke up. "That's one of the best things about that camp—flushing toilets and hot showers. I can't remember the last time I took a shower."

A fellow Guardsman eyed the mud-covered soldier. "Damn sure can't tell by looking at your filthy ass." He looked over at Mel and Bobbie. "Sorry, ladies, I'll try to mind my manners."

Mel laughed. "I think right now your language is the least of our worries."

"I think this stuff is hot enough," Thad said as he raised the top from one of the trays and steam rolled out.

Mike slapped his hands together. "Let's eat!"

Chapter 26

"Dammit, Doc! I ain't asking you if I'm fit to leave, I'm telling you that I'm leaving," Sarge barked.

Doc shot Ted a look, then looked back at Sarge. "I really think you should wait another day."

"I can lie around there just as good as I can here, better actually."

"I'll go get the captain," Mike said as he headed for the door.

Doc walked over to Kay. "See if you can talk any sense into him."

Since his injury, Kay had stayed close by Sarge. Knowing that he was a friend of Jess's had made her open up to him, and over the past few days, she and Sarge had talked a lot. She enjoyed his company, and liked that he was a bit rough around the edges. And he loved that she doted on him, bringing him food from the kitchen. It was the beginning of what seemed like a great friendship.

"I think you know better than I that there is no talking to him about this," Kay replied.

Doc shook his head and walked off. "Hardheaded sumbitch."

Ted smiled as a frustrated Doc walked away, shaking his head. In short order, Mike returned with Captain Sheffield and Lieutenant Livingston.

Sheffield crossed his arms over his chest as he looked down at the old soldier. "Just can't wait to get out of here, can you?"

"My job here is done! These boys need a break."

Sheffield looked at Ted with a smile. "They need a break, huh, not you?"

Sarge jerked his head around. "With all due respect, Captain, kiss my ass."

Livingston doubled over in laughter. Even Sheffield laughed at Sarge's response.

"Your respect is duly noted," Sheffield said, trying to get serious. "Are we going to be seeing you boys again? We're working on things, but I'm used to having support."

"And you'll have it. It's not like I'm dropping off the face of the earth. You'll be able to reach me by radio, and we'll be around if you need us," Sarge said.

Sheffield let out a sigh. "All right, thanks. Go ahead and take some time, just keep your radio on."

"Why, thank you, Captain, but for the record, I wasn't asking for your permission."

Sheffield smiled as he shook his head. "First Sergeant, I can only imagine the string of wrecked officers lying in the wake of your career."

Sarge grinned. "Some mustangs just can't be tamed, Captain."

Once the two officers left, he called Ted over with a whistle and a jerk of his head.

"Time to get your scrounge on, Teddy. Go find that knuckle dragger and get what we need to set up camp."

Ted shook his head and made for the door. He tapped Kay on the shoulder. "Would you mind giving me a hand real quick?"

"I thought you'd never ask," she replied as she got up.

They went outside together when Mike pulled up in a Hummer, blaring the horn. As Ted got in the passenger seat, Mike asked, "Time to go shopping?"

"Saw that coming, huh?"

"Of course. You know how he is."

Together the three proceeded to grab supplies from the stores of the DHS. Since Kay had intimate knowledge of not only what was on-site, but where it was located, the looting of the food stores didn't take long. Their booty consisted of everything from food to cots and blankets. They weren't selfish in their gathering, just getting enough for their needs. The one thing they did take in excess was coffee. When Mike and Ted saw the freeze-dried bags of coffee, they couldn't help themselves.

"Can you guys think of anything else?" Kay asked.

Mike and Ted thought about it, then shook their heads. "No, I think we've about covered it."

"I know of one more thing. Pull up in front of that second connex on the right up there."

Ted pulled the Hummer to a stop in front of the container. "What's in here?" Mike asked.

"You'll see," Kay said as she got out. "Follow me."

Mike stood at the door, when a large cardboard box shot out, almost hitting him in the face. "What is this?" he asked as he turned the box around. "Ah, yes, Kay, we need this too." He tossed the big box of toilet paper into the back of the Hummer.

Ted looked back and started to laugh. "Thanks, Kay!" he yelled out the open door.

Kay came out with another box and tossed it into the back of the truck as well. "You're welcome," she said as she shut the door. "But one of those is for the girls."

"You mean Jess and Fred?" Mike asked.

"Yep, I think they'll appreciate it," she replied.

They rode back over to the infirmary. Sarge was up and sitting on his stretcher when they came back in. A crutch rested beside him.

"Took y'all long enough," he said as they walked in.

"Yeah, yeah, you ready to go?" Ted asked. Sarge stood up, resting his weight on the crutch, and walked toward the door.

"Hey, Doc, you coming?" Ted asked.

"No, I'll have to wait a day or two for that one to heal up," he said, pointing toward Aric.

"Where's Fred?" Aric asked, sitting up. His BDU top was gone, replaced with gauze and bandages.

"She's out helping some friends. She'll be back around," Ted said.

"Oh, okay. Am I going to be able to leave here once I heal up?"

Sarge was still making his way to the door. "I don't see why not." He stopped and turned to face him. "Just remember whose side you're on. And if you ever make the mistake of pointing a gun at me—"

Aric waved him off. "Don't worry, I promise that'll never happen again."

Chapter 27

Sleeping inside an actual house was a nice change of pace. It was the first time in a long time that I felt like I could relax. Knowing the DHS was no longer a threat removed a huge weight off my chest. Mel and I took our time getting up the next morning, just talking and laughing like good old times.

However, even after our relaxing morning, we couldn't lie around all day. There was a lot that needed done—we had to turn this place from a house into *our* house. I needed to get the solar stuff set up and connected to the house and see if the well pump still worked. Running water would truly be a luxury, and I kept my fingers crossed that it would work. Mel woke the girls up and put them to the task of sorting out the living room. Naturally, they were a little grumpy, but Mel got them into gear pretty quick.

I went out and started working on the power plant. I decided to use a method for connecting generators that I had used in the past. Pulling the wires off the bottom of the AC breaker mounted on the side of the house, I connected the leads from the inverter, then connected the neutral. With the connections made, I went around the house and shut off the main breaker at the meter before going inside the panel.

At the panel I shut off all the breakers, then went back out to the trailer, which we had parked close to the house the night before. After another quick check of the connections, I turned on the inverter and grabbed my multimeter. After verifying the power there, I headed back inside and flipped the AC breaker on, which energized the entire panel. This process is known as backfeeding, and while it's not legal—not that there was anyone to complain—it is totally functional. Checking the panel schedule, I turned on the breakers for lights and receptacles. Shouts of joy coming from throughout the house told me that the lights had come on. Sadly, the only breaker I couldn't turn on was the hot water heater.

Once all the breakers I thought we would need were on, I went around and checked all the lights. Two rooms needed bulbs, but other than that they all worked. Fortunately, the trees on the property covered the front of the house for the most part, allowing me to set the panels up off the end of the house beside the trailer. As I was wrapping up the panels, Danny walked over.

"How was it last night?" he asked.

"Best accommodations. Four stars. How about you guys? How was it in the house?" I asked.

"It's kind of tough to see everything you own destroyed as it is. Bobbie seems to be taking it better than me. She was up half the night cleaning things up."

"You know how she is, she's got to clean," I said with a laugh.

"Yeah, you got that right. You try the well yet?" Danny asked.

"Nope, was just about to."

We walked over to the well house. After opening the spigot on the bypass, I looked at Danny, said, "Cross your fingers," and flipped the breaker on. The contacts snapped shut, and I could feel the pipe vibrating.

"Is it running?" he asked.

"I don't think so. I think it's bound up," I said as I flipped the breaker off.

"Think it sat too long?"

"I don't know. I'm going to try bumping it." I started to flip the breaker on for a second, then off, then on, then off. After doing this several times, a loud gurgle came out of the spigot. I smiled. "That sounds good." Brown water started to flow out the spigot, a trickle that quickly built up in volume and pressure.

"Close the valve. Let's see if the pressure switch and tank are any good."

Danny and I both watched the pressure gauge as the needle started to move, slowly working its way up from zero toward thirty pounds. The needle passed the thirty mark and kept climbing. At forty-two pounds, the pump shut off.

"At least all that works," Danny said.

"Yeah, I'll just have to keep an eye on the tank for a while, make sure it's not leaking."

Danny stuck his head in the small shack. "Looks pretty new, it should be all right."

"Let's go in and get some running water," I said as I extricated myself from the small building.

As we came in the back door, Mel looked over. "The toilets are making noise."

"That's a good thing. Let's see if they work," I said, right before the sound of a toilet flushing drifted from the hall bathroom.

Little Bit came out hitching her pants up. "The bathroom works," she said with a smile.

"Guess that answers that question," Danny said.

"Let's go see if we can get power back on over at your place," I said.

"That'd be nice. It would make cleaning a lot easier."

When we got back to Danny's place, Jeff, Thad, Jess, and Fred were standing on the porch with Bobbie.

"Hey, Danny, thought you could use some help today," Thad said.

"That would be great, thanks, guys."

"We're going to see if we can get some power back on over here," I said.

"Power? How are you getting power?" Fred asked.

"I've got a small solar system. It won't run much, but it's something."

"You two go on ahead and do that. We'll help Bobbie get some of this stuff out of here," Thad said.

While they all headed in for the cleaning detail, we went back to where we had set his system up before. Being as his house was already set up for it, it didn't take long to get it hooked up again. The hardest part was getting the panels back on the roof. Unlike at my house, his pump started right away, and there was soon running water in his house as well.

When we got inside, Bobbie and Jess were doubled over laughing.

"What's so funny?" Danny asked.

Bobbie pointed at the spray nozzle at the kitchen sink, she was laughing too hard to say anything. Fred was laughing but managed to calm down enough to tell us. She held up a rubber band. "They wrapped this around the sprayer," she managed to get out.

"You mean, with all this other shit they did, one of them actually wrapped that thing so it would spray?" Danny asked.

Bobbie looked up with tears in her eyes. "Yes, it's just so

funny that they would think of this. I mean, how long did they think it would be before it would even be possible? No one has running water."

"That is kinda funny," Danny said.

"Yeah, there's someone like you working for them," Thad said, pointing at me.

"What the hell is that supposed to mean?" I asked with a laugh.

"You know exactly what that's supposed to mean. Always the jokester," Thad replied with a laugh.

"I guess you got me there."

Everyone pitched in to help clean their house. Bobbie and Danny went through everything as it was brought out, deciding what to keep and what to throw on the pile to burn. Once all the broken or thoroughly nasty stuff was brought out, the ladies set to work on the scrubbing while we turned our attention to another unpleasant task.

"Man, that is nasty," Jeff said as he stared down into the toilet bowl in the small bathroom.

"Yeah, Danny, I don't think there's any saving that thing," Thad added.

"That's what I was thinking. I think I'm just going to pull it out."

"That's probably the best idea, but I ain't going to do it for you," I said with a chuckle.

Danny pulled on a pair of nitrile gloves and started to unbolt the toilet, using his Leatherman tool. I ended up breaking down and helped get it out of the house, carrying it out back into the woods.

"We'll find you another one somewhere," Thad said as we set it down.

"I've got one in the barn over there. I'll get it put in later. I'm not too worried about that right now," Danny said.

"Good, 'cause Thad knows about friends and plumbing," I said.

"You guys want to help me with the doors, see what we can come up with?" Danny asked.

"Sure thing," I said as Danny headed for the barn.

Danny found a tape measure in the shop and we headed for the front door. It was a standard 3-0 door, not that that did us any good at the moment, as there weren't any replacements around. We spent most of the afternoon constructing a makeshift front door out of lumber Danny had in a rack. There wasn't enough plywood to sheath it with, so we cut one of the one-by-fours in its place. Getting it into the frame was going to be a challenge, but we were up for it.

In the end, we used a couple of strap hinges Danny had in his never-ending bins of stuff. While Frankendoor wouldn't close into the jamb, it did close flush to it. A hasp and bolt on the inside kept it secure. The two French doors were going to be another issue. One set came off the downstairs bedroom. Danny decided to just close that one off entirely. Thad and Jeff said they would handle that while Danny and I worked on the other.

A set of French doors wasn't a possibility, so we framed in one side of the opening and made a door like the first one. Danny ran a screw in on one of the one-by-fours then held the cordless drill up and looked at it. "Man, could you imagine doing this without these tools?" He laid the drill in the bag with the rest of the tools. In the bag were a reciprocating saw, circular saw, and impact drill.

"Yeah, cutting all this with a handsaw, not to mention turning screws in by hand—that would suck," I said as I flipped the door over to do the other side. "Where in the hell did you get all this lumber?"

"Remember when I worked for that builder?"

"Yeah, what were you doing, stealing from him?" I asked with a laugh.

"No, I just went through the trash piles on the jobs. Soon as a house was framed I was there. They left a lot of stuff behind. No sense in hauling it to the dump."

"Guess not. Your pack-ratting really paid off here."

"It does have its benefits."

Once the doors were taken care of, we took a break. No one had eaten anything all day, and all of this work had built up our appetites.

"Hey, I'm going to go over and get Mel and the girls. I think it's time for some lunch, or breakfast," I said.

"Cool, we'll get some MREs out," Thad said.

I left to go get the girls, surprised at the amount of work they had done while I was gone.

"Wow, you guys have been busy," I said, coming in the back door.

"We want to get things settled, try and make it feel like home," Mel said as she wiped the kitchen counter.

"I can't believe no one broke in here. It's so nice inside."

"Well, from the outside, it doesn't look like much. Speaking of which, that'll need to change."

I started to laugh at the thought of a honey-do list. "Sure thing, babe. But for now, let's go over to Danny's for lunch."

"Yeah, lunch!" Little Bit shouted and ran for the door.

We all walked together over to Danny's. Everyone was on the back porch. A couple of open cases of MREs sat on the table.

"You girls pick out the ones you want," I said.

"I like these things. They're cool," Taylor said.

"Me too, they're fun!" Little Bit said.

I went through the boxes after everyone had theirs and picked one out for myself. While I knew these weren't the greatest things in the world, today, they tasted wonderful. After so long of eating what we could find and catch, the variety of flavors in each spoonful was impressive.

After lunch, Jeff threw all the wrappers on the burn pile. "Danny!" he called out. "You want me to burn all this for you?"

"Sure, thanks."

"You two go round them up. Me and Jeff will take care of the trash."

"You guys going to get that couple from the campground?" Bobbie asked.

"My friend is moving here?!" Little Bit exclaimed.

"Yep, they're going to live here."

"Where are they going to stay?" Mel asked.

"I was thinking Mark's house. We know he isn't coming back."

"That's good, they'll be right across the street from you," Danny said.

"You ready to go?"

"Yep, let's go."

I looked at Mel. "We'll be back in a little bit."

She smiled a sweet smile. "Hurry back."

"I ain't starting on your honey-do list today, or even this week."

"Sure, okay," she said with a wink.

Danny disconnected the trailer and we loaded up and headed out. We didn't talk on the ride, just enjoying the scenery and the beautiful weather. For a moment I was able to ignore the reality of our current life and drift back in time, back to when it was such a normal, not-even-worth-thinking-about event to be driving down the road. Only the litter on the road prevented the scene from being exact.

Brandy was alone by the fire when we pulled up. As I got out, she ran up, looking relieved. "I'm so glad you guys are here!"

"Why, what's up? And where's Tyler?" I asked, looking around.

"He's off in the woods," she said, pointing off into the bush.

"Why's he out there?" Danny asked.

"These guys came through earlier, three of them. They seemed creepy, the way they looked at me."

Tyler was carrying his rifle as he walked up. "Hey, guys, did y'all see anyone when you came in?"

"No, there's no one back that way," I said.

"What'd those guys do?" Danny asked.

"Nothing really. They didn't say much, it was just the way they were looking at Brandy—they wouldn't stop looking at her."

"Well, I guess we're just in time, then. Let's get you guys loaded up," I said.

A big smile spread across his face. "Awesome, let's do this."

"Hey, Danny, why don't you keep watch while I help them load up?"

"Sure."

I followed Tyler up to the camp, where Brandy was already packing their things. I was surprised at how neat and tidy the inside of their tent was. Save some sand on the floor, it was clean. Being as everything at the camp had gotten there on two bikes, it didn't take long for it to be loaded. In less than an hour, we were headed back.

"This is so exciting! I didn't even dare think about living in a house again," Brandy said.

"I'm glad we came across you guys. It'll be good to have some friends around for Little Bit," I replied.

"I can't tell you guys how much we appreciate this, guys, really," Tyler said.

"No problem, we can use some help and you guys surely can as well," Danny said.

"Are we going to be living near you guys?"

"Right across the road from me," I said.

"Oh cool! Whose house is it? I mean, could they come back?"

I thought about how to answer that. "No, they are not going to come back. It belonged to Lake County sheriff's deputy, but he died."

From the back I heard Brandy. "Oh."

"Not in the house, though. Don't worry about that," Danny said.

"Oh, okay, good. I was worried there for a minute."

"I don't think he'll be haunting you," I said with a smile, then thought, *But he might haunt me.*

As we pulled up to the house that would be theirs, I saw a Hummer sitting at Danny's gate. Pointing to their new house, I said, "This is your place, but we're going down here real quick."

"Sure," Tyler replied.

I pulled up into my yard and parked near the fence between our houses.

We found everyone sitting on the back porch, along with Sarge, Mike, and Ted.

"You finally get cleared by Doc?" I asked, stepping up on the porch.

"I don't need to cleared by no one. I cleared my damn self," Sarge said from where he sat sprawled on the big lounge chair.

Little Bit was sitting beside him. When she saw the kids, she hopped up. "Mister Sarge, I'm glad you're back, but I'm going to go play with my friends now." Sarge smiled as she wrapped her arms around his neck and quickly ran off. From the amount of squeals from the two girls, you'd have thought there were thirty of them.

"So you guys heading down to the river?" I asked.

"Yeah, we're in vacation mode now," Ted said.

"There are extra houses here if you guys want to stay," I said.

"No, we want to go to the river, it'll be nice down there," Sarge answered.

"Cool, you guys just drop by for the hell of it?"

"They brought us a present," Mel said, kicking the big box of TP.

"Well, aren't you girls lucky," I said with a smile.

I pointed to Tyler and Brandy. "For those of you who haven't met them yet, this is Tyler and Brandy. They're going to live here as well."

"Nice to meet you all. This is really something, so many people," Tyler said.

"Yeah, we're like grapes, come in bunches," Mike said.

Sarge looked at him, shaking his head. "More like a basket of fruits and nuts."

Looking back at Tyler and Brandy, I said, "You'll have to forgive him. Sarge here is our resident curmudgeon."

Sarge leaned forward. "Come a little closer, sweetheart, and I'll club your mudgeon."

"Don't worry, Morg, a newborn could outrun him right now,"Ted said with a laugh, without thinking of where he was standing. Sarge's crutch quickly came around into his kneecap. He was leaning against a post and nearly fell over when he jerked his knee up.

"Ow, dammit, old man!"Ted barked.

Sarge was laughing. "One mudgeon crushed."

Tyler and Brandy looked unsure about what they'd just seen, so I reassured them. "Don't worry about him. Contrary to how it may appear, he's actually a nice guy."

"Are you guys hungry?" Mel asked.

"Uh, I hate to say it, but yes, something to eat would be nice. Thank you," Brandy said.

"Don't thank us yet. This is all we've got right now," Thad said as he passed a half case of MREs to Tyler.

While they ate, we all talked, mainly about all the work that lay ahead of us.

Sarge said he didn't know what was going to happen next. "That's above my pay grade. All I know is what I was asked to do"—Sarge jabbed his thumb toward Mike and Ted—"and these guys went above and beyond."

With a big cheesy grin, Mike said, "Was that a compliment? Did that grumpy ole bastard just give us a compliment?"

Ted reached over and covered Mike's mouth. "Shut up and take it for what it's worth."

Mike mumbled through Ted's fingers for a second, then let out a sigh.

"You two about ready to go? We have to get things set up before it gets dark tonight," Sarge said.

Ted and Mike both got up. "Yeah, let's get this show on the road,"Ted said.

We all walked out to the Hummer, saying our good-byes. It was nice to know they were *temporary* good-byes. These guys were safe—for now.

"It's all downhill from here, Morg. I think the hard part's over," Sarge said as he closed the door.

"Really? I think the hard part is just getting started," I replied.

Taylor was standing beside me. "Dad, is this the end? I mean, is the government still going to try to kill us? Are they going to leave us alone now?"

I looked at Sarge. He gave a little shrug, then I looked at Taylor. "To borrow a phrase from history, 'it's not the end, it's not even the beginning of the end, but it may be the end of the beginning.'" Sarge winked at me and slapped the side of the truck.

Mel looked at Brandy. "Let's get you guys settled."

As the Hummer pulled down the street, the three youngest kids chased after it. The afternoon was beautiful and with all the laughter from the kids it was like being transported back to a happier time. I hoped that the move back here would bring us full circle—that we'd find real happiness again. A lot of work lay ahead of us, but it was good work: rebuilding our home, our community. We were on the road to recovery. I didn't know the path we were on to get there, but I had high hopes for it.

Also in the Survivalist Series

978-0-14-218127-0

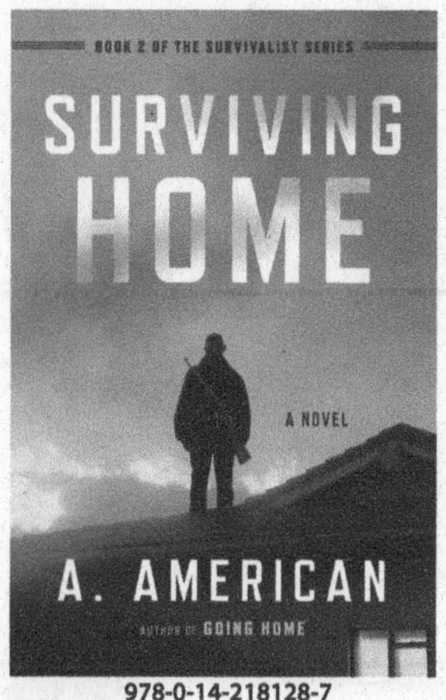

978-0-14-218128-7

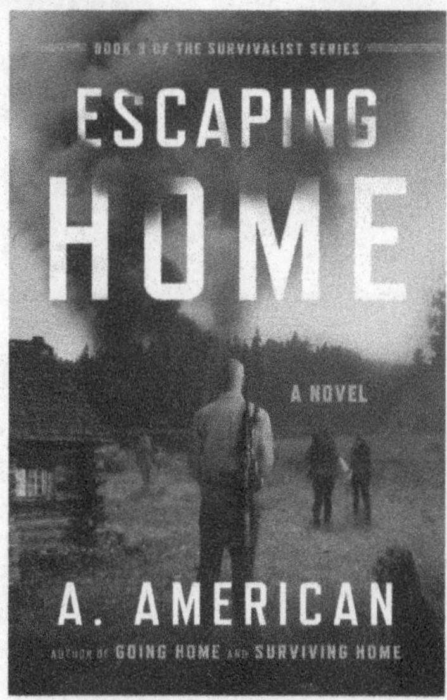

978-0-14-218129-4

Available wherever books are sold.